THE ELDRITCH HUNT

SEASON OF THE RUNER
BOOK III

———◇———

ABIGAIL LINHARDT

Edited by J.H. Flemming. Cover art by Andre Bat. Chapter font *Comic Runes* designed by **takuminokami**.

Also available in audiobook and ebook.

Paperback ISBN: 978-1-957175-11-9

Hardback ISBN: 978-1-957175-13-3

Ebook ISBN: 978-1-957175-12-6

ACKNOWLEDGMENTS

As always, I owe the completion of this book to my two most loyal fellow author friends K.N. Nguyen and Kate Segar. I still owe you a black oath of my own. Three years going on more. Couldn't have done it without you.

And thanks to J.H. Flemming my editor. Yes, I cried when I saw the hundreds of comments left in this document that tense September day. But I wouldn't have the confidence in these books that I do without your help. Thank you.

Also thanks to Andre for dealing with my long periods of silence while he was just trying to make me the cover I asked for. He's a true artists.

Last, thanks to Aaron my narrator. He's been patient with me, worked around my terrible lifestyle. He's the voice of the Runers, of the dark world they live in. Thank you for giving my words a voice.

THE ELDRITCH HUNT

SEASON OF THE RUNER BOOK III

ABIGAIL LINHARDT

For Joshua and his bun, whether he likes it or not.
Hope you like immortality, bucko.

CONTENTS

Why d'ye come to me dark shores
Bound 'hind waves of salient green
Gods here walk, our lands destroyed
A plea for life we pay in blood
Bended knee we bow on moors
Hunt again, our clans war on.

Flee ye thralls and 'ner return
Maids, ye sword yer valor wrought
What worth find ye here in ice
Where Reks take on a wild shape
No hearth can melt nor forge 'ere burn
The god-touched land beyond these shores.

--From *The Song of Caerwren* sung by Aivar the Wayfaring Bard

CHAPTER 1

THE NECROMANCERS

AL'MYRAHN SAND WHIPPED LIKE SHARP GLASS OVER Tarkan's exposed eyes as he scanned the storm-ripped horizon for the cave entrance. Holding on to the reins of his camel, he grounded himself against the powerful wind, head down. The animal knew where to go. He could trust it to pull him in the right direction. A powerful gust swept up from the south, bringing with it the smell of fire and ash. He braced himself against the camel. The beast stood lazily, chewing on the bit, waiting for him to give it a command. The storm didn't bother the desert mount. A small, exhausted grunt behind him made him turn. He struggled against the shifting sands to get back to his adopted daughter.

"Stand up, Zeva," he said, trying to haul her to her feet. "The caves are near."

Zeva, his young ward, moaned sadly. "I'm sorry, Tarkan," she sniffled. "This storm has exhausted me. The winds won't stop!" She looked back. "And Jasmin."

Her horse had fallen on a dune the night before. She'd had to walk then. The horse had been a gift for her eighteenth name day. But when it fell, breaking its ankle, Tarkan had no choice but to leave it behind with the storm. It would have hurt Zeva to see it raised and watch it lumber, dead and unstable, over the sand. He couldn't torment her like that.

He slid his arm under hers, supporting her. "I know. But we're close. Just a few minutes more."

Tucking her between him and the side of his mount, he pushed his head down into the wind and marched on. The sandstorms had blown up as a result of a maelstrom off the eastern shore near Singad, between the Shezai Ocean and the Caravan Sea. They'd been in Singad when the storms came in, devastating the seaside cities. They'd fled inland, hoping the storms and wind would stay near the coast. As if an unseen god had pushed the storm towards them, it had born down on them in the weeks it took to flee to Ala'Nar. They needed to get back to Singad to follow a lead he couldn't speak to Zeva about. Not yet. Since they were close to Ala'Nar, he wanted to check on the remains of his people to confirm a suspicion. A pair of Runers who had hunted him over a year ago had burned his tribe. He'd not returned to Ala'Nar since, fearing the city would be on the lookout for necromancers still.

Those Runers haunted his dreams, the woman Runer especially. On nights when he was particularly tired or anxious, she lay before him like a ghost in his dreams, white and glowing. At first, she appeared far away, crying for help. Each night, her prone form moved closer and closer to him. He often saw the dead's souls wandering the earth. Unlike them, Sybal was farther away, behind a veil. And he'd rarely seen a spirit lying down as she did. In the dreams, she haunted him from the east, towards Singad and the storm in the Caravan Sea. Just last night, she'd hovered before him, struggling to wake.

Could the lady Runer be dead? Had she, perhaps, died thinking about when they met in Ala'Nar? Where she mistakenly thought he'd killed her family? Sharar had murdered the woman's mother and brother before his very eyes, leaving him to take the fall. Perhaps that was why she haunted him in her death. Remembering the would-be sorcerer's face lit a fire in his blood. Ever since the Runers had helped him and Zeva escape, he'd sought ways to strengthen his own power, never again wanting to be helpless and weak. Never again being powerless to save her. There was only one mantle that would bring him that kind of power, and he had to become worthy of that title before another necromancer did.

"Tarkan!" Zeva shouted. "I see the opening of the cave!"

The necromancer glanced up, seeing it, too. A black, yawning entrance amidst the whipping sand. Careful not to run on the wind-swept sands, fall, and be buried alive, Tarkan gripped the saddle of his camel and led Zeva to the mouth of the cave. Familiarity with the cave came back to him from over a year ago. Once on the solid sandstone ground, he jogged deeper in until the wind became a distant howl, and the sand no longer tore at his flesh.

Gasping in the clean air, Zeva giggled and threw her head coverings off. She shook her long black hair down. Tarkan watched her black locks tumble. He almost smiled at her glee until his eyes landed on the scars covering her face. Despite the damage Sharar had done to her in his months of torture—disfiguring her—Zeva's face glowed with beauty.

"At last!" she called, singing into the echoing cave. "I'll have sand in my scalp for a year," she joked, picking at the top of her head. "When do you think the sandstorms will stop?"

"Soon," Tarkan replied, turning to go deeper into the network of caves and tunnels. They were outside the province's major city and had a small amount of safety from the storm and the people in the cave. "Best to stay quiet. We don't know what lurks in these caves during this storm."

"What are we looking— Ouch!" Zeva tripped over a rock in the path and fell.

Tarkan caught her and apologized, lighting a torch. She couldn't see in the dark like he could. "Any signs that someone has been here," he answered. "You remember the crate?"

Zeva made a delicate sound, showing that she did. He knew she had never been fond of the dead cargo, but—like most things about him—she accepted them with grace. He didn't deserve her. "It contained your tribe and a few others," she went on. "The Runers burned them. Did that happen in here?"

"Yes," Tarkan said. "But not all of my tribe were amongst them when they destroyed them. There was one who left us—even leaving his wife, Elahel, with us. Ashkan."

"Are you looking for him?" Zeva asked. "Are you hoping he tracked them down? Would he come back for her?" The hopeful tone Zeva adopted when dreaming up romantic images overtook her. "You said he loved her like the frozen fires of Nah'jaha."

A small twitch snapped over Tarkan's face. "Ashkan was a wild man and a fierce necromancer. Elahel didn't return his love as passionately. But she loved him in her own way. As we all do."

Zeva hummed sadly. "Any kind of love is preferable to loneliness."

Tarkan's still heart stung. "Ashkan was an ambitious necromancer. With no Necro'Khan in Porsh, I assume he may be seeking trials to make himself worthy. He may have come to find his tribe. To find Elahel."

Zeva shivered. "I can't imagine anyone wanting to be the Necro'Khan. The things you have to do to become such a creature are horrible."

Her words struck him deep. "Sometimes we must choose the lesser of two evils. Taking a darker path to protect that which is ours to keep safe."

"Is it the lesser to not make me Scriven?" she asked.

"Zeva," he snapped, turning to glare at her. "I will not hear of you becoming an Apostle again. I've said this a thousand times. Necromancy is not the life for you. For anyone. Do not mention it again."

Her eyes widened at his harsh tone. She dropped behind him,

unable to look him in the face. He knew her sensitive nature would silence her. But he grew tired of the argument. Zeva often asked to be Scriven: to have the necrotic scriptures tattooed on her flesh and start her education in the necrotic ways. But he'd not have it. He wanted to preserve her. Keep her sweet, naïve, and pure. It had been simpler before Sharar hunted them down. The evil that he'd opened her eyes to had made her more persistent. But she didn't need the black oath; he'd protect her. He'd commit any atrocity to let the necrotic gods see him as the only one worthy of being Necro'Khan.

Her silence after his hard words hurt. He took her hand, pulling her abreast with him. He gently ran his thumb over her forehead. There, just above her elegant brows, he'd put the only mark he hoped ever to scrawl on her. Like all necromancers from Porsh, each one marked themselves by their familial houses. The symbol for his family was a tiny black star with long, cruel points—a likeness to the star, Mirzam. The star that never moved.

"It killed me to mark you this way," he went on. "I could not bear to hurt you again."

She smiled apologetically. "You are my father. I needed you to know that." She mimicked his caress, running her finger over the matching star, hardly visible amongst the scriptures running over his flesh, but she knew where it was.

Over an hour of silence and exploration passed before he found his way back to his old hiding place. Ahead, he saw the skeletal remains of his loyal dragon and the remnants of the crate of bodies. He handed the reins to Zeva and proceeded to the detritus alone.

Kneeling, he inspected the ashes for signs that it had been disturbed in the last year. It didn't take long for him to find what he sought. He knew every one of his tribe's skeletons by heart.

"Elahel *is* missing," he said, crouching by the bones of his tribe. "She had the scriptures engraved on her spine, ribs, and other bones. She's not here."

"Why did she engrave her bones?" Zeva asked, keeping her distance.

"A different house from Porsh," Tarkan said with a sigh, standing up. "They tried to hide their marks. It didn't always work. Ashkan must have been here. Taken her. But only her. Even death could not stop his love."

"Do we follow him?" She shuffled her feet nervously.

Tarkan walked over to his dead dragon and ran his hand over a giant, curving rib. "Raised him from an egg," he said absentmindedly.

"Before me?" Zeva asked.

He nodded and sighed heavily. "Nearly a century before you. My father gave it to me on my eighteenth name day. I called him Rakthar, since he was a western dragon. He didn't belong on Al'Myrah." He stopped before falling too deep into his memories. "Perhaps I've lived too long." A heavy weight bore down on him. He stayed in this world for her. To protect her. Keep her safe. There was only one way to ensure nothing ever harmed her again...

Zeva took his hand and looked at him. "Not long enough yet."

He allowed himself to smile down at her. Her amber eyes twinkled in the darkness.

"We should try to head back to Singad," he said at length. "Ashkan has tribe members there who left Porsh when my father became Necro'Khan. He'll seek their council."

Zeva moaned. "Can we buy another mount? Or join a caravan? The elephant traders from Bahratt often cross this time of year. We could bargain for a ride."

He had nothing to bargain with. And it would be too dangerous. If they were found, he could be easily overtaken, tied to a stake, and burned. But she needed to be cared for. "I'll think of something," he promised her. "Let's move back towards the opening and rest. One should not sleep so close to the dead."

ব

"TARKAN!" Zeva called, frightened.

He woke from his half-sleep and pushed himself up. The fire had gone out, but he could see the tribe of approaching wanderers. She crawled close to him, making herself small behind him.

"Do you hear that?" she asked, unable to see them. Her panting pulsed hot against the back of his neck.

"I see them," he told her, standing up and wrapping an arm around her protectively. "Twelve. Four horses. Two wagons." In the darkness, the hair of the horses glinted like diamonds as they passed under the shadow of the cave opening. "Akhelatek horses," he whispered. "They're Porshain."

"Tribesmen?" she whispered.

Tarkan stepped forward, reaching out with his tattooed hand towards the travelers. The scriptures on his flesh crawled, warning him of danger. "Yes," he answered. "But they bring darkness with them. Stay."

"Don't leave me!" she hissed, terrified, grasping for him in the darkness.

He turned back and gently clasped her head with both hands, kissing her forehead. "Stay."

Facing the entrance, he took a dozen steps towards the oncoming pack. They did not light torches, for they were able to see in the darkness and avoid the crags and rocks. He stood still, wondering if they'd branch off down another passage, essentially leaving him and Zeva alone. They didn't.

One stopped mid-step. He'd been spotted. Behind him, Zeva gasped and covered her mouth.

"Friend or foe?" the voice of a young man asked from the caravan. He had the strange accent of Caerwren looping around his words.

"Neither. Brother," Tarkan offered. "Akhelatek horses come from Porsh."

An audible sigh of relief and whispered conversation went up from the tribe. A torch blazed into life, briefly blinding Tarkan. The tribe came closer. A young necromancer led the pack, holding the fire. His eyes were so blue they almost vanished into the whites of his eyes. His skin, under his black scriptures, shone like clouds, whiter than any Tarkan had ever seen. His hair was yellow, braided, and beaded with silver.

"Caerwren?" Tarkan asked, wondering if the pale man came from the country of white men.

The necromancer nodded. "Yes. I came to Al'Myrah as a child. My parents were black powder traders before joining the Palace of Apostles."

His shoulders were broad, his bare arms knotted with muscle. The people of Caerwren were giants, tall and strong enough to break an Al'Myrahn warrior's neck with one hand. Seeing such a brutish man covered in the scriptures sent a shiver down Tarkan's spine.

"The Palace fell decades ago," Tarkan informed the man cautiously.

The white man gestured to the older Porshains behind him. "But its spirit travels with the nomadic tribes. The man who made me Scriven walked the desert sands with his people, as I do now."

Tarkan pushed Zeva back. If the man wanted a fight, Tarkan wouldn't be able to stop him. He might be able to hiss the scriptures in his mind that would bring up the bones of his dragon, but he didn't have the power to use the scriptures without speaking them aloud. And this huge man could stop him before he did.

"No fear, though," the younger man said, seeing the visceral reaction. "I am merely searching for one who can help us."

"I felt something when you approached," Tarkan warned him anyway. "What is among you that makes my scriptures stir?"

Coming closer, the younger necromancer beckoned his tribe

forward. Older men and woman stood among them, tired and weather-beaten. All of them had the scriptures on their flesh—except one, a young woman with chestnut hair and bright green eyes in her honey-colored face. A noble house of Porsh used to have such women, their gem-like eyes giving them away.

"I am Arne, and this is my tribe." He motioned them forward and the others began to unload their burdens.

Not having asked them to stay, Tarkan's guard went up. They were vastly outnumbered. Not that those in the brotherhood of the necrotic scriptures were natural enemies. They were not friends, either. And with the mantle of Necro'Khan open, all there were competition. He stood stiffly, calculating how to run should they need to.

Arne went to the wagon and helped the jewel-eyed woman down. She moaned and fell against him.

"What's wrong with her?" Zeva asked.

That was when Tarkan felt it. Behind the woman on the wagon rested a large, square crate. It was painted black and bound in orichalcum chains. He realized this was where the pulsating darkness came from.

"This is Ishtar," Arne said, lowering her to the ground where one of his tribesmen re-kindled the fire. "Soon to be my Apostle. And also my betrothed."

When the fire glowed inside the cave, Tarkan looked more closely at Ishtar. She looked very sick. From the way she walked, he guessed she'd given birth recently. His eyes flicked back to the black, chained box. Repulsion pushed against him.

"A drekavac?" he guessed darkly.

"That is what a Runer called it," Arne said quickly. He glanced back at the box and then at his tribe. "We could only pay for the binding. He would not slay it."

Tarkan withdrew closer to Zeva. "It's the consequences of your own actions." He couldn't keep the blame out of his voice. He pointed to Ishtar. "Did you not tell her what happens when someone lies with the likes of a necromancer? Same as with a Runer. Nothing that comes from that coupling will be sentient. A drekavac is the monster you birthed."

Ishtar moaned and began to weep, face in her hands. "I thought I'd die. They cut it out of me. It's not living. But at night, it crawls toward me. Weakening me. Taking my life. So the Runer said."

Tarkan nodded. "It's more spectral than flesh."

"We tried burning it," Arne went on.

Tarkan shook his head. "You need a Runer."

The other necromancers mumbled and cursed among themselves.

"We tried," Arne said. "But the cost. And he threatened us. Dirty scoundrels, the lot of them. Ala'Nar is impossible for us to pass through. We have been searching for a stronger necromancer, one who might banish it for us."

A small hitch of interest touched Tarkan's chest at this. Could he dare try the rituals that might banish such a monster? Something of that caliber might make the black oath look on him with favor—a favor towards gaining the power he needed to protect Zeva forever.

No, he couldn't. Not yet.

"The best thing to do will be to find a Runer," he said, his throat stiff with the effort of not taking on the task himself. "Have him perform the ritual that will cleanse the drekavac and make it a guardian spirit."

Arne exhaled in desperation. "That spell requires a post, a lintel. A home. We have none. I see from the fade of your scriptures that you are an old necromancer." He gestured to his tribe. "We are not. We do not have the strength to perform the rite. Isn't there something you can do? I can offer you an oath of my own as payment."

Tarkan scoffed darkly. "This is the kind of thinking that got you into this. Young, stupid necromancer, throwing out blood oaths."

"Then don't take an oath," Zeva said to him. He faced her, glaring. She didn't back down from his icy stare and simpered sadly. "He loves her. It was an accident. Help them."

The way she clasped her hands and how her eyes begged in the fiery darkness melted his cold guard. Gently, he caressed her cheek with his thumb. She smiled hopefully.

"Zeva, leave," he ordered.

"But—" she started.

"No negotiation," he snapped. She did not need to see what he was about to do. "I don't want you witnessing this." She'd only watched him do a few spells. Nothing like what he was about to do. He wasn't sure if it would work, and it was dangerous. But for her, he'd try. And to gain favor with the black oath. Like other magic wielders of the map, necromancers were bound to the necrotic gods that gave the scriptures on their flesh their power. His gods were not as strict as others. But if he wanted to ascend and take up the mantle of Necro'Khan, then he needed to gain favor with them.

One of the older necromancers, a woman with a gray and white braid, took Zeva by the hand and led her farther into the cave.

Tarkan watched them go. "If one hair on her head is harmed, I will slaughter the lot of you."

Arne's eyes teared up. "We mean you no harm, sira. We are just desperate."

The honesty in Arne's eyes reminded Tarkan that not every necromancer—or sentient being—was as vile and evil as he'd come to expect. Still, he did not want to be taken advantage of again.

"Then prepare yourself," he growled softly. "Bring any goats, chickens, or sacrifices you can spare. We need their blood."

TARKAN TOOK his black box out from the saddle bags of his camel. The flesh-like outer coating always made him squirm. He opened it, revealing a ritual dagger. Cutting his wrist deeply with a silver-handled ruby blade, Tarkan quoted the necrotic scriptures for the spell in a deep, guttural mumble. He only heard the first few syllables before the black wind swirled around him, swallowing them up. He dribbled his blood in a circle on the cave floor before handing the knife to Ishtar.

"Come into the circle," he told her. "Do you have any pacts or oaths upon you already?"

Ishtar shook her head. "I am not an Apostle yet, either. I have no ties. No black magic."

He nodded, pleased. "Open your blood."

"Taking on her wounds?" Arne asked, recognizing one of the five spells of the necromancers. "What good does that do?"

Tarkan realized the younger necromancer was uneducated in the necrotic ways. "It takes on curses, covenants...and haunts."

Ishtar moaned, opening her own arm with the ritual dagger. Weak, she sat inside the circle and handed the dagger back to Tarkan. "Will it haunt you, then?" she asked, confused.

He nodded. "Then I will open the Blood Path."

Several of the witnessing necromancers gasped and touched their black scriptures like a blessing.

Arne's eyes went wide. "The Blood Path? The pathway to the God Deep?" he whispered in horrified awe. "Can you do that?"

Tarkan wasn't sure. But if he could, the gods would be in awe. He held his bleeding arm out to Ishtar. She pressed their wounds together and they grasped each other's forearms.

"Your blood, my blood," he said, and she repeated it.

"Your wounds unto me," he said, and she replied,

"My wounds unto you."

"Your pain fills me," he whispered, feeling every ache and pain transfer from her body to his.

"I give it freely," she whispered, her cheeks flushing red.

He took her wounds into himself. Something in Tarkan's stomach churned, and his unbeating heart twisted in agony. Something else besides the horrifying birth haunted Ishtar. Something inside her body. The pain almost made him stop. Had she been feeling this just moments ago? Her weak state suddenly made sense.

Then he felt the eyes of the drekavac on him. "It sees me," he grunted.

Behind them, on the wagon, the black box shook and the chains rattled. He prayed to his necrotic gods that the chains the Runer had forged would hold the thing. He had no way of controlling it if it escaped.

Suddenly strong and rosy, Ishtar asked, "Now what?"

As she spoke, he took in her face. Her shoulders were squared and she stood tall, as if years of pain had been lifted. A sudden weakness engulfed Tarkan. He shoved her out of the blood circle, still bleeding. "Do not close your wound. You will take back your pain." He motioned for the other necromancers standing by with the sacrificial animals to come forward. "Cut two in half," he ordered from inside the sanguine circle.

Startled, they did as he commanded. The goats bleated furiously as they killed and divided them, their insides spilling grotesquely over the cave floors. He showed them how to place the two halves facing each other inside the blood circle. The lined-up creatures, split in two, made a sick, bloody pathway. The screaming animals echoed down the caves to where Zeva and the older necromancer waited. Knowing his daughter would come at the gratuitous sounds, he hurried.

"Ishtar," he commanded, holding his bloody hand out to her. "Walk the Blood Path with me." He frantically prayed the black oath looked on him with pride as he attempted the dangerous spell. He'd been a follower of the scriptures for over eighty years. Surely he had gained enough favor.

She came between the carcasses, grimacing the whole time. Together, they walked up and down the path the dead animals made.

"Swear to take your wounds back when I am finished," Tarkan said darkly. The black wind rushed again.

"I swear," she said.

Facing the head of the Blood Path, Tarkan focused on the dead, sanguine carcass. "Open this door to the Deep," he growled, thrusting his hands forward as if to grab an invisible gate. "I, who have taken the necrotic oath onto my undying flesh, beseech the God Deep to open to me."

Covered in his own blood, surrounded by the dead, he held his hand out to Ishtar one last time. "Give me your power."

She held her bloody arm out to him. He dug his fingers into her wound and then consumed her blood. The foul wind picked up stronger. It was working. Excited, Tarkan begged once again that the God Deep, the realm of the gods, be opened and flung his arm wide. The others, outside the Path, could not see what he and Ishtar did.

A hot, fiery wind pushed back his hair and robes as a small sliver crackled before him. He gasped in surprise. Through it, he saw the world of the gods. Laid over their own world like a fiery veil, sandy dunes covered in flames sprawled out before him. In the distance, almost impossible to see in the blinding red sun, a huge serpentine beast dived into the sand, shaking the earth.

The scriptures on his skin crawled, pulling to the east. Something inside looked for him. Nothing threatening, but something cried for his help. Distracted from the task at hand, he leaned into the call, listening.

Who are you? he cried internally. *What do you want?*

Sensing more than seeing it, a white shape—a ghost of a girl—called out to him. Her words were unintelligible, but her spirit was restless, fearful. The more he tried to find her, the weaker he felt. Holding open the spell drained him of his living blood.

Come east to Singad. She's waiting there, the sensation said.

"Brother!" the tribe behind him screamed. Something metal cracked, giving way, and the Porshains cried out.

"Bring the drekavac!" Tarkan shouted, coming back to the world outside the God Deep. Despite his shaking arms as the spell drew the blood out of his own body, a thrill filled him. *I'm doing it!* he thought triumphantly. How many other Apostles had been able to crack open the God Deep like this? At last, the power he'd been searching for, sacrificing for, seemed within reach. But the toll it took sapped his strength. Still, he held on, hoping his god saw. Hoping it found his effort praiseworthy.

In a panic, Arne and three other necromancers picked up the black box. It shook, a roaring scream coming from inside.

"A chain has broken," Arne called.

"Cast it before me!" Tarkan ordered, feeling the thing clawing at the inside of the box. It wanted release from its supernatural prison. It wanted him.

Something to his right caught his attention in a soft, white glow. The lady Runer, Sybal, screamed from the distance. Calling for help. He'd seen her ghost in his dreams, but had never heard her before.

The voice came from inside the God Deep.

Grunting, he shut out the other voices that tried to pull his attention away. He had to focus. His grasp on the Deep began to slip through his fingers. He was too weak.

Arne heaved the shackled crate down, and he and Tarkan kicked it into the crackling opening. The longer he held the spell, the more his blood drained away until he saw it being pulled from his very body like a wrung-out rag. The agony overtook him.

"Leave the circle!" he shouted to Ishtar. He needed the drekavac to break free now, body and spirit in the Deep.

Ishtar jumped out and the monster burst free, the orichalcum chains bursting. The monster looked around, its hideous, fetal head snapping its too weak neck. Confused, it fell from the box and crawled in circles until its white, ghostly eyes landed on Tarkan. Opening its lip-less mouth, the monstrous child screamed, inhaling

Tarkan's life force. His hands, holding open the portal, sunk to shriveled, skeletal limbs.

Clapping his hands together, he closed the opening to the Deep before the thing crawled towards him. With a thunderous boom and a sizzling crackle, it slammed, locking the creature inside. Crying out, Tarkan collapsed backwards in the now still silence. Too weakened to even breathe, he let his body crumple.

He had reached beyond his rank and his strength.

"Ishtar," Arne called, pushing her gently back into the ritual center. "Say the oath is fulfilled."

The cave ceiling wavered in fiery light before Tarkan's eyes. He couldn't lift his head. The spells had drained him of his blood, more than he'd expected. Ishtar's illness permeated everything inside him. He needed blood. The woman knelt over him and claimed her oath fulfilled. When she did, the split animal carcasses burst into flames, taking the circle with it.

"Bring the flesh," Arne ordered another necromancer. He reached into a black box similar to the fleshy one Tarkan carried and brought out a human heart. "Consume," he ordered Tarkan, holding it to his mouth. "You need to replenish yourself. The blood is dead, but the heart was a servant of ours. You do not need to fear possession."

Eagerly, Tarkan bit into the heart and drank the blood from its fresh arteries.

"Take it all," Arne offered. "I have plenty."

Satisfied, Tarkan laid his head back down and finally caught his breath. His heart beat once...twice. His head fell to the side to take in the spot where he'd done what very few necromancers before him had. Opening the Deep was a good sign that his black oath looked on him with favor. But the joy he felt as the fresh blood trickled from his mouth vanished. Zeva stood in the darkness, tears falling like rain from her eyes. She shook, her eyes locked on him.

"I told you to leave!" he roared at her.

Beside him, Ishtar moaned and held her chest. Zeva dashed away into the dark cave, audibly weeping at what she'd just witnessed him do. With a grunt, Tarkan sat up and reordered his robes on his thin figure. He glared at Arne and Ishtar. Zeva's fearful eyes burned into his brain.

"Thank you, brother," Arne wept, kneeling and taking Tarkan's hand in his. "I will pray that the scriptures look on you with favor, should you hunt the mantle of Necro'Khan."

"Thank you for the blood," he replied from a dry throat. "You did not have to give me the strength back."

"I did," Arne mumbled, his voice still shaking. "You have saved us. Never have I seen an Apostle open the Deep as you just have. Surely our god will favor you."

The other Apostle's words encouraged Tarkan. Perhaps he wasn't as weak as he felt? Had the favor of the necrotic gods finally turned to him?

As the tribe settled in, Tarkan packed his own things away once he could stand again. No desire to stay near them remained. And Zeva needed comforting.

Before he left, he took Arne aside. "I say this only as advice for you. I see how much you love her. Are you going to put the scriptures on her flesh, make her a Scriven?"

Arne shook his head. "I thought I would. But she deserves to live. The drekavac was my fault. I owe Ishtar her life. I see that now."

That was what he was afraid of. "She is ill, Arne," he whispered. "I felt it inside when I took her pain. You could do the same, but it would weaken you and your magic."

The younger necromancer's eyes went wide. "Ill?"

"Dying, actually," he corrected. "She is in great pain. She has maybe months left to live. Bearing the drekavac weakened her further still. Let her take the oath. She will never be as strong as other necromancers, but the unlife we share will save her."

Arne's face contorted in agony. "It is no life for one such as her."

Tarkan glanced away. "I know," he said softly. "But if you love her, you will save her. Scrive her."

༄

HE FOLLOWED the tracks of the camel deeper into the cave, to an underground river that flowed out the back towards Ala'Nar. The thing had run off during the ritual, so he carried his black box with him. The success of his sudden decision to tear into the Deep filled him with hope. For too long had he been weak, taken under another man's boot. This was a good sign.

Zeva walked back and forth outside the mouth of the cave, something in her hands. Cautiously, he went to her, fully aware of the blood still caked on his body. When he entered the early morning sun, he realized she was picking flowers. The black-petaled flower, called midnight sun, grew out of the sand and rocks surrounding Ala'Nar. They were large and thick stemmed to bear the winds and heat. Zeva had at least a dozen in her arms and searched out a final, perfect flower.

"Zeva?" he croaked. "You should not have seen..." He stopped as she straightened up, facing him.

Her face was red and her eyes were puffy, but she smiled meekly at him. "I love you, Tarkan," she said tenderly. She held up a midnight sun to him. "This one's for you. But the rest are for me."

Shaken, he raised his skeletal hand and took the proffered flower. His blood-stained fingers touched the black petals, turning them red. He swallowed hard, unable to speak. He did not deserve her. She held up the bouquet, and he saw now that she'd used their thick, rubbery stems to tie them into a laurel. She placed it on her head. The rising sun cut through the petals, making spikes of sunlight burst around her head in bright, warm flashes.

"What do you think?" she asked.

Even with her scars marring her face, he'd never seen a more beautiful girl.

"Better than an Al'Myrahn sunrise," he whispered.

She lurched towards him, hugging him around the waist and pressing her cheek against his blood-soaked chest. Giving in, as he often did with her, he kissed the top of her head and wrapped his arms around her. When he closed his eyes, drinking in the scent of the flowers around Zeva's head, Sybal's cry of terror filled his waking mind. He gripped Zeva tighter. He hadn't seen the Runers in a year. How could he hear her so clearly now? Only the dead cried out like that.

Sybal? Dead? Her plea had come from the eastern coast.

She'd put herself and her mentor in danger, confronting Sharar and his djinn for him and Zeva almost two years ago. The months of torture they'd endured at the would-be sorcerer's hand still filled both their nightmares. If the Runers had not hunted him down—had not been willing to hear his tale and let him go—Zeva might be dead, and he'd still be enslaved to the scholar. What humanity was left inside his undead body pushed him to listen to Sybal's harrowing cries.

He gripped Zeva even tighter, never wanting to let her go. "We have to go east back to Singad," he said. "The Runers need our aid."

CHAPTER 2

ZEVA

THE STORM IN THE EASTERN SEAS CALMED AT LONG LAST, taking the inland winds with it. Zeva followed Tarkan back to Singad without complaint. They wrapped themselves in soft cotton, covering every inch of their bodies to avoid the prying eyes of the elephant traders. Despite their disguise, a cat-like Masahk eyed Zeva up and down. By the way his slitted pupils examined her, she thought he might want to eat her. But his flirtatious smile fell when Tarkan glared from behind her.

The week-long trip went by filled with song from a young, handsome driver of an overly elegant araba. A fat, rich woman inside the araba joined in now and then. The singer stopped when they reached small towns and villages buried in the sand. The hurricane had left devastation in its wake. The closer they got to the eastern shore, the worse it looked. But at long last, they reached the vibrant, buzzing shores of Singad. The city had been covered in sand, and patchwork fixes showed where the winds had ripped through, but the busy, ever-moving people of the port city pushed the invading sand out and returned to their quick, bustling lives.

Zeva walked the lanes near the docks of Singad between

merchants and rushing sailors. She held a white scarf over her face so only her dark, amber eyes peeked over the cotton folds. Tarkan ordered her to cover her face whenever they were in a city. Hardly remembering Moshav, her mentor keeping away from large settlements, Singad was perhaps the biggest city she'd seen. Even Hatal didn't move as fast as Singad. Tribes of Masahk made their cawing and wild language heard over the bustle of tradesmen, merchants, swindlers, and thieves alike. Some of them resembled humans more than others. A pod of some kind of ocean tribe of Masahk lingered in the shallows with wide, white eyes in black, scaly faces. White glowing dots tracked down their spines to their fishlike tails. Men and women from Caerwren hid under awnings, their pale skin red and tender from the Al'Myrahn sun. One had hair the likes of which Zeva had never seen: red, long down his back, but curly and wild like the wind. She found herself staring when the man met her eyes and raised a metal tankard to her. He had foam gathering in his matching red mustache from drinking.

Sticking out into the ocean, the city's surrounding villages always smelled of salt and sunlight. It might have made some wince and feel dirty, but Zeva loved the buzz. It reminded her of what little she remembered of her childhood in Moshav, before Tarkan. They had not been completely happy years, but Moshav's markets had always delighted her. Even if she did have to hide now, she still liked to touch the wares coming off the ships: silky fabrics from Xia, spices from Bahratt, and the shiniest gold from Alika. Farther inland, the chaos slowed down as the roads split to their respective villages. The main road to the city of Singad was busiest. All sentients disembarking from the ships would caravan through the mountains and then out into the different provinces of Al'Myrah. Tarkan had come to the ports to look for signs of Ashkan and the lady Runer he'd heard in the Deep.

She ran her hand over long, rectangular swaths of beaded and mirrored fabric from Bahratt. The woman selling it quickly placed it into her hands and rattled away in some dialect she didn't under-stand. Her adoptive family in Moshav, before Tarkan had stolen her away, had taught her many languages—even the tongue of Caerwren, which was oddly similar to Al'Myrahn—but this one eluded her. The merchant tried to drape the glittering fabric over Zeva's shoul-ders, showing her how to wear it, but to no avail. Zeva smiled at the altercation. She loved times like this: she rarely experienced anything outside Tarkan's company. Ever since he'd rescued her from the sorcerer, he'd forced her to hide. They stayed in the shadows, trav-eling at night, stopping in caves or crypts to rest.

The merchant came around her stall to get closer to Zeva.

"No, thank you," Zeva said quickly, using both hands to place the Bahratt fabric back in the woman's hand. When she did, she dropped her face cover.

When it fell, the merchant woman stopped, gasping and recoil-ing. Zeva's face burned and her eyes watered at the woman's reaction. She gripped her face to hide the scars and burns that mauled most of the left side. The burns flowed down her honey skin to her neck and disappeared into her dress front. Fumbling with the headscarf, she pulled it up to cover her disfigurement and wrapped it around her neck to hold it in place. Then she turned and ran from the horrified merchant.

She couldn't stop the tears that flowed down, dampening her mask. She often forgot the scars were there. Tarkan always stroked her cheek, kissed her forehead, and looked at her with affection. It made her forget what that man had done to her over the months of her imprisonment. She knew those scars—especially on a woman—would be memorable to anyone who saw her. That was why they had to hide. That, and Tarkan was a necromancer. *The* necromancer of Al'Myrah. The one who'd devastated Ala'Nar, who'd put the sultana of one of the greatest continents on the map into an apocalyptic frenzy. She couldn't hate Tarkan for what he'd done, even though it had made Sharar hurt her. In those long nights and agony-filled days, she'd known he'd come back for her. But now the entire country hunted for the necromancer who had destroyed Ala'Nar.

Making her way back closer to the port, losing interest in the cacophony of life around her, Zeva leaned against a wooden post with an oil lamp atop it. She watched the sailors and crews lug huge boxes from far away down the gangplank and stack them on land to be sorted by a port master. An accountant with a quill and board marked things off, checking their foreign labels and shouting for dockworkers to move them to their respective areas for delivery. A little anxious from the crowd, she wondered how Tarkan expected to find the Runers in the throng.

She glanced over her shoulder at Tarkan. Wrapped in black so only his blue eyes were visible—his hands wrapped to hide his rings and the scriptures on his fingers—he bargained with a man at a post board about something she couldn't hear. She knew he was taking a risk coming to Singad. She was content to follow him over Al'Myrah, but his other investigations began more and more to look like they led to Alika. He didn't have to tell her what they were looking for before the search for the Runers had interrupted it, but she had a guess. Though Tarkan might love her, care for her, and protect her, he was still a Porshain. A necromancer. There were others like him, and each one knew the Necro'Khan was dead. He wanted to go to Alika and hunt for the Mahit'onomicon, to find it before any of his brethren and decode its dark secrets.

Zeva pulled away from the center to escape the busiest part of the port and watch a pack of pirates from Bahratt. The darker skinned men clinked and glittered in gold, laughing and telling stories among themselves as they trod down the gangplank. Zeva ran her eyes over their ship, admiring the bright red and blue paint, when something odd caught her eye. A girl, near her age, rose out of the ocean waters below the dock like a ghost. No one else noticed her as she passed through the wood until she stood on the shores of Singad. With elegant Xian robes and long, whip black hair, the girl looked like royalty. But she was made entirely of flickering white and green light. Zeva gasped. It was indeed a specter of some kind, and only she could see it.

Clasping her hand over her mouth, Zeva smiled in joy but shook in fear. All her life, she'd begged Tarkan to make her Scriven, to allow her to learn the one spell to raise a ghost. He'd refused, and yet here one stood, visible only to her. But with no protection from possession, like the runes of a Runer or the scriptures on her skin, she shrank away. One last Bahratt pirate walked ashore, passing through the girl. The ghost's calculating eyes swept the port. Then, with a ghostly, echoing tone, the ghost said, *It was my wish that brought you here. Where are you?*

Zeva held her breath, eyes glued to the specter. She heard the Xian girl.

Where are you? the ghost asked again. Then, her eyes landed on Zeva. She smiled kindly. *There you are.*

Shaking, Zeva took one step forward. "You can see me? I can hear you."

Then it is you, the Xian replied. *I don't know who you are, but she does.*

"Who?" Zeva whispered. "What do you want?"

The Xian ghost stepped towards the next berth, taking a dozen steps in her foreign robes. She waved her hand. *She comes. I died, granting my wish that she would find her way home, and that someone who could save her would be here to find her.*

A familiarly shaped piece of cargo caught Zeva's eye. Four men carried a long, rectangular crate—a coffin painted with the protective black—on their shoulders with poles, and disembarked from a Xian ship. The sailors spoke in the rapid tongue, but she caught their words. They'd sailed into a storm, thinking they would never make it out again. It was a miracle they'd lived.

"The ship held steady," one said. "Like it rested in the palms of a goddess, guided here."

As they spoke, she heard others had not been as fortunate. Many ships were lost in the maelstrom and the raging storms over the last several weeks. But not theirs.

Zeva looked back at the ghost girl. "How did you come here?"

The girl smiled. *I'm not as human as I look. I will be drawn back to where I belong as soon as my wish is fulfilled.*

The men set the crate down with a grunt, pulled the poles out, and went back to the ship to continue their work. Zeva slowly slinked through the crowd towards the coffin. She'd met enough Porshains before Sharar took her and Tarkan hostage to know what lay inside a box such as this. She gently ran her hand over the top, wondering who or what lay inside. As she did, her fingers traced the lettering on the cargo instructions. The letters were Xian, but the looping, elegant script suggested a formally educated Al'Myrahn writer. The destination: Abigor Sharar; Albayda, Hatal.

Zeva's blood chilled to a stop in her veins. That was when she recognized the scholar's elegant handwriting. She'd seen it in his journals, had watched him write most nights while he held her prisoner. She looked up, but the Xian ghost girl was gone.

"Wait!" Zeva called, turning on the spot to try to find her. A few sentients looked at her, frowning.

She pushed herself up and ran to her mentor. "Tarkan," she hissed as he joined her, pushing through the throng. "I found something."

His eyes never stopping as they flicked across the port searching for any danger, Tarkan grumbled, "What are you talking about?" He counted the coins in his hand. His brow furrowed despondently.

Understanding he was set back again, she tried to keep her voice calm. "I saw a specter. She showed me that crate." She pointed discreetly. "Painted black. It's labeled in Sharar's handwriting."

At this, Tarkan met her eyes with concern. She could only see his icy blue orbs amongst his black wrappings. "Are you sure?"

She straightened up, looking to make sure it hadn't been moved yet. "Yes. She said we were meant to come here! It's a coffin. Come and see!"

She took his hand and pulled him to the crate plastered in Xian writing, stamps, and instructions. Paid couriers from different parts of the continent were already checking the items around the crate and loading them onto their wagons for delivery.

With so many bodies milling about—parcel snatchers and traders there to pick up their goods—no one noticed the two of them inspect the coffin-shaped crate. Zeva watched Tarkan's eyes whip across the many pieces of parchment pasted to the crate.

"But it came from Xia," he mused, looking out towards the east.

"Yes," Zeva breathed, excitement pulsating in her blood. "I've seen so few ghosts. But this one saw me! Like she knew I would let her speak to me."

"Zeva," Tarkan warned, glaring. He hated her desire to join the ranks of the necromancers. But hadn't this been a good sign? Tarkan turned back to their find.

Crates and boxes of all shapes, sizes, and makes were being pried open by people around the docks. A few were haggling with traders, some most likely thieves. Singad was a lawless wasteland where a postmaster might sell one's goods to a thief for extra coin.

"Hand me that," Tarkan hissed, pointing to a pry bar on the open back flap of a wagon that belonged to a master builder.

Zeva meandered casually through the goods and saw the courier run up front to stop a man from untethering his horse, shouting curses. She seized the tool and passed it quickly to Tarkan. Then she stood in front of him, covering most of him. He pried at one of the thin, wooden slats and angled his face to look inside.

"By the Dokhma," he gasped.

She spun to look but couldn't see inside. "What is it?"

Tarkan stammered. She'd rarely seen him at a loss for words.

"I don't know if she's alive," he breathed. "We have to move her."

Zeva understood his tone. "Do you know her?" she asked excitedly.

"Yes. It's her." Tarkan dropped the bar and immediately scouted for an unattended wagon. "It's Sybal. She..." Discreetly, he slipped a hand inside the crate, his eyes unfocusing. "I don't think she's entirely dead. We have to take her away from here, somewhere we can safely discern what happened to her."

Glad that he wanted to save the woman, she pressed the slat back down and followed his lead. "Who is she?"

"A Runer," he shot back, head tossing back and forth for a means of transportation that might not ask too many questions.

"Where will we go?" she asked. "Porsh?"

Tarkan stopped, thinking. He shook his head. "It's too far. Her master, the man she follows, might not be far behind. At least, I hope he's not." He glanced back down at the label. "Hatal," he whispered.

Zeva clenched her fists over her heart. "No. I don't want to go back."

Tarkan gently took her shoulders in her hands, urgency tightening the marked skin around his eyes. "There is a place. Makan Almyat: the place of the dead. Many tombs of ancient Hatal lay in a valley there, surrounded by black sand mountains. It will be safe for us."

"You hid there when you first ran from him," she remembered. He didn't nod, but she understood. "We could hire an araba?"

Tarkan straightened up, clearly glad she would follow him without question. They spotted the ornate araba from before, with red wheels and golden tassels hanging from the top. The driver, a young man with long, glossy dark brown hair, sang to a pining older woman.

"It's not very covert," Zeva said.

Tarkan sniffed in agreement. Something close to a smile creased his barely visible eyes as he looked at the singing man. "It helps when you know the right people." He pointed to the merchant from

Bahratt who sold the glittering wraps. "Buy one of those and put it on. You'll be our sheikha." He pressed the coins into her hands and vanished into the throng towards the driver.

Sighing to gather her courage, she went back to the woman. She spun the coins around her fingers out of nervousness.

"Oh, sabi," the woman said to her in Al'Myrahn. "I apologize for before. Please, I meant no harm. I am a stupid woman."

A little taken in by the woman's adamant apology, Zeva smiled and relaxed. "I need your most beautiful piece, please."

"Of course, sabi." The woman pulled out a few pieces.

Zeva had never shopped for fine clothes, not even when she was a girl living with her foster mother. Unsure what she was looking at, she asked the woman to pick.

A moment later, she was armed with a pink and green wrap, glittering with golden adornments. Zeva hid her face in her white covering and let her long, black hair tumble down her back. She supposed this was what a wealthy woman looked like. By the time she found Tarkan and the stolen araba, he'd gotten the black coffin with the woman inside safely tucked onto the back.

"How did you..." Zeva started, but the appearance of the young, handsome driver stopped her words.

"By the gods," the young man cooed, holding out his palm to her and smiling dazzlingly. "I am very glad to make your acquaintance, Zeva."

"We're very much out of coin now," Tarkan grunted, shoving himself aggressively between Zeva and the young man to pay a few dock workers, who helped them lift the coffin onto the araba.

Zeva blushed as the man winked at her.

"Don't be like that, old friend," the young man called to Tarkan. "I'm doing you a favor. Oh, no, dear. Sorry. I have to go."

The old woman who had been listening to him sing came around the corner of the araba, fanning herself and carrying a pile of new silks, calling his name.

"But you promised me tonight." She sighed longingly, taking his glossy hair in her hands. "My husband won't be back for days."

"I know." The singer matched her melancholy coo with his own, giving her a quick kiss on the tip of her nose. "What a grand time we would have had, too. Now run along. I see your next engagement eyeing me with daggers already."

The woman sighed sadly but moved through the crowd to a corpulent sheikh who sat waiting at a hookah tent. He glared at the young man, like a jaguar eyeing a gazelle, before leaving to grab the camel and transfer their packs.

"Who are you?" Zeva asked once they were alone. Everything from his startlingly bright eyes to his alabaster brow took her breath away. How did Tarkan know such a man?

"Vicdan Nashira." He smiled, kissing the back of her hand. He led her around the back of the araba but quickly dropped her hand when he spotted Tarkan fasten the drop-down back wall of the araba. "I saved your old man's life once, too. How's my handiwork holding?" He smirked, slapping Tarkan hard on the chest.

The necromancer coughed, the wind knocked out of him, and gave Vicdan a death stare.

"Aye, Tarkan, eat some beef or something," Vicdan said, shaking his hand. "I think I just hit pure bone. I hope he takes better care of you than he does himself, my desert rose."

Ignoring Vicdan, Tarkan climbed into the araba with the box and motioned for Zeva to join him. "I will take your offer of lawless thievery, Vicdan. But I will not tolerate your incessant talking. Don't speak to her." Another threat obviously lingered on his tongue, but he held it back.

"I'm so glad we ran into you, Vicdan," Zeva chirped. "Company is rare for me." She blushed again. Unsure what made it happen, she didn't like the heat that rose to her face when the man looked at her. Maybe the sun was extra bright today?

The roguish young man smiled crookedly until Tarkan's sharp as ice eyes sliced through his smile.

"Always happy to tag along for adventure," he said tactfully. "Where to?"

"Southwest," Tarkan snarled, eyeing death threats at Vicdan. "Hatal."

Zeva touched the box as Vicdan clicked his tongue and flicked the reins. The two white mares started a brisk trot, pulling them away from the ports and out onto the roads that snaked between the city and the villages.

"What's in the box?" Vicdan asked.

Zeva almost replied, but looked to Tarkan first. "You said she was a Runer?"

"I never told you how I found you, saved you from Sharar," he replied darkly.

She noted how his voice dipped. He never shied away from showing emotion to her, but it still didn't happen often.

"Remember the Runer who hunted me?" he asked.

She nodded. "You said, 'What a fool. He thinks I am some base beast he can slay.' " She shook her head. "I don't miss your pride."

Her remark clearly stung him. She regretted her words. His pride —rage—had led to her capture. His continued defiance of the evil man had led to her months of torture.

"She is his apprentice," Tarkan said after a melancholy moment of silence. "She helped free me and save you. She stood up to Sharar with us, gave Tzarik—her mentor—the strength he needed to face him."

"Sybal?" Vicdan shouted from the front. He pulled hard on the reins, stopping the araba, and spun around.

"Don't stop!" Tarkan roared. "We need to get out of sight."

"Is she...?" Vicdan stood up.

"She's alive," Zeva piped up. "Her spirit is strong, or he wouldn't have caged her in black." She cocked her head to the side. "Is she a Runer, too?"

"Yes." Tarkan snapped his fingers for Vicdan to drive on. Reluctantly, he did.

"It's Sharar's handwriting," Tarkan mused as they rumbled through the inner circle of the city to back streets with less traffic and fewer curious eyes. "But the labels are from Xia."

Zeva watched him, thrilled that not only had a ghost appeared to her, but Tarkan was not shutting her out.

He went on. "The Runers had to have been in Xia. If Tzarik saw this box, he'd follow it to Hatal."

"And you're sure we'll be safe?" Zeva asked, some of the hot thrill of adventure turning cold. "Won't Sharar come looking for her?"

"He won't go to Makan Almyat," Tarkan said with a dark grin. "Even an army of Runers cannot stand up to all the haunts and specters there. The dead are our allies."

"Bad memories of Hatal?" Vicdan asked Zeva.

She nodded mutely.

The young man smiled, making his honey-colored eyes sparkle in the Al'Myrahn sun. "I'll show you a much better Hatal. You won't even remember the worst hours spent there."

Zeva smiled kindly at him, taken in by his joy. He didn't understand. Nothing could make her forget. But at least he'd offered. Perhaps it wouldn't be so bad to have him walk her around the glittering city's streets. The spear of ice shooting from Tarkan's eyes told her it might be difficult to sneak away with the charming singer.

Glancing over her shoulder at the coffin, a new kind of wonder filled Zeva's chest. A lady Runer? She'd never heard of such a thing. Tarkan's last apprentice had been a woman. There were woman warriors. The sultana was one of the first women to rule Al'Myrah. But a Runer? Never. The desire to save Sybal ignited and burned even hotter in her now. Not only had this Runer saved her, stood up to a dangerous man, and worked in a monstrous world, but she did it all alone. Zeva had the company of Tarkan and loved him. But she could not even imagine what it would be like to speak to a woman like that. She wondered if Sybal would like her. Be willing to speak with her about things she could never talk to Tarkan about.

"We will need money for shelter and food when we reach Hatal," Tarkan said when they hit the open road.

Vicdan sang a long, high note. "No worries there, old man. I've gone up and down this continent and have never wanted for food or a place to sleep. Leave it to me."

Zeva reached across the araba and lifted the slat Tarkan had pried off. Looking inside, she beheld the lady Runer who had helped save her over a year ago. Her Al'Myrahn skin shone pale and patches of the roots of her yellow hair had whitened. Black veins stood out against her skin.

"Don't Runers have white blood?" she asked Tarkan.

"She's poisoned," he replied. "Her heart is not beating strong, and she doesn't breathe. But I can still feel her soul inside."

Zeva shivered. "How terrible." She looked in again. She could tell when the woman stood, she'd be at least six feet tall. "She looks like a shield-maiden from Caerwren. She's beautiful," she added. Carefully, she reached inside and pushed a lock of the Runer's hair out of her face tenderly, then sealed the box back up.

The road to Hatal would be littered with cold nights, thirst, and empty bellies. If they could save Sybal, it would be worth it.

CHAPTER 3

MAKAN ALMYAT

The jongleur grated on Tarkan's nerves, never stopping for breath between Singad and Hatal. He continuously told Zeva of festivals, rowdy public houses, and other adventures he'd had inside the capital city of Al'Myrah. Her eyes grew wide, and he sensed the anticipation she held for when they entered the city. Tarkan chose to have them go the long way around the main city. They were tired, thirsty, and hungry, but he wouldn't risk the brazen jongleur whisking Zeva away in the night.

The tombs of Makan Almyat lay outside the city, a black spot near the shore closest to Porsh. The night was old when they reached its borders. The light from the moon did not hit it. The malignation from the black and necrotic magic that permeated it kept all natural, living things at bay. The haunts were kept inside by hundreds of tall, black obelisks lining the perimeter. Tarkan and Zeva would be protected from possession and curses from the haunts, Tarkan by his black scriptures, and Zeva because she was a blood promise, bound to him. She would be covered by his blood. Tarkan smiled darkly, hoping a specter might possess the jongleur.

They entered the boundaries of the obelisks. White, black, and gray stone made up every monument, mausoleum, and pyramid. Each tomb looked different from the next. Once inside, the light from the moon vanished and pure darkness engulfed them. Vicdan lit a torch for him and Zeva to see by.

"Reminds me of Porsh," Vicdan mused softly, as if he might wake the dead.

"You've been to Porsh?" Zeva asked innocently.

Vicdan nodded, his eyes darting to something in the shadows that moved. "To the house of Mirzam, actually." He smiled at her, gently prodding the star on her forehead. "With our mutual friend some time ago. Terrified me then, but little did I know it was my first act as a great hero in a dangerous adventure."

"This is the best place to hide," Tarkan assured them both. "We will be safe from Sharar, and Tzarik will head for Hatal. We must be on the lookout for him. The malignation will keep out all others."

"We called it a blight," Vicdan offered.

Tarkan took the opportunity to educate the jongleur. "A blight is a curse. Typically won't pass from one place to the next. A maligna-tion will if it grows strong enough." He pointed to the stone pillars that dotted the perimeter. "These obelisks have sigils that keep it inside. For now. A blight can be placed by purposeful magic. A malignation is never intended; it is the inadvertent result of powerful, black magic."

Zeva smiled politely and hugged Tarkan's arm. Getting through the valley of tombs took longer with the araba in tow. The wheels constantly hitched on the blasted, glassy waves of the streets. Even Tarkan slipped a few times on the rough terrain. Having spent ample time in Porsh and Makan Almyat, he knew hours had passed and that the moon must have risen outside the dead borders when they reached the center tomb: a pyramid made entirely of ghostly white stone.

"We're going in there?" Vicdan asked, a slight quiver to his tone.

"There is nothing to fear," Tarkan quipped.

The three of them lifted the black coffin and marched under the post and lintel of the tomb. The smell of the cold crypt brought back calming memories for Tarkan. When they passed the entryway into the foyer of the tomb, his scriptures did not crawl; nothing haunted the space tonight.

"We're safe," he assured them. Zeva gasped as a bat flitted past them. "Nothing is moving now."

Tarkan led them down a side hallway made of the same white stone. Reliefs of histories none of them knew covered the tomb walls. A few pedestals of artifacts from the dead's long-ago lives lined some small alcoves. At last, they passed into a smaller room with three stone coffins. Tarkan signaled them to put Sybal down at the foot of the other three.

"What will you do?" Zeva asked once they all stood around the box. "That sorcerer will know she's gone missing. He'll come looking for her. He might guess we've taken her."

Without verbally answering, Tarkan lifted the slat and pried the others off. He instructed Zeva to bring his fleshy black box to him and had Vicdan help remove the rest of the top. With the coffin open, they looked in.

"Oh, Sybal." Vicdan sighed sadly. He knelt next to her still form and reached in to touch her, gently stroking her face.

The necromancer motioned for Vicdan to help lift her. They laid her on top of one of the other stone resting places and Tarkan took the box from Zeva. Vicdan sniffled softly and watched.

First, Tarkan paced slowly around Sybal, examining her with only his eyes. The long tail of an inky black rune coming from the corner of his eye stirred as he used the powers of the scriptures to look for her spirit. Mumbling the verses, his eyes caught a quick glimpse of it inside her body. It flickered and snapped like a tongue of white lightning.

"She's still here," he breathed, reaching toward her. In his necrotic vision, his own ghostly black hand stretched toward her white spirit. Her form flickered and vanished in a bright crackle. It reminded him of the portal to the God Deep closing.

He paused, lips parted partly in horror.

"What is it?" Zeva asked, seeing the change in him.

"Sacrificed," Tarkan mumbled, lowering his hand and going to Sybal's side now. "She wasn't just killed; she was given to a god against her will. But she never fully died."

"What?" Vicdan gently stroked Sybal's icy hand on the other side.

Tarkan looked up, meeting the jongleur's eyes. "Everyone has their gods. Some sacrifice to them to gain favor. As I do. Each god prepares an afterlife for their followers. The one for good, called Janna, on Al'Myrah. And one for bad: Nah'jaha, a place of eternal ice, fire, and darkness."

Vicdan quickly drew a holy circle over his heart, but nodded, showing he understood. "As they taught us all. I forgot other countries and religions sacrifice sentients to their gods. What horrible gods."

"In most places on Al'Myrah, you do not sacrifice...other sentients," Tarkan went on, opening his black box and carefully selecting a silver blade, knowing the orichalcum one beside it would harm the Runer if it cut her. "But not every people are such as we are."

Zeva and Vicdan both grimaced sadly, understanding.

He finished, "When killed as a sacrifice, your spirit does not get to experience the paradise or hell set up for you by your god. Instead, you go to *them*, the one you were sacrificed to. Your spirit enters the God Deep, a spectral realm laid over ours like a mist, where they walk as we do."

He gripped the Runer's armor to remove it, but his fingers fumbled with her laces. He'd opened just a fraction of a doorway into the Deep in Ala'Nar for the other tribe. It had nearly drained him.

Only an ascended Necro'Khan could really force the Deep open, go inside, pull a soul out...

The gods in Al'Myrah mimicked their people: quiet, what some might call civilized. Other countries, where the gods were more savage, had a thinner veil between the mortals and their gods. Places like Caerwren. He calculated quickly, knowing the western winter approached. That was the time the barrier was thinnest; the perfect time and place to try again. To gain favor.

"Tarkan?" Zeva whispered, lightly touching his shoulder.

He came back to the present and finished removing Sybal's armor. With much prying and difficulty, he took it completely off. Carefully, he prodded at her sides and mid-section. The stiffness had taken her entire body. With the armor off, he could see clear bite marks on her neck.

"So, you think someone sacrificed her?" Vicdan asked, eyes filling with sadness again.

Tarkan didn't reply yet. He ran his hands over the bite and leaned to look at the back of her neck. Something there caught his eye: glistening, white blood. It was dry now, but the mysterious sulfates of the Runer blood still caught the dead light. He motioned Vicdan to help him push Sybal onto her side. When they did, he lifted her black tunic. Zeva whimpered and turned away, touching the scars on her face.

Crisscrossing over Sybal's back were deep, bloody lashings. Pale patches of flesh on her side showed where bruises had blossomed before her death. Someone had beaten her near to death before administering the bite. Tarkan shifted to look at Zeva. His ward had tears brimming in her eyes. She understood this kind of torture.

"Was it *him*?" she asked, her voice quivering.

"I don't think so," Tarkan replied, laying Sybal back down. He touched the bite again. "Masahk, maybe. A serpentine immortal with venom." He pushed Sybal's sleeves up and saw the burns and white bruises around her wrist. "Crucified on a cross, tied," he added. "A part of a ritual killing. That must be what put her into the God Deep."

"Well, get her out of it," Vicdan snapped, running his hand under his nose.

Tarkan glared at the younger man. "It's not that simple." Unless he could ascend. Better him than another necromancer. He had, after all, killed the last Necro'Khan. It was rightfully his mantle.

He took up the silver knife again and pressed it onto Sybal's forearm. Grateful that neither of them stopped him, he cut all the way from her wrist to the crook of her arm. No blood spilled from the wound, further confirming his suspicion.

"The venom from a viper Masahk congeals the blood of mortals," he explained. "Runer blood is not living, so the effects might be different."

Making smaller incisions on either end of the longer cut, he slowly peeled back an opening in Sybal's flesh. The light from the flickering torches hit the exposed muscles, veins, and sinews inside Sybal's arm, refracting the light into colorful specs on his black robes. Despite their white blood, the muscles inside Runers usually remained at least a pale shade of red. But not in Sybal.

Curious, Vicdan and Zeva looked over Tarkan's shoulder.

The muscles in Sybal's arms were the color of pearly ivory, almost glittering from the hardened sulfates inside her veins. The black he'd seen in the veins from the outside was actually a dark, deathly purple. Tarkan touched the muscle. The hardness did not penetrate all the way through. The surface of the muscle still depressed when he poked at it, but just underneath the soft top layer, it was hard and almost unpliable.

"Like it's turning her to stone," Zeva whispered.

"We have to do something," Vicdan shouted into the echoing vault of the crypt.

"I don't know how," Tarkan started, stepping back from the

prone Runer. "In most cases of a venomous bite, one can drain the poison."

Vicdan shoved past Tarkan and gave Sybal's other arm a small squeeze. "She's not entirely taken over. Maybe we can..." He gulped. "Drain her of the poison anyway?"

Tarkan pointed to her whitening muscle. "You need Runer blood. Impossible for me to make, let alone find the ingredients."

Vicdan rubbed his chin. "And I suppose red blood is out of the question?"

The necromancer nodded. "It would break her oath to the runes to go back on the white."

The jongleur sighed loudly and turned on his heel, marching to the stone steps leading up out of the crypt.

"What are you doing?" Zeva asked, trotting after him.

"Finding a Runer," Vicdan called back. "She can't go on much longer like this, as the old man said."

"You think you can find a Runer?" Tarkan called to him doubtfully.

Vicdan turned to face them. He shrugged. "I am better at words than you are. I may be able to get what we seek. But you're right. Come with me and help me find one of these blaggards."

"And a proper coffin," Zeva said, running to catch up with Vicdan. "She deserves better than that box."

ZEVA GAVE up trying to convince Tarkan to come with her and Vicdan into Hatal to find a coffin for Sybal. She didn't hear what he said, but watched Tarkan hiss a warning at Vicdan as she climbed onto the araba to head into the city.

"He's so charming," Vicdan muttered between his teeth when he joined Zeva.

Zeva nodded, agreeing. "Do you think we can find a Runer who will sell us his blood?" she asked. She gripped him hard when the araba started its wobbling trek over the malignant ground.

"Perhaps. There are ways to find people, even in a big city like Hatal." He smiled down at her. "But I need distraction from poor Sybal's fate. And you need to experience the city."

She glanced up at him, confused. He smiled ahead.

"I will show you the best the city has to offer now that we've got the dark cloud of Tarkan off our backs. A few days in Hatal as we search for a Runer should brighten your spirits."

When they entered the city, Zeva insisted on finding a coffin first. Realizing she would not take in the glory that was Hatal until they had the morbid thing strapped to the araba, Vicdan gave in. A morgue waited on a corner near a temple with a large graveyard within the city. A man stood atop the minaret, loudly shouting a call to prayer. Zeva marveled at the architecture of the place of worship and the graveyard.

"They honor their dead so well," she mused.

Even the morgue boasted beautiful stone carvings, gem-encrusted decor, and elaborate carpets spread over the floor. Vicdan let Zeva pick out the coffin, then paid the man extra to have him help them strap it to the araba before they continued on.

Once they had it secured, Vicdan said, "Now, we catch some street performances and find a place to pass the night away."

Zeva looked up from admiring the black and silver coffin. "We're not going back now?"

Vicdan shook his head. "Makan Almyat is a few hours' drive, and the sun is setting. The best performances are at night." He held his hand out to her.

Smiling shyly, she took it and let him lead her through the streets. They tied the horses and araba to a public hitching post and meandered through the gilded streets. Wealthy sheikhs moved about in their silks covered in gold. A group of powerful quadis argued outside a courthouse. Street urchins ran, hiding from angry shop owners. Blacksmiths' bellows belched smoke up and sparks flew from stone wheels where they sharpened blades.

Vicdan took her to a public house where they watched a dancer and her remarkably trained goat do magic tricks. He bought her food and wine, but after a few sips, the world began to wobble and she stopped drinking. She kept her wits about her and looked for the tell-tale black leather of a Runer, but found none that night.

The next day, he led her to a shop that glittered more than the sultana's palace. Outer stalls shone with golden necklaces, ruby rings, and large earrings like sun-disks. Zeva couldn't stop herself from gasping as she ran to the shop. She'd seen a few ladies dripping in gems and gold, but had never touched it before in her life. Smiling shyly, she caught Vicdan beaming at her.

"Pick something," he said, grinning at her delight.

The merchant came out of the main shop, tucking a single round lens into his chest pocket to greet them. "See something you like, sabi?" He smiled kindly. He was older and had gray hair under his head wrappings.

"Everything!" Zeva beamed, grabbing a handful of coins. They turned out to be a belt of gold coins and links that clinked delight-fully as she picked them up.

The merchant smiled. She met his eyes and his fell a little. Real-izing he'd seen her disfigured face, she blushed and ducked her head into her shoulders. But the man said, "I think earrings."

Gently, he reached up and pulled her head scarf down. Her eyes flitted to Vicdan, unsure what to do. He simply smiled at her. The man picked up a set of long, dangling earrings of gold with red stones on the end. "Fulgurite glass," he said. "From Singad's red sand." He held them up to Zeva's ears. "They frame your face nicely."

She blushed again. "I don't think... I don't know..." She could never be bold enough to wear earrings like that, with her face uncovered.

"Perhaps," Vicdan said, picking up quickly on her discomfort. "A ring." He reached across the table and picked up a ring made of the same gold and red fulgurite. He gently took up her small hand and poised the ring over her middle finger. "May I?"

Giddy, she nodded. When he slipped the ring over her scarred hand, it almost made the marks of torture invisible. "Oh," she breathed.

"That settles it." The merchant beamed.

Vicdan paid him and the pair walked on down the street.

"It looks like a rose," Zeva said, holding the ring up so the stone caught the sunlight.

"A perfect desert rose for this desert rose," Vicdan said, kissing her hand before holding it.

Zeva giggled. "Thank you, Vicdan."

After an afternoon of looking for a Runer and finding no success, Zeva insisted they go back to Makan Almyat before Tarkan worried. They stayed a second night and headed back in the early morning. Unwilling to hide her new ring, Zeva didn't wrap it, instead letting it shine on her finger. If Tarkan noticed, he didn't say anything.

Two days later, Tarkan begrudgingly sat in a rowdy tavern deep in the province of Hatal. After the mistake of letting Zeva and the jongleur go into the capital alone, he wouldn't risk it again. They had no doubt been seen. Even the most uneducated in Hatal would have recognized the mark of House Mirzam on Zeva's face. They'd been too brazen. They needed to find a Runer to preserve Sybal and get back to hiding as fast as they could.

Vicdan worked the patrons, looking for a Runer who might have extra sulfates they'd be willing to part with. Over the years, Al'Myrahn Runers had faded more into legend. Meeting Tzarik and Sybal together were the most Runers he had run into in the last twenty years. They mostly traveled alone or died soon after their first few hunts.

The crowds in the city made Tarkan silent. He withdrew into his deep cowl, wrapping his face and hands in soft, black cotton to hide his telling appearance. That night, Zeva sat with him in a dark corner, far from the bright hearth where a toothless woman told a dirty story filled with clever innuendos. Zeva didn't laugh at the jokes, not understanding them. Instead, she tended to the pipe Vicdan ordered and drank mint tea sweetened with honey. She leaned up against Tarkan, sharing her warmth with his cold body.

"This is the coldest winter I've ever felt on Al'Myrah." She sighed, watching Vicdan whisper with a mysterious woman in a deep, red hood. "Even Moshav never got this cold."

"Times are changing," Tarkan agreed.

Zeva took his hand. Her warm, living flesh heated his palm instantly. "Oh, you're freezing." She smiled, putting her other hand on the back of his to warm him.

The red ring glinted in the firelight. He wasn't angry at Vicdan for buying Zeva a gift; he was angry that *he* never had.

The woman in the red hood nodded to Vicdan and reached her dark-skinned hand up for his. Golden chains bound to rings around her fingers marked her as an apprentice magi. Underneath the gold, dark brown ink spun around her palms and wrists in magical circles and patterns. The stargazers from Bahratt claimed to read palms, tea leaves, and to be able to tell the future through mysterious magical means. The woman gently traced the lines in Vicdan's palms with her long, red nail before turning her head to face Tarkan. Her eyes glowed like warm gold from inside her deep hood.

Tarkan stirred, not sure if she saw him or simply turned her head in his direction. The woman did not smirk like so many of her kind did. Instead, she pressed her forefinger to Vicdan's brow. He nodded and then scampered over to Tarkan and Zeva. He dug a coin purse out from his satchel.

"Well?" Tarkan asked.

"Well," Vicdan repeated, "I am off to a night of prophesying. Don't wait up."

Zeva's hand shot out and stopped Vicdan. "Wait. Did you find anything?"

The jongleur smiled. "I will after tonight. The magi have this kind of sex magic—"

"Go," Tarkan cut in, glaring at Vicdan. Zeva frowned, confused and a little annoyed that Tarkan didn't let her in on what was going on. "We'll head back to Makan Almyat. Find us tomorrow."

"Nonsense," Vicdan said, appalled. "You will not sleep outside in the sand like vagabonds or among your precious dead." He dug into his coin purse and pulled out a handful of rupees, handing them to Tarkan. "When you travel with Vicdan, you sleep inside." He winked at Zeva and turned to follow his magi up the stairs.

Tarkan prepared to protest, but Zeva's face lit up. "It's been so long since you've slept inside," she whispered. She shot forward, kissed Tarkan on his sunken cheek, and ran to the thin innkeeper to pay for a key. The woman's eye flitted to him, then back to Zeva. She handed her a key to a room and left out the back.

Stealing himself, he realized he'd have to bear Vicdan filling Zeva's head with the wonders of the city while they hunted down a Runer. It could be days. Days of torturous melodies from Vicdan's mouth and the buzz and clatter of the city.

CHAPTER 4

THE BUTCHER
OF ALA NAR

CROSSING THE SHEZAI OCEAN TOOK ONLY A FORTNIGHT
with the wind at the back of the Al'Myrahn vessel. The seasoned
seamen ran about joyfully, crying out thanks to Layth'asad, the lion-
shaped prime god of Al'Myrah. The familiar tongue chorusing
around the weather-beaten Runer brought a weary smile to his
parched lips.

Tzarik trudged across the deck of the big ship to take in the
sunrise in the east and his homeland to the west. Across the golden
waters of the Al'Myrahn shore, the tang of spices, sweet meat, and
ripe fruit drying in the sun met him. He took in a deep breath, filling
his aching chest with the smell of home. On the back of his head, the
sun hit him warm and welcoming. It glittered off the red, ruby-like
sand of Singad.

The seaside province always buzzed with eternal life. Being the
main port for trade with Xia, Alika, and even the rare ship from
Oceanya, Singad boomed with life, never sleeping. This was good;
Tzarik needed a hunt, a bed, and to find a lead on the cargo Sharar
had sent ahead of him. Somewhere, Sybal's body was locked in a box,
and he had to find her before the scholar did. Surely Sharar had left
Xia before him, sailing into the storm. Perhaps Yui's curse had
waylaid him, blowing him off course.

Tzarik led the three horses—Mamun, the Akhelatek, and Sybal's white mare—down the gangplank and into the port part of the city. The outer ring, like most cities on Al'Myrah, was the dirtiest, loudest, and fastest moving part of the larger main city of the province. He pushed through the throngs when his sulfates suddenly rushed in a cold surge. Spinning around, he instinctively put his back to Mamun and laid his hand on the hilt of his scimitar. Eyes watched him. Leaning into the warning from the sulfates, he scanned the crowd. Too many sentients roamed the square for one to stick out, but something had its eyes on him. Not one sentient glared at him.

Satisfied, but still on edge, he waved down a messenger boy, who was in the midst of gathering up a pile of missives to distribute. The boy had long, tangled, yellow braids and pale skin. Tzarik only knew a handful of words in Caerwren but recognized its people. He'd been told by the monk to go to Caerwren, but hadn't made up his mind yet. Angry that some god played a trick on him with the boy's ethnicity, he moved towards him. He took Sharar's letter, the one the Masahk on Xia had intercepted from a correspondent of Sharar's that mentioned Tarkan appearing and taking the cargo. He held it out to the boy. The elegant, looping Al'Myrahn letters on the front would be his best bet.

"Can you read this?" Tzarik grunted to the Caerwren boy in Al'Myrahn.

"I can read anything for a rupee," the boy said slyly. Then he asked something in Caerwren, which Tzarik was shocked to find he understood a word or two.

"Speak Al'Myrahn," he growled. Tzarik dug in his belt and found an Al'Myrahn coin amongst his Xian ones. He would need to hunt and acquire coin if he wanted to start tracking Tarkan. He didn't need shelter, just food and water for him and the horses. He flipped the coin to the child, who caught it deftly. After biting it to ensure its authenticity, the boy narrowed his eyes at the letter Tzarik held.

"All right, but it'll cost you more." He winced up into the sun to look at Tzarik and smiled.

When Tzarik glared down at the foreign boy, his smile slipped a little. The messenger scoffed lightly and shook his head. "Fine," he moaned in Al'Myrahn. "It's almost the same, you know. And you're a Runer. How do you not know Caerwren?"

"Read," Tzarik barked.

"It's an address in Hatal," the boy said simply. "One of those fancy scholarly men. A whole bunch of them live on that street near the seminary. Has a good view of the sultana's palace as well."

"What street?" Tzarik asked. "There are at least three seminaries in Hatal."

"It said Albayda." The boy pocketed the coin and grabbed up a few more missives to deliver to others in the city. "When you find the city square with the alabaster fountain in it, you're close." He leaned over the letter again, frowning. "This," he pointed to the looping script, "is the house number. Same shapes we use on Caerwren. It means twenty-seven. Odd number, on the left side of the street when you face east. Just find the fountain."

Tzarik knew it. "Thank you." He tossed the boy another coin. Sharar had sent Sybal's body ahead of him. She'd be gone from Singad by now. The couriers would take her to the address, which Tzarik presumed was the scholar's home. But the letter had said that Sybal was missing and had mentioned Tarkan. If Tarkan had found her somehow, would he deduce that Tzarik knew to follow them to Hatal?

He mounted Mamun and prepared to leave Singad. The horse snorted excitedly as its hooves pushed into the sand. Even Mamun was glad to be back on their home shores. No matter if Tarkan had taken Sybal or if the couriers had, Hatal would be the place to start. And it would have a hunt for him.

Letting the noise and familiar smells and conversation wash over him, the Runer kept his head down under his black cowl and made his way towards the western end of Singad. The sandstone buildings harkened to his memories. The sun winking through a line of wooden supports made him wish Sybal were there so he could tell her a story that started with, "Once, Azar brought me to Singad for a hunt…"

He'd not walked in silence like this since before Sybal. The sun reached its zenith when he came to the western gate of the main city. The sands of time moved quickly with no one there to keep him company. Deciding, since he didn't have to stop at night and let Sybal rest, he left the city gates and journeyed out into wild mountains of the province. He knew the trails through the sandy hills well, and wouldn't need more than the light of the moon above. The night would be chilly with the winter approaching, but the cold wouldn't bother him.

Almost in a trance, Tzarik marched on, stopping only when thirst drove him to find a stream or when Mamun whined and snorted to rest. A nomadic tribe in the sand mountains between Singad and Hatal paid him to find a plant that would cure one of their number from a curse of pox from a witch. Tzarik knew from the way the man scratched at his skin that it wasn't so much a curse as a bottle of flees dumped into the man's clothes. But a nettle that grew in the harsh sands tended to drive such pestilence away. Finding the nettle and brewing a tincture from it, he healed the man and was paid a few coins.

Before he knew it, the glittering capital city of Al'Myrah, the home of the sultana, rose over the golden sands. Hatal was only rivaled in wealth and beauty by Ala'Nar.

He stood a moment on the cresting dune, looking at Hatal light up in the sunset. Mamun nudged him, panting eagerly. The horse knew the city just as well as he did, and knew it meant clean stables, fresh hay, and cool water.

"We can't stop," he murmured. His voice barely cut through his dry throat. His stomach roiled with hunger.

As if to disagree, Mamun turned one ear down, looking him in the eye. The other two horses snorted in accord with Mamun.

"You're right," he sighed, trudging into the city. "I'm no good to her dead."

The Albayda district was made of white sandstone and marble. Golden and pearly facades lined the streets where dignitaries and political citizens milled around, going about their final tasks of the day. Feeling very out of place, Tzarik ducked into the nearest public house he could afford at the edge of the district. He paid for three stalls for the horses and a little extra to have them scrubbed down with cool water. The inside of the house hummed softly with the din of travelers, pirates, nomadic Masahk, and dignitaries from other parts of the map.

Trying to stay low, he moved to the stretch of countertops that separated the innkeeper from the dining area, where the smoke from hookahs filled the air. An Al'Myrahn woman with thick black hair and soft, oval eyes washed a pile of metal tankards on the other side. When he approached, she faced him, drying her hands on a rough cloth.

"Hazil!" she shouted towards the back, calling someone by name. To Tzarik she said, "Ten for the night, fifteen for a bath. Dinner is lamb. No morning meal."

Without question, Tzarik plunked down fifteen rupees. Only a few more clinked in his satchel. "I need a hunt," he said.

The woman smiled, pressing her red lips to the side. "Not much haunts in Hatal," she started. When her large eyes landed on him, she paused in her chore and narrowed her eyes. "Do I know you?"

Finally allowing himself to meet her eyes, Tzarik scanned her face. She was young, pretty, but he didn't know her. "I don't think so," he replied cautiously. "I'm looking for acquaintances of mine. A man, much like a Runer, and a girl with him."

She didn't speak, her mouth slowly opening as she tried to place his face. At length, she shouted again. "Hazil!"

A young boy burst from the back, covered in feathers with straw in his hair. "I was plucking the chicken," he panted, wiping sweat from his brow.

The woman grabbed his arm, hissed something into his ear, and shoved him back out the way he came. Smiling at Tzarik and handing him a small brass key, she said, "I'll get the bath ready for you."

꙳

TZARIK REMOVED HIS LEATHER ARMOR, eyeing the tub of hot water. Mentally taking note of everything in the saddles, he realized he only had one bottle of sulfates. He needed to hunt, and would have to be very careful. Perhaps he'd find small jobs that didn't require combat and the risk of injury. He'd make more eventually, but first, he wanted to find Sybal. He'd risk the Runer's death as long as he could if small jobs wouldn't present themselves.

He tossed his belt aside when a soft knock sounded on the door. Taking up his knife from his boot, he pressed himself against the wall and gripped the black iron door handle. Then he flung it open and braced for an attack.

The boy, Hazil, stood in the dark doorway holding a bowl of lamb stew. He blinked up at the Runer. "I'm not that bad of a cook," he said, entering. He walked across the room, undeterred by the threat, and set the bowl down on the stand near the straw mattress.

Tzarik watched him, waiting for him to leave. When the boy didn't move, he quipped, "What do you want?"

Hazil clasped his hands behind his back, rocking on the balls of his feet. "Can animals have ghosts?" he asked.

Taken off guard, Tzarik blinked, shaking his head. "I've never seen the ghost of a dog or horse. But that doesn't mean they couldn't." He didn't know which sentients were allowed souls and which ones weren't. "Ask a priest or a kehann."

"Something is in the alley out back," Hazil said quickly. His eyes turned hard. "Come and see."

More confused than before, Tzarik eyed the boy. "Have you seen something?"

"Please come and see!" he begged harder. His hands shook.

Even if a ghost of the boy's dead pet didn't linger in the alley, something did, and it frightened him. It would be worth a look if it led to payment.

"Show me," he said.

Tzarik followed Hazil down the steps. Being late, the tavern was empty now except for two dark-cloaked figures sitting away from the smoldering embers of the fire. The boy led Tzarik out the back way through the kitchen, which was miraculously scrubbed to a shine. Gripping his knife, he took a deep breath to get the sulfates ready to pick up on anything amiss.

The alley behind the public house was dingy and dark. A notice board stood on the other end of the alley, its patents flapping and hissing in the light night breeze. Hazil stopped and pointed further down the alley. Cautiously, Tzarik turned to walk into the darkness. That was when something caught his eye. A certain patent on the notice board also showed the face of the guilty person it called to be brought to justice. Even though he couldn't read, Tzarik knew the sum at the bottom was significant. Looking at the sketched image, his stomach dropped out.

It was his face.

"What is this?" he barked to the boy. Hazil had taken several steps back towards the entryway. His face glowed pale in the lamplight. "What does this say?" he growled.

The boy shook. "It says you're the butcher of Ala'Nar." He gulped, eyes going wide. "I'm sorry."

A wild rush coursed through Tzarik's veins. From the shadows, a figure leapt out cloaked in all black. The white flash of a blade told him the man was there for his blood. Tzarik ducked out of the way, easily dodging the assassin's sloppy stab. Twisting around, he slashed with his knife. The strike missed but made the assassin spin.

The man charged, grappling Tzarik now. A black mask was wrapped around his face, hiding his features. The two entangled themselves in combat until the assassin got a solid kick into Tzarik's chin. The blow shot white light through Tzarik's eyes and he fell onto his back. The stone street sent a shock wave through him worse than the initial hit. He staggered to his knees.

The assassin reached for a small crossbow on his thigh. Behind Tzarik, Hazil cowered against the doorframe, watching.

The world came back into focus as the assassin aimed. Tzarik could tell from the tilt of the assassin's wrist that he was too weak to properly aim the bolt. It would miss him by a foot, but it would hit the boy behind him. Roaring, Tzarik charged the man to stop him from firing. His shoulder connected with the man, driving him into the street. Grappling again, the assassin pulled a bolt from his belt and attempted to shove it into Tzarik's neck. Blocking with his forearm, he brought the knife up under the assassin's chin. The man gurgled and froze. Then he went limp.

Panting, Tzarik stood up and spun to face the boy. Hazil's eyes filled with fear and tears. He dashed inside.

Before following him, Tzarik inspected his would-be assassin. To his relief, it was just a common bounty hunter. No white cloaks of a Reaver or their mysterious weapons that now were so familiar to him. Seething, he ran inside after the boy.

The place was empty now, the mysterious cloaked figures by the fire gone. The innkeeper came running in from the front door, freezing when she saw Tzarik. He lunged at her, easily locking her arms painfully behind her back. With her kicking her legs, he slammed her face into a table and held her there. The woman screamed, begging him not to hurt her.

"I'm sorry!" the woman cried, cringing from his snarling face. "They said you were with the deathfiends! There's a patent out on you. They paid me a finder's fee. I need the coin. My sister owns the public house on the other side of the city and she saw them." She panted, catching her breath. "When I saw you, I knew you had to be the one who destroyed Ala'Nar with them."

"Deathfiends?" Tzarik repeated. "Necromancers?"

"Yes, yes!" The lady sobbed, pulling uselessly against his brutish grip. "They're here in Hatal. Have been for days. We couldn't find Reavers. We needed Reavers. The report from Ala'Nar last year said a Runer was with the necromancers. But I couldn't find one." She gasped, tears soaking her face. "Please, don't hurt me."

Tzarik leaned closer to her face. "Did you send an assassin after them, too? Are they alive?"

The woman wailed. "I don't know!"

"Yes!" a high voice cried.

Tzarik spun around to see Hazil standing in the doorway, eyes drowning in tears. "I saw them when I took her a wagon of cheese last night." He gasped, clearly fighting to stand his ground while resisting the urge to attack the much stronger man grappling with his mother. "The other assassin just left. He went after them: a man, all in black, and girl in white."

The Runer's heart leapt: Tarkan and Zeva. Somewhere, Tarkan had Sybal, and had no idea assassins had been paid to find and kill him.

"Are you sure they're here?" Tzarik asked, finally releasing the woman. She fell to the ground, sobbing.

Hazil nodded. "Saw them myself. They have been looking for a Runer for days. They come and go from Makan Almyat." He shivered.

Tzarik glanced out the open front door at the purpling sky.

Fear stabbed at his chest. If they were at the public house, sleeping, they were vulnerable. Perhaps they were unaware that someone had sold out their presence to a bounty hunter. If the one cloaked man had just tried to kill him, the other would be on his way to find Tarkan. Running past the boy, he galloped into the street to mount Mamun. He prayed he wasn't too late.

CHAPTER 5

UNSPÖKEN

IN THE COLD, BLUE LIGHT OF MORNING, TARKAN WATCHED
Zeva walk the round pen beside the stables. She spent time with each
horse and camel, petting them, whispering sweet words to them, and
even brushing a few. She'd woken early, too excited to be laying her
head in doors to actually sleep. He also rarely slept. He fought the
urge to follow her out, letting her be on her own for just a moment,
though still within his sight. Now that she was older, she'd become
bolder. She didn't ask for his permission to walk away as often. She'd
venture out on her own and didn't cling to him as much. He should
have wanted her to find her independence, but something held him
back. He wanted to keep her like this forever.

On the other side of the wall, he heard Vicdan stirring. Good; he
wanted to leave the city. Hopefully the magi had seen during their
night and could tell them where to find a Runer willing to sell his
sulfates. Something thumped hard on the other side of the wall and
two voices giggled softly. He glanced over, hoping the jongleur would
hurry. When he turned back to the window, Zeva had vanished from
sight.

His heart leapt and beat once in panic. Rushing to the edge of the open casement, he scanned the pen for her white garments. The door to the stable hung open. He was just about to push away from the window frame to gallop down the stairs when a black-cloaked figure frantically dashed around the stable, coming to the open door. Tarkan glared down at it. The figure stopped, taking a second glance into the stable, then skidded to a halt.

"Zeva?" the figure's deep voice called.

Now Tarkan's heart pounded. The man knew her. Abandoning the room, Tarkan fled down the stairs and out into the pen. By the time he reached the stables, Zeva's voice called out, "Who are you? Stay away!"

With no weapons, nothing to raise, and no way to ward off her attacker, Tarkan galloped into the stables and threw himself at the man. His thin body collided with the other's solid, muscular frame. He grappled with the cloaked figure, wrapping his arm around the other's neck.

"Run, Zeva!" he shouted through teeth gnashed with the effort of holding onto the man. But Zeva didn't run. She hesitated, face pale with fear.

The other man grunted and fought against Tarkan's hold. He easily slipped his fingers under Tarkan's arm, and with a wild swing of his upper body, flung the necromancer over his head. Tarkan landed hard on his back, his head buzzing as his skull cracked against the hard dirt. The other man pressed his boot into Tarkan's neck and pointed the curved edge of a shimmering scimitar into his midsection.

Suddenly, the man froze. "Tarkan?" he asked, quickly removing his boot. The scimitar disappeared from his vision, too. "You're alive."

Gasping, Tarkan looked up into the black hood. Icy blue eyes peered down at him. "Tzarik?" he coughed.

A wild cry made them both look over to where Zeva had seized a pitchfork. She raised it and prepared to charge at Tzarik.

Tarkan sat up, raising his hands for Zeva to stop. "Wait, Zeva!" he called. She froze, but her face remained wild with fury. He stood up and faced the man. Looking at him front on, he recognized the Runer who had saved his life and helped him rescue his daughter. He motioned for Zeva to come forward. She did, albeit cautiously.

The Runer smiled in relief. "She's wilder than I thought she'd be."

"A Runer?" Zeva gasped, dropping the pitchfork. She dashed to Tarkan's side, shrinking beside him. "We need your help."

"I'm glad to see you're alive. I need your aid. I've been looking for you," Tzarik confirmed. He stumbled over his words, trying to organize his thoughts. "Do you have her? Is she here?"

Tarkan nodded silently, not even caring how the Runer knew he had Sybal or how he'd tracked them down.

An audible sigh of relief tore from the Runer's chest. He stepped back, taking a breath to steady himself. "Is she alive?"

Zeva understood who Tzarik was now and moaned sadly.

"What is it?" Tzarik asked.

As best he could, Tarkan explained what he'd found that day in Singad, bringing Sybal to Hatal, and what he'd discovered once he'd opened her up. The Runer's face darkened the more he spoke.

"But if we can bring life back to her body," Tarkan finished, "we may yet put her spirit back. But going into the world of the gods is dangerous and difficult. And there is only one who has the best chance."

Tzarik waited for the necromancer to go on, but he dared not. Tzarik said, "I was counseled to travel to Caerwren, where the barrier to that place is weakest."

Understanding dawned. "The Eldritch Hunt," Tarkan confirmed. So, their paths would intersect. He almost smiled. "I met some of my tribesmen on their way there. The time of Vasaras, winter, is when the barrier between us and the God Deep is weakest on Caerwren. It's naturally weaker on that continent, so Vasaras will make it even simpler." The Runer did not know that only a Necro'Khan could enter the Deep to retrieve a soul. It was true he wanted to ascend before any of his kin, but he could not bring himself to sacrifice what was needed for such an ascension. But if he had reason to try...

Seeing his hesitation, Tzarik said, "I intercepted correspondence on Xia involving you, Tarkan. Sharar knows you took Sybal. He left Xia long before I did, while the maelstrom devoured the Shezai Ocean. I was hoping it had waylaid him long enough to allow me to make it back before him and find you before he did." The Runer paused a moment, then went on. "If you go with me, at least you will be on the move. And I will need you once we are there—as you said."

The Runer was trying to convince him. His eyes almost shone with desperation. Tarkan saw Tzarik's jaw clench as he spoke, trying to find the right words to convince Tarkan to travel to the west in the winter. Should he tell Tzarik his desire?

"If Sharar still wants you," Tzarik was saying, "he will seek you until he finds you and has you bound and shackled. Especially since you took his prize." The Runer's blue eyes flicked up. "Where is she?"

"Makan Almyat," Tarkan replied. Good. The Runer had stopped his groveling. "I will show her to you."

"Tzarik!" a melodious voice shouted from above.

Tarkan noted the shocked, confused, then doleful expressions flash over Tzarik's face as he looked up at the public house. The jongleur waved energetically out the window, half his body sticking out. He was entirely naked. Tarkan slapped his hand over Zeva's eyes.

"You've found us," Vicdan called. "How marvelous. We're all together again." He turned to speak to the magi, who said something to him inside the room. "Yes, you were right. You said I would meet a Runer, and here he is!"

Tᴢᴀʀɪᴋ ᴡᴀɪᴛᴇᴅ ᴏᴜᴛsɪᴅᴇ to be joined by the others. Vicdan ran out only half dressed, his shirt unlaced and one boot on. He flung his arms wide and dove at Tzarik, exclaiming a long, high joyful note. The Runer dodged the incoming embrace.

"Don't be like that, old friend," Vicdan simpered, recovering from the snub. "I was worried about you. And with good cause, it seems."

"I'm sorry Tarkan and Zeva ran into you," he said, mounting Mamun. The other two appeared and Tarkan helped Zeva up into the araba.

"Well, I'm not." Vicdan smiled, taking the reins of Sybal's horse from Tzarik. He mounted the white mare, much to Tzarik's displeasure. "This has been a wonderful adventure. And Zeva has been a delight."

The girl smiled over at them from her perch next to Tarkan, dropping her head with a blush.

"Ah-ah, Zeva," Vicdan said joyfully. "What did I tell you about receiving compliments? What do you say back to me?"

The girl blushed even more deeply. "You're not so bad, either." She giggled nervously.

The jongleur beamed. "Exactly."

Tzarik caught Tarkan's blue eyes ice over at the interaction. Deciding it was in Vicdan's best interest to be separated from Tarkan, Tzarik rode ahead of the araba and Vicdan followed him, hungry for every detail of his adventure on Xia. Tzarik indulged the younger man, answering every question he lobed at him every few sentences or so. Vicdan constantly interrupted Tzarik's replies with his own stories of travel or similar experiences. One terrible story involved conjoined twins and a very angry, rich silk merchant who turned out to be the husband of the jointed women. Vicdan also interrupted to explain long, ancient histories of the Xian provinces and explain the beliefs behind certain symbols and creatures.

When Tzarik began to discuss the Wushito and their ways of containing monsters, Vicdan quieted down and listened. He frowned, genuinely interested, and allowed Tzarik to at last finish his tale. He spoke until his throat got too dry and he'd exhausted himself and driven Vicdan into quiet reflection. In the silence, Zeva told a godtale about a woman who could spin wool into gold.

By the time the sun set, the black valley of Makan Almyat loomed below them.

"Here we are." Vicdan sighed after they all looked into the maze of tombs and pyramids. "She's just inside."

The haunting pathways through the graves didn't frighten Tzarik at all. He eagerly followed Tarkan towards the great tomb. The closer he got to seeing Sybal again, the more his heart hammered in his chest. What if he couldn't save her? What if once he asked Tarkan to sail to the frozen land of Caerwren, the necromancer refused? He had no reason to follow Tzarik into the west.

The party stopped outside the tomb's doorway.

"Tzarik," Zeva said gently, "you go ahead."

A quick glance at Tarkan showed him waiting, still as stone. Vicdan dismounted but held on to the Akhelatek's reins.

"Go on," he said, waving his hand as if at a petulant child. "We'll be right there."

Tzarik turned his back on them and used every ounce of his strength to not dash over the malignant earth to find Sybal. He conjured up the last time he'd seen her in life. She'd come to him in a strange dream when he'd almost fallen to his death off one of the many cliffs of Xia. She was beautiful then, just like the first time he'd seen her in the courthouse where she'd fought for her life, brazen and bold.

But before the dream, he'd watched her turn and run back into the Hallow City. She'd all but told him goodbye before dashing back into the mouth of the beast they'd eventually slain. She'd known in that moment that she wouldn't come back out. Why? Had she intended to kill their enemies, testing her oath to the runes?

He slipped down the stone steps into the crypt. He checked a few burial rooms hesitantly without finding where she lay. The hesitation melted away and soon desperation overtook him. He whipped around the corners of the crypt, eyes scanning the empty rooms. Finally, a black coffin amongst three stone ones appeared behind one of the last corners he checked. He gripped the ornate stone wall to hold himself steady, wanting to run to her and not see her all at once.

Knowing no one was there to witness his weakness, he dashed to the coffin and gripped the lid. He didn't look inside until he'd lifted the lid entirely, giving him vision of her whole body.

Sybal lay perfectly still, pale, with blackish veins under her now ivory skin. The warm, golden Al'Myrahn hue had left her flesh. Unable to hold back, he reached in and touched her face. His skin pressed warm into hers. With his other hand, he stroked her blonde hair. Unlike her flesh, her hair was still soft and silky. As he ran his fingers through her locks, patches of stark whiteness flashed into the firelight where it had lost its color. His gentle touches stopped. Besides the beliefs of Xia, there was only one other thing that made a sentient lose the coloring of their flesh and hair: the touch of a god. They called them god-touched. He'd seen it once, and then it had resulted in madness and death. Worse than that, there was only one outcome for a sentient touched by a god, if not death.

With a loud grunt, he slipped one arm under Sybal's legs and the other behind her shoulders, lifting her out. Unable to bear her long body, he collapsed onto the ground, cradling her. The weight of her unconscious form on him broke the last wall of defense he had. Silently, he dropped his head onto her chest and gripped her tightly. Her body fell forward, limp enough to hang on his arms. He embraced her so tightly, he expected her to gasp, but no sound came from her. With her cold and stiff, he only had Tarkan's assurance that she was not dead.

He pulled his face away and gently tucked her loose hair behind one ear, then set her up with the last vial of sulfates he had, as Tarkan had advised. He placed his hand against her back to lay her down. Through her thin, black tunic, his hand felt scars on her back. He dared not inspect her body like this. Closing his eyes, he pressed his forehead to hers and breathed in her scent.

Not sure how much time passed, he opened his eyes when a gentle hand touched his shoulder. Vicdan knelt next to him silently. Tarkan stood a good distance off, watching him. Zeva must have waited outside.

"I need your help," Tzarik finally said to the necromancer. With Sybal in his arms, he couldn't wait any longer.

Tarkan nodded almost imperceptibly. "I know. There's only one way I know to get her back."

Vicdan frowned slightly, looking up from Sybal to Tarkan. "What are you thinking?"

"Can you do it?" Tzarik asked. "A monk I met said you could. But..." He tried to gauge the necromancer's reaction, but his face was a mask, like the statues of sheikhs around them.

"I desire such a task," the necromancer whispered hoarsely.

Tzarik suddenly felt like he wouldn't have to convince Tarkan. The necromancer had already thought about it. "I don't understand," Tzarik said. But it didn't matter. "Can you save her?"

The necromancer's eyes broke their connection with Tzarik's, turning distant. "It requires...great sacrifice."

Tzarik understood. He turned his face back down to Sybal and gripped her tighter. "I can find another," he grunted.

At the suggestion, the necromancer dropped his crossed arms. Vicdan looked up, curious at the sudden reaction.

"I will find a way," Tarkan said quickly. "Tzarik, only a

Necro'Khan can return a soul from the God Deep. I will not stand by and watch one of my tribesmen take the throne I suffered for."

"Necro'Khan?" Tzarik asked. "Lich king? You do not bear that mantle."

"But I can," Tarkan whispered, leaning close. "It's what I've worked for ever since breaking from Sharar."

A slight hesitation hooked Tzarik at this. He glanced at the stone coffins, much like the ones on Porsh, where Ishmael, the last Necro'Khan, had lain. Tarkan had killed Ishmael, severing his head and taking his heart. If Tarkan was willing to do that to his own father, he couldn't fathom what another necromancer might do to take that title. It was a risk he'd have to take if he wanted to save Sybal. She'd put her life in his hands two years ago and he'd not protected her.

Taking in her pale face again, his heart twisted. "As you wish, Tarkan."

ـﻰ

"Because you've never experienced it, I suppose," Vicdan cut in to Tzarik's thoughts, answering a question Tzarik had not asked as they crossed part of the vast, open desert that was the center of Al'Myrah.

With Tarkan's camel and the horses Tzarik had with him— Sybal's white mare, Mamun, and the Akhelatek Hiro had given him —all four of them could ride the distance. They'd spent the first two nights in awkward silence, even Vicdan and Zeva. But now, of course, the jongleur had to speak.

"Don't presume to know my thoughts," Tzarik mumbled back.

Vicdan smirked. "It was hard to miss your thoughts last night. It was too quiet. Why do your blue eyes insist on brooding around campfires? Ugh! I wanted to sing, to tell a story—something! Two nights of silence, Tzarik. So, I had only one occupation for my energetic mind: staring at you."

Slight revulsion came up Tzarik's throat.

Vicdan said, "I think I counted two minutes total during camp that you were *not* looking at Tarkan and Zeva. Staring is rude, Tzarik." He grinned playfully. "And I thought to myself, what is he looking at? Surely not the girl. Then I realized, 'Vicdan, you silly goat. He's marveling at both of them. Poor lad's probably never felt love.' Then I thought, 'Well, but this look says he misses that kind of thing.' But there was too much regret in your icy orbs. So, then I thought, 'Gods! He's fallen for our Sybal.' But do Runers do that? Then I got sad and stopped thinking about your depressing life." His face turned a little softer and he cocked a brow towards Tzarik. "Eh, Runer? There's no shame in it, you know."

Tzarik wanted to snap at Vicdan and make the young man recoil from his harsh tone. But that would push him away. He didn't want to be alone right now. Honesty would sound juvenile, but he didn't know what else to say.

"I don't know, Vicdan," he confessed, despite his misgivings. "The thought of losing her brings back the dark place I used to be in before her. Now that I've known something else—friendship, perhaps—I don't want to give it up. I don't want to again be the man I was before her. I wouldn't survive it. Not this time."

"Ah, a godtale as old as time." The jongleur sighed, smiling. "They say that finding love won't make your life better or fix your problems, but I have found that to be vastly untrue. There are people who are wrong for you. There are people not right for you. Then there are people who see the best in you and don't think about unearthing it because they know you can get there on your own, that you just need a little support. If I may, Tzarik?"

The Runer waved his hand for the jongleur to go on, knowing he wouldn't stop, even if he put his fist into his teeth.

"Don't fight it," Vicdan offered. He smiled sadly. "I know she won't hate you for showing your feelings. I saw how she felt about you that night we met on the river caravan. I also saw how you felt about her." He made a terrified face, remembering the interaction two years ago when he'd first tried to bed Sybal. "They say don't take a rabbit from a wolf, but I learned that night never to take Sybal from Tzarik. I thought it was strange, but I also saw how neither of you were going to speak your feelings out loud. Her, because she wanted you to stay. You, because you thought it was foolish. Well, I have news for you, Runer. Love makes fools of us all. And it's wonderful."

Tzarik grunted in agreement, then looked at Tarkan and Zeva ahead of them. There were stranger versions of affection. Or love? Yes, he didn't doubt Tarkan's fatherly love for Zeva.

Emboldened by being allowed to speak so much, Vicdan went on. "There is something else I swore to do once I met you again. And it will make these nights around the fire much more enjoyable. We have several nights before we reach Bagdula and find a ship."

The Runer glared with trepidation at the younger man. "And what was that?"

"Reading and writing," Vicdan crowed. "I bet you thought I'd forgotten about my threat to teach you your native tongue. Did you know that the tongue of Caerwren is very like our own? We share many words. The barbarians in the west do butcher our inflection, though. They treat the words very poorly. But it should be very simple for you to pick up, I think. Especially if we're going to that godsdamned frozen west."

His first reaction was to shut Vicdan down, to refuse. But too often had he been at a disadvantage because he couldn't read his own language.

When he didn't reply, Vicdan rummaged in his pack, looking for something. "You will learn to speak this language at the very least, and you'll thank me later. Then, you can read everything for yourself, and you won't have to listen to me talk on and on."

Tzarik perked up. "Let's get started, then."

The jongleur smiled graciously at the jibe. Finding ink, paper, and quills, he closed the flap of his pack with satisfaction. "Yes, we will start tonight. Caerwren's alphabet has only twelve letters. They don't write nearly as much as we do. Most in Hovandel and Gidenmore use Al'Myrahn letters to sound out the Caerwren language and in Rom it's practically Al'Myrahn. It's all very mixed up, but will make it quite simple for you. Half their tongue doesn't have a written equivalent. It's utter barbarism, if you ask me. But that will make it easy to learn, since they are derived from the same old tongue."

Regretting his decision as Vicdan droned on about linguistics, he caught Zeva smiling at him.

"Don't worry, Tzarik," she said kindly. "I'll help."

Looking ahead, Tzarik saw the central desert stretch on and on. He'd trade the darkness and snow of Caerwren right now to take back his agreement to learn language from Vicdan.

CHAPTER 6

TO THE FROZEN SHORE

TZARIK FILLED THE JOURNEY FROM HATAL TO THE boundaries of Bagdula with Vicdan as the jongleur showed him the straight and sharply angled letters of Caerwren, making him speak the words the two languages had in common and then using those to teach him the unfamiliar words. They put aside the Al'Myrahn alphabet once he had it memorized and focused on writing and sounding out the far simpler western characters. Vicdan picked up quickly that Tzarik learned spoken words faster and leaned more into speech than the letters after a few nights.

Too often in the last two years, Tzarik had been at a disadvantage because he could not understand the language of a people. His time on Xia had driven him to near madness with not being able to understand basic conversation. He had no desire for it to happen again.

He sat with his back against Sybal's coffin, having removed it from their now rickety wagon as they made camp. He didn't want her to be alone.

Zeva joined him as Vicdan spoke very slow Caerwren to him, writing a single word every now and then. She reached over to the parchment he worked on and wrote the elegant, looping Al'Myrahn letters under the matching ones from Caerwren. "Their letters look like the trees of Caerwren: stiff, straight, and angled. But these are the same." She pointed to three symbols that Tzarik now saw were very similar.

"This is true," Vicdan said, and he launched into a long oration about how Al'Myrahn explorers brought written language to places like Caerwren some thousands of years ago. "You see, the yellow-heads of Caerwren were voyagers long before we were. In fact, the only other sentients they found were most likely Xian or Alikan. Rhostrana grew quickly once they had ships. So, a Reks from Caer-wren—that's like a sultan—came to Al'Myrah and they used to raid our shores for slaves." He wrote the word out in Caerwren.

"Then why is it written like a name?" Tzarik interrupted, frowning, and checking back at a previous line of the of angled letters to see if he'd gotten a name right.

Zeva and Vicdan leaned closer. "Oh, yes," Vicdan murmured, checking the Caerwren word. "Reks," he repeated, thinking. "I'm not sure. It is written like a proper name, but we don't do the same with our honorifics unless they are paired with a name. Except for you, Runer."

Tzarik traced the mysterious letters with his eyes, over and over, until he memorized them. He was afraid now to ask why the word Runer would be written out like a name. Vicdan might go on for an eternity.

"Runer is a Caerwren word," the jongleur went on, seemingly reading his mind. "But my profession—jongleur—is a Rhostranan word."

"Zeva is an Alikan name," Zeva chimed in, loving the game. "Vicdan is Porshain."

The younger man looked up, brows raised. He didn't say anything for a moment before suddenly smiling. "It is." He elbowed Tzarik. "Where does your name come from? It's rather mixed up, isn't it? Is it tsar, like Rhostranan royalty? Or is it like tzadik, like the holy people of ancient history?"

Tzarik shrugged. "Azar named me. My father never gave me a name."

Vicdan smiled kindly. "The Al'Myrahns' had written language before most civilizations did and introduced it to the west. For all the good it did the brutes," he mumbled, correcting one word Tzarik wrote with a quick accent above a line. "They don't have a single monarch, each canton battling the next for land and sentients to sacrifice to their gods. They're vastly less civilized than even the mountain villages of Bahratt or the nomadic tribes on Alika. However, they don't have slaves in the traditional sense anymore, thank the gods. The Rekses still indulge with thralls, though."

Tzarik focused on the words he penned. To him, the letters of Caerwren looked like sharp, mountainous peaks. Others reminded him of the straight, leafless trees he'd seen in paintings of the wild, western country. Beside it, where Zeva had written the Al'Myrahn equivalent, the Al'Myrahn letters sloped and swooped in elegant dunes like the desert they came from. They made a small ache stab at his heart for the home he was about to leave again. He stopped tracing, looking down at the Caerwren word for "hunt." He mumbled it out loud to himself, sounding it carefully.

Vicdan beamed. "Well said, Runer. Are you sure you've never read before? You're soaking it up like a tavern-dweller would spilled wine. You would have made a wonderful scholar. Nothing escapes that brain of yours. And your accent was good, too. But most of Caerwren sounds like grunting and grumbling to me."

"It is more like old Al'Myrahn," Tarkan said, adding on to what the jongleur had imparted earlier. "In Porsh, we wrote in old Al'Myrahn. Our written word is too sacred to adhere to the modern language."

Tzarik's eyes moved the necromancer's exposed fingers. Now that he'd spent days studying the looping letters of his native tongue, he recognized them on Tarkan's pale skin. They were more complex, but familiar now.

He put the parchment aside and Vicdan handed him a book filled with stories in the eight dominant languages of the map. He flipped to one about a princess from Al'Myrah who saved herself by telling stories for days. He knew that one. One was about a djinn. Zeva had commented on how the stories were for very young children, but it was all he could read in his own language so far. He didn't tell them, but being able to read even a single word sent a thrill through him that he was not accustomed to. Silence fell in the camp as the others let him read, but Vicdan had to fill the quiet with the droning of his wheel fiddle.

Vicdan took to humming softly and drifting in and out of sleep after thirty minutes. Zeva breathed softly, but Tarkan's blue eyes never closed. Tzarik finished the Al'Myrahn story, then found one in Caerwren. The written language was far less refined than the Caerwren words Vicdan and he had been speaking. Uanble to undertand, he handed the book to Vicdan.

Happily, the jongleur took it and began to read the story in slow, careful Caerwern. Tzarik understood the spoken words far more easily and even heard the ones they shared with Al'Myrahn.

The story was called *The Ayin*. It told the godtale of a man from Al'Myrah ordered by the sultan to deliver a message to a man in charge of a tribe on Caerwren, a Reks. Vicdan had said it was like a sultan, but Tzarik deduced from the context it meant something more like a chief. But the man in the story, Ayin, feared Caerwren and wouldn't go. So, he'd taken a ship to sail anywhere else on the map but to Caerwren. The ship that carried Ayin ran into danger on the sea: a storm, a kraken, pirates, and others until the captain decided Ayin was the curse, running from his duty. So they'd tossed him overboard. Because Ayin hadn't completed his mission to Caerwren, Rhostrana had attacked, stealing away a certain people called a word Tzarik couldn't translate: Vaeson. When he asked Vicdan, the jongleur was embarrassed to admit he didn't know what it meant. Whatever Vaeson were, the absence of them on Caerwren threw the western continent into a rage and they'd attacked any Rhostrana trader on their shores. The last page of the story explained that the sailors of Caerwren now called anyone with bad luck an Ayin. An image at the end showed a frozen shoreline, waves covered in ice, and tall, imposing white cliffs. The strange, straight trees without leaves dotted the white-capped mountains of the picture.

"We'll need money for warmer clothes," Tzarik said to Tarkan after another hour of quiet contemplation. Beside him, Vicdan snored. "I should find a hunt. Something small to get us coin and fur."

The necromancer remained still, his daughter sleeping soundly against his chest. With his cold eyes, he peered into the darkness beyond their campfire to the west. "It is winter. The cold is the one hindrance we can prepare for."

WESTERN BAGDULA FADED from green to gold sand as its rain season dwindled, but still harbored a vast green prairie where Tzarik was able to dispatch a swamp creature for a single mother with seven children. Six, now that the monster had moved inland to escape the deep, colder ponds to feed for the winter. She was so grateful, she gave him a fur-lined coat and a nugget of unrefined gold she'd gotten in Ala'Nar. Tarkan and Zeva stayed with their wagon while Vicdan made the rounds in a bathhouse full of rich traveling men, liberating a few valuables from their abandoned cotton pants.

"Aren't you afraid you'll get caught?" Zeva asked Vicdan when they all met up again outside a furrier with a shop on the seawall.

"Have been. It's not always hard to get out of that situation, though." Vicdan smiled. He went into the shop to get the rest of them some fur-lined cloaks while Tarkan and Tzarik eyed the ships moored in the docks.

Tzarik picked out an enormous ship from Rhostrana with its

many masts and white sails, and even one of the angular ships from
Xia. Most were Al'Myrahn traders and sailors. He was thinking
they'd have to barter with the Rhostranan captain, ask him to make a
stop at Caerwren, when Tarkan lightly tapped his shoulder and
pointed offshore. There in the distance, a longship with a menacing
dragon-shaped figurehead bobbed in the waves. A single square sail
was being unfurled even as they watched. Tzarik took in the shallow
draft. The ship was for shallow waters, coming close to land and
leaving quickly. A smaller version at a dock, one with no sail, waited
with several yellow-haired men and women aboard. They were
arguing with the harbormaster. They had small axes, but looked like
traders, not fighters.

Tzarik motioned for Tarkan to wait and walked with purpose
towards the foreigners. His mouth went dry and his head buzzed as
he anticipated speaking in a new language. He knew he'd sound
childish, as many foreigners did to him when they spoke Al'Myrahn.
But he had money.

He marched up behind the shouting harbormaster and looked
down at the woman he argued with. She had two long yellow braids
and wore dark green cotton under a thick brown fur cloak. The
conversation, as he understood, was about mooring overnight
without paying.

Her eyes snapped to him when he came up behind the
harbormaster.

"What do you want, Runer?" she shouted up to him from the
rowboat in smooth Al'Myrahn. "We have no ghosts for you."

He glanced at the harbormaster who started to rage at the yellow-
haired woman. Then, he decided to play into her favor. It was her
boat he needed after all. He pointed to the dragon-headed longship
and asked in Caerwren, "Your boat?" His voice shook as he tried out
his new language skills on a native of Caerwren.

A small, impressed smile quirked up the corners of her mouth.
She shook her head and spoke slowly for him to understand, using

simple sentences to cut out the harbormaster's involvement. "Captain Sigmund's boat. Traders, not warriors. We have no quarrel with anyone," she added in a growl, glaring at the harbormaster.

"You moored here last night!" the harbormaster shouted for what must have been the dozenth time. His tone sputtered as his beady eyes darted between Tzarik and the woman. Tzarik understood the harbormaster's frustration too well. He reveled in being on the other side of the language barrier.

The man gripped an abacus and a metal pen in his hand like they were a bit of driftwood he clung to in the ocean. "You have to pay!"

"I paid him!" the woman snapped, shaking the rope that tied the boat to the dock. "I gave it to that little rat of an apprentice he has." She spoke only to Tzarik, in slow despite her anger.

"She says she paid you," he told the harbormaster in Al'Myrahn.

The harbormaster sighed and rubbed the bridge of his nose under his spectacles. "These barbarians have no sense of decorum," he mumbled to Tzarik.

Tzarik dug in his belt pouch and held up three gold coins Vicdan had liberated from the rich men. The round man's eyes went wide, and he stammered. Tzarik pressed the coins into his chest and shoved the man along as he tripped over his words. The yellow-haired woman glared at him.

"I *paid* the scoundrel," she said hotly, still in Caerwren. "They try to trick us. Make us pay twice."

"I don't doubt it," Tzarik replied, or tried to say. By her expression, he might've fumbled a few words. But she gave him a gracious shrug of her shoulder. He knelt on to the dock. "How much for passage for me, some cargo, and three others to Caerwren?"

Her keen, green eyes flitted back to the wagon and the other two he'd left behind. "Sigmund doesn't like Runers," she warned him. "Thinks they're bad luck."

He frowned, trying to understand her rapidly quickening speech.

She no longer spoke slowly for him now that the harbormaster had gone.

She tapped his chest hard. "Runer. Bad luck."

"Ayin?" he asked, recalling the story, and hoping he'd heard her correctly.

"Aye," she nodded, hauling up a coil of rope onto her shoulder. "Ayin."

Tzarik held up the golden nugget, twisting it to catch the sun. Gold was a universal language. Her eyes sparkled.

"However," she said with a smile, speaking slowly again, "he's a reasonable man." She snatched the gold, pocketing it with the speed and dexterity he'd only seen Vicdan use with such things. She flicked her head towards her crew mates. "Get the cargo. We need to catch this wind."

The western winds cut through the cloaks, burned Tzarik's skin, and froze the tears it pulled from his eyes onto his cheek. The farther they got from the golden waters of Al'Myrah, the angrier the ocean became. The waves crested high, turning to an almost sky-blue. Shards of sharp, white ice soared over the waves, showing just how cold the water turned this far west. The inky sky contrasted sharply with the blue waves, highlighted by bright white cracks of lightning. The wind picked up the salty water and flung it into his eyes.

He watched the enormous captain stagger over the pitching deck. The sailors from Caerwren were massive, taller than even Sybal. Their shoulders were broad and their hands huge. When they had boarded, standing closer together, Tzarik's head only came up to the captain's lower chest. Some godtales said the sentients of Caerwren were descended from giants. He realized now where Sybal had inherited her height from. Her mother, Freja, had been from the west. He remembered her being tall and imposing, just like Sybal. Their massive frames weathered the storm well, beards and braids frozen stiff from the cold wind.

"Where are the Al'Myrahns?" Captain Sigmund shouted over the gale-force zephyr.

The first mate, a man with a sea of red tangles and tiny braids whipping from his scalp, scowled into the wind, nodding towards the back of the ship where Tzarik huddled with the others. "Hiding."

Turning to look where his mate pointed, the captain spied the black mass huddled in a corner near the tied-down cargo. The desert dwellers clutched each other under the black wings of their new cloaks. Tzarik realized how pathetic they must have looked. He met Sigmund's eyes through the sharp wind and saw a glint there he did not like. He could tell their mood and what they read on the wind by how quickly they spoke. When at ease, the seadogs spoke slowly, like the roll of a huge, turquoise wave. When something foul crept up on the weather, they spoke quickly. Vicdan had been right: he picked up the language quickly. He attributed that to the shared words and what the jongleur called the grammatical structure. Whatever the hell that was.

"This storm has pulled us off course by a sunrise," the red-haired first mate shouted so they could hear. "Taking us towards Northica. We should have been home by now. We don't have the supplies to last long off course. And it's Vasaras. The men will not want to dock on just any shore."

This last warning made the first mate lower his voice. Tzarik realized this was what the sea dog feared more than the other misfortunes.

The captain, Sigmund, glared at them through his wild beard and sea-crusted hair. Some strands of his white and yellow hair didn't move in the wind, frozen stiff. "After the misfortune in Al'Myrah, the men are angry." Sigmund sighed.

Tzarik gripped someone's hand under their yards of fur cloaks. It had to have been Vicdan or Zeva, because their flesh was warm. He didn't care right now, he just needed to keep his sulfates flowing. How did the Runers on Caerwren stave off the cold? The sulfates were not entirely like the blood of cold-blooded snakes, but they weren't near as warm as red blood.

Sigmund lumbered over to the Al'Myrahns. He had a massive axe wound on one leg that he'd told them a story about on their first night on the ship. It had never healed properly, giving him a permanent lopsided gait. It made the huge Caerwren man look like a moving mountain with his swaying steps. He loomed over them, looking down as they tried to crouch below the side of the ship.

"Get inside," he grunted, pointing to the tiny door that led to a small cabin area. The longship had no lower deck. "You cannot stay in there forever, but you may die if you do not ease into the cold."

Not arguing, Tarkan and Tzarik stood up quickly, each hauling up Zeva and Vicdan. Tzarik's legs buckled against a massive wave that knocked Zeva down. She cried softly, miserable in the wind and never having sailed before. Tarkan wrapped her in his arms and pushed his head down against the wind, heading into the small cabin.

"Thank you," Tzarik mumbled. He held Sigmund's gaze for as long as he could in the biting gale.

"Don't thank me yet," Sigmund mumbled. He glared back at his crew. "This lot don't think I should keep you. Think you're an Ayin."

Recognizing the term and name, Tzarik's guard went up. Instinctively, his hand went to his scimitar.

"Don't, Runer," Sigmund warned. "If this storm passes and we see no snow in the air by tomorrow morning, you'll be safe."

Inside the cabin, Tarkan stood apart, letting Vicdan engulf Zeva in his warm embrace. The necromancer looked out the tiny porthole, which was open to the ocean air. Tzarik joined him, watching the icy, bright green waves rise and fall. The farther they got from Al'Myrah, the greener the ocean became until it was almost a sky-turquoise hue. It looked cold.

"Will the ship tip over?" Zeva asked, her voice muffled through her hands.

"No," Tzarik supplied. "They're made to stay on top of the water, ride the waves. It won't capsize."

Zeva's wrinkled brows showed she didn't quite believe him. But she stayed quiet, and they sat close together again as the sun, hidden behind swaths of gray clouds, sunk towards the horizon.

The jade medallion lying on Tzarik's chest was as cold as ice. He touched it with his fingers, tracing the image of the dragon there. He'd only prayed to a god once in his life, never believing in them or their power. The last time he'd sailed from Al'Myrah, he'd seen something in the clouds above the unfamiliar country, something he'd sworn was a white dragon. It had circled the top of Xia like a guardian. Closing his eyes and pressing the jade into his chest, he begged the dragon—if it were real—to let them enter Caerwren alive.

Eventually, despite the terrible waves and the boom of thunder on the horizon, he drifted off.

A CRY of anguish stirred Tzarik from his nightmarish sleep. His head turned as a particularly powerful wave spun the ship like a top. Another voice cried out a name, but the wind ate up the sorrowful call. Tzarik had spent little time at sea, but knew what the cries of a man falling overboard sounded like. He stiffened, realizing the storm had claimed one of the men.

"Where is the Runer?" Sigmund's voice shouted from above the cabin ceiling, muffled by the wooden deck. "The sea has taken enough from me!"

"I knew it," Tarkan hissed beside him, already awake. He kicked Tzarik hard, pushing the last of the drowsiness away. "Hide!"

Jolted by the necromancer's hard kick into his stiff leg, Tzarik jumped up, bracing himself against the beam in the center of the cabin.

Sigmund threw open the door, several faces following him, making a ruckus so loud the fish below could have heard. The men shouted, called for action.

Zeva made a high-pitched gasp and scrambled to disentangle herself from the wool blanket the sailor had given her during the night. Next to her, Tzarik rolled to the side, looking for his scimitar.

But there was nowhere to run or hide in the tiny cabin. The sailors flooded the lower room, lanterns and weapons in hand. Two of the brutes grabbed Zeva by her wrists as she tried to shield Tzarik. She screamed, yanking at her captors.

"Don't touch her!" Tarkan growled. Two more seized him, pulling his arms so hard behind him that he lost his footing. Another put his great boot against Vicdan's chest, stopping him from rising. The rest surrounded Tzarik.

"What's happened?" the Runer demanded, empty-handed. Looking around, he realized the items had shifted in the storm. His belt must have slid somewhere under the cargo. Defenseless, he raised his hands to chest height to show he had no way to fight back.

"You and your curse have been on this ship long enough, Ayin," Sigmund grunted. "Peradon, the god of the sea, has taken my young nephew, Nohr. Even now his brother cries at the stern, watching his brother's frozen body drift farther away. I will have to tell my sister I have lost her son. We are too far off course; we don't have the supplies to weather this storm anymore. No more. I'm sorry, Runer. There are a lot of things the men can stand, but an Ayin is not one of them." He motioned for his men to move in.

"Don't come any closer," Tzarik growled, but the men moved in, pinning his arms behind his back and kicking him behind his knees to make him fall.

"A curse. Bad luck," Sigmund said sadly. "Runers are always bad luck, but never this bad. I've worked with many before. But..." He sighed, glancing over at Tarkan and Zeva. "You have something worse with you. The sea is punishing me for letting you board my vessel, for bringing you close to my home. Once you're gone, the storm will pass. Always does."

"What?" Zeva cried.

"No!" Tarkan jerked against his captors. "Superstition among ignorant sea rats."

"*You* are going over with him," the captain snapped. "I don't know what you are, but you anger Peradon, the god of the sea. Of *life*."

"We can't be that far off course," Tzarik tried. "Give us a boat. We'll paddle to shore."

Sigmund laughed and the other sailors scoffed. "Not in these waves. Some are ten feet high. You'd capsize. Besides, I cannot risk the gods knowing I aided an Ayin. You must be given to Peradon. You go over."

"Over?" Tzarik gasped. "I can't swim."

"That's the point, Runer." The captain reached over and grasped Tzarik by the back of his neck. His large hand easily gripped the Runer, covering his string of runes so he couldn't grasp them. Sigmund pulled him out through the door. The red-haired first mate did the same to Tarkan.

"Don't," Tarkan pleaded, thrashing against his captor. "You don't have to do this."

"Don't take him!" Zeva wept audibly, tears staining her face. The crew pulled the other two up after their captain, forcing them to watch.

"What kind of a man sacrifices another to a god?" Vicdan asked, also terrified. "That's barbaric!"

The first mate laughed darkly. "Welcome to Caerwren, lad." He ordered one of the other men to take Vicdan and Zeva. "Tie them in the cabin. They will see the ocean calm."

"Wait!" Vicdan shouted, grunting and struggling against their captors. "Just take us to shore. I can see it through the rain and snow. Please!"

Sigmund reached back and backhanded Vicdan hard, shutting him up. Tzarik thrashed against the captain's giant-like strength to no avail. Zeva and Vicdan's cries were cut out by the wood of the ship and howling gale. Sigmund marched to the rail. Tzarik kicked madly while his fingers pried at the Caerwren man's hand. As the captain had feared, the morning had brought more wind, more savage waves, and the air had turned white with thick flakes of snow.

The soft flakes landed on Tzarik's exposed face like tiny pricks of cold steel. He gagged against Sigmund's iron grip, trying to offer a different resolution. Up on the stern, a boy shouted out into the wild waves, crying for his brother.

"I offer you this Ayin!" Sigmund shouted to the waves. "We seek recompense! Have him and this marked pagan as a sacrifice and bless us with smooth waters and gentle winds!"

"Don't," Tzarik wheezed as Sigmund lifted him up. With a final desperate attempt, he kicked, hitting Sigmund in the center of his face.

The man's fortitude astounded the Runer. He heard the nose crack and blood dribbled down his chin, but he didn't relinquish his grip.

"I'm sorry, Runer." With a shout, muscles straining, he tossed Tzarik out.

Tzarik fell through the freezing, rain-soaked air for five night-marish seconds. His gut flipped over in fright. Before he could gasp, a giant, blue, icy wave reached up like a vindictive hand and submerged him. As the wave crashed, it pulled him under.

Water alone terrified him. This angry, thrashing, frozen ocean nearly drove the last of his sanity away. Once the wave had him in its grasp, it tossed him head over heels, filling his nose and mouth with salty water. It burned inside his skull and a cough rose in his throat.

Forcing it down, he knew if he coughed, he'd gasp, and that was when the drowning would start.

He kicked into the darkness, arms pinwheeling in sheer panic. Within seconds, he lost all sense of direction. The air bubbles from his nostrils swirled away from him as another wave spun him around, not helping him find the surface. The water took away all feeling in his body. The only sensation was a burning in his lungs.

Finally, his head broke the surface. He knew because the air was colder than the water and it burned his cheeks. Screaming and gasping, he drank in the air. Everything around him was shrouded in darkness. The only light came from the lamps bobbing on the back of the ship—already yards away.

"Tzarik!" Tarkan's voice cut over the wind and roar of the waves. It sounded so far away. Distant.

Flailing his arms to stay above the raging sea, he caught the dark form of the necromancer to his left. Tarkan's white head dropped below the waves.

Finally, getting his feet kicking, Tzarik fought to find the rhythm of the waves and keep his head above water. He slowed his panicked movements, feeling the rise and fall of the water. Once he made himself wait for the waves, they helped keep his head up if he worked his limbs with them. Not sure if he made any progress with his arms, he paddled towards Tarkan as hard as he could. It took several minutes to find him, and when he did, Tarkan slipped in and out of consciousness. Tzarik gripped him under his arms, put his back against the sea, and kicked with all his might. Despite the necromancer weighing almost nothing, the extra weight pulled Tzarik back under several times. Each dip filled him with fright as the turquoise waves swallowed him and Tarkan up. He gasped when cresting a wave, desperate for air and not sure when the next chance would come. The cold air cut his insides.

After what felt like hours of fighting the storm, his lungs and legs burning in exhaustion, he washed closer to the craggy shore. Using the last of his strength, he clutched Tarkan tight to his chest to stop the sea from ripping the necromancer out of his arms. Rocks cut through his flesh as he tumbled over them, but he didn't feel them. He angled himself between the light necromancer and the sharp, black rocks to the brunt of the impact. At long last, a final, colossal wave lifted them both, smacking him down hard on the shore.

The cold filled his veins and limbs, stiffening him much like the Runer's death. The same pain shot through him with every crawling movement as he hauled himself and the necromancer onto shore. He lay still, numb and exhausted.

Opening his mouth, his lungs creaked, and only a strained, hoarse cry came out. His body was so frozen that speech was not possible. He lost his breath, waiting for the sulfates to pump some kind of warmth through him.

"Tzarik?" Tarkan's voice whispered, cut into fragments by the wind. Tzarik blinked the stinging sea water from his eyes. "Get up," Tarkan croaked. "We have to move before we freeze."

Tzarik forced his numb arms to push himself up. He limped over the sharp rocks, pulling Tarkan with him towards a white, chalky pathway leading up the cliffs they'd seen earlier. Torrential wind shoved salty spray into the already misty land.

A group of four men with a small fishing boat watched the strange pair, nets suspended before them.

Tzarik wheezed, speaking in Caerwren. "A city? A village?"

The oldest of the men pointed towards the path and the cliffs. "Follow the cairns. Northica to the north, up the mountain. But Altevine will be easier to find, over the moors and prairies."

Squinting into the gale force wind, Tzarik hardly made out a tall pile of rocks marking a trail. He understood as the words were the same in Al'Myrahn. Just to be sure, he pointed to the rock marker and repeated the word. The fisherman nodded. Hunching down, Tzarik led the way.

The cairns marked the path. Some had flickering peat torches on them, making them easier to spot. Others had blown out in the wind and rain. The higher they ascended, the more the wind ripped their wet clothes. Tzarik looked around for some kind of shelter, kindling, or life. Nothing but dark moors rolled out towards a cluster of sharp, steel-colored mountains. The grass somehow looked gray and a thick, bluish mist constantly flickered and wafted over it, tossed in the wind. The unmistakable scent of fire and ash permeated the air despite the wind.

The ground shook. Tarkan jerked Tzarik around by the arm he had over his shoulders. The source of the rumbling shake slowly lumbered past in the distance. His frozen breath caught in his throat.

Beyond the range to the west, up in the clouds, walked the definite outline of a lithe dragon. The shape of the colossus jutted out over the mountain tops as if the peaks were a mere stone wall keeping in a dog. The titan was so far away, they could glean no discernible markings. Tall and slight, like a deer, it had a long, serpentine tail. Above glowing white eyes, branching antlers arched up to the sky in sharp waves where a crackle of bright, green lightning snapped between the tines. With every step it took, the earth rumbled. The Runer and the necromancer watched in paralyzed silence as the thing marched on until it finally vanished into a thick mist of clouds. The earth-shaking steps vanished with it, leaving behind the smell of brimstone and fire.

Tarkan gasped, mouth agape, taking in the surrounding moors. "Runer," he whispered, "where have you taken me?"

CHAPTER 7

AWAKENING IN THE DEEP

At first, the only sensation Sybal registered was one of being hunted. Something watched her, hungry for her while she could not move. She gasped, almost crying, trying to move her body, to hide from the predator. Not only did solid darkness fill her vision despite her eyes being wide open, but her limbs couldn't feel anything, let alone move at her command.

Gods, help me! she cried. *Tzarik, where are you?*

She remembered the flogging. The beating. The fangs in her neck. The memories brought a fresh wave of pain and weeping.

I've got you, the familiar, gentle voice of the Xian princess Yui whispered now and then. *I used my wish. You're safe. But it's coming. They gave you to it. I cannot stop it hunting you. Once you touch Al'Myrahn shores, it will come for you. Run when you see it.*

Struggle as she might, something stopped Sybal from seeing and moving. Almost like she'd been caged inside a box that suppressed every feeling. Trapped and hunted, she waited. Unable to see Yui, she only felt her and knew the princess's spirit guided her on the rocking, sea-like journey. Slipping into this dream and then back out into pure and total darkness became the norm. Until one day...

A burst of orange and white light pierced her eyes. A familiar, dry warmth touched her icy, stiff flesh. But she couldn't move her body. She could see, but not what awakened her. She lay on nothing, hovering above a rocky ground, sand whipping back and forth in infinite circles.

"Al'Myrah?" She gasped. Her voice didn't travel far, muffled just beyond the tip of her nose. She tried to pull herself up, but couldn't, like in a dream paralysis. She resigned herself to looking up, and the faint outline of a hooded face looked down at her. She didn't know if it was part of the dream or if her eyes were going. "Help me," she said to the figure, trying to sit up once again. Familiarity radiated from the face. It knew her.

Her strength spent, she collapsed onto her back and drifted into the dark again. This waking and sleeping came and went again and again until it built up a rage in her. The black, faded figure came and went. Sometimes, the feeling of the thing hunting her jarred her awake. She looked around for it but saw nothing. Yui had said it was coming. They'd given her to it. And it was on its way.

Sometime later, she came to full consciousness, back into the white dream world. This one was different. A cold wind cut through her thin cotton tunic and cloak. Her light, leather Runer armor blocked the tearing fingers of the icy gale from touching her chest, but it slipped in through the gap near her arms, making her shiver awake. She still lay flat, hovering, but the confines of the invisible box had vanished.

Gasping, she rolled and fell to the rocky earth, landing hard on her hands and knees. She sank an inch into the cold mud. Focusing on the soft ground, she found something similar to ectoplasm squirming and writhing underneath. She gasped and pushed away. Her eyes darted around.

Wide open moors sprawled out around her, but she couldn't see far. Green mist, ghosts of trees, and rock formations blocked her view. Her sulfates rushed down the back of her neck. Spinning around, she felt she faced east—the direction the deity that hunted her came from. Unable to see far, she realized it was still coming towards her, but from far away. Her senses maddeningly heightened.

She felt it wanted her. It wanted to bite her, swallow her. It had been denied the pleasure of devouring her.

Checking in with herself, she found her runes around her neck and her scimitar at her side. She breathed, her heart beat, and she could feel her boots on her feet.

"I'm alive," she gasped, her voice cracking. "Where am I?"

Crouching low, she marched into the mist. Sounds of movement crackled and slithered all around her. The ectoplasmic snake-like worms in the ground moved with a constant, slimy hissing. A raven cawed somewhere far off. A hawk screamed. She even caught what she thought might be the rumbling roar of a tiger, but it had a more horn-like quality. Like a kind of bugle.

She followed the most open paths until she came to a forest of strange trees. They grew straight up, their branches covered in tiny, thin needles. They smelled fresh. She stopped outside the canopy and narrowed her eyes to scan under the trees. Things moved in the darkness. Thick, glittering white webs wound from tree to tree. As she looked, another sound rumbled beneath the others.

A deep, throbbing beat pulsed under her boots. She looked back down at the crawling mud and waited. It beat again. Like the earth had a heart that thumped under the ground. As she focused on it, the ectoplasmic snakes slowly reached up, slithering around her ankles. She hissed in disgust and shook them off. Trying to listen to where the beat came from, a scream shot up from the mist behind her. She spun on the spot, looking for the source of the terrible cry. A roar in the distance confirmed that something hunted in the dense mist. Black forms and shadows ducked and rushed just out of sight. Like ghosts and green and blue fog, they wavered and appeared. She thought the moans of specters filled the air just under the stifled silence. There were things walking about; they were just invisible. Her sulfates tingled cold, telling her she was right. There were hundreds of ghosts all around her.

Gripping her scimitar, she dashed into the dark trees. Whatever walked out in the moors sounded big and might not follow her into the forest. It wasn't until she was deep under the trees that the cold hit her. The green mist soaked through her thin cotton and chilled her skin. The slightest wind made her shiver. She pulled her cloak up over her head and tighter around her shoulders, but it did little to warm her. That was when she spotted signs of campsites throughout the forest.

Small fires left their black, ashen marks here and there. Someone had even entwined thin branches to make a kind of canopy of sticks. A few patches of unmelted snow lay in the shadows near the trunks of the moss-covered trees. The deeper she shambled into the forest, the darker it got and the more webs she found. The mist sunk into the trees as well, not giving way to vision.

Deciding to see where she might be, Sybal touched the trunk of a tree. This one branched out, old and thick with gnarls and branches perfect for climbing. She looked up and saw a mass of branches duck behind the trunk. The long, hairy, jointed branches curled into the shadows, clicking and snapping. She froze, trying to decipher what she'd seen when a soft moaning caught her ear.

"Hello?" she called, spinning around. The thick green mist made the sounds come from every direction, carried on the cold air. She shivered. Bending down, she picked up a fallen branch and inspected it. It was not dry enough to light, nor was the moss at the base of the trees.

The voice moaned again. It came from her right, above her.

Dropping the branch, she stumbled over the mossy, icy ground to an immense pile of rocks. The boulders piled high, stacking up to the base of a mountain. Dens and openings dotted the side of the cliffs. All of them glittered with frosted webs.

"Can...you help me?" a weak, female voice begged in a Caerwren dialect.

Sybal clambered over the unfamiliar rocks and stopped short, facing a wide-open cave. Slick webs covered most of the ground.

Small, round swathes of webbing bundled around formless shapes along the wall and ground. Her eyes followed the glittering webs up to a wall of cold stone. There, a woman hung, pinned to the wall, wrapped in a huge spider's cocoon. Sybal's breath immediately picked up as she took in the sight before her. The other bundles looked similar in shape. The woman was so pale her skin melded perfectly with the white-red hair that tumbled over her bare shoulder. Besides her head, the only part of her Sybal could see was her naked, bulging belly. Near the bottom side of her stomach, another patch of white webbing splattered over her.

"What happened?" Sybal cried in Caerwren, scrambling to reach the woman.

In reply, the woman screamed, thrashing in her stringy prison. "They're moving! They're inside me!"

Sybal's eyes went to the woman's stomach. Just beneath the flesh, something stirred so violently she could see it moving in the dim light.

"Those things," the woman wept, gnashing her teeth in pain. "Bolemesh's spawn. The spider goddess. It put them in me!"

Just as Sybal reached up to hack away at the spider wrappings holding the woman, something pierced out from the flesh of the woman's stomach. The woman screamed. "Run!"

Sybal fell backwards over the other wrapped victims, terrified at the jointed, hairy leg that protruded from the woman's belly. "What the hell?" she shouted.

"Run!" the woman repeated. Just as she gulped in air to cry out again, her torso burst open in a rain of blood and flesh. Dozens of spiders, some as big as cats and others the size of mice, poured from the now-dead woman.

Knowing she could not possibly cut them all down, Sybal took the woman's last words to heart and dashed away into the forest. The spiders, hissing and snapping their pincers, gave chase. Faster than she was, they soon caught up, slinging webs towards her and leaping over her. One aimed for her head. Spinning, she sliced it in half. The two halves split on her scimitar blade, falling on either side. Seeing this, the monsters halted, clicking nervously.

"Come on!" she screamed, brandishing her orichalcum blade. The spiders seemed almost sentient. Their shiny black eyes flicked between each other, Sybal, and her sword. Some clicked and hissed. Sybal quickly glanced at her scimitar. "You didn't think I could I hit you," she said. "Never tasted the blade of a Runer before, monster?"

Just as one of the larger ones had leaped at her, a brassy bugle tolled through the woods. The spiders shrank, hissing. Sybal almost swore she heard their raspy little voices saying a name: *Mjordir*.

Mjordir, they whispered in fear, in one haunting voice. *He is here. He crosses over. Run.*

Suddenly, the spiders scurried away, close to the ground. Sybal watched them go, then spun and galloped out of the forest.

☉

EVEN THOUGH THE mist hung thicker outside the forest, Sybal felt safer. Once the dark canopy lay far enough behind her, she took stock of her surroundings once again. Looking to the west, deep behind thick clouds, she caught sight of a white orb sinking below the horizon.

"Sunset," she mumbled to herself. She whipped around, looking for some kind of shelter: a rock to lean her back against, a cave— anything away from the spiders and the eerie ghosts lurking just behind the blue and green mist. She couldn't build a fire out in the open. The land was so flat, everything within miles would see it.

Tzarik had once said the best hiding place was movement.

Tzarik! Where was he? Her heart skipped a beat, and she couldn't stop the call. She shouted his name, scanning the ground for his short, black form.

"Where are you?" she cried. "Where am *I*?" Her calls roused something farther out on the moors and the deep, underground heartbeat came back to her attention. Something like ashes and cinders wafted up to her.

Facing the west again, she focused on the setting sun and marched towards it. Every few steps, she chanced a call, looking for her mentor. That was when the memories of what had happened came back in shattered pieces. She'd been in the Hallow City, saving Yui.

Yui! The princess's voice had guided her, had said she'd protected her. "Her wish," Sybal panted, listening to the sound of waves lapping nearer. "She used it to get me home to Al'Myrah." The cold air, dry grass, and strange trees told her this was *not* Al'Myrah.

"For Krishvu's sake, where am I?" she shouted. Her boots stomped into salty, cold water. The wide expanse of water and gray waves stretched out. "Tzarik?" She gasped, a sob rising in her throat. "Where are you?"

Out here, near the ocean, the sounds of mysterious, stalking animals and the caws of the ravens were quieter. Deciding it was as good a place as any, she gathered driftwood (blessedly dry) and set about making a camp. As she worked and kept her sulfates on high alert, she realized the creatures, perhaps ghosts, moved around her still. They were invisible. Once, she even thought the cold touch of a specter dragged down her spine. There were things moving in the green mist that she could not see.

Once the sun vanished, the night got so cold Sybal couldn't move from the shaking in her bones. She sat as close as she dared to her tiny fire. She waited until it almost burned her flesh before running out to gather more wood. Dragging her knees up to her chest, her hood over her head, she shook, hoping maybe some kind of sleep would overtake her. But she didn't feel drowsy. As she sat, her eyes drifted down to the sand and pebble beach. She thought about the last thing she remembered: looking for Tzarik on the Xian horizon. She'd believed he would come back for her.

"You can't think like that, Sybal," she chided herself. "You know he would have." Had he come back looking for her? Had he made it out alive? Had she? A conversation she'd had with the Di-Huan floated up to her memory: *our hells are each other's countries.* She'd been taught since she was a little girl that Nah'Jaha, the hell most on Al'Myrah believed in, was a land of fire and ice, always frozen and covered with snow yet burning for eternity. This could have easily been Nah'Jaha. Glittering white frost covered every surface and the air reeked of ash and cinders.

She noticed she had two shadows on the sand. Flicking her eyes up, she found one moon behind her in the west and another in front, in the east. The western moon was larger.

What had she done to deserve to go to Nah'Jaha rather than Janna? She laid her cheek against her knee and let the tears fall. No one could see her weeping. Would she ever see Tzarik again? Would she ever...

A gigantic shadow passed over her. She recognized the shape as that of a winged creature. Leaping up, she unsheathed her scimitar and slipped her runes out from under her armor. Her eyes, tired and sore from weeping, scanned the skies. While the moons were bright in this cold hell, no stars dotted the blackness. This made finding the black creature difficult. She glanced at her fire. No, there was no point in snuffing it now. The thing knew she was here. And after she dispatched it, she didn't want to have to bring the fire to life again.

Listening hard, she actually heard the beast land on an outcropping of rocks to her left. She guessed at the size of it from how much rock tumbled to the ground in the darkness. Talons scraped and feathers ruffled. Her eyes trained on the area, waiting. Despite her Runer vision, she couldn't see the thing.

Behind her, the water rippled. With that slight, watery sound, all others stopped. The soft rustling in the grass silenced itself. Even the wind stopped.

Sybal straightened up. "What the hell?" She turned to face the water.

Like a blast of twelve cannon balls hitting the water at once, a flurry of black, slimy limbs shot out of the green waves towards her. The ocean spray soaked her, almost instantly freezing. Her sulfates rushed in her veins, fueling the power she needed to dodge one tentacle and hack another. She didn't have time to stop and watch as they slapped at her, whipping around in lithe curls as they tried to grasp her. She hacked at the thrashing limbs and made her retreat as best she could. To her left, the giant winged beast cawed.

After slicing four or five tentacles, watery and black blood splashing over the sand around her, the thing pulled back into the ocean. The water still roiled, as if it thrashed in pain under the surface. Then, out on the horizon, a form rose out of the black water, a mass the size of a mountain with glowing white eyes. It overtook the horizon. Atop it, many-pronged antlers rose, grasping at the moon. Sybal's mouth fell open in horror. This colossus raised up rippling arms the size of trees.

"Oh, shit!" Sybal screamed, dashing back inland. The thing was going to bring the limbs down onto the beach, swatting at her like a fly. Sheathing her scimitar, she ran as fast as her long legs would carry her. A smaller version of the colossus rose out of the water. Its limbs shot out, grasping the rocky cliff, and it hauled itself up onto the beach. Sybal quickly drew halat, stopping one swiping tentacle on the white shield. The creature gave a squealing roar and started its attack anew.

The winged beast cawed and finally flew into her vision, swooping down close to her. She drew buhkar, turning to black mist to avoid a flap of its great black wings. Just before she re-materialized, the sea monster clutched at her, passing through the mist. With another squealing roar, it fully pulled its grotesque body up onto the beach. Now she saw that it, too, had sharp antlers. Using its powerful limbs, it made a crawling motion towards her as the colossus watched. She had to stop now and hack a few more times to deter the monster. She drew halat, spun, and sliced another tentacle.

But it wasn't enough. One finally grasped her ankle, and the thing gave a cry of delight. It jerked her so fast and hard, she didn't have time to hit the ground before she dangled upside down. She fumbled with her scimitar, cutting herself on the curved blade as she screamed and tried to maintain her grip. Finally, she dropped it. Her runes hung down into her face and she couldn't get ahold of them with the swaying gait of the sea monster on land. The thing cried out to the colossus in the ocean as if showing off a prize. A deep, other-worldly bellow replied to it.

The monster, using the tentacle holding Sybal to walk, slammed her hard against the ground just as she grabbed buhkar. She dropped it, her head ringing. Writhing in its grip, she caught sight of the winged beast. It was a monster-sized raven.

Every creature is huge, she gasped in her mind. That seemed fitting for a hell.

Then the creature holding her thrust her even higher into the air, over its antlers. Her gut flipped in fright, and she begged the thing to not drop her. Held over its central body, she saw something open up. Between the two prongs of antlers, a slit split open, revealing a maw filled with teeth. The red throat spiraled down, all lined with more sharp fangs.

With a cry of determination, Sybal flipped herself up and grasped the tentacle holding her ankle. Unable to find buhkar and without her scimitar, she bit down into the black flesh. The thing trilled in pain and flailed. Its icy blood filled her mouth and she gagged. But it was enough to stop the thing from dropping her into its slit-like mouth.

The raven called, diving at the monster, pecking fiercely at where its face might be and sinking its silver talons into its soft, black flesh. Shaking Sybal like a rag doll, the creature dislodged her. Buhkar fell into her face, brushing the bridge of her nose. Grasping it, she drew it, not caring how high off the ground she was. Misting, she slipped from the grasp of the thing and plummeted towards the ground.

Just as the sandy beach rose to meet her and she rematerialized, a feather storm engulfed her, catching her in a perfect swoop to break her fall. Since it had helped her escape, she clutched its feathers, burying her face in its neck when she slung herself onto its back. With a final caw, the raven soared away from the beach, taking her with it and away from the tentacle monster.

Chancing a glance back, a horrible sight came into view. The colossus grabbed the smaller monster in its tentacles and put it in its own vile maw, eating it whole. She made herself watch, telling herself that could have been her.

Readjusting on the raven's back, she looked ahead.

"Thank you," she shouted over the wind from its flight. Of course, the bird couldn't understand her, but that wasn't the point. She patted its silky black feathers, then wondered how to tell the thing to put her down. She glanced over the edge. The ground shot past her so quickly that she gasped and clamped her thighs down tightly around the raven's body to hold fast.

Lowering her head to its neck to avoid as much wind as possible, she hunkered down and waited out the ride.

Eventually the raven made tighter and tighter circles. It reared back, sticking its silver-taloned feet out to land gracefully on the ground. As it did, Sybal had to slide off its angled back. She landed far less gracefully. Once on her feet, the raven eyed her with its glittering emerald eyes.

"Thank you," she said again, then repeated it in Caerwren. If a bird could talk, surely it would use the language of the continent she thought they were on. Even standing, the raven was so large she had to look up at it.

"You are quite welcome, lass," the bird replied.

Sybal gasped. She stumbled back one pace, eyes wide and locked onto the emerald eyes of the raven.

If a raven could smile, that's what this one did. Its blazing emerald eyes creased in what could only be a grin. "Apologies," he said kindly. The bird cawed and a flurry of feathers burst out towards her.

Sybal shielded her face and took a few cautionary steps away from where the bird had vanished.

Where the raven had been now stood a man, a bone mask and helmet over his head. The same blazing emerald eyes looked out from underneath. His tall body was clothed mostly in furs and soft leathers. His legs were bare under the furs, except for thick animal-hide boots. He wore bits of bone hand-tailored to his other animal-skin clothes as armor. His raven hair was platted in a storm of braids and elegant waves.

Sybal gulped, taking in the wild man. "Are you...?"

He held up her scimitar to her. He must have grabbed it with his talons. "I'm a Vaeson, a god-shaped. What your country might call a werecreature. My name is Kjarton." He held his left hand out to the side, fingers splayed as if to grasp something. A metallic whooshing flew towards them. With a thud, the man caught a huge silver sword by its hilt. He'd summoned it to his hand with that simple motion. "Like you, they sacrificed me to a god."

Sybal glanced around with only her eyes, her mouth open. Slowly, she took her sword from the man's other hand. "Vaeson? Sacrificed to a god?"

Kjarton nodded, slinging the enormous sword he'd summoned onto his back. "Yes. This is the God Deep, the place for the souls forcefully given to a god not their own. Come, we must find shelter. If you haven't seen the god that pursues you, it's still coming. They hunt their sacrifices most viciously beneath the moons."

CHAPTER 8

RUNERS OF CAERWREN

Zeva went hoarse from crying and the entire underside of her arms and fists were bruised from pounding on the door. She didn't even notice the pitching and screaming wind had lessened significantly over the last hour. Vicdan stood leaning against the wall, his arms wrapped tightly around himself. She was about to ask him how long they'd been held when the jongleur pushed himself up, eyes brighten in alert.

She heard it then, too. With the storm gone, the thud of the captain's boots rang through the hull of the ship.

Sigmund threw open the door to their holding place. A gray sun shone behind him, and the horizon bobbed gently.

"You monster!" Zeva screeched. All fear of the waves gone, she charged Sigmund and hammered uselessly on his back. The captain easily shoved her off so hard she fell against the deck of the ship. She scrambled to her feet, tears and rain drenching her hair. She dashed to the rail of the ship.

"Zeva, don't," Vicdan cried, grabbing her around the waist and pulling her back from the edge as she screamed Tarkan's name. "See? There's the shore. We were close to land," he shot at the gritty sea dog. "You could have given them the raft."

Sigmund shook his great head. "I will not risk the wrath of my gods, lad." He pointed to the back, where the horses stood blindfolded. Sybal's coffin had thankfully not moved during the storm. "You should be grateful we didn't destroy your cursed cargo," the captain went on, marching past them to the rudder. "We could sell you both for sacks of coin, but now that the storm has passed—as I knew it would—I will spare you. You may go ashore."

"Sell?" Vicdan gasped. Zeva felt him grip her tighter against his chest. "Are there still slave raids on the Black Road?"

Sigmund nodded, glaring up into the sky. A single ray of sun split through the clouds. "Rhostrana guards it more than ever. Without an Al'Myrahn or Rhostranan shibboleth, one cannot take the Black Road and hope to walk off it. Unless they are selling or have a guardian." He eyed them again.

A chill colder than the winter rain and ice shot through Zeva. "Please, don't," she begged. "We'll leave." She looked up at Vicdan, then to the distant shore. A small dock waited there with no ships in the berths. No sign of Tzarik or Tarkan showed on the frozen shores. "We have to go. We have to find them!"

The waves calmed drastically as the captain glared at the two Al'Myrahns, clearly deciding what to do. The leveling ocean seemed to have a soothing effect on the hardened captain. The quickly calming ocean drew Zeva's eyes to it. The shore was not far.

"Very well." Sigmund sighed. He shouted to his men, signaling them to sail up alongside the dock. "Take your damned dead with you. If you value your life, stay away from the Black Road. Rhostrana uses it for trade with Al'Myrah and your black powder. They will not be friendly with you just because you are from Al'Myrah. Rhostrana still has a slave trade. Ask any Masahk. And my countrymen who maraud along the Black Road will not be kind to you, either."

Zeva couldn't find it in herself to thank the man. Vicdan mumbled a begrudging thanks, but she hated the man, despite his warnings.

The sleet made even the horses shiver as Zeva and Vicdan led them down the unsteady gangplank to the wooden docks. None of the crew left the ship.

"This is a kindness," Sigmund said to her. "Don't forget it."

THE OCEAN CALMED, but the rain still pelted down, hard and sharp. Vicdan found two long pieces of driftwood amidst huge, sharp rocks along the shore. Using some of the rope from Mamun's cargo, he lashed the coffin to them like a sand sleigh and roped it down with Sybal inside. Then he tied the makeshift sleigh behind her horse. Once everything was secure, they trudged towards a valley between two great ranges of mountains.

Caerwren was bare and desolate. The green prairies stretched out, up hills into rocky moors. Sharp mountains loomed in the distance, gray against the dark sky. A few small homesteads dotted the horizon. Sharp stones jutted up out of the moss and grass like they grew that way. They cut their boots on them and stumbled on the crags. They couldn't see far in the thick rain and frozen snow.

"Tarkan!" Zeva shouted into the biting wind.

"Zeva," Vicdan hissed, shaking under his colorful coat. He gripped her arm and pulled her closer to him and the horses. "Don't shout. We don't know what might be out there."

"But..." she started, unsure how to argue. She just wanted to find him. To know he was safe. "We haven't been separated like this since Sharar..." She grabbed her head covering and wrapped it around her scarred face. "That was the only time we've been apart. I cannot bear the thought of it happening again. I just can't." Her mind ran wild with possibilities. Had Tarkan drowned? Been swallowed up by a sea monster? Would she be alone forever now?

She let out a sob.

Vicdan stopped walking and drew her into a wet, cold hug. "I know his type, sabi. He's tougher than you think, despite being all skin and bone. And I know Tzarik. He won't let Tarkan get hurt. Now." He scanned the little hills before them. "Let's get up onto one of these grassy mounds and see what's out there."

Gathering her courage, Zeva followed Vicdan inland. For hours, they trudged against the muddy ground and into the whipping wind. The mud was harder to tread over than the shifting sands of Al'Myrah. Trying to watch her footing, she trained her eyes on the grassy, damp ground, but it didn't matter. She slipped on a sharp rock under the moss and cut her knee. Landing just right on her joint against the gray stone made instant tears fall. Vicdan knelt to check the damage.

A loud bugle sounded over the hills.

"What is that?" Zeva gasped, pulling her knees in close as the pain reverberated through her leg.

Vicdan stood up and unsheathed Tzarik's scimitar from Mamun's saddle. He moaned slightly and turned the blade over in his hands. "This blade really is unbearable. I feel it in my veins already."

"There!" Zeva pointed. An enormous creature in the shape of an elegant horse—almost like a gazelle— crested the hill. Its fur was golden, almost pearlescent. "What is it? It has trees sprouting from its head." She stood up, placing Vicdan between her and the creature.

The beast threw its pronged head back and bugled again; the sound flying all the way to the tops of the mountains in the north. Zeva followed the sound with her eyes. The mountains in the north stood tallest, capped in snow. From where they stood, she spotted something that might have been a bridge stretched between the peaks. The unmistakable sound of a horn replied to the creature.

With a quieter, animal grunt, the creature bobbed its head and turned to leave.

"A radjur. It's rather majestic," Vicdan noted. "Terrifying and strange, but glorious."

"Will it eat us?" Zeva asked, watching till its antlers passed from view.

Vicdan shook his head and almost laughed gently. "Eyes on the side of its head. It's not a predator."

Impressed, Zeva smiled weakly. "Has our Runer inspired further study for this jongleur?" she asked.

"Well..." Vicdan blushed. "I like to be prepared. My run-in with the Runers surely has expanded my horizons and fueled my hunger for adventure. But this." He waved his arm to the expansive plains before them. "It's been some time since I've left Al'Myrah."

Hours later, they crested a hill and found a small village nestled among the bogs between the hills. Dozens of small mesas shot up from the marshy ground with dark sides and green tops. Pathways of wooden landings made up most of the entry to the village over the bog, though the water was frozen and bright green. Others sprawled between the mesas, connecting the broken landmass. A gravel pathway led into the village through a small arch with a single large lantern above it.

"Should we go in?" Zeva asked.

Vicdan nodded. "Tzarik would look for a village or a city."

"Tarkan!" she shouted, her heart racing then. Surely they could not have landed too far from where Tarkan and Tzarik would have washed ashore.

Vicdan tried to grab her back, but she dodged his worried grasp and charged into the village over the shaking wood and rope walkways.

"Tarkan!" she shouted again, head whipping around, taking in the people. Every villager stood massively tall, making it impossible to see far. "Tzarik?" she chanced, in case they had gotten split up.

Her eyes landed on a group of men leaning against a ramshackle stable outside a kind of public house. Their hair shone almost stark white and their eyes icy blue. Huge, straight swords in the shapes of crosses hung on their backs. Strings of runes lay on their chests, out in the open for all to see.

"Runers." She gasped. "Greetings, Runers," she said in Caerwren.

As she trotted up to the cluster of monster hunters, one stood up straight to greet her. He stood easily two feet taller than her and eyed her up and down like a lion spotting a wounded gazelle. She noted the strange gaze but thought perhaps that was just how these kinds of men looked at people. But this Runer was Masahk, unlike the others. What she'd thought was a cloak of feathers behind him she now realized were his long, bird-like wings. Two softly feathered ears stuck up out of his black cloak. On his exposed forearms, she noted tiny, soft feathers along the top. He whistled at her, calling the other Runers' attention to her presence. The way he leered at her made her steps falter.

A few snickers and laughs went up from the other Runers when they turned to see the small Al'Myrahn girl calling to them.

"I am looking for my father," she said. She couldn't say why, but felt compelled to clutch her skirts tightly. "He should have washed up on shore. With a Runer. Please," she added when they only ogled her, "we've come a long way and have been walking for hours."

"Are you alone, lass?" the Masahk one asked coyly, leaning back against a wall. He was handsome, but the gleam in his eye made Zeva stop cautiously.

"Are you lost?" another one asked. "Do you need a big, strong man to look after you? See to your needs?" He gripped the front of his huge black belt and stuck his hips out in an imposing stance.

Zeva shrank away just a little. "Can you help me?" she asked, beginning to doubt the Runers. Her eyes darted around the muddy hovels of the town, unconsciously looking for an escape route. Where had Vicdan gotten to? Why were the Runers sending fear into her? "They're about this tall." She held her hand just above her head. "Blue eyes, both of them. One is a Runer. Al'Myrahns."

The Runers all stood up and slowly meandered towards her. They broke off to encircle her. Only the Masahk one stood back, arms crossed now, unmoved from where he leaned against the wall of the public house. He watched with bored interest.

Her heart leapt into her throat. *What do they want?*

"Poor little lost desert rose," the closest Runer said with a smirk. He reached out and touched her long, black hair. "Want to know my crime?" he jeered. The Runers behind him laughed. "Old Yorn knows it well. Beat a man to death with my bare hands." He held them in front of Zeva as if the blood still lingered there. "Old Yorn takes a beating well. Gives me a thrill bringing him to the edge. Coming close to breaking my oath. I like thrills." He leaned over his shoulder to the Masahk Runer, who stood back. "Young Ragnall, where is old Yorn? I haven't loosened any of his teeth in a good while."

"Dying somewhere," the Masahk called Ragnall replied, looking away from Zeva and her herd of predators. His long, feathery ear twitched. "Useless apprentice. Waste of time runing an old man like that."

"Worth it when you killed his old hag, though?" the first Runer asked with a chortle.

Zeva gulped. "You killed someone?"

Ragnall shrugged. "What was she going to do without her husband? Die frozen and alone this winter? It was a mercy killing." He smirked, laughing. "What are they going to do? Condemn me to a runing?"

"And what about you, lass?" the Runer asked, his rough hand touching her face. His eyes flashed, showing he was about to strike.

Before Zeva could recoil, a savage shout behind her made her duck down. The opaline arch of Tzarik's scimitar cut over her head, slashing to ward off the Runers. The group of them took a step back. Zeva looked up. Vicdan stood in front of her, brandishing the scimitar sloppily towards them.

"Hands off, Runer scum," he growled.

The lead Runer held his hands up, laughing. "Apologies. We

thought she was alone." He took a second glance at Vicdan, taking in his brown eyes. "Where'd you get that sword, lad?" he asked, realizing it could not belong to Vicdan.

"Just back off!" the jongleur shouted, his voice shaking. He pulled Zeva close to himself and backed away.

The other Runers laughed dryly at the little man and his stolen orichalcum blade. "Don't cause trouble, little Al'Myrahn," the Masahk one warned with a wicked grin. "We are above the law here."

Vicdan nodded, grasped Zeva's hand, and marched back to the horses. "*Never* run off like that again," he gasped, giving way to quaking in fear. He sheathed the sword back in its protective black leather. "Do you understand? They would have hurt you, Zeva, in ways I don't want to fathom. Runers are vile men. We are lucky to know the good ones. And while, of course, I am concerned for your safety, I do not want to imagine for one moment what Tarkan would do to me if I let you get hurt." He shivered dramatically.

The danger of the situation finally landed in Zeva's mind. "Oh, gods!" she cried. "I didn't know what they wanted. I thought they'd help me."

"Oh, you sweet sabi." Vicdan looked around, unsure. "We don't have enough coin to stay in a proper room, and my fiddle is quite drenched through. I can't play for a room tonight." He slung the instrument off his back to his front and gave the wheel a few turns. It screamed like a dying cat. "That won't do. We could stay in a barn. Sleep with the horses."

Zeva didn't protest. Shaken, cold, and just wanting out of the rain, they paid every coin they had to feed the horses and be allowed to sleep on the floor of the stall. A single brazier lit the way between the walls of stalls. Once the sun had gone down, Vicdan closed the stable doors to block out the wind. They sat near the brazier for warmth, shedding as many clothes as they dared to dry them out overnight. Tzarik's horse, Mamun, had blankets, a few scraps of dried meat and soggy rice, and one dry cloak. Vicdan gave the cloak to Zeva and curled up near the brazier.

He fell asleep quickly. Zeva eyed the black coffin, lying awake. She lay before Vicdan, his chest pressed into her back for warmth. Slowly, she picked his arm up off her waist and slid out from under Tzarik's cloak. She crawled across the hay to the coffin and opened the top. Inside, the lady Runer lay cold as ice and still as ivory. Zeva brushed a few strands of her blonde hair off her face and braided it down the side to keep it neat.

"I know," she mumbled, as though coming back to a conversation that had been interrupted. "You're probably scared, too. But I swear, we'll find him. Vicdan says he's tough. He's looking for you, too. I know it."

Reaching into the coffin, she pried Sybal's arms up and folded them onto her stomach. She ran her hand over the Runer's hardening flesh.

"He gave you the last of his blood," she whispered. "He must really love you. Tarkan told me about you two. How you saved him. And me." She held Sybal's hand. "I never thought I'd be able to thank you. I wish now I could speak with you." She laughed flatly. "I love Tarkan, but he's hopeless about anything I want to discuss. He hates when I try to talk to him about my feelings or experiences I want to have. He's always studying, looking for that book. I bet you'd have an answer to all my questions and could give me advice."

The woman in the box was beautiful. Zeva loved her yellow hair and muscled arms. She was tall, too. Zeva guessed she'd be a strong, elegant fighter.

"You know," she went on, "I've never really had friends. Tarkan hates most people. Living people. I hope..." She had to swallow to steady her voice. "I hope when you wake up that you'll be my friend. Childish wish, perhaps. But Tarkan is very fond of reminding me how young I am." She rubbed Sybal's hand with her thumb. "Could we be friends?"

She imagined Sybal smiling, nodding. She'd say something about how she'd never had a little sister and how they could be close.

"Thank you," Zeva whispered to the Runer.

Checking over her shoulder to make sure Vicdan still slept, she crawled over the side of the coffin. It was large enough for them both. She gently pushed Sybal over a few inches and lay on her side next to the lady Runer.

"My mother gave me away." She yawned, loving the sensation of sharing her innermost stories with another woman. "To take another man as her husband. That's what Tarkan told me, anyway. Then my father promised me to Tarkan. Well, promised him the first thing from his house, should he win a battle." She snuggled closer to the Runer. "That was me. And I'm not sorry about it. He's been so good to me. I'm not even sorry about the year we spent imprisoned by that sorcerer. He hurt us." She looked up at Sybal. "Are you sorry you became a Runer?"

The woman remained passive and beautiful. Another yawn stopped Zeva's questions and she drifted off to sleep.

CHAPTER 4
THE BLACK ROAD

THE CLATTERING OF STALL DOORS SWINGING IN WOKE Zeva. She snapped her eyes open. Above her, an old man with a long white beard gazed down at her. His eyes, one icy blue and the other a muddy combination of brown and blue, peered at her beneath bushy brows. Zeva screamed and sat up.

"He won't harm you," a deep, smooth voice said to her.

The Masahk Runer from before, Ragnall they had called him, opened a stall and led his golden-colored mare out. The mare's saddle bore all the now-familiar tools of his trade: saddle bags full of vials, a sword of plain steel, a crossbow, and other such things. He slipped a small, black, fleshy box into his saddlebag before tying it down.

"His name is Yorn," Ragnall went on. "My apprentice."

Zeva crawled out of the coffin, shutting it back up, and huddled down to make herself small. Vicdan was gone. She eyed the old man where he squatted near the brazier. "He's so much older than you. Or..." She nervously looked Ragnall up and down. He was Masahk, after all. She couldn't tell how old he was.

The younger man scoffed. He slipped the reins onto his horse. "I'm twenty-five. Very young for my kind. Been hunting for five years. Not long, but long enough. Yorn here is nearing sixty. Runed only a few months ago."

Gathering the blankets and cloak, Zeva kept her eye on the older man. He hadn't moved. His pale skin nearly hid the veins underneath, white with the poison. They bulged, casting a shadow over his flesh. "What's wrong with him?" she asked. "I've seen very few Runers. He looks ill."

Ragnall nodded. "The oath is rejecting him. He'll be dead soon. His mind went with his red blood. Yorn!"

When Ragnall shouted the old man's name, he jumped like a scolded dog and ran to his mentor's side where he crouched again, clinging to Ragnall's cloak hem. Zeva's heart broke for the old man.

"I hope whatever his crime was, it made up for this," she said sadly. She rolled the blankets up and went to the stall where their horses waited, keeping Ragnall in her view.

Mamun made a snorting sound and put his ears down. She calmed him with a few pats. His head followed her movements, led by his nose, attracted to Tzarik's cloak. The horse sniffed it excitedly, then scanned the stables, ears pricking up. "He's not here," she whispered to him despondently, patting his neck. "Sorry, old boy. I'll tell him you miss him, though."

"His crime isn't worth *this* kind of suffering." Ragnall sighed, shoving Yorn out of the way with his avian foot. "Something about land and living on his wife's property. I don't know. Shouldn't matter on Caerwren. Outside Rom, the only cantons that claim land belongs to one sentient are Hovandel and Gidenmore. Even those are thatched barns by Al'Myrahn standards." He locked his blue eyes onto Zeva and looked her up and down.

She noted a shift in the Runer then. The steely, vile demeanor melted just enough for her to look into his face. She liked his angled features, sharp nose, his soft feathering. The way his long ears twitched and turned to listen to sounds she couldn't hear. She took in his long, black-clad legs. His feet were bare but were those of a bird, like some of his other features. His long wings, hanging like a second cloak behind him, brushed the ground. She wondered if they were soft or if he could fly like the angels she'd read about in stories.

His hard eyes softened. "You're lost and afraid," he mused without any threat. "You're ignorant, too. If you're not careful, that will get you into trouble."

Zeva's cheeks flushed with indignation even though she knew he was right. She was innocent and ignorant; that was what Tarkan always told her. She realized Ragnall had seen that in her and that was what had made him look at her like prey. But it also made him change now. His eyes drew her in. Something in the pit of her stomach dropped and her heart picked up its pace.

"If you want to get to the main villages of any canton, take the Black Road," he said.

"Oh, no," she said quickly, snapping her eyes up to his face, hoping he hadn't caught her staring. "The captain said not to." She left out the part about being bought and sold as a slave.

Ragnall laughed darkly. "Sea dogs don't know what goes on here. They're wary of the trade ships. Most likely pirates. Take the Black Road. It's full of traders and all sorts. If your lost Runer is here, he'll head to larger clanlands in search of villages, cities. The ones who pillage the Black Road won't be interested in you. Rhostrana is only interested in Masahk slaves, not lasses like you."

That mysterious, ravenous glint returned to the Runer's eyes. Zeva shivered and looked about quickly for Vicdan. The scimitar hung in its sheath on Mamun. She could at least run for it if he moved towards her.

"You look like the lasses I see from Hatal. Rich. Soft."

She took two steps back.

"I mean you no harm." He smiled. "Come with us." He indicated the mute man at his feet. "We're taking the Black Road towards The Empty." He glanced over his shoulder quickly, then said, "Do you know the Court of Deliverance?"

She shook her head. He considered her, then half tilted his head in a sort of shrug.

"Forget I mentioned it, then. But there are ways to remain safe on the Black Road. Stay to the west, stay in the caravan. Vilderkin pillage the Road sometimes, too. And Sjörna-Reks has broken her pact with the Warpath alliance, taking captives for her hunts. But you want to find her clanland. She's the Reks of Altevine, the closest canton with a large village."

Zeva scoffed. "Doesn't sound safe at all. You said Rhostrana takes Masahk slaves." She looked at him pointedly. "The captain said Rhostranans watch the road. Aren't you worried?"

He shook his head. "I make my own choices. Just like you can. You don't have to do as some cowardly sea dog said."

A small, unfamiliar sensation plinked into Zeva. She'd never been told to make up her own mind. In all her eighteen years, Ragnall was the first to tell her to do such a thing, to tell her to think for herself. The cold sun glittered on his white flesh and feathers.

Maybe she could choose her own road.

"You'll be safest in the caravan. Trust me," he added when she opened her mouth. "There are worse dangers outside the Road. Wisps on the moors, kuri lurking in the shadows, a helhest drumming its hooves against hard stone. And Vasaras, our winter, is upon us. The wall between us and the gods is thinner than ever. Even during midsummer, you can find a god walking amongst the mountains. Now?" He grimaced in genuine yet controlled fear. "It's a dangerous time, lass. Clans hunt sentient sacrifices. They don't come to the Road. Except Sjörna-Reks. But Skarde-Reks in Northica will deal with her soon enough. You have nothing to fear."

The images that filled Zeva's mind thrilled and frightened her. She could not look away from Ragnall's clear, terrifying eyes. Everything about Caerwren sounded terrifying. And Tarkan was not there to tell her what to do. Yes, Ragnall frightened her. But on the Black Road, the caravan would be safer than wondering the mountains and frozen hills of the cantons, hoping to find a village. Ragnall knew Runers; Tzarik would go for a larger city.

"We're paid up," Vicdan said, entering the stable. "We should get moving. You!" He rushed to Zeva's side when he spotted the Runer.

"Vicdan." She turned and grasped the front of his coat. "We don't know this place. I know the captain said not to, but I think we should take the Black Road. It will have others on it. Traders. A caravan. No monsters."

The jongleur glared over her head at the Runer who now led his golden mare out of the stables. "Did he tell you we should take it?"

She nodded. "But I don't think he was lying. We'd be safer in numbers. Tzarik would go to a city and Tarkan would follow him."

Vicdan called out to Ragnall and his retreating apprentice. "Is there a safer road?"

The Runer turned in the great stable doors. "You could go south towards the canton of Hovandel and cut through their mountains." He eyed them. "You said they washed ashore? In the storm?"

Zeva nodded.

"That storm carried most ships off towards Zealmor. If they came ashore where I think they did, they'd be close to the Black Road, towards Altevine." He said the name of the canton as if it were a curse not to be spoken out loud. "Sjörna-Reks and her clan are on a crusade in Altevine. A part of the Black Road goes near her clanlands, but she shouldn't get too close." He said to Vicdan pointedly, "It would be wise to travel in the caravan."

THE LATE AFTERNOON sun hardly warmed Zeva's blue fingers on the road. She clutched one of the blankets around her shoulders. Soft, dry flakes of white began to fall. She walked behind Sybal's horse, close to the coffin, while Vicdan rode the glittering Porshain horse. Mamun had protested when Vicdan tried to ride him.

The caravan was not unlike those that plodded over the sands of Al'Myrah. Wagons of nomads, groups of wary soldiers, a mysteriously cloaked rogue, and a handful of Masahk made up this part of the caravan. A rabbit-type Masahk with white fur and long, soft fingers approached Zeva with a wooden cup. It steamed with something that smelled sweet and fresh. She held it out. Her nose wiggled like her more primal counterparts.

"Mint tea, Al'Myrah?" she asked, calling Zeva after her country of origin. "It's rare up here in the west, but I have my ways." One of her long, white ears twitched mischievously.

"Thank you." Zeva gasped, clasping the warm wooden mug in her hands. She took a drink. It burned, but she didn't care. "It's wonderful."

The rabbit woman smiled, her buck teeth showing. "I saw you join us out of the village. You looked so cold, I couldn't help myself. I don't have much, but I'm pleased to give what I can."

"You're too kind," Zeva sniffled, running her hand under her dripping nose.

The rabbit's nose twitched faster and her eyes darted around. "I'm an emissary for the Court of Deliverance; helping is what I do."

"The what?" Zeva asked. "I heard that from a Masahk Runer."

The rabbit Masahk smiled, her soft, white cheeks bulging. She turned and hurried back to a human man with a mess of curly dark hair. She put her hand on his shoulder and followed him off a thin path, heading northeast, breaking from the caravan. Zeva sipped again at the tea. She'd rarely had mint tea. It was popular in Al'Myrah, but Tarkan hardly ever took her into a large city where they could get it. The most recent time had been not long ago, on her eighteenth name day. He'd bought her horse, Jasmin, and had taken her to a public house for tea. She closed her eyes, drinking the memory as she filled her lungs with the smell of hot mint.

Whispers started to ripple through the caravan and the group spread out.

"What's happening?" Vicdan asked, pushing up in the stirrups.

Behind them, Ragnall called to his old apprentice, who trotted alongside his horse. He heaved the old man up behind him and commanded him to hold on. "The Vilderkin," he whispered. "Get your swords."

Zeva ran to the side of Vicdan's horse. Without delay, he reached down and pulled her up. "What are they?" she asked.

"I'm not sure," he replied. "I've heard songs about them. Not good. They're nomadic, barbarian tribes that live in the mountains. The songs say they look like beasts. They ride huge—"

"Wolves!" a woman screamed from the front of the caravan.

Like a well-rehearsed dance, the caravan split down the middle. The travelers ran in all directions. Horses snorted and charged, pulling wagons and other loads haphazardly in all directions. Children and the old—those who could not get out of the way—were knocked over. Zeva saw one get trampled right away by a frightened horse.

"Vicdan, what do we do?" she cried, gripping his waist.

Her companion kicked the horse and wheeled it around in an attempt to free them from the maddening throngs. Then she spotted the attackers. Huge men and women adorned in animal skins with antlered skull helmets charged at the caravan among massive wolves, horse-sized falcons, and elegant prong-horned radjur. The human riders straddled the backs of great white and gray wolves with cruel tines growing from their foreheads. Using some kind of crossbow, they fired ropes into the caravan. These ropes swung around sentient creatures and bound them. Then the riders pulled them in. They did the same to wagons and coaches, but those ropes had barbs at the end. They chanted strange names, calling them like a prayer.

As they dashed past one such wagon, full of a traveling tribe of nomads, four or five of the people called Vilderkin shot their roped arrows into the wagon. They heaved and toppled the thing, nearly dislodging Zeva and Vicdan as the horse dodged around the wreckage. The people inside screamed and spilled out. When they did, the

Vilderkin set upon them. Blood splashed over the dry grass and finally the sound of steel against steel rang within the valley.

Zeva reached down to the saddle and pulled a crossbow from where it hung, tied. She had to fight to release it, and was jostled about violently by their fleeing. But soon enough, she had the small bow in her hand. In a panic, she set a bolt in the flight groove. She couldn't pull it back. She screamed in panicked fright as something hissed past her ear.

Just as she finally bent the limbs, one of the weighted ropes spun around her body, trapping her arms to her sides. The lead weights hit Vicdan hard and he fell forward. Then, with a powerful jerk, Zeva soared off the back of the horse and into the air. She clutched the little crossbow, preparing to fire when she landed. The ground hit her backside hard and jostled all the air out of her. With a gasp, she raised the bow and fired into the antlered face that appeared to gather her up.

The warrior's head jerked back with a shout as the black shaft buried deep in its skull. With her attacker dead, she stood up and dashed away from the wolf riders, flinging the ropes off. She leapt over bodies, ducked another fired rope, and weaved between the madness out beyond a rocky outcropping. Turning to hide behind a great gray boulder, she found a tiny incision that led into a small, dark cave. She ducked inside, closing her eyes and covering her ears.

She counted to sixty ten times before opening her eyes. A tiny ball of soft white light bobbed before her with the erratic movements of a moth investigating a flame. All the sounds of the raid died away. She took several deep breaths, watching the ball of light.

"Oh," she breathed, gazing into the white depths of its light. She suddenly felt as if the thing beckoned her.

She stood up and took one step towards it. It jolted backwards and the faintest sound of tinkling reached her ears. Delighted, she followed the orb. The gentle light soothed her almost instantly, so she focused on the middle of it. She couldn't decide if she saw a tiny figure in the center or not. It didn't matter. The light creature whispered, *This way! Follow me. They like you. You are strong. We feel your power. I'll take you to safety. They want you, but we'll have you first.*

Her back faced the attack as she followed the wisp of light out and away. A giggle escaped her throat as she followed the thing. The valley stretched on until she came to a rise in the earth, a hill that spilled up towards the mountains. The wisp of light hovered over a small, smooth gray stone.

"What have you got there?" Zeva asked, crouching near the stone. With her icy fingers, she pushed aside the grass. Two eyeless sockets in a skull looked out at her from the side of the hill. She cried out and stood up. Her fingers brushed the skull and for just one moment, her vision went black. A terror filled her like no other, ripping a scream from her throat. She fled several paces before stopping.

"Where...?"

The wisp had vanished and fear soaked throughout her. Something behind her sent a chill down her spine. She turned, but nothing was there.

"Vicdan?" she screamed into the open air. A cold wind picked up as the sun finally appeared beneath the clouds, setting. Her voice echoed across the rocky hills. She was alone.

Backtracking as best she could, she ran with the sun at her back. She called out her companion's name and listened for signs of the raid. She'd wandered off farther than she'd thought. The more she tried to remember where she'd come from, the more that creature with the glowing eyes loomed in her mind. At long last, moans and pleas for mercy reached her ears. She rounded one more hill encrusted with glittering gray stones and found the remains of the caravan. Every last one of the sentients faced one direction, hands either above their heads as they begged or clasped before them in thanks.

"Please, mercy, Sjörna-Reks," someone sniveled. They quickly added, "We are grateful you saved us from the Vilderkin. They fear only you. You are great, strong. Let us pass. Please."

The new intruder the caravan faced—begged mercy from—was another wolf. But not a wild wolf at all like the last ones. This one, red with glowing emerald eyes, surveyed the begging people with far more intelligence behind its eyes than the others. The red wolf stepped into the crowd of desperate sentients. It towered over them, the size of a draft horse. With each step, more of its wolfish nature melted away and it shrank. The form it revealed was more terrifying. A woman, the tallest woman Zeva had ever seen, took its place. She had long, tangled red hair and the same blazing green eyes surrounded by black paint. Her savage armor was cruel, made of teeth, claws, and bone. The pauldrons on her shoulders looked like dragon fangs lashed together with leather. She pushed a skull mask up onto her head to show more black war-paint on her pale flesh. Her arms were thick as young trees, corded with muscle. She eyed the sentients as she walked among them, accompanied by a man just as tall as she. He bore a massive axe in his arms and only had one good eye, the other covered by a patch. The woman held her left hand out to the side. A metallic wind precluded a huge, ornate axe flying through the air. The thick haft thudded into her hands as she caught it. This made a few sentients kneeling before her quiver, ducking out of the way of the curved axe blade.

Zeva stayed crouched a good distance away, not rejoining the herd. The woman, whom they called Sjörna-Reks, spoke.

"Every day the Black Road comes closer to Altevine." Her voice, to Zeva's surprise, was smooth, deep, and almost melodious: sensual, beautiful, and terrifying. "And every day the Vilderkin move in closer. You bring danger to my canton with your very existence. By simply walking by." Her green eyes met each face she passed. Her gentle tone made them quake in fear. She stepped high, every movement of her long, bare leg making one more sentient flinch. "I know what they say about me, that I have broken the Warpath alliance. But

Zealmor and Northica—our brothers in the alliance—stand by and offer no protection for you. I am the one who must sacrifice my honor in the alliance to keep the Road safe. Who among you will give themselves up to keep the peace?" she finally asked.

Now soft cries went up and heads bowed.

"Skarde-Reks has warned you to stay inside the Warpath," a man offered. "The Black Road is not the alliance's concern. We owe no sacrifice!"

"My god is hungry," she snapped, raising her pale chin to glare down at the man. "The barrier weakens every day of Vasaras, and Raudnir must be fed. The Eldritch Hunt is upon us. I must satiate my god." Her eyes narrowed. "If you will not give, I will take."

As the woman spoke, Zeva spotted Vicdan in the throng. Ducking low, she ran towards him.

"Sjörna-Reks!" Ragnall the Runer shouted. He stood up, seizing Vicdan by the arm, heaving him up from a throng of cowering sentients.

Taken by surprise, Zeva gasped and struggled through to them. Ragnall hissed at her to get back. He pulled Vicdan up and stumbled over the destroyed, disfigured body of old Yorn.

Sjörna-Reks looked up, her red brows moving up her pale forehead in amusement. "A Runer," she mused. She spotted old Yorn. "And your apprentice. Dead."

"The Runes did not take to him," Ragnall said offhandedly, spitting onto his dead apprentice's face. "Take this foreigner and leave us be."

"No!" Zeva shouted, pulling on Vicdan against the Runer's iron grip.

"Let us go," Vicdan warned. This interjection brought Sjörna-Reks' eyes to him as well.

She looked amused. "Two from Al'Myrah in one caravan on the Black Road. Rhostrana must not have its fill of the desert rats from Alika."

"What are you doing?" Zeva asked Ragnall, choking on her words. Somehow, his betrayal hurt.

The man with the eyepatch growled at Vicdan as he fought against Ragnall, reaching for a blade.

At first, Sjörna-Reks looked only mildly interested in what Ragnall had proposed. The closer she got to Zeva, the more her face fell, turning serious.

"Please, leave us be," Zeva begged. "I'm looking for my father. Don't take us and sell us. I must find him."

The wolf woman shook her head. "I am not here to take and sell. I need bodies, blood, and souls."

Vicdan exhaled harshly. "That's so much worse."

Finally, Sjörna-Reks stood just inches from Zeva. Ragnall's arm shook as he put it out between the Reks and Zeva, letting her know he feared the wolf woman just as much as the others. A wave of gratitude at the Runer's small gesture flooded Zeva, even though he'd been terrible before.

The woman raised her hand to Zeva's face, brushing away the mud that covered the mark on her forehead. Sjörna-Reks' eyes widened.

"The star of the necromancer," she said. "Raudnir has heard my prayers. My Volra saw the star in their visions." She stared at the mark for another long moment. "Take all three of them," she ordered her party.

"Three?" Ragnall shouted as two great men pulled his arms behind his back. "I offered them to you!"

Sjörna-Reks smiled, bored with his begging. "I've not sacrificed a Masahk soul before. Could be worth more than all the rest." She glared at Ragnall. "Thank you for stepping forward. Don't disappoint me."

"Wait!" Vicdan shouted as two more of the giants bound his arms behind him at his elbows. "Where are you taking us?"

Overcome, Zeva cried and struggled uselessly against the two women who bound her as well. The tears froze on her face. With her arms pulled tight behind, the cold wind cut through her thin front and chilled her. Grateful it wasn't them, the rest of the caravan let the invaders take Ragnall, Vicdan, and Zeva without a fight. They didn't care for the vile Runer, and even less for foreigners.

"Please, no," Zeva cried as they were each lashed to a massive, antlered wolf. "I have to find him. I have to know if he's safe."

Sjörna-Reks stepped up beside her, looking down at her like she was a rare animal to be hunted. "I promise you, we *will* find him." She smiled darkly, her wolfish fangs showing behind full, red lips.

Despair filled Zeva as they pulled her, bound and freezing, into the mountains of Caerwren.

CHAPTER 10

THE WAY OF THE WEST

AT FIRST, TZARIK THOUGHT STOPPING DURING THE NIGHT would be a deadly idea. Sleeping, lying still in the frigid air of Caerwren, would paralyze them, maybe even kill them. But walking through the night proved just as painful and dangerous. Shadows of creatures dashed to and fro in the darkness, and beasts flew overhead he could not see. The constant marching made him leave Tarkan behind more than once. The third night, he built a fire and hunted. Weakness from hunger made him dizzy and stumble over the uneven earth. He was sturdy and had gone days with no food before. He wasn't sure how Tarkan fared, and it seemed rude to ask.

Without speaking, he got a fire going. The dry bog moss all around them burned hot and bright. To their right, in the north, a spine of mountains jutted up, white-capped and imposing. In the darkness, Tzarik could make out tiny specs of light: pyres. There was life on the peaks.

"I'm going towards the tree line." He indicated to his right. "I have to find something for us to eat. Once you're warm, find water."

The necromancer silently agreed and Tzarik headed out to hunt with nothing but the curved blade from his boot. He'd never been much of a game hunter. Runers often worked in cities where lodging and food was plenty. Right now, in the dry wind, he wanted water more than food. Unsure about Tarkan, he hadn't spoken during their march simply because his mouth was too dry. Just thinking about a cold spring drove him wild with thirst. Surely a river or spring flowed somewhere nearby?

Drawing atan quickly, he scanned the earth for tracks of creatures. The ground was dry, but a few broken sprigs of the tough undergrowth showed where something had tread. Reaching down, he touched the broken bits. The liquid life of the plant hadn't frozen yet. He stayed crouched, scanning the area. The creature was close, whatever it was. He hoped it could be eaten without causing illness.

He repeated these steps until ending up deeper in the forest than he'd wanted to be. Thirst clawed at his throat, and the rage that came with an empty belly made his mind irrational. His legs shook while his mind spun circles in his skull. Exhausted, he leaned against the trunk of a tree. He needed to rest. Just for a moment. Laying his head back, his fingers spun the jade bracelet around his wrist. He'd memorized every inclusion and swirl, looking every day for a crack to form. The monk told him if the bracelet broke, it meant the one wearing the other had perished. Tzarik didn't believe in luck, gods, and especially not trinkets like this. But he'd examined the bracelet every day anyway. It remained whole, giving him hope.

A wild whoop shook him alert. He coughed, his dry throat sticking together when he inhaled suddenly. His toes had gone numb and the skin on his face burned in agony. He blinked, grabbing atan to look for whoever had made the war cry.

"Don't!" a voice hissed. "They're hunting."

Slowly, and quietly as a cat, Tzarik got to his feet but stayed low. A man crouched next to him, holding a waterskin.

"Here," the man offered, seeing the glint in Tzarik's eyes. "Quietly, though." He pointed behind them. The man wore a green cloak, clasped with an elegant broach made of wood and carved in the likeness of a leaf Tzarik didn't recognize. The man held a long, strongly curved bow in his other hand. A quiver of green-feathered arrows stuck up over his right shoulder.

Without waiting, Tzarik grabbed the waterskin and poured the sweet, clear liquid down his throat. He coughed, but pushed through, guzzling down half the contents.

"Steady now," the man said with a smile. "A ritual for the Eldritch Hunt lies just beyond that ravine. We don't want them to spot us."

Slightly satiated now, Tzarik craned his neck to look. Wild figures clad in fur and bones, all wearing crowns of antlers, ran back and forth in firelight. Each one held a torch. Some rode horses, others giant wolves, and a few sat astride a creature like a gazelle with branch-like horns.

"Lowland hunters taking Northica for sacrifice," the man explained in a quiet, sad voice. "But I see you are not from our shores."

"Thank you," Tzarik said quickly, wanting to show the man he appreciated his aid. "I don't suppose you have food with you?"

The man made a noise indicating he was smiling. "My wife has found your companion. Do not fear. She is making a stew as we speak." He checked over Tzarik's head to watch the wild hunters move farther away. "Good. They are moving towards Northica. The inlanders like to take the redhairs from Zealmor. Think it makes for a better sacrifice."

The man stood up, still cautious, and bent low.

"What were you thinking, wandering the moors of Caerwren in naught but the cotton of Al'Myrah?" he asked softly, leading Tzarik back the way he'd come. "And sleeping under the trees. You would have frozen before sunrise."

"Trying to hunt," Tzarik mumbled, slipping his knife back into his boot. "A seaman we paid to bring us across from Al'Myrah threw us from the ship."

The man nodded, understanding. "Sea dogs are very superstitious. I'm surprised they took you on at all."

The man expertly navigated the frozen bogs and tiny ravines back out to where Tzarik had left Tarkan. A much brighter, taller fire blazed there now. A strangely shaped figure stirred a pot over the fire. At first, Tzarik couldn't see Tarkan, but then spotted a cloak of furs with Tarkan's pale face illuminated under it.

"My wife, Fjonya, is a little overbearing when it comes to caretaking," he apologized.

"If I didn't take care of you, Aivar, no one would," Fjonya replied, handing her husband a bowl of stew.

Now that they stood in the ring of firelight, Tzarik realized the woman's figure looked strange because she was a rabbit-like Masahk. She stood tall, on round, thick legs covered in white fur. She wore a wool coat, dyed blue, over her furry body, and black woolen gloves.

The man in the green cloak, Aivar, handed Tzarik the hot bowl. Grateful beyond measure, Tzarik took it and drank half the bowl in one motion. It burned his throat, but he didn't care. He glanced over to make sure Tarkan ate as well. His companion sat swathed in the skin of some huge, gray creature. His eyes had brightened considerably, but he didn't speak. He also held a bowl of steaming stew. Tzarik joined him near the fire. With food in his stomach and water finally thickening his blood, he could think clearly for the first time in three days.

The couple exchanged a few whispered words while Fjonya served up two more bowls of the stew for her and her husband. Soon, the four of them sat around the campfire consuming the thick broth.

"Won't the light attract the ones we saw in the forest?" Tzarik asked.

Aivar shook his head, giving Fjonya a quick kiss on her soft, white cheek, thanking her for cooking. "They are no doubt taking their captives to the summit of Tyrmagnar."

Tarkan glanced at Tzarik just as he did the same towards the necromancer. He saw that Tarkan also knew the legend. Tzarik was unfamiliar with a lot of history and legends from the map, especially the east and far north, but Tyrmagnar he knew.

To make sure he'd thought of the correct legendary savior, he asked, "The giant who slew the god?"

"He slew Mjordir, sending him back to the God Deep," Tarkan added, speaking for the first time. "The prime god of Caerwren who pulled the mountains from the earth. He gave sentient kind the mountains as a gift, protected them from other gods in exchange for their blood. A river, red and sanguine, runs through Caerwren, invisible to our eyes. Mjordir drank from this river. Tyrmagnar, a mortal man and a blacksmith, took it upon himself to break sentient kind from Mjordir's grasp."

Fjonya nodded, her long, floppy ears dancing. "Tyrmagnar stood up to the god, fighting it and the others back into the Deep where they belong, giving sentient kind a chance to have free will. Those in Zealmor say their prayers to Mjordir still. The mid-west bows their heads to Tyrmagnar, giving him god status. They will take those they capture from Zealmor and sacrifice them in the skull of Tyrmagnar."

"His remains still stand?" Tarkan asked.

Aivar handed them the waterskin again. "Aye, lad. As do most of the god's skeletons. Stay clear this time of year, my friends. The Eldritch Hunt makes savages of us all."

Taking a chance, Tzarik asked, "What does that mean? What is the Eldritch Hunt?"

The couple gazed cautiously at each other. Fjonya said, "Vasaras is the time of darkness, the season of the Hunt. We never know when the power of the gods will leak through the barrier." She motioned to the sky above. "For now, we get to see the sun rise. But soon..." She held her arm out flat to represent the horizon and moved her other fist along the line, sinking it lower and lower until it didn't break over her arm. "The sun will not come up again for weeks. That is when the God Deep is nearly open upon our continent. Specters, monsters, long sleeping gods—they all surface. They walk among us."

Tzarik still didn't understand. He'd never believed in a god, let alone the kind of monster he and Tarkan had witnessed on their first day. "But why the sacrifices?"

Tarkan took the skin from him and drank deeply before replying. "Do you know the one thing gods don't possess?"

The Runer waited, studying his companion.

"Blood." Tarkan's voice dropped dangerously. "Red blood." His eyes went glassy. "Something I and my tribesmen cannot give them from ourselves."

"Your god demands blood?" Tzarik asked.

The Masahk and the man watched Tarkan carefully now; their suspicions confirmed. Fjonya nodded and sighed. She stood up, lashing her pot to her pack now that it was empty.

"Where are you going?" Tzarik asked.

Aivar flipped his hood over his head. "It is not out of malice that we leave you, Runer." He politely inclined his head to Tarkan. "Please, keep the fur cloaks. You will need them."

"Wait!" Tzarik jumped up to chase after them. "We need to find a city. Where is the closest civilization?"

Fjonya's nose twitched in amusement. "Civilization on Caerwren?"

"The closest canton is Altevine," Aivar said, taking his wife's hand. "You could go to Northica, but they are defending their bridge from the lowlands. What do you seek?"

Tarkan stood up and his voice came gruff and deep. "My daughter. We were separated on a ship coming here."

At this, Fjonya's soft lips parted and her eyes widened. "The girl," she whispered to Aivar. "With the star on her forehead. I gave her tea. She was so sad."

"What girl?" Tarkan threw the fur cloaks aside and took two threatening steps towards the couple before Tzarik stopped him.

"Oh, lad." She sighed, her whiskers falling. "We met a lass. On the Black Road. We parted from them just before... Well, we heard it was dreadful. The Vilderkin and Sjörna-Reks' clan clashed in the valley."

"What does that mean?" Tzarik asked, pressing his hand into Tarkan's chest as a warning when he felt the necromancer tense up again.

Aivar's face fell. "She could still be alive. But she *will* be in Altevine. Sjörna-Reks, the Reks of Altevine, is gathering souls for a great sacrifice. The other Reks are calling her a heretic. They think by the time Vasaras reaches its zenith, she will begin whatever eldritch ritual she is preparing."

Tzarik's throat tightened. "Was the girl alone?"

"No," Fjonya said quickly. "She had a young man with her." Her cheeks pinched in a grin. "And horses. And a box like a coffin."

Hearing this, Tzarik's own heart rested and raced at the same time. He faced Tarkan, knowing that both he and the necromancer would want to march towards Altevine now.

"Don't leave the firelight," Aivar counseled them once again. He took a branch from it and lit a torch from his pack. "The creatures will be wary of the fire. Guard yourselves, as any hunters may spot it and come for you."

Understanding, having been abandoned many times as a bad omen, Tzarik let them go. He turned towards the direction of Altevine and glared up into the night sky.

"I don't care about their gods. We leave at sunrise."

Tarkan lightly touched the star on his forehead. "For a man who hunts monsters, you have a powerful disdain for gods."

The Runer took up one of the cloaks and wrapped it around himself, pulling up the hood. His ears immediately burned as they thawed out, away from the wind. "I've never needed a god. The ones I've seen have only brought hurt and punishment."

"You may need my god and meet its demands if you ever want to see Sybal again," the necromancer whispered.

ঽ

WITH FOOD IN HIS STOMACH, a fire, and a warm cloak wrapped around him, Tzarik slept deeply that night. His mind filled with images of giants and monsters. Huge, glowing eyes watched him over the peaks of mountains and up from the depths of the ocean like they waited for him to make a move.

Tarkan kicked him awake. Once again, a gray sheen lay over the land, blocking out the sun. Tzarik was beginning to wonder if the sun ever rose in Caerwren.

"There have been packs moving toward the mountain," Tarkan supplied as Tzarik got his blood flowing again. "I heard a bell early this morning. There must be a city or village close."

With no ceremony, the two of them followed a trail of marched-down grass towards a valley. They didn't speak for fear of causing a rage or urgency in the other. At least they knew the others were alive, moving. The trail they followed led them up over a side of a smaller mountain so they could see out into the space between the greater of the peaks. To the north rose the huge peak of Northica. Before them, hills and rolling valleys stretched out. The first part of a city, surrounded by impossibly tall walls, hid nestled between the land masses. Two nearly straight ridges rose just outside the city. The man-made structures crawled up the sides of the hills until they came to a grassy hilltop. There, a freehold of smaller homes and a great, thatched longhouse watched over the city below. Smoke rose from the freehold.

Tzarik followed the rising hills out of the settlement with his eyes, curious. They looked manmade. The slopes met the side of a mountain, and from the earth rose a colossal human skeleton. Shaken, Tzarik took a step back. The giant's ribs had crashed onto the mountain it rested against, like a warrior taking a respite. It had to be thousands of years old, but flesh and sinews still covered part of it. A huge, straight sword stuck out of its chest.

"Tyrmagnar," Tarkan said solemnly. He pointed to a line of tiny torches trailing to the top of the mountain to the giant human skull. "They bring him sacrifices. A godslayer turned god to them."

His eyes taking in the myth, something akin to caution and doubt bloomed in Tzarik's chest. His mind went back to the creature he'd seen on their first day, walking over the crags of the mountain. Wordlessly, he followed Tarkan towards the walled-in city. The closer they got, the more the wilds melted away, and sentient chatter, smells, and movement soothed their worried minds.

A deep esker surrounded the city, with a stone bridge as the only access point. No guards checked who came in or out. Packs of clansman filtered in and out in ruckus, roaring clamor. Once over the bridge, the din of life grew louder. The muddy streets were lined with folk from all over Caerwren, some bound and tied, being led by others. These shouted that they were headed out the back of the city, to bring their prisoners as sacrifices to Tyrmagnar or Raudnir or some other god.

"Sentient sacrifice," Tzarik mumbled in disgust.

Tarkan slowly turned his own icy eyes to meet Tzarik's. "You may want to prepare for the inevitability, Runer. Some realms of this world can only be reached by such a sacrifice."

"The true gods will have their vengeance!" a man tied to a pillar shouted. His black curls flew in the light wind and the mad shaking of his fervor. He wore the full white robes of the philosophers of Rom. Tzarik had only seen illustrations in books, but recognized it. Some from Al'Myrah went to study in the academies of Rom, with their alabaster pillars and long-winded orators. The man looked as though he'd been beaten into captivity. "You are a savage people!" he went on as watchers laughed at him, deep into their drink already. "A veritable god will thrive upon your worship alone. They do not ask for your blood. Stop giving in to death and sacrifice! Why can't you see reason?"

"What are we looking for here?" Tarkan asked as they eventually reached what had to be the city square.

While the walls were made of stone, every roof was thatched, and the streets were made of mud. Tzarik spotted a few blacksmiths, but none worked in metal armor. Thick leather and simple, straight blades peppered the stalls.

"Travelers from the Black Road," Tzarik replied. "And sulfates," he added when he spotted a pack of Runers outside a smith. He'd need more to replace the poisoned ones inside Sybal.

He broke from Tarkan and approached the towering group of men. Each held a new orichalcum blade, inspecting them for blemishes. The smith behind the forge wrung his hands nervously as he waited, his eyes darting to each hunter in turn. Every smith Tzarik dealt with treated him like a thief or a murderer. They never showed fear like this one here. He'd almost forgotten about how Runers were far more feared and respected on Caerwren.

"Not bad for your first attempt," one of the Runers said in a gruff, sneering tone. "He was right to recommend you to us." He jerked his head away and the pack turned to leave.

"Um, sir," the smith babbled with apprehension. "Payment? Orichalcum is dangerous, and the way your blades must be heated is—"

One of the Runers rounded on the helpless smith. Tzarik saw from the way his weight fell on his boots and how his hand gripped the handle of his blade that the Runer meant to strike the smith.

"Runers," he interjected, stepping apart from the crowd. "A word, if you would."

The others turned to face him. Their hunters' eyes slowly roved up and down Tzarik's body. One smirked and whispered something to another.

"Ah," the one who'd threatened the smith said to him. "A whiteblood brother from a foreign land." His eyes went to Tzarik's belt. "Where's your sword, Runer?"

Tzarik braced himself. "I've come far. I need sulfates and information about the caravan that was attacked on the Black Road."

The Runers—all four of them—gave each other meaningful glances. Tzarik's sulfates rushed in his arms. His fingers twitched for a weapon. Unsure why he got the sense they would attack, he took a step back.

"I don't have much," he started.

"We don't want your foreign coin," the Runer scoffed, a wicked grin pulling his pale face into a leer. "It's the time of the hunt. And murder was not my crime."

The man sprang at Tzarik. With a cry, Tzarik dived under the man's swinging arm to the forge, where an unfinished blade sat near the anvil. He gripped the straight blade clumsily, unused to its weight and design. He hardly had a moment to brace it against his palm when the other Runer's blade hit it hard. The taller man bore down on Tzarik easily. A few cries from nearby citizens went up, but no one paid much mind aside from moving out of the way. Tzarik slipped out from under the larger Runer and ran.

"Get him!" the other Runers cajoled, laughing heartily at the fleeing Al'Myrahn.

Tzarik was able to duck under the smith's table and roll out of harm's way for just a moment while the bigger man clambered over it. This gave him just a moment to regrip the blade and see it was also orichalcum. Good; it would sting the Runer whenever he landed a hit. He parried the oncoming blow and caught Tarkan's dark shape scampering out of view in his left eye. He hissed some incantation as he evaded the fight. The necromancer would have no defense in the city, so Tzarik moved to put himself between the Runers and Tarkan to protect him.

As he danced around in the quickly emptying square, he summed up the Runer's Caerwren armor: the chest piece was black leather like his. Unlike his, curved pauldrons protected the taller Runer's shoulders. His dark pants were not full and billowy, either, showing Tzarik exactly where to cut at his legs. With a quick disengage, he lunged with the point of the foreign sword, nicking the inside of the Runer's thigh. The man roared in pain, reeling back. The cursed metal worked on Runers just as well as monsters.

But this hit signaled the other three Runers to rush Tarkan. Tzarik kicked the wounded Runer hard, knocking him over as he clutched his now bleeding wound. One Runer lunged at Tarkan, but missed. The necromancer wavered and vanished into the air, turning partly invisible. Even Tzarik halted in stunned surprise. Tarkan's solid form rippled as he fled a few steps away.

"What monster is this?" one of the Runers roared.

Tzarik fended off two more Runers before the first swung his long, muscled legs from the ground. He caught Tzarik's shins, knocking him flat on his back. As the first scrambled to his feet, a second lunged at Tzarik with his glittering blade. Tzarik shoved his sword up, piercing the side of the attacker's leather armor, causing him to back off. The first got to his feet and kicked Tzarik hard in his chest just as he rose. The man's enormous foot knocked all the wind out of Tzarik. Then the man reached down, gripping the front of his armor, and lifted him easily. With a wicked grin, he shoved a tiny orichalcum blade just below Tzarik's ribs. The cursed metal sent pangs of agony through his entire body. His hot, white blood leaked out. A few cries from onlookers went up.

Suddenly, the Runers behind them shouted in surprise. The clang of Runers' blades told him a fifth had entered the fight. His captor dropped him, flipping him around, pulling the blade from his side, and held it to his throat. From the mixture of his sweat and long hair in his eyes, Tzarik couldn't see the newly arrived Runer. He heard the moaning of the other three to his satisfaction.

"I should have known it was you, Jyrgon," said the new Runer.

"If you loved goats a little less, your crime would stop you from bloodying our streets every other day."

Unwilling to be held captive, Tzarik drew buhkar and slipped out of his captor's arms. The man shouted in rage. Before he could move, Tzarik slipped behind him, drew halat, and shoved it at the Runer, sending him flying forward. The one who had intervened stepped into the man's path and used the momentum to toss him over his shoulder. The man landed with a thud. While his savior dealt with the savage Runer, Tzarik stumbled to his feet.

The orichalcum did its job. His wound wouldn't close up fast enough, even if he drew artiah. He stumbled to the forge, where he lay against the stone wall for support. He blinked the sweat out of his eyes, scanning for the Runers' horses. Where there were Runers, there were sulfates within their black boxes.

"Tarkan?" he called, too weak to move.

The necromancer wavered into view, appearing at his side. He muttered some kind of excuse for not helping more, but Tzarik waved it away. He knew how the necromancer fought, having witnessed it many times. He wasn't a sword fighter nor a sorcerer who could hurl lightning with his bare hands. Tzarik didn't blame him for running.

"He stabbed me with orichalcum," Tzarik mumbled. "Can you see their horses? They should have a black box somewhere with vials of white sulfates."

Tarkan glanced up only momentarily. "You're bleeding too much."

Tzarik nodded, sliding down the wall to sit on the muddy earth, tired and in pain.

Without warning, Tarkan loosened the laces on the side of Tzarik's armor and slipped his long, bony fingers under his tunic. His cold hand on Tzarik's flesh made him gasp. Before he could ask what Tarkan was doing, the pain from his wound vanished. With a groan, Tarkan fell back onto his heels, gripping his side.

"What the hell did you do?" Tzarik asked. He pulled his armor aside and inspected his now scarred flesh.

Pressing his hand onto his side through his black robes, Tarkan mumbled, "One of the five spells of necromancy. Taking on the wounds of another. My blood clots, Runer. And your rune will help me."

Moving quickly, Tzarik pulled artiah from his leather cord and drew it slowly over Tarkan's fresh wound. He did it twice more until the stab wound scabbed over fitfully. Together, they stood up and looked for the one who had saved them. A tall, white-haired Runer gave the last of the attacking foursome a swift kick to their backside as they retreated. Then he turned to face Tzarik.

"Still getting into trouble, Tzarik?" the Caerwren Runer asked with an artful smile.

Tzarik recognized the pale Runer now and gasped. "Korvoth?" Relief at a familiar face doused the fire of despair. He and Sybal had run into Korvoth nearly two years ago on Al'Myrah when they had searched for an answer to what they now called the Runer's death. He had been gracious then and proved once again now that he was not like his Caerwren brethren.

"What brings you to my shores this time of year?" Korvoth asked, leading them away from the prying eyes of the quickly refilling square. "And I apologize for our whiteblood brothers. Runers are killer imbeciles at best," Korvoth reasoned. "During the Eldritch Hunt, they are possessed with death."

"That's why we're here," Tzarik said as they turned down an alley.

Korvoth took in Tarkan now and his eyes dimmed. "Where is your lady Runer?" He asked it cautiously, no doubt remembering the conditions of their first meeting.

"Somewhere supposedly near Altevine," Tzarik replied. "We've been through much since we saw you last. And..." His throat seized up. "Her fate is my doing. I brought this upon her. Korvoth, I need sulfates for her. And I need to find her. Do you know anything about the caravan on the Black Road?"

The pale Runer nodded. "Sjörna-Reks has been haunting that road, taking prisoners."

"So we've heard," Tzarik confirmed. "Sybal was on that road with two companions. We need to get to Altevine."

Korvoth led them to a hitching post outside a rundown inn where his own huge black horse waited. He dug into his saddlebags. Tzarik noticed a wrapped sword hanging from the saddle, its orichalcum blade broken. Korvoth pulled out a fleshy black chest and opened it, retrieving one vial of sulfates.

"I cannot spare more than this," he said with warning. "But the mori and nolrieth are simple to track this time of year. If you need to, you can find them near Altevine. You know to be cautious when hunting them."

Grateful, Tzarik nodded and took the proffered vial, stowing it in his belt satchel. "Can you tell me anything about this Sjörna-Reks? Why is she taking captives? Are there clan wars brewing?"

Korvoth's eyes went to Tarkan behind them. "I'd be wary of going into her clan's land, Tzarik. Blood and gods are the way of life here on Caerwren. But Sjörna-Reks has drawn the scrutiny of other Reks, even from those in her northern alliance they call the Warpath. This Vasaras, she gathers more blood and souls than any other Reks. She fills the bogs around her clan's land with their bodies and souls. If she has taken your lady and her companions..." His blue eyes filled with doubt.

"There must be a way to know if she took them," Tarkan growled.

The pale Runer met the necromancer's eyes. His face contorted as he did battle with himself.

"What is it?" Tzarik asked.

"She's been brazenly on the hunt for one who can raise the dead." His tone dropped low and serious. "Years ago, she called

Runers to her to hunt down and find one who could perform such a rite. Only three were brought to her in all those years. Two did not survive, one eventually escaped. Ran."

"Then it should be simple to find her," Tarkan said quickly. "No mortal sentient seeks out a necromancer."

Tzarik gripped Tarkan's arm to stop him from taking off. "I'm not handing you over to a barbarian to be slaughtered on her altar."

Tarkan threw his arm off. "That's not what she wants. Even if it were, I'd die for Zeva. Just as you would for Sybal. Don't pretend this isn't the best path forward."

"Noble of you, my necrotic friend," Korvoth said, taking in the black tattoos on Tarkan's face now. "I cannot say why she desires such a sentient. But I would caution you. The hate between the Warpath alliance—Altevine, Northica, and Zealmor—has grown too much for the rest of Caerwren to bear. They don't care what the more barbarous cantons do."

Tzarik considered Tarkan's fervor. The dark, bloody stain on his robes lingered in his eyesight. Tarkan had taken on his wounds without question. He had followed him this far, trusting him to find the way. They were all but sure this mountain queen, Sjörna-Reks, had taken Zeva and Vicdan from the caravan. Something inside him told him Sybal, Zeva, and Vicdan were in Altevine.

"This is your choice," he warned Tarkan.

The necromancer cut him off. "I don't expect you to stay behind, Tzarik. If you get the chance, after Sybal is revived...run."

CHAPTER 11

BOLEMESH

AFTER FLEEING THE COAST AND THE WATERY MONSTER, Sybal followed Kjarton into the green mist. Panting and her heart racing from the fight with the horrid monster, she didn't ask questions. The man's pale legs flashed as he ran in the darkness. She kept her eyes focused on them since his black hair and sparse, dark, animal-skin garb blended into the surroundings. Things moved in her peripheral vision: a green specter, a tiny white monster, a black shadow. They were there; she just couldn't see them through the thick blue and green mist.

Kjarton ducked into a maze of rocks left behind by what looked like an avalanche. Sybal followed and found herself in a network of underground tunnels underneath an elaborate stone circle. At first, the stones appeared strange, too smooth. Then she realized they lay arranged in a spiral pattern with intricate lines of river stones. The opening of the caves sat at the base of a pile of mountainous boulders that had fallen from the peaks and settled there.

She kept glancing back to make sure none of the spiders or the other monsters mentioned had followed her. "I saw something in the woods," she stammered to the raven man, using the Caerwren language. "Heard a name from a swarm of spiders. It made them stop chasing me."

"Mjordir," Kjarton replied, leading her in. "The prime god of Caerwren, the one who guards Tierheim. He loves the Hunt and moves between the Deep and the living world. You won't see him, unlike the other gods. No one does. But you will feel his presence."

Inside the cave, a warm fire glowed, with the furs of strange creatures spread all around it. Kjarton had made a sort of short table of wood and bone.

"You don't feel hunger or thirst," he explained, moving around the space. "But that's part of the curse of being sacrificed. You can still die of hunger and need for water. You just won't know until it's too late."

"Die?" she repeated. "You said you—and I—were sacrificed. Doesn't that mean we're dead? This isn't Janna, is it? Or is it Nah'Ja-ha?" Had she not been a good Al'Myrahn? She'd prayed to the east, had memorized the mihals. Or was her crime enough to damn her to this place in-between? The oath to the runes was supposed to expunge her guilt.

He shook his head, motioning for her to take a seat by the fire. "I wouldn't be in your hell, lass. My god is the Valravn. Not whatever you Al'Myrahns worship."

Sybal sat where he indicated and watched him as he gathered some more logs and brittle white sticks for the fire. The fire instantly warmed her wet clothes. "Uh, Vaeson?" she stuttered. "I know what a werecreature is, but—"

"Because you're a Runer?" he asked, inclining his head to her pearlescent blade and runes. He stopped and made eye contact with her. "I've never met a lady Runer. Al'Myrah must be an advanced civilization."

It was, but she glossed over his compliment, used to people having the same reaction upon meeting her. "Even my mentor wouldn't know what a Vaeson is."

"Clan royalty," he replied easily. "It's not well-known off the continent, but you're not going anywhere, are you?" His words were ominous, but his emerald eyes smiled.

Sybal blinked, shaking her head. "How long have you been in..." She thought back to what he'd called it. "The God Deep?"

"Time is irrelevant to the gods," the man replied, removing his bone helmet and quickly tossing the logs into the fire. The straight, pale bridge of his nose was flecked with tiny freckles. "I cannot say. Perhaps years." His green eyes looked up from where he gathered a gray, dry meat laid out on a stone slab. "What year was it when you were alive?"

The way he framed his questions made fear mount. He'd said she'd been sacrificed. She supposed that might have been what those crosses were for in the Hallow City. It seemed just the other day she'd run through the thick rain of Xia to face off against the serpentine Masahk. And save Yui. Overcome, she knelt by the fire and pushed her hands out towards it.

"I was on Xia," she began. "It was just turning to winter. I was twenty-six years old. The year was 312 by the Al'Myrahn calendar. Xia's summer had been fading."

The man's grimy face brightened as he handed Sybal a skin of fresh water. "Caerwren uses the same calendar. It was the year of the Yarrow Tree, 307, when I was sacrificed to the antlered dragon god of Northica and their lesser radjur god."

Sybal coughed on the water. Apologizing, she didn't mention her mother was Northican. Clearly hadn't been clan royalty, though.

His eyes went to the fire, consumed by memories. "Five years, I suppose. My son will be fifteen now. If only he..." He stopped. "It matters not," he whispered hoarsely.

"I was beaten," Sybal went on after taking a drink of the hot water. "Killed on a Xian cross. I didn't think Xai'long took sacrifice. But the spirit I see in my sleep is a snake, not a dragon."

Xia had many gods, most forgotten, since the country worshiped the White Dragon primarily. Wu-Zhiang must not have worshiped the White Dragon and had offered her soul to some other god.

"The Valravn?" Sybal asked when the man offered no more conversation. "Oh, and thank you for saving me," she added when he didn't move. "What was that thing?"

"I try to avoid them." Kjarton finally sat. He took up a wide swath of black fur and stitched it together with a strange, pale, leathery thread. "The God Deep is the home of the gods," he offered. "Some long forgotten. They pass through it on their way to and from our clanlands, homes."

"Nah'jaha is said to be a land of ice and fire," she said, praying this wasn't some cultural misunderstanding. She had to be sure she wasn't in hell.

"No," he cut over her quickly, sensing her fear. "As I said, this is not Tirheim, either. Our hell. The God Deep is a place for souls not given to their own god. The gods feed on the forcibly given's blood and life here. The Deep is a layer over our world." He picked up the hem of her thin, cotton cloak, laying it over his palm. He tucked it between his fingers so the cloak took on the shape of his hand. "You are on Caerwren, inside the God Deep. If you were on Al'Myrah, you'd see your gods and spirits in the desert. But here, you will see ours. Few gods remain on this side during the Eldritch Hunt, more satisfied to cross the barrier into our realm and see the bloodshed in their honor." His eyes unfocused. "I once saw the Valravn, observing me through the mist in Altevine. It felt glorious to know my god's eyes were on me."

Her brows shot up and her breath hitched.

"I will show you." He looked up, out the entrance to his hiding place. "There are many things in the Deep to be wary of. Some secrets I still don't know, but I'd rather not learn. We must journey further inland, towards Altevine. This is just one of the places I go, but I dare not stay away long."

Sybal frowned, reimagining the map in her mind. "I must have been near the shore between the nameless mountains. Between Hovandel and Northica. I didn't see so much as a village. Aren't there villages along the coast?"

Kjarton nodded. "You will not see them here."

Her heart sank while her mind spun. She dropped her face into her hands.

Kjarton shuffled over next to her. He tenderly raised her chin with his cold fingers. "I am not as a brave as you. The way you fought the sea god was thrilling. I don't have that kind of fearlessness."

His softheartedness shone on his kind face. She smiled weakly. "Thank you. I wasn't always this way."

"I will show you the monsters and secrets of the Deep so you know how to defend yourself against more death. Will you come with me?"

She checked that her runes remained around her neck. They did. And she had her Runer blade. She wiped it on her pants, knowing she'd need it clean for the next day. If the Deep was full of hunting gods and prowling monsters, she'd need to be ready.

ᚴ

THE JOURNEY towards where Kjarton said Altevine lay did not pass in sun rises and sets. The sun in the Deep had no pattern, and two moons in the sky often glowed at the same time. Sometimes, the sun vanished and long stints of darkness followed. This darkness brought out monsters she could not see that hissed and prowled in the shadows despite the two moons in the sky. Eyes peeked out from long reeds, and the soft pattering of bare feet flitted behind them. Kjarton always moved with caution, taking no risks and only stopping when they had the safety of at least one rock wall to lean against. She privately judged his fear, wanting to search to the very corners of the Deep.

He showed her which tiny creatures he'd eaten from the bogs

that hadn't made him ill and which plants wouldn't poison her. At last, they reached their destination. After passing out from beneath the nameless mountains, a great moor stretched before them. In the distance, what looked like a short, jagged mountain range arched over the grasslands. Sybal examined it, confused by the shape.

"It looks like a god dug out the center of that mountain," she mused. "The edges are so perfectly round."

Kjarton almost beamed at the strange landscape before them. "The city of the thronehall of Altevine lies within that crater. The story says that years ago, one god made the grasslands. To spite him, a goddess put a single mountain there. Angered, the god tried to destroy it. But the edges remain."

"Any of your gods?" Sybal asked.

He shook his head. "Our ancestors took it for its defensibility."

As they stood looking at what must have been Kjarton's homeland, a crack of green lightning split the sky. Sybal instinctually ducked. Behind the dark clouds, the lightning lit up the shape of a huge, antlered dragon. When the green flashes faded, only a distant roar remained.

"They're moving," Kjarton whispered. "Let's get to safety. The lightning in the sky is far from us. But when it comes from the ground, avoid it."

Sybal quickly looked down, taking a few steps back. "Lightning from the ground?"

The raven man nodded. "You'll learn in time. But now, we need to run."

He led the way, sprinting across the marshy, writhing ground. They ran past more black shadows in the green mist and one white, naked body—man or woman, Sybal could not tell— standing still as stone. Kjarton's hiding place near Altevine was much the same as the previous one. They waited out the lightning storm in silence. The earth shook and harrowing screams rose from outside the cave. Sybal wrapped herself in her cloak and stared into the fire.

"Is there a way out?" she asked once the spirits and gods quieted. "The magi say the barrier is thin in Caerwren."

The raven-haired man looked at her with pity. "I will show you."

ả

KJARTON CAME with her when she finally ventured out, looking for anything that might help her find a way out. He'd started by leading her towards a tower mesa. When very little activity greeted them, he followed her quietly as she investigated. She looked for any sign of hope over the frozen, dark moors. For Tzarik. He hadn't come back for her on Xia. He never came for her. She always chased him down. But now she couldn't. Would he leave her at last?

Sybal clung to the sharp rocks as one came loose; she'd been distracted by her sad thoughts. She gasped and pulled herself closer to the cliff face as she scaled it. Above her, Kjarton's raven-shaped shadow passed over her and he cawed loudly.

"I'm fine," she shouted up, hauling herself up onto the new plain. She rolled over and gasped for air. The mist, even during the time the sun shone, lay so thick she could not see far. It also chilled her skin, making the cold air sink deeper into her. But now she wore the black fur cloak Kjarton had made. She wasn't sure what she was looking for, but knew wallowing in misery and hiding in the caves wouldn't help her find a lead.

Crouching, she looked forward into the dense fog. Whispers and screams became common. Never really catching the frightful things causing the sounds made it much worse and more terrifying. She tuned out the sounds to pick up the one sound she'd come to dread. The slithering of something colossus had woken her the night before, and the feeling of great, slitted yellow eyes on her had made it impossible to sleep. She'd seen the monster before, coming for her across the ocean. It had finally landed in Caerwren. The longer she watched, the more another sound approached. A skittering accompanied by the softest trilling.

Carefully, she ran, ducking into the tall grass towards the sound. Unsure what she was looking for, her eyes jumped to every shadowy movement in the mist. What she thought was the thumping of her own heart rose louder. Footfalls. Someone ran towards her. She stopped, waiting. A scream cut through the mist just as the dark, sharp shape of a piney forest covered the horizon.

A terrified weeping announced the arrival of a woman covered in mud with lips blue from the cold. The woman ran like a drunk, head tossing left and right in horror.

"Go!" she shouted in the common speech of Caerwren when she spotted Sybal. "Bolemesh is coming!"

Above her, Kjarton screeched. "Run, Sybal!"

The skittering she'd heard arrived just behind the lady.

"Wait!" Sybal shouted, grabbing at the woman as she careened towards the cliff Sybal had just scaled. But the woman didn't stop.

Another gruesome scream shot through the mist as the woman went over. But Sybal didn't have time to contemplate the fear-driven suicide. The woman had looked familiar, and when the herd of spiders broke into her view, Sybal knew where she'd seen the woman before. She'd been the one tied in the spider web, the one who had burst open from the inside, hundreds of spiders pouring out from her belly. She was still alive?

Sybal couldn't take in the horror before the herd of arachnids was upon her. Swinging her curved sword, she cut through six of the dog-sized spiders and their rabid pincers. Their shrieking rose and fell in bellowing calls as their venom splashed over her face. With a savage cry, she cut through two more, leaping over the wounded to get away from the drop behind her. Kjarton cawed and dived, turning into a black arrow. He took two in his silver talons and cast them into the mist over the edge.

Drawing buhkar, Sybal misted away from two that nipped at her thighs, somersaulted for distance, then shoved a quickly drawn halat into them. The runic barrier hit the monsters hard, crunching their pincers and making their heads bleed. They writhed on the cold, hard ground, making that bellowing sound again and clicking in fear.

The ground shook.

Sybal whipped her head back to the tree line, but nothing moved. Through the mist, she made out the sparkling of thick, white spider webs. These monsters must like the shadows of the trees and the myriad of opportunities for webs the branches provided. She made a note to steer clear of forests.

Just as she turned back to the right, a scream leapt from her chest. Her body, driven by her sulfates, ducked and rolled to avoid mandibles the size of her entire frame. Just as she came up from the roll, she leapt to the side to avoid a hairy leg as thick as a tree trunk. She drew halat out of instinct and dashed towards the trees. Then she glanced over her shoulder. Standing near the edge, a colossal spider loomed in the green mist.

The thing was pale, with spiny black hair covering its entire body. But it was more horrifying than just its size. A kind of human torso was attached to the bulbous backside. Large, feminine breasts swung below it with every step of its wide, spindly gait. The face was also human. Clearly the giant face of a woman, its eyes lulled in their skull-like sockets, tongue hanging out at a rabid angle from its mandibular jaws. Sharp antlers arched up from its grotesque head like black lightning. The thing made Sybal want to scream and vomit all at once.

This had to be Bolemesh, the spider goddess.

Sybal screamed. She ducked and ran at a diagonal away from the trees but also away from the dangerous precipice. Her hand instinctually went to her thigh, but her small crossbow was gone. "Kjarton!" she screamed, waving her hand.

The Vaeson, in his raven form, dived and weaved, trying to get close to her, but shying away from the arachnoid goddess. She moved to leap up onto his back to safety, but Bolemesh snapped at her when she neared the raven. With that attack, she sliced at one of the goddess's legs with her orichalcum blade. The titan screamed and jerked the wounded leg back. A thick glob of blue liquid leaked from the wound and saliva from the lolling tongue dripped down her exposed chest.

With that one moment of hesitation, Sybal dashed again, her long legs pumping like a terrified horse against the ground. She slipped under one of Bolemesh's spindly legs, but the titan was ready.

An earthshaking thrust of the spider's thorax shot a stinger the size of a spear into Sybal's face. She rolled on instinct again; the stinger punctured her fur cloak. As it did, a spray of rope-like web shot out. Sybal didn't want to imagine the sticky threads filling her insides if it had stabbed her. Grabbing buhkar, she drew as slow as she dared while running, and misted to the left back towards the cliff of the mesa.

"Go!" she shouted to Kjarton, signaling him to drop over the edge.

Bolemesh latched its rolling eyes onto Sybal now that she ran in the open. She stopped to face the titan. It screamed with a million voices and thrust its stinger at her again. This time, Sybal put all her energy into quickly drawing halat and atan in the same hand and screamed as she threw the glowing barrier at the monster. The webbing hit it as the runes brought it back up. The monster roared as her own webs crashed into her human face, blinding her at the same time.

Satisfied, Sybal ran to the edge, preparing to leap onto Kjarton's feathery back. But as she came close to the edge, something black and green warbled from the ground up to a spot about ten feet above. Her sulfates rushed and sweat immediately beaded on her brow. Skittering to a stop from her wild gallop, she fell to the blighted, writhing ground. Behind her, Bolemesh shrieked and clawed at the webbing on her face. The light that sprang up from the ground crackled and split like lightning. Something inside gave a ghostly cry and the green, translucent shape of a specter shot out and tumbled down the cliff face with a howl. Something told Sybal not to run into the green lightning.

Shaken, she crawled backwards away from it, covering her face from the blasting wind emanating from it. Behind her, Bolemesh gave a satisfied growl. Realizing the goddess must have freed herself, Sybal scrambled to her feet and went around the now charred spot where the lightning had sprung up, giving it a wide berth. She leapt, falling towards the raven. She clung to him, panting, a wild smile easing the tears of fright.

"Tzarik will not believe this!" she shouted over the wind. She patted the raven's shoulder.

He gave a nervous laugh in reply and spiraled gently down towards the ground.

"And what was that cracking thing? A specter came out of it." She craned her neck back to look, but the rift vanished.

"Let's get on solid ground first," Kjarton replied. "It's what I was looking for before. To show you."

Once they arrived back at the safety of Kjarton's cave and he forced several gulps of water down her throat, he explained. "In Caerwren, there are divine grounds where sacrifices are made. Some places, like the stone circle outside Altevine, have the thinnest barrier between our world and the God Deep, because of how many souls have been given there. But others are newer. I believe—and I could be wrong—that the lightning strikes are where a new sacrifice was made, tearing open a part of the Deep to let in a slaughtered soul. Most likely they're for the Eldritch Hunt, where hunters are out on the moors and planes gutting those from other clans. I've seen some like us pass through. But most are not strong enough, and come in the forms of ghosts—weak, frail souls."

Sybal poked at the fire with a long femur from some unknown creature. "Have you ever tried to go through? From this side?"

Kjarton shook his head. "Once, I saw a man turn to fire and ash when one hit him. He didn't come back. There are laws to death that the keeper of death enforces. You cannot cheat your fate."

It made sense to Sybal. If the lightning strikes were openings, and she slipped through one back into the living world, she might be a ghost. She'd never seen a sane spirit wandering the living world. When Kjarton had first started speaking about the lightning, she'd wondered if she could pass through. It seemed a wrong choice now.

"'A cure for fate is patience,'" she quoted. "A verse from the mihals," she said when Kjarton's emerald eyes glittered curiously. She weakly smirked. "There are some near Al'Myrah who try to defy death. But they are never good men."

She took another drink from the waterskin, wishing they could make something stronger. "Come back?" she asked, repeating what he'd said about the man who'd burned up in the lightning.

His thick lips turned down and he looked away from her. "Yes. It will be easier to show you. Or..." His hands nervously went to one of the many tiny braids in his hair. "Later. We cannot go out now."

The sun blacked out early and Kjarton insisted they stay in the caves, taking no chance out in the Deep during the dark time. He mended her cloak with a bone needle in silence. Sybal sat near the fire, the cold the only ailment she'd felt since waking in the God Deep. She glared up at Kjarton, wishing he'd be less cowardly and venture out with her again. She tapped her nails along the blade of her sword. If she sat much longer in silence, she'd run out without him.

"Not all sacrifices are as simple as the Eldritch Hunt makes them out to be," he said at last into the silence.

Sybal tore her eyes from the fire. "What's that?"

Outside, a howl broke the cool air and a distant moan of agony rose from a dark valley. They both turned to look out the dark opening.

"Do you know where your god is, Sybal?" Kjarton asked.

Frowning, she shook her head. "The priests say that's why it's called faith. We have prayers we say every day. We hang the mihal above our doors to show reverence. Things like that. He doesn't appear to us."

Kjarton nodded, biting off the string he'd been sewing with and tied the end off. He inspected his stitches. "The gods walk among us on Caerwren. The continent has rested over a thin barrier to the world of the gods for centuries. They come and go as they please. Some find it terrifying. Others, divine. Some reach out to that power, wanting to take it for themselves, become a sorcerer. Touching the source of their power. But it's not for mere mortals like us. Even blessed sentients like Vaeson and Masahk should not consume a god's power."

She laughed lightly. "So, if you were clan royalty—as a Vaeson— you were a Reks? That's the correct word? Are all Reks Vaeson?"

Now he took a deep breath, held it, then let it out. His green eyes sparkled. "Aye. Kjarton-Reks of Altevine."

Sybal's inner eye ran over the memories of the map. Altevine was close to Northica, further inland, and was one of the most barbarous cantons on Caerwren. She eyed the meek man. "I never would have thought you were a Reks."

Kjarton's emerald eyes turned down, not arguing with her assessment. "I wasn't born to be Reks. My love sought me out, lifted me up to her throne. I owe her everything. This is why I stay so close. The mountain spine you saw in the northwest? That is the backbone of my canton. My clansmen live between there and the White Spear in Northica, to the borders of the sea. I was sacrificed to Strigganoct and the radjur on Altevine's land. It was a curse for our people and an insult to our god, Raudnir, and the Valravn."

Sybal swallowed and made a small sound of disbelief. "If they sacrificed a Reks to a god, then no one is safe."

At this, something pained him and he winced, his face darkening. "To this day, I cannot say whether I went willingly or not. Love is the cruelest of all powers, Sybal."

"Someone you love sacrificed you?"

His eyes glittered with sudden tears in the firelight. "Have you ever loved someone so much, you'd die for them? I loved her. It hurt so much. I couldn't stop them from killing me. I did it for her."

Suddenly, a sensation she'd never felt marred her every nerve. Her chest constricted and her breath caught. Eyes burning in hot tears, she choked. At first, she thought it must be the Runer's death, but she had her blade and runes. Confused, she clenched her hand tightly, turning her arm over to inspect her veins. Her mind did not slow. In fact, it filled with images and memories of Tzarik. Each one flashed past so quickly, she wanted to reach out and snatch it back to take it in, cherish it. Beneath her ribs, something felt like a collapsing cavern, aching. He had been so frustrating on Xia. The way he'd gotten annoyed at the weather, the food. He'd constantly complained. She missed it.

She remembered standing on the balcony with him one night. She'd leaned in, sure of her actions, taking a chance. He'd frozen solid. His ever-impassive face had given nothing away. She couldn't read him in that moment like she used to. He was annoyed, confused, or didn't reciprocate her intent at that moment. She'd given in to her feelings for him while they'd fought on Xia. Long ago, she'd loved— yearned for—feelings of love and romance. It seemed so silly now. Tzarik was not that kind of man. He'd never give in to his emotions, even if he felt them.

Wiping her face, she shook her head. "No. I was in love once, but only as a silly girl engaged to a prince. I was to marry upward, and I was well aware. I would have been queen, maharani of Jarabu on Bahratt, once he became maharajah." Speaking the truth out loud took her by surprise. She'd almost never thought about it. "I knew I was lucky that he'd chosen me. I knew he'd chosen me for my family's status. But we did love each other. I think it baffled my mother."

Kjarton narrowed his emerald eyes. "That's not the love you mean to speak of. I saw something else on your face before. Who is it you'd die for?"

She clenched her eyes tightly at the lie. She'd loved Rahul, yes. But in a giddy, laughable way. The first time she'd seen Tzarik, in the courthouse, something new and powerful had been born in her. At the time, she'd thought her feelings for him were irrational, brought to life by knowing he was the only one who could save her at that moment. But that was a lie she'd told herself these last two years. No, she'd loved him from the start. She just hadn't known it. Now, it hurt to think about, especially since she was sure he didn't care for her like that. Yes, Kjarton was right. Love was cruel.

She took her black cloak that Kjarton had mended and slung it over her shoulders. Facing the opening, she sat with her back to the fire and watched the sky, waiting for the gods to bring the sunlight back.

CHAPTER 12

CIRCLE OF DEATH

At the first sign of sunlight, Sybal took up her sword and runes and went out to hunt. She needed to shake the emotions off that had consumed her so easily. That girl she used to be —the weepy one, the weak one, the one who let her whims be her lodestar—could not come out again. The Deep was too dangerous for that. She needed to control herself and survive. And the realm of the gods boasted enough monsters to satisfy her wants.

She left before Kjarton stirred and went back to the mesa where Bolemesh had appeared. There had been tracks there for something she guessed was a great snake. It had to be the one from Xia. It had followed her all the way across the ocean in the Deep. If that thing wanted to hunt her until it found her, she'd make it easy. At the base of the white crags, she expected to find the woman's body. Nothing lay there. No broken corpse on the sharp rocks. A quick glance around told her the woman had landed there. Blood speckled the area. But her body was gone.

At first, she couldn't find any sign of the snake god, so she had to go deeper towards the forest. There, she hacked on branches attached to the long threads of the spider, shaking them. If the snake would not appear, perhaps Bolemesh would want another fight. A few of the small spiders the size of rats scurried along the vibrating webs, but she easily dispatched those with a series of savage curving strikes.

The earth sloped down, making the sylvan canopy feel more like a dark cage. The writhing earth under her boots turned softer. Looking down, she found moss covered every rock and branch along the ground. When she raised her eyes back up, the forest grew so dark that nothing beyond the first few rows of trees met her searching gaze.

"Shit," she murmured, snapping her head around to try to find the way she'd come. With the darkness, she couldn't discern a single direction. So she continued on. Surely the spider goddess would be close. Her vile spiderlings skittered over the branches, hissing and whispering.

A soft moaning made her stop several minutes later. Swallowing hard, she snapped her eyes from tree trunk to tor looking for the sound. Realizing it came from behind a tree to her right, she drew her scimitar and slowly walked towards it. The trunk of this tree was thick and had abnormal bark patterns. Strange knots and gnarls protruded from it. At first, nothing seemed out of place other than the usual eldritch atmosphere. Then, she realized what she was looking at. A single, wide, terrified human eye swirled in the trunk of the tree. Once it came into view, the other knots revealed themselves to be the curves and angles of a man inside the tree. His mouth stretched open in a permanent scream, but his lips were made of bark. A single green sprout stuck out from his throat. The moaning came from him.

Fear ripping through her, Sybal gasped and ran. She didn't care what direction she went in. Anything would be better than looking at the poor amalgamated man. She tripped over a tree root that she swore rose up to inhibit her escape, but pushed herself up quickly. The blackness between the trunks of the trees turned gray: sunlight.

With the exit in sight, she stopped and turned to look back. Eyes watched her leave, and long fingers made of branches slowly came around the trunk of a tree. The wooden face of a giant monster gazed at her.

"You cannot have me!" she shouted at it. She turned and got a face full of sticky, thick spider web. The ground shook with the beat of eight colossal legs. The watching eyes in the forest blinked, then vanished. Something larger came to their door.

"About time," Sybal shouted, emerging from the forest to see the shape of the goddess lumbering out of the mist. She gripped her scimitar and pulled the runes to the outside of her armor. She didn't know if she could kill the thing, but she'd give it a try. After all, it was just an oversized monster. Tzarik often said it was a Runer's job to dispatch monsters no matter what shape they took.

Bolemesh reared up onto her back four legs, her front four clawing at the air like a rearing horse, showing she remembered Sybal. Somehow, the monstrosity looked smaller now.

With a scream, Sybal ran towards it. She planned her moves. She'd go under it again. It hadn't enjoyed having its sensitive joints hacked with her magical blade, so she'd start there. The goddess whipped its hideous head around, trying to watch Sybal and jab at her again with her horrid stinger. Misting once, Sybal drifted to a far back leg under the ugly goddess and slashed. Bolemesh screamed and large drops of spittle rained from open mandibles. While the goddess reeled, Sybal shoved a quickly drawn halat to the other leg, the one holding the majority of its weight.

When the barrier hit, Bolemesh slipped like a dog on ice. Her soft underbelly fell towards Sybal. Gauging the distance, Sybal slashed upward with all her strength. A rain of blue fluid gushed from the wound onto her. Unfazed, she cut again and again, making the spider scream until it got its feet back under it. Bolemesh tried with clumsy strikes to pierce Sybal with her stinger, but the wound was too great. Limping, the spider veered away to regain its ground.

Sybal turned to face her, wiping the ichor from her eyes. Panting and grinning in victory, she prepared for her next attack.

The earth rumbled. She froze, and so did Bolemesh. Something moved beneath the surface at such a rapid pace, the entire cliff face shuddered. Sybal took a few steps back, trying to track what direction the underground monster came from. Before she could pinpoint it, the ground exploded before her. It reminded her of how they'd used black powder to dig deeper into her family's mines.

A white streak of shining scales shot up from the ground between her and Bolemesh. The spider goddess cried out in its eerie thousand voices, cowering. Sybal recognized the thing now. A giant white snake with yellow eyes and a thick, whipping, purple tongue slithered out of the ground, coil after coil. The white scales and vicious fangs reminded her of Wu-Zheng.

"So, you're her god?" Sybal said flatly.

Unlike Bolemesh, this god's eyes looked more alert. More sentient. She didn't care. Regripping her scimitar, she faced it. The spider goddess cowered into its forest, a thick trail of blue slime flowing behind it. The snake finally flicked the end of its tale out of the hole, slithering over the grassy ground, making a deep hissing. A voice came to Sybal's mind. It didn't speak to her; the words just appeared as if she'd overheard it.

Mine, it hissed. *Blood for me. Oceans I crossed. Long I have hunted for blood given!*

Its tone raged in anger.

"Of course!" Sybal shouted up, wrapping her runes around her left hand. "Come and get your blood." She smirked. "You won't like it. I've heard it tastes like rot."

The snake had been slowly slithering towards her until she spoke. Her sulfates rushed in her veins and every muscular twitch and tensing of the snake showed to her trained eye before it moved. She saw it recoil ever so slightly, preparing to strike. Her mind fired off possibilities of maneuvers. Her first instinct was to run, but she knew there was no way to outrun the snake god.

Its head struck down at her, triangular maw snapping open. The memories of her nemesis doing the same move drove her to draw halat quickly. The snake, like its worshiper, struck against the magical barrier hard, bloodying its nose. With that moment, she misted and landed several quick, arching strikes against the snake's white body. As she did, she sensed its rage at her vanishing.

Drawing a quick jiun, she smiled at the snake god's annoyance. "That's right," she mused to it. "You don't know about runes where you're from. Enjoy the chase."

Under her flesh, the sulfates ran hot from the fury rune and she moved quickly, kiting more on instinct than thought. She landed several more strikes, then dove into the coils of the snake. She misted to move and not get caught, having experienced that before. Just as she planned, the snake struck itself in vicious attempts to get her. It drew its own blue ichor out and slowly became more and more enraged.

Mine! it screamed in its godly voice. *The stench of barbarian gods maddens me! Come to me, little sacrifice, and let me flee this place and its animals.*

Sybal found the more she continuously drew the rune, the more exhausted she felt. Jiun wore off, slowing her more than she'd anticipated. She'd never drawn so quickly and guessed the rapid use had tired her. With flaps of scaly flesh finally hanging off the stacks of coils, she quickly drew jiun once more and misted out of the sticky mess. When she rematerialized, she stumbled and panted.

Her blood screamed for her to turn around. She did, grabbing halat as she turned, knowing a strike was coming. The world slowed as her blood told her what was about to happen: too late, it said.

The white barrier flickered to life before her, but just a fraction of a second too late. A huge, hot maw, dripping with venomous fangs, clamped over her. She screamed but cut madly, fumbling for her runes. Something pierced her thigh. Instantly, her veins filled with venom. The same sharp fang punctured her very middle. At this, she froze, her guts lacerated and destroyed. Suddenly, the snake lurched and cast her from its mouth onto the ground.

With a wet, bloody smacking sound, Sybal fell several yards from its fangs to the hard ground. Every bone in her body broke from the forceful fall. She tried to gasp for air, but her lungs collapsed. Her white blood pooled under her, seeping out in torrents. The wound in her stomach was so massive, she couldn't even cover half of it with both her hands. The snake's fang had gone through her.

Foul, the voice hissed in her mind. *Not living blood.* The god's eyes narrowed as it glared down at her. *Bad sacrifice. Your blood belongs to another god. I cannot take you...*

Sybal managed a gurgling laugh. It hurt, pulling a moan from her. But she still smirked up at the disappointed god. "I told you," she said, gasping. Her runes were still wrapped around her left hand. She tried to move her fingers to get to artiah, to heal herself. "I'm foul. Like rot. I'm a Runer."

Her vision went gray and her brain screamed for oxygen. Somewhere between fighting for breath and groaning in agony, she blacked out, but then came back. Someone stood over her.

"Kjarton?" she moaned. "H-help me."

"I told you not to go out." The raven-haired man sighed and shook his head. "It's best you die, Sybal. Trust me. This is what I was trying to tell you." He held his left hand out and a metallic whoosh preceded the appearance of his massive blade landing in his hand.

She gasped as her heart fluttered in her chest, panicking for its own life. "Wh-why?" she stammered in fright. "I have to get out of here. I have to find him. I need t-to tell him..."

The moment of death became familiar. She'd felt this before. She'd already died once. Wasn't that enough?

"Don't worry," Kjarton said, gripping his sword and turning to fend something off. "Come back here when you resurface. Don't panic. Keep going until..."

His voice drifted farther and farther away as he kept talking. He was trying to tell her something. Keep going? Going where?

∂

ONLY DARKNESS and suffocation came to her for several agonizing moments. Slowly, the sensation of cold water touched her outstretched fingers. As she panicked for air, a white, glowing spike like a tower flickered into view far away. Then, a single, enormous blue eye turned to face her.

I see you, a crackling voice, like what ice might sound like if it spoke, said to her. *You have been touched. Touched by a god. Not by me, but by one of my children. Useless, dead god-touched. I will have you nonetheless. You will be mine. You will cull servants of lesser gods. I will guide your blade.*

As the voice spoke, it turned familiar. Feminine. It almost sounded like her mother, Freja.

Suddenly, mud and water pressed down on Sybal so hard she could barely move her arms and legs. At least they were not broken. She'd blacked out and somehow ended up under a dark, swamp-like river. The sludge moved around her, carrying her farther away from where she'd woken up. Her lungs burned for air and she clawed upwards. Kjarton had said she'd died. If she didn't escape these watery surroundings, she'd die again. Drown. Huge, worm-like creatures writhed next to her, grabbing at her and pulling her down. She shoved through them, disgusted by the feel of them on her body.

With a scream, she filled her chest with the cold, familiarly stale air as she broke the surface. Her hands splashed into the thick mud and she pushed herself up. The surrounding trees were only shadows and her hands touched a disgusting, thick, spongy moss. Blinking, the familiar mist and open plains of the Deep came into focus. She gasped, loving the feeling of her lungs inflating, and crawled out of the mud.

Pushing herself over onto her back, she panted. Underneath her, the ground turned more solid. Savagely wiping the mud out of her eyes, she looked around. Her breath came in gasping growls and she realized a kind of madness seethed inside her. In a rage, she leapt to her feet, feeling more alive than ever. Her heart slammed against her chest. Glowering, she snapped her head around, looking for the damned snake that had tried to eat her whole. No sign of it appeared.

"Where the hell am I?" she mumbled, checking her side. Her scimitar and runes remained with her. She stomped the ground; it thudded solid. As solid as the malignant ground ever was in the Deep. A few more calming breaths later, she spotted the cliffs to her left. The spot where the woman had crashed against the craggy earth remained red.

Sybal raised her hand up to her face and inspected the mud covering her. The woman before had been covered in mud. A theory came to mind. Now that she knew where she was, she marched back towards Kjarton's den. On her way, she inspected her midsection for any marks. To her horror, her flesh had scarred, but no wound showed. From the top of her belted hips to her first rib ran a red, textured scar. Without a care as to who or what might see, she dropped her belt and pulled her left leg out of her black pants. Where the other fang had hit her, another scar ran halfway across her thigh like a corded, fleshy worm. So she had been touched by the god. With a groan, she redressed and found her way back.

Kjarton waited for her with a fragile pack on his back made of bone and branches. He didn't look shocked to see her.

"The first death is always the worst," he offered, handing her a water skin.

She snatched it roughly and guzzled down half the contents. "Not my first time," she mumbled, handing it back to him.

So that's what he'd meant on their first night together. She would die if she let herself. At least she knew she could come back, even though it meant fighting her way up out of the accursed ground. But she would. She'd die and claw her way out a thousand times if it meant surviving until Tzarik came for her.

She picked up her scimitar and began to clean it, keenly aware of Kjarton's eyes on it.

Kjarton sighed heavily. "Sybal, I want to show you something."

KJARTON LED her over small foothills and over steep crags for two days. During their hike, they hunted something Kjarton called a skygge. The thing came ambling over a tor they passed. It was a woman, pale, bloated, with white, unseeing eyes. Her head lulled to the side with each step she took. Her black tongue hung out from between blue lips. Sybal watched her amble over the rocky ground until she reached out to her, growling. Realizing she meant her harm, Sybal leapt aside and severed her head with a quick stroke. Black blood spurted from the neck and the body fell to the ground. She watched in disgust as the tendrils underneath slowly snaked up from the boggy grass. They wrapped around the skygge and slowly pulled her under.

"A spirit that has spent too long in the Deep," Kjarton explained. "Too many deaths. They lose their minds. They are little better than a risen dead. It is the fate of us all."

More skygge than sane spirits like her and Kjarton wandered the ghostly moors. Sybal swept her eyes over them. Had it been her death that now let her see them? The Deep teemed with spirits and mindless skygge now. A few green and blue ghosts reached out to her but recoiled when they came too close to her black armor. They seemed almost harmless, defenseless. Somehow, knowing the creatures had been sentients that no longer fought to live in the Deep disgusted her. Taking out her scimitar, she walked into the mist. Spinning her scimitar, she made a handful of ghosts dissipate and went for a skygge. Easily decapitating one, she moved to another. Then another. A gray-skinned Masahk skygge lurched at her, growling from the mist. Its clawed hands slashed at her. This one didn't care when she cut its guts, spilling them into the marshes. It snapped its jaw at her, trying to bite. She stepped back, wound up, and with a particularly savage strike, cleaved it clean in two.

Smattered with ectoplasm, she looked at Kjarton and his massive sword that came to him when beckoned. "None of the others have their blades," she mused, sheathing hers. "Just you and me."

He didn't reply, setting his face in determination. Sensing this might be what he'd wanted to show her, she didn't press the matter. He pointed to a piece of ground that bubbled like boiling water. "Lightning," he mumbled.

Exhaling sharply, Sybal stumbled back several yards as a flash of the green light crackled up. A wisp of a white ghost floated like steam, vanishing into the blue and green mist. She looked back down at the charred spot and noted the roiling ground that preceded the lightning. She'd died once already. She didn't want to experience it again. Or die so many times she became a skygge.

Sybal looked down, lifting one foot. The malignant forms writhed, gently reaching up to try to grasp her. "Are there many trapped in the ground?"

Kjarton stopped and turned to look her in the eyes, his own going dark. "Many souls. Thousands of lifetimes' worth."

As if to illustrate his point, Sybal spotted a single, pale hand reaching up out of the blighted earth that squirmed with the worm-like ectoplasm. The hand was stiff, frozen in a claw-like shape, reaching for air. When she spotted one, more became obvious. Things she'd thought were rocks were sentient heads covered with moss, half poking out of the crawling earth. Eyeballs rolled backwards in their heads, looking to the sky for aid. Other things she thought to be branches were arms or legs, dripping in black moss. Souls that had given up on crawling out of the earth, given up on the eternal life of the Deep.

On the second day of their hike over the caldera to where the center of Altevine would be, they finally stopped atop an escarpment overlooking a strange expanse of land. Sybal tried to focus on the rotting foliage and the dark shadows and reflections of the land below, but had never seen anything like it.

"What is this?" she asked.

"An opening. A place of great sacrifice," Kjarton answered. "A body pit."

Now that he'd said it, Sybal saw the reality of the shadows and shapes below. It was a bog. Clumps of peat floated here and there, as did the skulls and limbs of sentients. Their faces twisted and decayed just a little under the doleful liquid. She let her eyes travel over the acres of bog filled with bodies.

"So many," she whispered.

Her companion's face fell into a wistful glare. "Places of sacrifice mar Caerwren. Some are vast, as you see here. Others are smaller."

Sybal swallowed but could not tear her eyes away. "Why are you showing me this?"

The raven man's face twisted into a sad grimace. "Because you are not dead," he whispered.

She spun to face him, a strange mixture of hope and confusion swirling inside. "What do you mean?"

He reached up and pulled her runes out from under her armor by their leather cord. "Caerwren is packed with Runers. I see them come and go. None have come through *with* their runes and their blade." He grunted, stabbing his massive sword into the earth. "There is a ritual for a Reks's weapon, a voren blade. It binds it to us, just as the runes and your magic steel are bound to your body. Once your body dies, the oath is fulfilled. If your oath were satisfied, if you died with the sulfates in your veins, you would not have them in the Deep. You'd be able to lay down your sword in the afterlife."

Her heart raced. "Then why...?"

"Because you're alive," he reiterated a little more forcefully. He started to shiver. "That's why I show you this. It is a point of entry. The Deep lies over our world like a veil. We cannot see manmade structures, so I do not see where my love rests her head." He stopped and gripped his chest. "But she is there. Even he who ferries the souls of—"

A crack like dry thunder shook the earth. Sybal ducked instinctually, looking for the bubbling earth. In a flash of green-blue light, a monster leapt out from the nothingness between the earth and the sky. Its six hooves hit the ground with a rumble. At first, she thought it was just a horse. But where the head should have been rose the pale, armor-clad torso of a man. Larger than a mortal man, the human arm clutched a foreboding weapon. A blade curved from one end of the haft to the other like a crescent moon and dripped with red blood. In the monster's other hand, a decapitated head swung from ropes of golden braids. She noticed now that the centaur-like creature had no head of its own.

Once it landed from its leap into the Deep, it walked past in solemn silence into the fog. Sybal laid her hand on the handle of her scimitar, watching with wide eyes.

"The Vorlamir," Kjarton whispered. "The reaper and guardian who travels from the Deep to fetch souls lost on their way."

Sybal could not take her eyes off the giant, headless creature and its bloody axe. "It comes and goes?" she asked. If that thing could cross from the living world to the world of the dead, could she?

"As all gods do," Kjarton said. "When the gods walk the same mountain range as you, you want to make sure they are pleased with you. And so these sacrifices are given." He gestured to the body pit. "But the Vorlamir is the guardian of death. He can take a soul, not sacrificed, from one side to the other."

Sybal finally tore her eyes away from the Vorlamir and back to where it had appeared at the edge of the escarpment. She reached her hand out to feel for it, remembering the magical opening to the Hallow City. "Can we open it?" she asked. Her heart raced. Was there a chance to escape, if her body wasn't dead? Could she find it?

Kjarton shook his head. "We cannot. But they might try to from the outside. This is why I brought you here. If you are not dead on the other side, you might be able to escape and return to your body. If someone on the other side could find a way here, you might be able to leave, since your body could take your soul back. I wanted to you show the circle of death and what happens when you die too many times."

She frowned at him, her hand still outstretched. "Why? If I cannot escape from this side?"

His sad smile made her pity him. "So that you have hope. So you don't continue to look for danger, to look for something to kill you, to hurt you. You could not be here, on Caerwren, if your body was not here. Do you see?"

She dropped her hand. "Then am I here?" she asked, pointing to the soil. Had they brought her body here? Had someone taken her? Was it Tzarik? "I must be. My spirit was attached to my body. Otherwise, I'd wake on Xia, in the Deep." Her throat went dry.

"That is why I do not stray far from my love's clanlands," Kjarton confessed. "I am a fool to hope, but I dream one day she will open a doorway to the Deep and save me from the depths. Somehow."

A whimper escaped Sybal's throat as her mind once again went to Tzarik. Clenching her fist, she swallowed the sorrow. She shut her eyes tight to stop the tears. Then they flew open wide. Had he found her body? Perhaps he'd brought her to the place the barrier was thinnest—Caerwren—to try to bring her back. Too often he'd left her behind, even fled from her. Was he now, finally, hunting her down?

"That's it," she said out loud. "I'm here. He's brought me here." Her heart hammered under her armor. "He's here."

Kjarton's emerald eyes scanned her face, understanding. "Someone loves you enough to come to our frozen shores during Vasaras?" He looked back to the horizon. "Love is such a master."

Love? She raised her right wrist. The jade bangle remained, the one that matched his. Something like the hot, shifting sands heated by an Al'Myrahn sun swirled inside, warming her against the cold air.

"He's coming for me," she whispered, her dry lips cracking into a smile. "Finally." She turned to face Kjarton, a wary smiling pulling on her lips. "He will find a way. May the gods help any who try to stop him."

CHAPTER 13

SJÖRNA-REKS

TARKAN SMELLED THE CLANLANDS BEFORE THEY ENTERED the borderless boundaries of Altevine. He and Tzarik followed the path of dead, trodden grass up the hill to the thronehall that overlooked the sprawling village. Through a winding road of dirt and small homes, shops, a smith, and other trades a queen would need nearby, they finally came to the ornate doors of the thronehall. The royal structure stood tall, perched atop a foundation of stone with hewn steps leading up. A banner of green with the symbol of a red wolf painted over it fluttered in the cool breeze. Where the truss beams crossed, the likeness of the antlers they'd seen curved out like open arms, praising the sky in dangerous points. Other monstrous carvings of wolves and ravens decorated the roof.

Before them, in a small square before the open stairs up to the thronehall, an effigy burned. Tall and made of wood, it depicted a haggard woman with only one eye that glared out towards the wider world. Three figures in white with crowns of dried twigs encircling their heads knelt before it, prayed, then rose, hands to the sky, and sang prayers with their eyes closed. The smell and smoke came from the burning totem.

"Likho," Tzarik explained. "An omen of death to these people. To burn an effigy of one is supposed to ward off plague, famine, and curses."

Tarkan glanced back and noticed a few eyes watching them making their way up. "Let's hope it's plague," he mumbled.

They skirted around the burning effigy and prayerful figures and went up the steps towards the hall. The stone foundation turned into a veranda that surrounded the entire thronehall, giving it plenty of walking space where one such as a queen might survey her domain. A horrid barking and whining to the right drew their attention. Off to the side, a golden wolf the size of a horse snarled and snapped, straining against a chain. A man with an eyepatch shouted at the wolf, beating it into silence with a stick before turning to glare at them. He stepped away from the submissive wolf and bore down on them.

"Travelers?" he growled at them. He sniffed the air, his nose twitching. "Long way from home."

Tarkan flexed his fingers, ready to cast a spell should he need to. "Where is Sjörna-Reks? She took something of ours." The big man didn't scare him. Surely Tzarik would be a match for him.

With a dark grin, the man pointed to the thronehall. "In the hall." He almost laughed. "Busy, but I'm sure she won't mind you waiting inside." His eyes quickly flitted over the pair. Seeing no weapons, he gestured for them to go in.

The ornate wooden doors depicted a red wolf on one and a black raven with outspread wings on the other, silver talons flashing. The doors were heavy and both Tzarik and Tarkan had to push on one to get it open. The man with one eye laughed as he watched them struggle. Inside, the thronehall looked bigger than the outside. It stood two stories high, with small transepts on each side. Some had curtains hanging over them, partitioning them off, but others didn't. Tables and braziers dotted the wider area where barbarous-looking folk milled about, doing their tasks. At the end of the hall, a raised stone dais held two simple thrones covering a back door underneath.

In the center, a large fire burned in a circular pit. A sort of priestly-looking man in scant white leather skirts stood by the fire, tapping bones in a rhythm while singing softly. A fringe of white leather covered his eyes, hanging all the way down to his black-painted lips. He faced a pile of furs and blankets that moved in a savage rhythm beyond the flames. The movement drew Tarkan's eye just as a mass of flaming red hair flipped upwards, followed by the bare chest and blazing green eyes of a woman. Her body shone with sweat as she forcefully moved on the man underneath her. Tzarik looked away upon realizing what they'd walked in on, but Tarkan held her gaze.

Her eyes flashed through the fire, locking onto his. Watching him closely, she leaned down and gripped the man's throat. He choked as she finished, eyes fluttering. Not wavering, Tarkan focused his gaze as she slowly stood up. From her smirk, she understood he was trying not to waver to show his resolve. Shadows from the flames danced over her pale, naked body. She put her foot on her unwilling victim and reached a hand out. A metallic wind rushed, followed by a sword the size of the woman. The hilt of the beautifully etched weapon thudded into her waiting palm, drawn to her by a mysterious magic. With one arm, she held the sword out and placed the sharp edges against her prisoner's chest. Tarkan kept his eyes focused on hers. The woman considered him before looking down at her victim.

"I'll let you live, Ragnall," she said dangerously softly. "I may have a desire for your body again." She sighed, dropping the sword down hard. It stood perfectly, the weight of it pulling it into the dirt floor. Wrapping herself in a fur-lined robe, she sauntered away from the panting victim in the pile of blankets and poured herself something from an ornate clay jug.

"Sjörna-Reks?" Tzarik barked, unable to stand the awkward silence anymore.

"As you see," she breathed. She took a drink and her eyes lost some of the dangerous sparkle they'd had just minutes ago. She sighed and ran her hand over her chest, down her stomach, and to her thighs. "Runers are useless. Trying so hard to protect me." She snapped her fingers and pointed to the man who had just started to roll over to crawl away.

Tarkan caught his white feathering and blue eyes before the man with the eyepatch swooped in on him, dragging him naked and exposed out the back door. He had been a Runer, but also a Masahk.

"That kind of coupling never ends well," Tzarik warned the Reks.

"So the godtales go, Al'Myrahn." Sjörna-Reks smiled gently, tapping her goblet with one long finger. "I know very well." She gathered the folds of her robe in one hand and ascended to her throne to look down at them. She crossed her legs, letting the fur fall, exposing her long, thick limbs. Tarkan noticed every knot of muscle on her giant frame.

Behind them, the doors to the hall closed as a gaggle of bearded, axe-wielding men and women filed in, going to work on the braziers and skinning animals brought in from the hunt. Tarkan noted Tzarik taking in the company and his eyes finding every exit quickly. The Runer was on edge. He didn't have Tzarik's sense of danger and so relied on him.

"You have something of mine," Tarkan said, approaching the edge of the stone dais. "I want her back."

Sjörna-Reks smiled, uncrossing her long legs elegantly to switch which one was on top. She bounced one foot in anticipation. "I'd ask which one is yours, but I can tell from your marked flesh of whom you speak."

Tzarik took a step forward. "Where are they?"

The Reks's lips parted in a smile. "So, she is a Runer? I wondered when I saw her blade and the runes around her neck." She clicked her tongue. "Al'Myrah, the hub of civilization, has made the first woman

Runer. Well done, little man. The women of Caerwren find themselves above such base mutilation. What happened when you runed
her?" A sick and twisted smile warped Sjörna-Reks's face.

Tarkan felt his companion about to snap, so he thrust his hand
out to stop Tzarik from charging. "I can help you," he spat quickly.

Sjörna-Reks raised her brows over her goblet. "Would you?"

"Show me Zeva is unharmed," he bargained.

The Reks uncrossed her legs and leaned forward, her face turning
serious. "Listen, necromancer. I have had three of your ilk pass my
frozen hall. Two failed me, defying me and forcing me to crush the
unlife from their frail bodies. One ran, unwilling to submit to me.
What makes you different from them?"

Unsure what she implied, Tarkan fought to find the right words.
"I've heard only rumors. You seem ambitious, Sjörna-Reks. I think
my ambition matches your own. You want to open the Deep. I can
do that."

Her emerald eyes narrowed.

"Not many weeks ago, I walked the Blood Path to aid a fellow
tribesman," Tarkan said with a crooked grin.

Her brows went up again and her green eyes rounded. "Did it
open to you?"

Tarkan nodded slowly. Beside him, Tzarik frowned and looked
from one to the other, confused.

"I don't know what you want inside the God Deep," the necromancer went on, feeling the power shift in the conversation, "but I
can open it to you. Caerwren already speaks of your hunt. They
know you are gathering souls. They fear you. All you need is me."

The Reks moved as if to push herself up to stand, but hesitated.
"How can you be sure you can do this? My Volra has read the bones
and has seen no lich in the prophecies." She indicated the white
leather clad man.

Tarkan tried to keep the doubt out of his face. The shaman, the
Volra of Caerwren, used old magic that had almost disappeared. No

doubt it was weak and could not tell the Reks anything his gods didn't want them to know.

At the mention of a lich, Tzarik glared over at Tarkan. Tarkan hoped the Runer wouldn't open his mouth and object. He'd hate to get rid of Tzarik after all he'd done for him and Zeva. Despite his facade, the Runer had a moral compass Tarkan would not follow.

"Trust my blood," Tarkan offered. "My father was Ishmael, the long-standing Necro'Khan of Porsh, until his demise two years ago at *my* hand."

Sjörna-Reks leaned back in her seat. A hunger ignited behind her eyes. She looked down on Tarkan now with admiration, hunger, and a twisted kind of desire. The desire made him uneasy, but he looked past it. He needed this opportunity to garner favor with his gods. Then they'd give him the mantle he so desired.

"Our needs walk a similar path," he urged her, holding his palms up. "Give me a chance to garner praise with my god, and I will ascend and open the Deep for you. Your winter is the perfect time with the barrier so thin."

"I see." She sighed, holding back a smile. "I understand. And you have come to me willingly."

"Necro'Khan?" Tzarik growled to him. The Runer clenched his fists, realizing Tarkan had manipulated him and Sybal was being used.

Finally, Sjörna-Reks took a deep breath and stood up. "What do they call you, necromancer?"

"Tarkan," he replied cautiously. No recognition flitted behind the Reks's eyes.

She nodded. "Yes. The girl has been crying for one by that name." To Tzarik, she said, "And what hand have you to play in all this?"

Tzarik gnashed his teeth, unable to answer. No guilt at having hidden his motive from Tzarik blighted Tarkan's mind. The Runer would never understand the ways and desires of a necromancer. It wasn't part of him. He had no doubt Tzarik's need to save Sybal would keep him steady on the course.

"The lady Runer," Tarkan offered for him. "We believe her soul is trapped in the Deep, pursued by a Xian god."

"She's dead," Sjörna-Reks shot back. "Same as my raven king..." Her hand drifted to the empty throne beside her.

"Where is Sybal?" Tzarik finally asked, forcing his voice to stay even.

The Reks set her goblet down and gathered the folds of her robe again. "I suppose I could show you a kindness and let you live, Runer. I have no need of you."

"He is not part of the deal," Tarkan warned the Reks.

She stopped, one foot on the first stone step down. "Oh, no, he is. You all are. You may come and go, Runer. But your woman stays. I've dealt enough with men like you to know that if I give you a long enough leash, I'll regret it. But my deal is with Tarkan." She stepped down, sweeping past them to the back door. "I'll show you your women."

THE STOCKADE behind the thronehall was a round building and the only one made of stone. The smoke from the effigy wafted over and around the thronehall, filling the air like the mist. For once, the sun shone, the sky empty of clouds. Tarkan couldn't help but raise his face just a moment into the warm rays and feel the familiar heat. Beside him, the Runer's presence intensified. Tzarik was astute. Tarkan couldn't hide his true intentions from the Runer anymore. Tzarik was also a man who—despite his arguing to the contrary— had a strong sense of decency, of right and wrong. Tarkan had understood from a young age that he and his tribesmen were not, and never would be, that kind of sentient.

Nothing stops you, Sharar had said to him once. *I need that kind of fortitude.*

He blinked away the memory. For a year, he'd tried to push everything the evil scholar had said to him out of his mind. He wasn't the only one who suffered from nightmares of his time under Sharar. He glared ahead as the man with the eyepatch opened the stockade door for Sjörna-Reks. The doorway loomed tall and imposing over the Al'Myrahn men.

Inside, a large anteroom with a few guards and other prison armaments waited to be used. Tarkan tried not to look at them, but couldn't help but recognize one tool amongst them: a scold's bridle hung near a rack of sizable chains and shackles. Tzarik followed his eyes, but the Runer wouldn't understand. He'd worn the damn torture device more than once. Sometimes Sharar forced him to put one on himself and hand over the key. Tarkan remembered the taste of metal well.

Beyond the door of bars, a huge, circular room of cells waited.

"Don't bother with him," the high, melodious, yet exhausted voice of a jongleur said from inside. "He's a brigand. Go back to tending to that three-legged rat you love so much. Though I think he soiled the blanket."

"Ragnall!" a tender, familiar voice cut over the first. "Are you all right?"

"Leave him, Zeva," the jongleur said again.

Tarkan's heart thudded once, madly, against his chest and he couldn't stop his lurch forward into the room of cells. He pushed past the Reks and her man, even clipping Tzarik's shoulder on the way in.

"Zeva?" he called, scanning the circumference of cells. In one to his left, the groaning Runer he'd seen before lay, heaped onto the floor and curling in on himself.

"Tarkan?" his daughter's voice rang out to his right.

He spun around. Zeva crawled to the bars of the cell and scampered up from under a thin blanket, reaching her arm out. She wept upon seeing him and pressed herself into the bars as if she might slip through. Tarkan dashed to her, taking her hand in his. He pressed her palm against his cheek and kissed it before reaching through to touch her face. He pulled himself to the bars, damning the cage that separated them. Zeva sobbed audibly.

"I thought you had drowned," she wailed, unable to keep her hands off him. Even through the bars, she wrapped her arms around his neck and hugged him.

"Are you all right?" he managed to ask. "Did anyone hurt you?" He held her out at arm's length now, inspecting her.

She shook her head. "They tried. But Vicdan fought them off."

The young man smiled guardedly at the necromancer. "She's impossible." He pointed to the corner. "Look. She's built a nest for a three-legged rat that comes and goes. She has no hate for anyone. Even that damned Runer there." He half-heartedly pointed to the one called Ragnall.

Of course she hated no one. Zeva was pure. Innocent and good. Tarkan took her face in his hands and kissed her forehead before pressing his to hers. He waited a moment before speaking. Overcome with joy at seeing her unharmed, alive, even safe, he would have promised Sjörna-Reks anything in that moment if she'd just let him hold Zeva.

Softly, he whispered to her, "I have bargained for your release."

He knew this would trigger memories for her. Her head shot up and her eyes went wild with worry.

"No," she stammered. "Tarkan, not again. Please, don't do this."

He shook his head. "This isn't like last time."

"You don't understand what she wants from you," Zeva hissed, voice wavering in fear. Her eyes darted to Ragnall, back to his, then to Sjörna-Reks where she stood waiting. She spotted Tzarik and offered him a weak smile. Her lips parted and shut, trying to speak.

Softly, she said, "She's mad, Tarkan. Ragnall knows. I can't explain it here."

He'd promised himself in Porsh a year ago he'd never let her be frightened again. To never be separated from her. To never be hurt. He'd failed. Not again. He opened his mouth to tell her his true intentions, though it pained him.

A hard, sharp snap interrupted them. "Lokhtar, that's enough," Sjörna-Reks ordered her guard, pointing to them.

The man with the eyepatch strode to Tarkan, hand outstretched. Tarkan backed away, but the man still gripped the hood of his cloak and pulled him away roughly. He tossed him beside Tzarik.

"And Sybal?" Tzarik asked, his self-restraint looking in short supply.

"Hello, Runer!" Vicdan called with a smile, joining Zeva pressed against the bars. "I knew you were too tough to let those icy waters get you. Didn't I say so, Zeva? Told you he'd come towards civilization. Well." He looked around dolefully. "Close enough."

Sjörna-Reks pointed to a solid wooden door on the opposite side of the circlet of cells. "You may see her." She signaled Lokhtar, who strode across the stockade and opened the door. Sjörna-Reks pointed Tarkan in as well. "I want you to watch him as he sees her," she said gently. "Make sure she's alive. That her spirit remains as they have said."

Tarkan followed Tzarik across the stone floor into the single cell. The only thing in the room, apart from shackles on the walls, was the familiar black box. Tzarik hesitated before Sjörna-Reks motioned to him with her head to open it.

Tarkan watched the Runer kneel and fling the container open. His movements were controlled but urgent. Tzarik removed the lid and then gazed down at his apprentice. Tarkan came closer, looking over his shoulder. Sybal was pale. The visible flesh he could see—her face and hands—were veiny, the white sulfates hard under her flesh. Tzarik reached in and took her hand, running his thumb over her cold skin. The Runer restrained himself in the presence of so many eyes. Tarkan admired it.

Tarkan knelt near her head and slipped his hand down the front of her armor to get nearer her heart. He hissed a few verses, reaching out to touch her life-force. At first, he found nothing. Pressing more into the death he knew so well, he found the tiny spark of her life. Under his cold fingers, her heart beat weakly, fighting for every life-giving flutter.

"Tarkan?" Tzarik asked, his tone strained.

The necromancer withdrew his hand. "She's still alive. But she's fading."

"Will the sulfates help?" he asked, going to his belt.

He wasn't sure. "It may ease the strain of the heart trying to pump the solidifying sulfates. She's struggling, but she's not giving up."

The necromancer understood the anguish in the Runer's eyes. To help ease his mind, he took Tzarik's hand and guided it under Sybal's armor. He felt the Runer halt when his hand touched her soft chest, but he forced his hand over her heart. He pressed his hand on top of Tzarik's, making him wait and feel. Sybal's heart thudded once. She was not going without a fight. Under Tarkan's hand, Tzarik gently rubbed Sybal's cold skin.

Tzarik stood up and faced Sjörna-Reks. "Where is my horse? I need something from it."

She nodded. "I was raised amongst Runers. I understand." She snapped her fingers again and Lokhtar hurried out to fetch his things. "So, necromancer, do we have a deal?"

Something in the red Reks's tone told him it wasn't really a question. He didn't glance at Zeva or Tzarik. Zeva softly cried in the stockade. Tarkan knew Tzarik didn't understand the full implications of what he would have to do to become the Necro'Khan. He might not even understand the power such a position held. But Tzarik wanted Sybal back. This was the only way, and she was running out of time. The Runer would no doubt follow his lead, no matter what.

"I must be allowed to hunt," Tzarik bargained. "I need to find the ingredients for our sulfates. This is all I have." He held up the vial Korvoth had given him. "I need some for myself and to keep Sybal alive."

The Reks smiled, her arms at ease at her side. "I don't care; do as you must. You'll come back. I know you will."

The thinly laced, threatening tone put Tarkan and Tzarik on edge.

"She will stay here." Sjörna-Reks pointed to Sybal. "That way, I know you'll be back. We have to bide our time until the zenith of Vasaras, and I have more souls to gather. Don't I, necromancer?"

Tarkan didn't acknowledge her. "Zeva must be released from the cell and be with me at all times," he added.

At this, Sjörna-Reks narrowed her eyes, considering. Finally, she said, "If you submit to be bound and shackled, she will walk free." A dark grin twisted up the right side of her lips. "She won't leave your side. I see that."

The air grew colder and a shiver ran down Tarkan's spine. He couldn't succumb to the past now. Zeva's huge, brown eyes sparkled desperately at him from behind the bars in the darkness. "As you command," he whispered hoarsely. Doubt suddenly filled him, but he fought to push it aside. He couldn't speak again for fear of giving away his unease.

Sjörna-Reks smiled at his submission. She turned to Tzarik. "You may come and go on one condition as well." She thrust her finger towards Vicdan and Zeva. "Take him with you. I want to kill him, but every time I tried, the girl put up a fight like a Vilderkin. Get him away from me. I cannot stand his mouth."

Vicdan smirked, leaning up against the bars. "I told you, you wouldn't mind my mouth if you'd give *me* one night with you. But no. You choose that Runer every time."

Sjörna-Reks glared at Vicdan, eyes emerald fire. "If you don't take him with you, Runer, I won't cut out his tongue. I will have my Volra take his voice from inside his throat."

Vicdan's face fell. "Of course I'll go with Tzarik. No need for threats."

$$\partial$$

THEY GAVE Tzarik his gear and Sjörna-Reks took Tarkan back to the thronehall with the help of the threatening presence of more massive warriors. Every sentient on Caerwren towered over them imposingly. Tarkan knew not to fight against those who could break his bones with one hand.

The Reks led him back to the base of the stone dais. She faced him, the great fire pit behind him and the thrones behind her.

"Kneel," she whispered, holding her head and mess of long red curls high.

Cautiously, fighting to keep his face blank, he grudgingly did as she ordered. Far overhead, above the thrones, he spotted a huge axe-like weapon hanging there. It had two heads, each so sharp it seemed to cut through the firelight that bounced off its glittering blade. One blade had a jagged break in it, like a wolf had taken a bite of the edge.

Sjörna-Reks motioned a warden forward, one who carried chains and the familiar bridle. Tarkan moved to rise, but Lokhtar took a threatening step forward and Sjörna-Reks raised her pale, red brows. She dared him to flee now. The front of her black fur robe hung loose and open, exposing a line of white skin from her chest to her hip. She had no fear, wore no armor. Reconciling to her test, he lowered his head.

"I require complete submission, Tarkan," Sjörna-Reks said softly, looming over him. "But have no doubt of my sincerity. I *need* you to open the Deep. I will not harm you unless you force me. But I will take no chances."

She reached her bare arm out to him, fingers splayed.

"Make an oath with me. A blood oath."

Tarkan snapped his head up. "A dangerous oath, Reks. Should you break it—"

"Should *you* break it," she interrupted. "Your blood and my blood. I want your oath. If you break it, may your god take you, turn you inside out, and give you eternal life on this side of the barrier." Her pale, strong hand did not waver where she held it out to him, waiting for him to take it and pierce her skin with the sharp, silver rings around his fingers.

He considered, knowing the wording of an oath was far more important than taking it. When he didn't reply quickly, she flicked her head, signaling her warden. The man lumbered forward with a coil of chains and shackles in his grip.

"Very well," he said quickly. "By my blood, I will open the Deep."

"And raise an army for me, one that adheres to my command," she added.

He nodded.

"And you will submit to me."

"You will not harm Zeva," he quipped.

Sjörna-Reks shook her head. "I will not." She flicked her head to the silver rings on his hand. "Your blood."

Tarkan removed the oath ring, pressing a small pressure point on the top that made the tiny needle-like blades snap out from the bottom. Sjörna-Reks put the ring on her finger and took his hand. The sharp needles stuck into his palm. He winced only a fraction of a second. She smiled. As they held their palms together, the small, clear gem on top started to turn black, filling with his blood.

The Reks took it off, handing it to him. "Take my blood, necromancer."

Tarkan gripped her hand as hard as he could. The sharp edges of his silver rings pierced her calloused palms. She moaned, but not in pain, as her blood filled the remaining hollow space inside the ring. Once it glowed red with her blood, Tarkan released her hand.

The Reks stepped back. She raised her hand to inspect the wound. "Lokhtar," she whispered.

Wordlessly, the warden shackled Tarkan's arms at his elbows, behind his back, then wound a thin rope over his hands, binding his fingers. Then the warden locked the end of the chain to a metal loop at the base of the dais. Tarkan waited for the finishing touch.

"You obey your oath well. I see what this means to you," Sjörna-Reks said gently, taking the bridle from her warden. She held it up close to his face. "You are familiar with it. One day, you will have to tell me why. What is that story, necromancer? Most of your kind rarely interact with those outside your tribe. But you have. You are just as bold and ambitious as you seem. Brave." She slowly licked the dripping blood from her palm.

She smiled and reached out to touch his long hair with her bloody hand. She let it slip between her fingers, making a sound somewhere between a moan and a hum. Her blood tainted the ends.

"I won't subject you to it yet, as you have submitted so willingly." She turned and marched up the stone steps to her throne, white legs flashing in and out of the folds of her robe. She placed the bridal there, then faced him one last time. "My place of sacrifice is filled with many souls. More than you need to please your god. I will show it to you when we are ready. But I am merciful and will let the Runer hunt to preserve his woman first." She smiled and her eyes drifted away. "Love is the cruelest gift of all, isn't it?"

She disappeared into the darkness behind the thrones. A door opened and closed.

Tarkan twisted once to test the restraints and his shoulders immediately exploded with pain. He groaned through gnashed teeth and fought to hide the pain from the watching, curious warriors left in the great hall. Closing his eyes, he prayed Tzarik hurried.

CHAPTER 14

SNÖW AND ASH

Tzarik stayed as they took Tarkan away. The massive warriors handed him the bags from his saddle, and he went to work on setting up the sulfates. He found his black box and took out the rubbery intestines with the needles on each end. As he stabbed one into the vial from Korvoth and the other into Sybal's pale arm, he remembered the last time he'd been in dire need of sulfates. It had been long ago. Or at least it felt like it. They'd been on Bahratt and she'd cut him deeply with his sword. He'd been poisoned by one of Tarkan's risen beasts—an undead crocotta—and had lost a lot of blood. Never had he been scared for his life like that night. His survival had depended on her taking his orders. She'd done very well.

He scoffed to himself as he turned the vial upside down and tapped the bottom. The sulfates started to fall down the tube and into Sybal's arm. "I thought you'd killed me," he told her in a soft mumble so the others outside in the stockade could not hear. "Not sure why I minded when it was all I wanted then."

He couldn't force himself up. They waited for him outside, but he wanted to stay with her. His eyes traced the slow-moving, glittering white sulfates as they passed into her veins. He reached down and touched the spot where the needle punctured her skin. Already she'd warmed a little, and the vein turned softer.

"I don't know what's happened to you," he confessed. "And that angers me. I don't know how to save you. Tarkan might, but I don't understand that either." He allowed himself to touch her placid face. Never could he do this while she was awake. She'd tried once, had leaned in, and he'd snubbed her. "Did you know my thoughts before I did?" he asked her, trailing his hand up to her golden hair. It matched the people of Caerwren, as did her height. "You always saw past my mask. Knew what I was thinking before I did. I think that's why you..." He choked, clearing his throat. "I think that's why I didn't like you. Years of bullshit were useless against you. You saw how I hid, but you never pried at my defenses. You were just...there."

Stopping his words, he realized it sounded like a goodbye. No, he wouldn't allow that to happen. He'd crossed oceans for her, to keep her safe, but he'd failed. Not now.

Pushing up, he stood over her until the last of the sulfates dripped through to her. He carefully packed away his things and wrapped her wound. Out in the circular cell room, a man called for him by his title.

"Time to go, Runer," Lokhtar called. "The Reks has left for the hunt, as you must."

Another warrior with a long chestnut braid and battle axes at his side opened the cell where Vicdan and Zeva waited. Zeva's scarred face still shone with tears and she shuddered, pressed into Vicdan's chest for safety.

"Where is he?" she begged as Lokhtar grabbed her arm and shoved Vicdan out at the same time.

Tzarik moved to them, reaching out to Zeva. She instinctually detached from Vicdan and fell against Tzarik's side, clinging to him. "Let her stay with Tarkan," he said. "She can do no harm."

"She will," Lokhtar grunted, leading the way out of the stone stockade. He made to grab at Zeva again, but Tzarik pivoted, holding his hand out as a warning.

Vicdan scurried to Tzarik's other side, arms crossed against the cold. "What are you going to do?" he asked. They entered the wind outside, the smoke from the effigy finally dissipating.

"Do as you must," Lokhtar growled over the wind. "Follow me."

The massive man led them back into the thronehall, past the pillory where the golden wolf had been shackled. Where it used to be, now a crumpled heap of a young boy lay, moaning in the wind. Zeva stopped. With his arm around her, Tzarik stopped, too. She unfastened the fur cloak she'd been given and moved to cover the shivering boy.

"Don't," Lokhtar snapped, reaching for Zeva. Tzarik placed his hand threateningly on his sword hilt and the big man stopped. "The boy is not to be pitied," Lokhtar said instead. "He is a wildling. Born in the shape of a wolf."

"Oh, a Vaeson," Vicdan said, solving some unspoken riddle in his head. "The Reks is a Vaeson. A wild-shifting tribe. Though none off these shores are supposed to know. It's the best kept tribal secret."

Lokhtar started, glaring at the jongleur.

"Then how do you know?" Tzarik asked, guarding Zeva as she moved to cover the boy.

Vicdan gave a coy smile. "I met a traveling bard once. She was lovely. A Vaeson herself. They rarely leave their home as most outside their country find it taboo to...engage with them."

Tzarik scoffed. "You have no such qualms."

The younger man clicked his tongue, pulling a face. "I did no such thing. I merely engaged in education, from one musical master to another."

"She'd be killed if she ever returned to our shores," Lokhtar added.

As Zeva came close to the boy, his mass of long, tangled braids shot up. Like the wolf they said he was, he snapped his human teeth at Zeva, snarling and whining as he pulled against his chains. Zeva cried out and stumbled back.

"Why's he doing that?" she asked.

"Wildling," Lokhtar reiterated. "A Vaeson should not conceive when in their animal form." He motioned to the growling boy. "Makes their sentient mind less, hardly more than the wild animal god-shape they are blessed with."

Tzarik noted how the boy was shackled outside the thronehall. Underneath the wild waves of his blond hair, his eyes shone green and glowing. He had the same slender nose as well. This was Sjörna-Reks's son. Chained like an animal, she let her indiscretion live on display for all to see and hear, reminding them of what she'd done before they entered her thronehall. She was fearless, brazen, and dominant.

"I want him to be warm," Zeva protested, still holding her fur cloak.

"If he becomes too cold, he will shift," Lokhtar growled, tired of the conversation. "Even an animal knows how to fight the cold here. Come, we must hurry."

Tzarik pulled Zeva away. "Tarkan waits inside," he enticed her.

She let herself be led away, glancing back at the wild boy. As they turned to go, a huntress passed the wildling and gave him a swift kick for snapping at her boots. The boy yelped like a dog and cowered against the tether post. Tzarik fortified his mind against the familiar image. He'd buried his childhood deep in his mind, but he could not forget the scars on his wrists from the many times his father had shackled him like that. He'd been so afraid of his father that being sold as a slave to a quadi on Bahratt had seemed like a good thing. For a fleeting moment, the urge to release the boy fluttered up inside him like a butterfly. Sybal would have.

Steeling himself, he followed Lokhtar inside to see Tarkan chained as well. He sat at the base of the stone dais, the thrones empty above him. He stood up when they entered and Zeva ran to him. Tzarik envied their reunion. Zeva threw her arms around her adoptive father now that bars did not separate them, crushing him against the stone.

Lokhtar took a fur cloak off a pile of them where a man and woman dried the skins. He handed it to Vicdan. "You will want your blood warm and flowing," he advised.

"How ominous," Vicdan admitted, taking the cloak nonetheless.

"Our Runers will supply you with better clothing," Lokhtar said to Tzarik. "Our Reks wants you back alive. We have called for one to help you on your way. Our lands are not your lands and you must be cautious. You," he pointed to Tzarik, "may come and go as you please. Our men will be watching your woman to ensure she stays and that you return. Go and hunt. Find what you need and come back."

"I will," Tzarik promised. "What happens once this is over and we aid the Reks in her quest for...?" He didn't know what. His eyes drifted to Tarkan, where he waited. Now wasn't the time to interrogate the necromancer. But something, not far beneath the surface, chilled the sulfates in his veins.

"That remains to be seen," Lokhtar said honestly. "Go."

ALL THE UNCERTAINTY weighed Tzarik down, but he had to bear it and put it aside. Lokhtar told them to head down into the small village before the inner city to find their horses and a Caerwren Runer guide who'd been summoned by the Reks.

"What are we looking for?" Vicdan asked, hurrying down the hill, trying to keep the sword he'd been given from bouncing with every step.

"There are two ingredients we cannot buy from an alchemist," Tzarik told him. "They must be given or taken."

The jongleur smiled. "Ah, the mystery ingredients. What an

educational experience I am about to have! I hope I live through it. Then, I can compose the 'Ballad of the Sulfates.' "

"You will do no such thing," Tzarik warned him, spotting Mamun outside a small, thatched structure that looked to be a merchant selling hunting supplies. "The ingredients are known only to Runers, handed down by Runers."

"And how do you know the ingredients?" Vicdan asked.

Tzarik sighed inwardly. "My mentor, Azar, taught me. As I will teach Sybal." He should have shown her long ago.

They reached Mamun, Sybal's white mare, and another gelding. Its hair blazed shockingly red against its black mane and tail. Tzarik looked around for the aforementioned Runer guide. A tall, lithe man exited the store and made his way towards them.

"Korvoth?" Tzarik asked. "Did you follow me?"

The Caerwren Runer smiled, his genial disposition still intact. His ashen head glinted in the bright winter sun. "Of course I did. I could not leave a whiteblood brother alone on foreign shores. And I need the hunt as well."

The three of them swung up onto their horses and Tzarik replaced his saddlebags on Mamun. The horse made a small, pleased snort at having its master back.

"I am glad for your company," Tzarik confessed. "I wouldn't know where to start."

"We don't have to travel far," Korvoth promised, leading them down the hill and into the city. "The mori live primarily on the backside of the peaks of Northica. That is still Altevine clanland despite Skarde-Reks and Yrsa-Reks moving farther down their mountain."

"The mori?" Vicdan asked, tilting his head.

"But first," Korvoth said, knowing to keep the runic secrets, "the Mahar'nolreith."

Tzarik nodded, flipping his hood up against the wind that had picked up. "As it must be. Do you know where one might lurk?"

Korvoth flicked his head to the north. "Where a nolreith sleeps, others gather to it." More lurked behind the Runer's words.

Tzarik took in the big man's equipment. His own sword was slung across his back and another with a fresh leather grip was tied down to his saddle. Two bedrolls were piled up behind him. However, no apprentice had joined them. Understanding, Tzarik realized Korvoth knew exactly where to find the monsters.

Sensing the Runer's reading each other, Vicdan squinted ahead. "Yes, where one gathers, there are more." He took a deep breath and quoted, " 'Where the god-touched roam, the darkness makes its home. Run from here, don't be near, the Dohkma comes at gloam.' " He smiled. "A rhyme from my childhood. It means that where something from the Frozen Nation has made its home—monsters and the like—more come. They are drawn to the darkness of the blackest god: the Dohkma. Some think he is *The* God, the first god, who made all other gods. Others believe he is the opposite of that first god. Where the first god would be good and kind, the Dohkma is as evil as the other is divine."

"I'm familiar," Tzarik grumbled. "It will be easier to take the nolreith down with the two of us."

Korvoth agreed. "And we have bait."

Both Runers looked at Vicdan.

"Oh, no." Vicdan sighed.

TZARIK COULDN'T SLEEP when they stopped to make camp. Vicdan sat apart and gently spun the wheel of his fiddle, humming some melancholy tune. Korvoth came back with a rabbit clutched between his hands. When he sat down near the fire to clean it, Tzarik noticed it had a small set of spidery antlers. The other Runer skinned it and skewered it on a rough spit over the flames.

He wasn't normally the type to ask questions. He'd not had the occasion in some time, and when he did, he often refused to ask. Sybal never had that fear.

"Does everything here have antlers?" he asked at long last. Korvoth raised his brows. Tzarik added, "We saw a dragon when we first landed ashore. Massive, striding over the peaks. It had antlers like that."

"Ah," Korvoth hummed, slightly amused. "You saw Strigganoct. The dragon god, worshiped by the mountain people of Northica."

Tzarik frowned, stopping his hand where it sharpened his scimitar. "A literal god?" The monk on Xia had said as much, warning him that Caerwren's gods walked among their people. Somehow, he hadn't imagined it literally.

Korvoth nodded. "As Vasaras reaches its zenith, the barrier between us and the God Deep grows weak, thin. They come in search of that which they do not posses: red blood. During our winter, we hunt and offer that red blood in the hopes that when the fourteen days of darkness come, the gods spare us."

Vicdan's eyes shot up, snapping between the two Runers. "Just red? They don't have a palate for, say, white blood?"

Tzarik understood. Their blood was made from the blood and marrow of undead, god-touched monsters. It brought them their magic, allowed them to use the runes and be near the magic blade without consequence. It also bound itself to them and gave them the instincts that allowed them to fight like the supernatural monsters they hunted. Tzarik knew he'd not tapped the full potential of the sulfates, but most Runers didn't. It was enough to wield the orichalcum and use the runes.

"Fear not, lad," Korvoth said bracingly, slapping Vicdan hard on his back. "We won't let them eat you."

"Eat?" Vicdan cried.

Korvoth laughed darkly, but in good humor. With Vicdan there to keep Korvoth entertained, Tzarik looked up at the sky. The moon didn't shine through and the stars had vanished. Distraught that the light of the moon could not guide them, Tzarik instead watched the soft white flakes fall. He'd never seen snow. He'd heard stories of it. Curious, he reached up and touched one of the fat, cold flakes. It broke apart on his fingertip and melted. The cold water slipped down his cut-off gloves.

"First snow fall?" Korvoth asked, taking in his Al'Myrahn companions and their wonder.

"How marvelous," Vicdan mused softly for the first time. "I've seen paintings of it before." He stood up to catch the drifting beauty.

Tzarik held his hand out, palm up, and let the snow land there. It didn't melt on his glove as fast as it had on his flesh. "My mentor told me stories about it." He swallowed. "He hated snow."

He imagined what Sybal would say. Probably something about how she'd studied various climates in her youth. She'd tell him how snow formed in the clouds or how it was birthed from the mountain tops—wherever it came from, it didn't matter. She'd have some story about a time her family had traveled to Rhostrana and met with a grand naiz and that it had snowed there and they'd engaged in some winter pastime only the wealthy enjoyed.

She'd look amazing, wrapped in white furs, her yellow hair wild and waving in the cold wind. Her blue eyes in her warm skin would glow. She'd tell him to run in the snow as it piled up around them. The cold wouldn't harm her; her blood was from these white peaks.

Tzarik pulled himself back to the fire and caught Vicdan looking at him over the flames. The young man's large brown eyes reflected his sadness back. The jongleur knew Tzarik's mind. For once, Vicdan didn't say anything and allowed Tzarik to wallow in his somber thoughts.

Just as he made up his mind to sleep, a different kind of white flake drifted past him. He tracked it, unmelting as it landed on a stone near the fire. It wasn't snow. It was a piece of ash.

CHAPTER 15

THE
MAHAR NOLREITH

"Wait," Tzarik hissed to his companions.

After two slow days of travel, the impassible ice-capped peak of Northica's border rose into the hazy white sunshine before them. A massive wall of blue ice and blinding snow blocked their path. Dotted around the base of the mountain lay helmets, frozen bodies, spears, and masses of fur that looked like wolves. Above them, he knew Northica defended a stone bridge over the rushing river they could hear. The bridge was the only way into their mountainous kingdom. But the bodies that had fallen from above were not what stopped him.

His sulfates tingled, alerting him to a supernatural presence. Slowly, he drew halat. The shimmering barrier crawled out from his hand where he clutched the rune. He continued to draw it as he walked closer to the cliff face before them.

In the early morning sun, he could see tracks in the snow. The first were booted, human tracks. They dashed to the right then turned into bear prints. Where this change took place, two long gashes appeared beside it, like the marks a hawk in the dive might leave if it plunged down to attack prey. After that, both sets of prints vanished.

Tzarik pointed them out to Korvoth. As the taller Runer tracked them back, Tzarik went further around the cromlechs of ice and rock. The prey appeared, heaped in the snow. Cautiously, looking up first to make sure the skies were clear of the predator, he knelt by the corpse. The surrounding snow had melted away a minuscule amount, but enough to tell him that the body had been warm just moments ago. Again, his gaze shot up. Nothing lurked in the crevices amongst the rocks and ice.

"What is it?" Vicdan's voice carried over on the cold wind.

With the heel of his boot, Tzarik turned the victim over. The man had died while transforming. A soft black fur covered half his face and sharp, ursine fangs protruded from just one side of his open mouth. The prints were his. He'd tried to shift into his bear form to escape the predator. Carefully, Tzarik turned his mutated head. There, in his muscular, veiny neck, were four savage puncture marks. Blood still trickled out. He'd seen the Vaeson transform; they were the size of horses. Only a creature sure of its strength would attack such a beast.

Again looking up, he unsheathed his scimitar. "Damn," he hissed, rushing back to Korvoth.

"Mori," the other Runer said when Tzarik came around the ice and stone.

"I know," he replied. "We have to find the nolreith before the mori finds us."

"Why?" Vicdan asked, eyeing the dead man cautiously. When neither answered, he asked, "Is this a Runer thing? One of the deep dark secrets?"

Tzarik looked up at Korvoth for a reply. The taller Runer shrugged.

"The marrow from the nolreith *must* be gathered first," Tzarik explained. "The blood from the mori must be mixed into it second."

Vicdan raised an eyebrow. "And I suppose the magic just knows when you don't kill this nolreith first?"

His sarcastic expression melted when both Runers glared at him seriously. "All right, fine," he mumbled.

Korvoth took the lead, putting Vicdan in the middle, and used his long legs to march over the piling snow. He made his way back towards the first face of ice they'd found.

"Don't underestimate the black oath," Korvoth warned Vicdan. "It knows if you do not follow its laws and mores. If one takes the marrow of the nolreith without the blood of the mori, a madness like you've never seen will overtake a Runer. The nolreith is a god-touched, made in the image of Mjordir. Maybe even a lesser god itself. The blood of the mori, a sentient who has taken on immortal life, gives it balance."

Vicdan puffed his cheeks out, blowing out a harsh breath into clouds of steam. "And most Runers are murderers. That must make it terribly difficult to take the blood of the sentient monster."

"You have no idea," Korvoth replied starkly.

While Korvoth spoke, Tzarik's sharp eyes found the gap in the ice they'd been looking for. The mori would hide from the sun. It had just fed, so it'd be strong, but asleep. The presence of it here meant the nolreith wasn't far, either. Ice, blue and glowing, lined the inside of the cave. Somewhere deep inside, a river ran. Darkness permeated the space around them except in small dots where the sun pierced through a crack in the rock above.

The Runers lit torches for Vicdan and to ward off any lurking haunts. From deeper in the ice cave, a chilling warble danced over the cold air to their ears. The ghoulish sound froze Tzarik in his tracks.

"A helhest," Korvoth supplied. "Do not look it in the eyes, red blood."

Vicdan's already fear-rounded eyes went even wider in shock. "What is it? What will happen?"

Tzarik smirked dryly and pushed his way to the lead. "You'd be a much better companion."

The younger man followed Tzarik's back with his eyes. "What?"

Korvoth slapped him jovially on the back again, pushing him

along. "It'll knock you mute if you do," he answered. "But I doubt it's lingering. It's drawn to the nolreith—won't stay long."

In a panic, Vicdan fumbled with his pack and pulled out a silken Al'Myrahn scarf. He draped it over his neck and followed them. "Should it appear, I am taking no chances. I will bind my eyes and not look even a fraction near it. I can't risk that, you know. Why, just before I found our necromancer, I was the companion to a wealthy sheikah who said my voice was like honey on warm stone. I'm not sure exactly—"

Korvoth turned and grabbed Vicdan, covering his mouth with his huge hand. Tzarik froze. He'd heard it, too. When Vicdan struggled, shouting into the massive Runer's palm, Tzarik glared at him and hissed for him to be silent. He tucked his hair behind his ear, tilting his head to listen. His nose caught the scent before his ears heard the footfall of the monster.

Ash. Hot, sulfuric, charred ash suffused the air. The virulent redolence of brimstone filled his nose and then his head. "The smell of a demon," he whispered. "There are many kinds of demons, but they all came from the same curse: god-touched, being touched by a god, succumbing to their overwhelming power."

Vicdan held perfectly still at this.

"They become slaves to the god," Tzarik finished darkly. "Demons."

The years of hunting alone made Tzarik blind to the other two as he waited, listening, smelling his prey.

Vicdan gulped beside him and shrank away from the wide-open arena they now found themselves in. "Have you fought one of these nolreith before?" he asked softly.

Korvoth moved protectively in front of the jongleur, drawing his long, straight blade from his back.

"Yes," Tzarik answered honestly. "Just once with Azar."

Before Vicdan could ask how he'd acquired sulfates, Korvoth replied for him. "I, like so many here on Caerwren, have fought it many times. We gather it, sell it to other Runers. Some Runers on this rock hunt it exclusively. Makes a lot of coin from desperate Runers."

Another footfall shook the ice cave, causing a crack to splinter above them. Vicdan looked up and shook. "So you know what you're doing, then?" he asked, his voice pitching up.

"We just need a part of it," Korvoth answered.

He gestured for Vicdan to come forward. When he did, Korvoth took his arm and made a small, quick incision on the younger man's arm. Vicdan shouted in protest but couldn't pull away.

"Tzarik, what the hell?" Vicdan cried as Korvoth rubbed some of his blood onto a stone.

"We need to draw it out," Tzarik replied. He gave Vicdan what he hoped was an apologetic tilt of his head. "It won't come to our blood."

The other Runer tossed the stone deep into the ice cave. It slid over the glassy surface and vanished into the darkness. No sooner had the skittering and hissing of the stone stopped than a roar rang up from inside. The crack in the ice above splintered even further.

"Stay," he ordered the other two.

Tzarik followed the crack deeper. He was surprised to find a wide set of stone steps leading up into the blackness. The halls of the mountains had been carved out by sentient hands here. Statues of radjur with magnificent antlers lined the steps leading up, chipped and faded from years of exposure. He ignored the calls of Vicdan from behind, hoping Korvoth would keep his eyes sharp, and jogged up the long steps into the utter darkness. He could see, but only just. The nolreith would be deep inside.

Atop the steps, also covered in ice, the opening of what had once been an underground city yawned wide and huge before him. In the darkness, the curve of hewn stone glittered with frost. Structures furrowed right into the stone showed where once a people had lived.

Pillars of black and gray stone made up a small square and reached up into the infinite darkness above.

A few calls followed him from behind, but he pressed on into the darkest parts of the mine city. Without the sun touching his skin, it got colder. He stopped to listen. The hissing and whispering of spirits wheezed out from the shadows. They had been drawn here, pulled by the power of the nolreith. Something shot out from the shadows above him, flying overhead. The beat of its wings made his heart skip. Could it be the mori?

He didn't have time to contemplate it long. The putrid smell of the demon suddenly overcame him in a wave of icy fire. The colossal footfalls of the beast running told him they'd called it out. He steeled himself. There was no one way to take down a nolreith. They didn't need to kill it. Like Korvoth said, they just needed a part of it. Fear gripped his lungs as he panted, widening his stance to meet the god-touched monster.

"Tzarik!" Vicdan's voice screamed from far behind. A few other shouts and grunts followed the cry from his companion. It had to be the mori. But he couldn't leave the nolreith.

With a leap that rocked the entire mine, the nolreith shot up from a chasm spanned by a network of stone bridges. When it landed, he beheld the grotesque shape. The primary body of the nolreith moved with the gait of a horse, six hooves clacking wickedly against the ice and stone. Not unlike a centaur from Rom, the body of a man rose from its hunched, spiny back where its head might have been. But that was where the familiarity ended. The head was formed from the bodies of humans, amalgamated sentients fused together by the god Mjordir himself. One set of legs bent up, branching out into bloody antlers that curved back and up in deadly points. Coming out from this was another human-like body, naked and scaly. This one hung upside down with glowing eyes of fire. Where it should have had arms came long, clawed, writhing tentacles. The same kind of deadly limbs whipped from the spines on its curved back in a thrashing nest of tendrils. Wherever its cloven hoof fell against the stone, ice and fire shot out like sparks from a forge. The flames froze, making a sharp, jagged path in its wake.

The mahar'nolreith towered over Tzarik, bellowing a frightening bugle to the stone ceiling. Between that, the cracking of the ice, and the thunder of the frozen fire, all other noises were drowned out.

I am a servant of Mjordir, made in his image, the creature roared in Tzarik's mind, *and you will not have my marrow today, little Runer.*

The nolreith lunged.

Tzarik drew halat as one of the long tentacle arms lashed out at him. The arm bounced off the barrier, but it shattered the shield, throwing the Runer back. He hit the stone hard and gasped before rolling out of the way with buhkar. The tentacle passed through the mist, making him shiver. When he rematerialized, the nolreith stamped at him with its sharp hooves, bugling again. Tzarik took this opportunity to slash at the back of its ashen ankle. He landed the blow but had to act quickly, misting away and shielding himself at the same time. He ran between its massive, fleshy patchwork legs, slicing upwards as he did.

This only enraged the nolreith. With another horn-like cry, it ducked its head to charge at Tzarik with its antlers. He hacked at it, severing two spikes of the ivory-like horns with his opaline blade. But it caught him as he swung. The branchlike tines slipped under his left arm, lifting him easily. His center of balance spun as the nolreith pitched him up and over its back. It tossed him towards the nest of writhing tentacles and spines on its back. As he fell towards it, he spotted a morass of sentient limbs and severed heads with faces twisted in agony tangled in the deadly nest. He wouldn't join them.

Hacking desperately, he drew halat to block the immediately onslaught that grabbed for his wrists and ankles. This allowed him to dodge most and roll over the sharp spines, protected by the runic shield. Some slipped past and punctured his new armor, drawing his white blood. He tumbled down and hit the ground after a brief fall. The landing winded him again. Smelling his blood the nolreith whirled around, bucking with its back hooves and charging again with its antlers. The hooves kicked over his head and he had to mist again to avoid the tines. He gasped for air, becoming quickly exhausted.

This time, the nolreith snapped at him. The horror of watching it open its fleshy maw paralyzed Tzarik. The center belly of the joined human torso opened wide, splitting the flesh and making it bleed. A long, serpentine tongue lashed out. Like a viper, it snapped and hissed at him, driving him farther back towards the network of bridges and the long drop they spanned. The fear of the drop tingled up Tzarik's knees, his eyes catching it as he fled. With a roar, he tried to push past the irrational fear, but his legs still weakened. This slowed his pace, allowing the nolreith to catch up.

His mind snapping between the monster and the idea of running across the narrow stone bridge crippled him. With this one moment of hesitation, the sharp, gruesome fangs snapped at him. He tried to parry the blow, but the maw clamped around his arm. Afraid it'd rip his limb off if he resisted, he let it jerk him away from the edge and fling him back across the room. With a cry of pain and anguish, he rolled over the tines he'd severed before, his blood splashing over the mine's stone. The nolreith gave out a gloating, rumbling laugh and charged him again.

As it thundered towards him, his eyes roamed to the tines. They leaked a crystalline marrow from the soft, spongy middle.

With a shout of triumph, Tzarik snatched up the tines. They were easily as long as his arm and had more than enough marrow in them for vials upon vials of sulfates. This was all he needed.

"Korvoth!" he shouted back, knowing the mori would attack the other two. "I have it!"

The nolreith swung its grotesque head, tentacle arms reaching out. Tzarik parried one and spun away, but the second clawed his face. One of the jagged, bone-like ends tore the flesh from his scalp, down over his eye, to his collarbone. His blood blinded him, so he hacked madly at the monster. It screamed as the curved blade of the scimitar met resistance. Putting his entire frame into the spinning slash, he severed the arm. With a wet plunk, it hit the stone, splattering him with the watery marrow and blood. The wet fluids made the air pierce his clothes, chilling him. The missing limb wouldn't bother the nolreith; Mjordir would find another arm to attached to its demon.

Emboldened, Tzarik kicked the useful limb behind him and slashed again to make the monster leap back. It did, and he drew his crossbow. Sticking his arm out, he shot the bolt as one of the twitching limbs from the nest on its back whipped out. It wrapped around his thigh, jerking him upside down. But the bolt flew. It landed in the back of the roaring throat, silencing the bugle that had just risen from its gullet. From where he swung, Tzarik spotted the opalescent arrowhead sticking out from the back of its throat. It had gone in deep, the feathered shaft beneath the soft flesh of its throat.

The nolreith dropped him, staggering back. Its voice now came in a strangled hiss. Korvoth made a grunting sound far behind him. The clang of orichalcum against stone drew Tzarik back to the other fight. The nolreith slinked away into the shadows.

Tzarik spun when he heard Vicdan make a suffocating moan. Whirling, he ran back towards the other two. He only just rounded a bend in the rock when he caught a horrid sight. A towering human form draped in graying, threadbare garb loomed back the way they had come. The mori held the jongleur in his arms, out cold. Vicdan's back arched over the thin arm of the monster, his own hands dangling limp behind him. The monster latched onto Vicdan's neck with its fangs. He could hear it swallowing greedily from here. Vicdan's eyes were unfocused, half shut and dancing back and forth.

"Vicdan!" he shouted, letting any conscious part of his

companion know he was on his way. The bite of the mori placated its victims, but could be thrown off if one had a strong will.

A quick glance showed where the mori must have flung Korvoth off after an attack. The straight, pearlescent blade lay on the stone floor. The pale hands of Korvoth gripped the rocky edge of a precipice that led farther down into a steep, jagged fall. Tzarik hesitated, almost diving to grip Korvoth's scrambling hands, but a weak moan from Vicdan stopped him.

"I'm fine!" the Runer shouted to Tzarik. "Get your lad before that thing drains him." Korvoth grunted, getting one elbow onto the ground to pull himself up.

Upon seeing the Al'Myrahn Runer, the mori straightened up and wiped the blood from its lips. Gently, it adjusted its grip on Vicdan so it cradled him, but it did not relinquish its undead grip. Its eyes focused on Tzarik, making his sulfates rush. Having the thing's conscious eyes bore into him unnerved him.

"Ah, you've traveled far for my blood, Runer," the mori mused in a deep, liquid timber. "And what a wonderful sacrifice you bring me." The mori ran its long, white-blue finger down Vicdan's face, his neck, then chest, where it had ripped his cloak away to bite. "This one's heart is strong and gladsome," it praised. "I like it."

Tzarik switched his scimitar to his left hand and reloaded his small crossbow with an orichalcum-tipped bolt. "Let him go, monster," he growled.

Unused to bargaining with his hunts, Tzarik wasn't sure he could kill the mori. The vampiric creatures of Al'Myrah were usually wordless, raging bloodsuckers. He'd had little occasion to have a conversation with the monsters he hunted.

With a sweep of its aging cloak, the mori lifted Vicdan off his feet and laid him down gently on his back. Tzarik watched him carefully. The mori's face said it wished to finish Vicdan off, drinking the last of his blood. But it held itself back.

"Is he alive?" Tzarik shot to the mori.

The mori nodded, standing up. "Now, Runer, what kind of monster do you think I am? This one is a fine specimen. His blood is so..." The mori squinted its red eyes, looking for the right words. He tapped the tips of his clawed fingers together. "Vibrant. It'd be a shame to snuff this one's life out. Like an avalanche taking the life of a beacon as it signals its people." He stepped over Vicdan, the high heels of its boots clicking on the ice floor as he approached Tzarik. "I see your hesitation. Have no fear, Runer. You're not my type." The red orbs tracked Tzarik as he walked a wide circle around the mori. "You could kill me," it mused, as it read Tzarik's oathbound crime on his face. "But you haven't. That's different."

With a last glance over his shoulder to make sure the nolreith had retreated and hearing Korvoth pick up his blade, Tzarik walked towards the mori. The creature was a man—or had been. His skin, old and long dead like most of his vampiric kind, had a blue-black hue to it where blood no longer flowed, chilling it. His red eyes matched his long, red hair. The mori dressed like a wealthy man from Caerwren might: embroidered gold thread, though old and faded, covered his graying cloak.

"Will you bargain?" Tzarik asked. "Blood for blood." His body throbbed, from the bite on his shoulder to the fresh wound on his face. The mori had to know he was bleeding out as well. But it didn't attack. Tzarik sensed the mori was fascinated by his restraint and willingness to speak.

"Most hunters who come to these caves are terrified, Runer," the mori explained. It adjusted its steps to take itself further away from Tzarik. "Terrified of me because they are killers. But know they cannot kill sentient kind, else the oath should take them. I know the look of a killer. You don't have it. But the light in your eyes says you are far fiercer than they." It held its head high. "The other Runers cannot kill me. But you... I'm not used to being threatened." The mori reached into the folds of its garments and produced a familiar-looking dagger. It had a glass channel running down the blade to the round, clear grip. Tzarik had seen one before. Sharar had used it to take his blood.

"You need my blood like I need red blood," the mori said simply. "You stop me from taking every last, vibrant drop?" He smiled down at Vicdan again. Then, slowly, his red eyes turned up to meet Tzarik's. "I believe you could. Let me have a look into your mind. I want to see what gives you so much damned courage."

Like the tentacles he'd just dispatched, something wriggled into Tzarik's brain as he looked into the mori's red eyes. A searching, prodding finger dug deep into his skull. To his surprise, pain accompanied it. The digging tendril struck deep until he swore he felt it in his gut. The mori narrowed its red eyes, focusing.

"What are you doing?" Tzarik grunted.

Behind him, Korvoth strode forward, sword posed to strike. "They're mind readers if you give them the chance," he growled. He hefted his great sword, ready to strike if Tzarik gave the word.

"Finding your intent," the mori agreed softly, his eyes unfocusing as he probed Tzarik's brain. "I can smell the fear on you, Runer. It is unlike any fear I have had the pleasure to drink up before. You do not fear *me*. You do not fear the mahar'nolreith. No..."

He glared at Tzarik now and the pain in the Runer's head mounted. Tzarik forced himself to remain standing. A light tingle told him his nose bled as the mori dug deeper into his mind.

Sybal's face burst before his eyes, as did every fear he held secret. Losing her. Dying on this frozen shore. Leaving her alone should he perish. Sharar hunting them for eternity. The hidden djinn that waited to give Sharar the powers to be a sorcerer. The worry he felt about letting Tarkan ascend. His fear of loneliness.

As quickly as it had come, the pain and the images vanished. When Tzarik opened his eyes, the mori stood before him. To his surprise, he held his arm out to stop Korvoth from advancing on the mori.

"So strong," the mori mused, lifting the sanguine blade. "You have found your purpose. But you guard it in secret. It makes you strong, allows you to resist death."

Running the back of his hand under his nose to wipe away the blood, Tzarik glared at the mori. Tears of leftover pain blurred his vision. The mori slowly slid the blade into its own chest and clicked the handle. Through the glass, Tzarik watched it turn red. The blood swirled and glinted, a pearlescent quality within it. The glass blade filled and the mori held it out to Tzarik.

Unsure, Tzarik slowly took the proffered blade. "Why?" he asked, catching his breath.

The mori smiled sadly. "I am old, Runer. Immortal. More immortal than the Masahk on Alika as no blade besides that of a Runer can take my life. But I see you won't. Though you could. This tells me something about you. I dare not interfere with one such as you." It scoffed dryly. "I have little care for what a few sentients do in this century so long as I live on in this mountain. But I do still live on this map. I wish it longevity. But your necromancer..."

Tzarik started. The mori had gone deeper into his mind than he knew.

"That is one creature I could not abide upon my map," the mori went on. "So you must promise me something, Runer. With my blood in you, stop him from ascending."

"How?"

"The law of sacrifice," the mori offered.

Not understanding but seeing Vicdan hadn't stirred yet, Tzarik knew he had to hurry. "What if I can't stop him? I don't understand."

The mori tilted its head knowingly. "Or don't want to stop him. He is avoiding the law of sacrifice." He looked curiously down at Tzarik. "You don't know the laws and mores of necromancy?"

The Runers exchanged glances. "Tell me what you mean," Tzarik ordered.

The mori nodded generously. "To reach into the Deep as he

desires—as you desire him to do—requires him to ascend to Lich King, or as you would call it within the eastern triangle, Necro-Khan. He must placate his gods' lust for blood if they are to favor him so. Otherwise, his ritual to ascend will only end in his suffering. The third law of sacrifice is to give lives not of your own." He waved his hand. "All know the red wolf has prepared such a sacrifice. I can smell it from here. Her pit of dead, rotting bodies abhors me."

Sjörna-Reks. She had mentioned a pit of souls. Tzarik hadn't cared or understood at the time what it meant.

"Your necromancer must give these souls to his god," the mori went on. "Do you understand? Killing thousands. Sending their souls to the Deep, forever parting them from their gods' paradise, taking them from eternity with their loved ones." A deep-rooted sadness overtook the mori's red eyes.

This was not something Tzarik believed in. "I don't know that I understand," he offered. "I don't believe in the gods, in their heavens and hells. There are just too many. What if you follow the wrong god?"

The mori smiled and licked his lips. "Choose a god, Tzarik, and be faithful. They reward faith. But when one sentient sacrifices you —blood and soul—to another god, you are separated from your god, your loved ones, for eternity, living out a hellish existence in the God Deep, neither heaven nor hell, with gods you did not honor. Eternally hunted. Eternally dying. Eternal torture."

The icy air around him suddenly felt warm compared to the chilling horror that filled him. Did Sybal experience that? Eternal torture?

"I have to save her," he argued. "He can pull her out. Her body is not dead. Our white blood preserves her." He pointed weakly to the tine in Korvoth's hand. "That's why I've come."

The mori nodded sadly. "And I have given you my blood. But is her soul worth a thousand others?"

Tzarik stopped. No words came to mind to defend himself with.

"But there is another way," the mori offered after a moment. "The first law of sacrifice is to give oneself. Well, that won't do for your necrotic friend. Already his gods own his body. His soul."

"And the second law?" Tzarik asked, seeing where the monster led.

The mori nodded. "That's the one. The second law of the necrotic scriptures states that if one were to give up one soul—the one soul they love and cherish most of all, that which gives them life even after a kind of death like his—he could be Necro'Khan, for he would have nothing left to love in this world. Only his god left to please. No pure thing to protect. Nothing holding him back."

Tzarik's heart turned to ice. "A soul that gives him life?" Sybal's dead face flashed before his eyes. She'd given him life, forced him to go on living. Suddenly, he understood.

"Zeva," he whispered.

CHAPTER 16

THE PRICE OF SACRIFICE

In the cold, quiet night of Altevine, nightmares consumed Tarkan's mind as he slept. The hard ground provided no comfort, and the fires had turned to hot ash hours ago. Sjörna-Reks had not reappeared and had not yet released Zeva to him for more than a few hours. Throughout the day, he'd not knelt so low as to beg for her to be allowed to stay the night with him. However, the dark memories of imprisonments past haunted his thoughts. In his dreams, Sharar was there. He dreamed in his waking sleep about the days before he attacked Ala'Nar. The Runers had desecrated his home. His sacred place. He didn't know why they had come after him so personally, but it burned him inside.

The nightmare reminded him of leaving Sharar's home in the wealthy city near the borders of Ala'Nar, retrieving his dragon from its hiding place, and going out to send a message to the Runers. Sharar had warned him not to leave, to retaliate. He'd paid dearly for that disobedience to the would-be sorcerer.

"Where is Zeva, Sharar?" Tarkan had roared upon returning.

Sharar had taken control of his dragon, forcing it to lie in the sun, burning. This gift had come with his first wish to the djinn he carried with him at all times: the ability to command base beasts, living and risen. Tarkan had stood in the open square of the wealthy man's golden halls, enraged and exhausted after his flight from the main city.

"I warned you," Sharar had hissed darkly, sweat beading on his brow under his gauzy head wrappings. "I gave you an order to stay away from the Runers. To leave Ala'Nar alone. You disobeyed me."

Sharar had not tied him down, but Tarkan had felt trapped. He'd glanced around the empty house again. "Where is she, Sharar? You swore she'd be safe."

The scholar had scoffed and smirked, spreading his hands wide. "You went against my orders, Tarkan. I had no choice."

The necromancer's eyes had darted to the locked cellar door. He'd known all too well it led to Sharar's dungeon. He'd made a lunge for it but had stopped when a blast from his black dragon cut across the floor, shattering the ornate stone pattern. Shards of sharp tile had cut his arms as he'd shielded his face. Below, a high, pained scream had torn his heart.

"Zeva!" he'd called. He'd faced Sharar, flexing his fingers. He'd reached out with his black magic, feeling for corpses—anything he could raise.

Sharar had smiled and shaken his head. "You are wonderful, aren't you? I had the tombs excavated months ago. I'm no fool, Tarkan. I know who I'm dealing with." He'd motioned to the hatch. "Shall we?"

With a strength Tarkan hadn't known the scholar possessed, Sharar had seized his arm and pulled him down the winding stone steps into his dungeon. Tarkan had spent time amidst the torture devices the scholar had collected and had hoped to never be amongst them again. But then, he'd gone willingly. He'd almost pulled Sharar along, eager to find Zeva.

He'd stopped once they'd entered the strange yellow light of the dungeon. His heart had beat just once in horror. Zeva had lain bound and shackled on a stone table. Above her, an apparatus had slowly dripped something yellow and glittery from an hourglass over her body.

"What have you done?" Tarkan had roared, throwing Sharar off. He'd run to the table and reached out to cover his daughter's face.

Her flesh had partially burned, slipping from the acid above. She'd wept piteously as a fresh drop splashed over her neck. Tarkan had instinctually wiped it away, searing his own skin. As he'd wiped the acid on his robe, it had corrupted one symbol on the back of his hand. Quickly, he'd said a prayer and pulled away. He could not break the scriptures on his skin should the oath be broken.

"What do you want from me?" he'd roared to Sharar, who'd stood by, watching curiously. When the scholar had simply observed, he'd scanned the rest of Zeva's body. Blood had stained her white dress over her ribs and shins. Frantically, Tarkan had ripped open her dress and examined the rest of her.

Scars, burn marks, puncture wounds, and a long, grotesque, horribly stitched scar across her abdomen had come to light. Tarkan's black blood had run cold.

"You can do what you like to me," he'd murmured, forcing himself to keep his voice even. His hands had shaken as he'd covered Zeva again. She'd passed out from the pain of the acid. "You can open me up again, rip my bowels from my flesh, strip the sinews from my bones, turn my joints to liquid, boil my teeth—I don't care. But Zeva is innocent. Let her go!"

The scholar had clicked his tongue and sighed, raising his brows. "You're right, my necrotic colleague. You don't care. And that's what needs to change." He'd pulled out a slim dagger that glittered: Orichalcum. Sharar had handled the metal without a care for the mutation it might bring him.

Tarkan had taken one step back, but not before Sharar had pounced on him like a tiger. He'd slammed the necromancer onto the ground and stabbed the knife deep into the center of his chest, deliberately missing his heart. Still, the pain from the magic blade had boiled his blood and shot hot agony through him. He'd chosen not to move or fight.

"Don't make me break the scar, Tarkan. I'd hate to throw away a perfect specimen like yourself." Sharar had slowly turned the blade, drawing more blood and an anguished moan from his prisoner. Then, even more slowly, watching Tarkan's face the entire time, he'd haltingly withdrawn the blade.

When Tarkan had felt it slip out, he'd gasped and rolled over to stand up. Once he'd gotten to his feet, he'd stumbled to Zeva again, hands outstretched. He'd cast the spell to take on her wounds, healing her. He could bear it. He couldn't go on seeing the scars, knowing he'd caused them. But there were only so many wounds he could take, and Sharar had more to give. The damned Runers...

Just as he'd reached for Zeva, Sharar had seized him again, dragging him away easily, back to his dark prison. Then came the days of his own torture. Sharar had muted him, burning his tongue with a hot iron so he could not cast his spells. But that had healed. When not inflicting punishment on Tarkan, Sharar had turned his attention to Zeva. Tarkan hadn't been able to see her, locked away in another part of the dungeon, but he'd heard her. Her wails of torment had pierced the darkness, bringing him more pain than anything Sharar had done to his body.

His own screams woke him.

Tarkan looked up into the thatched roof of the thronehall. The pain in his bound shoulders reminded him of where he was. Still bound, but at least he was far away from Sharar. The thronehall was nearly black with only one torch lit. He shivered, the cold finally registering in his numb limbs. Trying to flex his fingers to keep his blood flowing, he remembered they were bound as well. His heart beat once, telling him the scar it bore still held fast. If all went well, he'd soon break that covenant binding.

The clinking chains mocked him, saying he had once again let himself become a prisoner. *But it will be worth the mantle of*

Necro'Khan, he told himself. Ishmael had often urged him to fight through trials, pain, and agony. *Suffering is temporary,* he used to say. *The reward is eternal. Especially for us. Bear it and you will taste that power.* It may take time. It may bring suffering, but once he was Necro'Khan, was there anyone who could stand up to him? Ishmael had been invulnerable to those wanting to shackle and bridle him. He'd destroyed his country. Tarkan wanted that kind of security.

A muffled sound came from behind the dais. A door opened, allowing in a gust of white flurries and a cold wave of mountain air. He hunched against it but noted the smell of wet dog.

A great red wolf gently walked out into the dim light from the flickering torch. As it passed behind the beam the torch was attached to, it changed into the tall, imposing form of Sjörna-Reks. She tossed her long red hair over her shoulder and motioned with her gloved hand for someone to follow her. Tarkan's heart swelled when Zeva came around the dais. Her eyes at first looked unsure, and she cast around, hands clenched over her chest nervously. Then she spotted him.

"Tarkan!" she exclaimed. She dashed to him, throwing her arms around his neck in a warm embrace.

Unable to return her embrace, he leaned into her. "Are you all right?" he asked, the dream lurking just behind his closed lids.

She nodded, kissing his sunken cheek. "Hungry and cold, but fine. I miss Vicdan." She opened the fur cloak he wore and snuggled in to his side.

Sjörna-Reks watched them long enough for Tarkan to wonder at her thoughts before she turned to the great fire, lighting it anew. "I heard you crying out," she said solemnly. "I am not cruel. I do not desire to inflict pain without need. She may sit with you tonight."

"Then why is he bound so?" Zeva shot, enveloping his chilled hands in hers.

The Reks faced them now that the fire in the great pit blazed hot and bright. "Because I need him. I cannot risk his flight. But I see how he loves you. And I honor love. It is the cruelest and strongest master."

Sjörna-Reks gathered the necessities for a stew and meat drying on horizontal poles, handing Zeva a loaf of oat bread as she prepared it. The girl bit into it ravenously and chased the mouthful with a sloppy drink of water.

Seeing her so hungry put an urgency in Tarkan. "Someone you love is in the God Deep?" he asked, watching Sjörna-Reks carefully.

The tall woman didn't reply, her green eyes focused on the flames before her. "Yes," she whispered. "Taken from me for my ignorance. His death was my fault. But he is mine and I will have him back."

Zeva swallowed and looked up at the solemn Reks. "Who was it?"

Tarkan let his eyes bore into the foreboding woman. She crouched near the fire, her bone adornments clinking as she did so. She reached her hand out towards the fire, dangerously flicking her fingers through the tongues of flame.

Finally, the Reks sighed and stood up to face the thrones. "My Reks. My beautiful raven lord." Her throat closed up, choking her with emotion. "My love, Kjarton-Reks."

Tarkan eyed Sjörna-Reks over the growing flames. "Your Reks?"

The tall woman nodded, moving to one of the twenty-four pillars that held up her great hall. "On Caerwren, the tribes believe strongly in a pair of rulers: one for waging war and showing might, and one for diplomacy and cunning. Both are called Reks and are revered by their clansmen."

Her hand reached out to the pillar, engraved in the likeness of what was obviously her and a man beside her. Tarkan examined it as she stroked it. The man stood taller than her, hair whipping out around them in a maelstrom. Raven feathers burst from his back.

"You are both Vaeson?" he asked.

Sjörna-Reks nodded, her hand lingering on the carving of her Reks. "Only Vaeson are Reks. Either blessed from birth like most, or given the god-shape when they take a thronehall. Well." She smiled at some event from her past. "If a god sees it should be so. Kjarton's clan was given their divinity by the Valravn, the raven god who watches from the skies."

"The eater of kings," Tarkan added. "The black raven god only accepts sacrifices of kings' hearts."

Zeva shivered. "Eating their own kind?"

The red-haired warrior queen closed her eyes, turning her face up to the thatched ceiling. "And I of Raudnir, the red wolf. The bearer of queens. Our union was not one of strength for our clans or our gods. It was a prophecy, designed by the gods themselves."

Tarkan saw where the story was headed, but he let the woman speak.

"You loved him," Zeva supplied. He heard her smile as she said it.

Sjörna-Reks nodded, turning back to face them, the decorative bones on her garments clinking. "To the point of cruelty. Other Rekses mate for power, unity. Not us."

At this, Tarkan stopped. He'd known cruelty. He'd known love. One could not lead to the other.

"Perhaps I was too passionate," Sjörna-Reks went on. "Our love led to a wildling child. Not one who can lead the clan after I am gone."

Tarkan remembered the golden wolf shackled outside the throne-hall. "Wildling?" he asked.

"We Vaeson should not mate in animal form," Sjörna-Reks said stiffly.

He couldn't even bring up that kind of image in his mind.

"My son, Signar, is mad. Feral," she added for clarity. "Mindless. When the other clans learned Altevine had sired a wildling, they attacked during the zenith of Vasaras, taking my Kjarton and sacri-ficing him to Strigganoct, a lesser god from the bastards of Northica. They are just as mad if they think Sjörna-Reks would crumple and let them have Altevine. If I do not bear another Vaeson, then I must choose a Reks. Or a Reks must rise from my clan." She clenched her jaw in a controlled rage. "I'd suffer neither. I want my blood on my throne. Northica should know the red wolf still rules Altevine."

Guessing at the Reks's motives, Tarkan understood. "Kjarton-Reks was given to a god," he began, watching the red-haired woman carefully to gauge her reaction. "He is dead. It's not like the Runer woman. Her blood keeps her alive, saving her from the sacrificial death. The venom that tried to take her life did not succeed. She is between life and death. Sybal can be retrieved as her soul is bound to her body still."

Slowly, smiling darkly, Sjörna-Reks turned to face Tarkan. Zeva shrank under her emerald gaze.

"Don't think you can fool me, necromancer," she said softly. She took long, measured strides towards the pair. "I have dealt with your kind before. Some are not strong enough to do what needs to be done. Some are unwilling. Your tribesmen wander far and wide to escape Porsh. I am familiar with your black magics."

Zeva looked up at Tarkan at this. He forced himself to lock eyes with Sjörna-Reks and not see his daughter questioning him. She didn't know his true intent with tracking Ashkan, with helping the tribe they'd met near Ala'Nar, and why he'd agreed to come to Caerwren. If she did, she'd beg him again to scrive her. To start her on the path he'd been forced into.

Sjörna-Reks went on. "I know you can do it. I know you want to. That's what will enable you."

He cut her off. "What I could bring back—what any Necro-Khan brings back from the Deep—will not be what you think. Kjarton-Reks was given to a god who will not let him go. He'd be a wraith, a ruination of what you knew and loved. An eidolon. A monster."

She towered over where he sat with Zeva now. Looking up at her in the flickering orange light, he reminded himself he was her captive. Willingly.

"You have not seen my wrath," she whispered softly. "Consider that a blessing. Do not think because I have been kind to you so far, my mercy will prevail. I am a slave to my cruel love. I do as I must to have it returned to me. Deny me and you will see the power of my displeasure." Her eyes flicked to Zeva.

Tarkan shifted his thin legs to sit up straighter as he faced her. "Our desires lie along the same path," he said cautiously. "I am simply warning you what might be pulled from the afterlife."

"I'm aware," she quipped.

A rush of cold wind whipped around them as Lokhtar entered from behind the dais. "The Runers have returned," he announced solemnly. "He wants to see his woman."

Sjörna-Reks stood up. "Bring the necromancer. I want him to see what has happened."

With little care to the pain in him, Lokhtar reached down and yanked Tarkan to his feet. He bit his tongue to stop the moan and leaned onto Zeva for support as Lokhtar shoved him out the back way. Lokhtar held his chains from behind.

SNOW FELL IN HEAVY, thick sheets from the black sky. Tarkan looked down at his black robes and watched the fat flakes land on the soft Al'Myrahn cotton. Zeva walked close to him, still huddled under the fur cloak. She gasped softly at the falling snow and looked up to see where it came from. Before them, Tarkan recognized Tzarik's horse outside the stockade. Knowing the Runer had come back alive put a kind of relief in Tarkan he had not expected.

Inside, no fire glowed. Zeva leaned in front of Tarkan to look inside the cell where the Runer called Ragnall had been imprisoned. She looked up to Tarkan's eyes, asking to leave his side. Wordlessly, he flicked his head towards the cell. She rushed over, kneeling and whispering the Runer's name. She hated no one. Her compassion outweighed any prejudice.

The door on the back wall hung open and Sjörna-Reks shoved Tarkan into it. Tzarik had opened the box and sat looking down at Sybal. Vicdan stood quietly behind, looking pale and exhausted. A bloody bandage was wrapped around his neck. Tzarik looked up when the party approached.

"Has there been a change?" Tarkan asked the Runer.

Tzarik reached down to Sybal's tunic and lifted it to expose her stomach. Tarkan didn't have to search for his soundless concern. A pale scar had appeared on Sybal's body, reaching from her ribs to the top of her belt. White, dried blood dribbled from the mark like she'd been cut open, bled, and healed in a matter of hours. Tarkan's eyes roamed over the rest of Sybal's body. She seemed unharmed. Then he noticed her hair. Once, only deep golden tones had glowed all over her head. Now white, ashen strands shot through her braid in thick streaks.

Tarkan knelt but could not touch the frosted locks. Squinting, he noted the diamond-like gleam in the candlelight. "God-touched," he murmured, half in awe, half in horror. "She's been touched by a god." He leaned to look at her midriff again. "Tzarik?" He inclined his head towards her.

The Runer reached down and gently rolled her nearly lifeless body onto her side for him to see. Bite marks wrapped her torso all the way around. Like a giant maw had bitten her. Tarkan swore softly.

"What does this mean, Tarkan?" Tzarik asked. The necromancer noted the slight edge to the Runer's tone. Tzarik had asked him, hoping his dread was unfounded.

He wasn't entirely sure. "I have a theory," he began, knowing how well the brutish Runer might take to such a vague answer. He stood up just in case. "She may have been pursued by whichever god should have had her blood. It found her." He remembered they'd come from Xia. Could be a serpent god. "It..." He braced himself. "It may have finally taken her."

"What do you mean?" Tzarik barked, emotion strangling his tone. "I've seen a god-touched, necromancer. Watched him die, succumbing to the curse."

To Tarkan's relief, Vicdan laid a quick hand on the Runer's shoulder, steadying him as he took a step forward.

"She can't die again, not in the Deep," Tarkan assured the Runer. "That is part of the agony of the Deep. Death over and over again. To suffer every day, should a god will it. Only to come back and endure it again."

The knowledge that Sybal could suffer death thousands of times twisted painfully on Tzarik's face. But what if they brought her spirit back into this body? Would she suffer the same fate as the last god-touched he'd had to watch die?

"You can stop her eternal suffering at any time," Sjörna-Reks reminded him softly from the shadows behind them. To Tzarik, she said, "She has the sulfates. It will save her for now. But will you allow her to languish any longer?"

Her ploy was obvious to Tarkan, but fell on desperate ears. Tzarik paced, his hands going from his long hair to the hilt of his sword. He hesitated. Even if the curse had taken to her somehow, he had to at least save her from the Deep.

"Tzarik," Tarkan said, his shoulders screaming in cold pain. The sooner he started the trials for the Necro'Khan, the sooner he could be unbound. "I can save her. We have a chance."

Tzarik stopped, his blue eyes glittering in indecision. "It's not as simple as that, Tarkan. I cannot ask you to do this."

"There is no other way," Sjörna-Reks hummed gently. "Do it, Tarkan. Open the Deep. Claim your mantle."

The Runer glared at the Reks. He'd clearly begun to understand her motive, but he didn't reply to her encouragement. Instead, his eyes fell back to his dying apprentice.

Unsure what ailed the Runer, Tarkan cast a glance over his shoulder to make sure Zeva still administered her attention to the imprisoned Runer. If she heard, she'd accost him with guilt at his hypocrisy. He'd denied her for so long, but now wanted more of that power for himself. Of course, there was no way to hide it from her forever.

"Where is your pit of souls, Sjörna-Reks?" he asked darkly. "Give me the payment and I'll show you what you desire."

CHAPTER 17

SCRIVEN

THE SHOCK OF TARKAN'S DECLARATION SHOT THROUGH Tzarik. How could he possibly think of dumping thousands of innocent souls into the abyss? The promise he'd made to the mori rang in his skull. It had only been an oath of words, not of blood. And Sybal was in more danger now than before.

"I will show you in the morning," Sjörna-Reks declared. She exhaled, raising her face to the darkening sky in jubilation. With a quick tilt of her head, she signaled Lokhtar to cut Tarkan's bonds. "Half a day's journey will take us to the bogs," she informed them. "There is a space for sacrifice there. It should do as a rift in the barrier —a weak point for you to open."

The Reks pushed past Zeva as the girl came back into the black room. Seeing Tarkan unbound, Zeva ran to him, allowing him to take her in his arms. Tzarik noticed the necromancer's eyes cloud over. Tzarik fought with what to say to Tarkan. He noted Sjörna-Reks's eagerness, how she tempted Tarkan. But he also saw and heard the desire in his voice. Tarkan wanted this as well. Had he done the wrong thing in bringing the necromancer to Caerwren? Positioning him to take up the mantle of his father? He knew little about

Necro'Khans, only the horror stories told around taverns. Maybe Tarkan would differ from the others before him? Was he imposing his own morality on his image of the necromancer? Perhaps he needed to speak with Tarkan, find another way.

"You're not really thinking of sending thousands of innocent lives into the Deep for torment, are you?" Vicdan said into the quietness, now bundled in three fur blankets.

"I cannot live any longer, as weak as I am," Tarkan murmured.

Zeva pulled back from her adoptive father and glared up at him. "Tarkan?" she almost snarled, showing a negative emotion for the first time since Tzarik had known her.

Tarkan coldly pushed Zeva away. "I have to do this. You know I have to. To keep you safe, to take a power so great that no one can ever harm you again."

"You don't know that offering all those souls will please our gods," Zeva shot back. "They could all be damned in vain! Tarkan, please. I love you; don't do this. Even if your gods deign to look on you with pleasure for this heinous act, do you expect to suddenly burst with power? That the necrotic magic will fill your veins?" She turned to Tzarik for support.

Haltingly, Tzarik confirmed, "The mori told us about the laws of sacrifice."

The necromancer's icy eyes narrowed threateningly at Tzarik. "I won't hear of it."

"Yes," Zeva piped up. "Tarkan, please! I've begged you for years. Let me be marked. Make me Scriven."

"No!" Tarkan growled back, turning violently away from her. "I've told you a thousand times, no!"

She ran after him. "You don't have to make me an Apostle. Just let me join you, please. Put the covenant scripture on my heart. Let me be a part of your world, to learn as you did." She glanced at Tzarik for backup. Quickly she explained, "Putting the covenant script on my heart makes the first oath, making me Scriven, putting the scriptures on my skin. It's only the first step. To make me an Apostle, to release the power of the scriptures on a necromancer's flesh, one has to break the covenant script." She tapped on her chest. "With that ritual, the covenant scar is formed. Breaking that scar will break a necromancer's powers. A stab to the chest, for example. But Scriven is not an Apostle, Tarkan!"

"And will you be satisfied?" Tarkan barked. "Or will you then demand I give you that scar, binding you for eternity?"

Zeva pressed her lips together hard, eyes watering.

Understanding dawned on Tzarik now. Zeva felt alone, despite the love she had for her father. Kneeling, he placed his palm against Sybal's cold cheek. Her skin grew whiter, the pearly scar prominent even on her paling flesh. Touching the white, crystalline strands in her hair, he felt the chill emanating from them. He'd seen them before. Azar was god-touched. It had led to his death. The madness that came from being touched by a god had been horrifying to behold. But Azar had rescued him from his bondage and Tzarik had done all he could to save him. He'd failed. If they pulled Sybal from the Deep, would the curse follow her? Was she doomed, no matter what? Would it be better than where she dwelled now, tormented for eternity?

I'd rather have months, even days, with you, than leave you to suffer forever, he thought. Was it selfish to bring her back and let her suffer another curse? At least then, she could die before succumbing to the god's curse and go to Janna, since she believed in such things. The only thing that was certain was her death: he'd explain, take her life before she turned into a slave of a god, a demon. Tears blurred his vision. There was no winning for Sybal. The choice lay with him. And Tarkan. The only sure way was the law of sacrifice. Tarkan's gods would accept that.

Tzarik shot up. "Do you *know* Sjörna's pit of souls will please your gods?" he shot to the necromancer.

Tarkan stopped arguing with Zeva and glared at Tzarik. "No," he murmured darkly. "There is no certainty. Only faith."

"You lie," Zeva hissed at him. "You told me to make a Scriven will elevate you. Tzarik heard of the laws of sacrifice from the mori—a monster that cannot lie. Make me Scriven." She narrowed her eyes. "Why won't you let me choose this life? Do you want me to leave you? Find another who will give me a chance to follow you into the dark?"

"Zeva," Tarkan begged.

Tzarik felt the hurt these words had on the necromancer. "Tarkan," he started, knowing he sided with Zeva for Sybal's sake, "at least she has a choice. You and I were not given one. Our lives were taken from us by those who swore to protect us."

"She doesn't know the life she's asking for," Tarkan shot back.

Zeva scoffed, crossing her arms. "You've been my father for thirteen years. I've followed you into the tombs of Alika. You and I have ridden on the backs of dragons. I've slept amongst the dead, tasted lives lost, heard wandering souls cry out." She dropped her arms, focusing on him hard now. "I've seen you do dark and terrible things in pursuit of the mantle of Necro'Khan. And..." She gasped, swallowing hard as she choked on emotion. Tears immediately spilled down her cheeks and her shoulders shook. "And I love you. Don't make me stand by and watch you do this terrible thing. Don't damn thousands when I am here, willing and ready."

An emotional silence arched around the cell when she stopped to take a shuddering breath. Sudden guilt clouded Tzarik's mind. His eyes shot from Zeva to Sybal.

"Don't, Runer," the girl suddenly quipped, pointing a shaking hand towards him. "Don't harbor doubt now. It's not a soul for a soul. I will not die."

"It's a black oath," Tarkan tried again, losing ways to beg his daughter to reconsider. "You don't understand what that can do to you. What your life will become. You must use blood magic, commune with the dead—"

"I've seen it!" Zeva cut in. Her tone said these would be her final words. "I know, Tarkan. I understand." She went to him, wrapping her arms around his neck and looking up into his eyes. "You won't lose me. I won't change. I know you think I am some precious thing to protect, to keep pure. It's how you've shown your love. But show me with this."

Tzarik's heart ached for Tarkan as he watched the two fight. He wished he knew what to say, that he'd not pitted them against one another. Would it be worth the short time Sybal would have left in this life?

Of course it is, he argued with himself. *We'll have a chance to find a way to save her again. And if we don't, she can enter her paradise.* Yes, even that was enough for him.

"If Sybal were here," he tried, speaking to Zeva, "she'd tell you to do as you saw fit. She *chose* Runing without fully under-standing it, but also said she'd not have changed her mind. She grew into being a Runer like she was made for it." He chanced a glance at Tarkan. The necromancer still looked torn. "When she comes back, she'll no doubt tell you how brave you were for giving yourself up for her. She'll also have words of encourage-ment that I—and Tarkan—never could speak. She'll understand why you did it."

Zeva nodded in finality. "And there will be no guilt." She turned back to look up at Tarkan. "No guilt," she repeated. She slammed her fist into her chest. "My choice."

At last, Tarkan spoke. "But you want me to ruin you so I don't bear the weight of thousands we've never met. How is what I want any different?"

She reached up and grabbed his chin, forcing him to look her in the eyes. "Because we *know* it will work. This is what your gods want. And when we die, we will be together. Until then, you will be

Necro'Khan. You will have the power you've craved since Ishmael cursed you. Let me give it to you."

Doubt again consumed Tzarik as Zeva spoke these final words. He needed a Necro'Khan to open a door to the God Deep. It was the only way to pass back and forth between the worlds. But what kind of power would he be releasing into the world through Tarkan? Ishmael, the last lich, had not been active in Tzarik's lifetime. Tarkan was over a hundred years old and had a century of malice and revenge to exact on a world that had turned their back on his country. Also, there was the time he'd spent in servitude to Sharar.

In agony, he forced himself to look at Sybal. "Is she really suffering?" he asked.

Tarkan took Zeva's arms from his neck and placed his hand on her cheek. Something inside him crumpled and Tzarik saw him surrender. "Yes," the necromancer answered. "The Deep is as I have said: eternal death and resurrection. Forever being hunted and devoured by the gods. Worse for Sybal, since she is alive in this world still. She will bear those wounds when she returns."

Then they were running out of time.

Zeva nodded, locking eyes with Tarkan. "Then we do it my way." She snapped her head back to Tarkan. She wouldn't threaten him, but the defeat pressing down on him showed as his eyes dropped away from his daughter.

"As you wish, Zeva," he murmured.

None of them spoke to each other for the rest of that night. Except Vicdan. Tzarik sat with Sybal with only the single flame of a candle for company. Tarkan and Zeva left the stockade, given somewhere to sleep together by Sjörna-Reks. He hadn't followed, knowing this night together would be hard for them. Vicdan hadn't followed them out, opting to stay behind with Tzarik. He sat beside Sybal now, plaiting her hair along the side of her head. At first, Tzarik wanted to swat him away, but realized the gesture shouldn't be treated so. Vicdan had put himself in harm's way for him and her.

Vicdan had been going on for ten minutes about how brave Zeva was. "I've never been able to imagine how agonizing it must be to become Scriven," he said, his fingers working Sybal's ashen hair. "It's not like one can be unconscious during the rite."

Tzarik looked around for something to fiddle with and keep his hands busy. "I've seen impressive marks upon some men's bodies," he mused. "They say tolerating the pain is a sign you are worthy of the symbols. It's probably no different for a necromancer." He settled on braiding a new leather cord for his runes. "Porsh was such a small country. No one on Al'Myrah thought it could be so powerful."

The jongleur sighed, raising his dark brows. "They've always had the Temple of Apostles," he said. "The storytellers say that the book of necrotic scriptures was found there."

"The Mahit'Onomicon," Tzarik offered. "So I've heard." His hands faltered in their task and he looked up. He'd only half believed in the book's existence. But the path to Necro'Khan was more than likely mapped out in the book. "Do you think Tarkan has the book?" he asked out loud.

"I'm not sure. Perhaps." Vicdan stood up and went to Sybal's other side, rubbing his hands together for warmth. His fingers no doubt were chilled from the cold emanating off her. "Or that dead bastard read it and taught Tarkan," he offered in reference to Ishmael. "A mistake, considering his own son returned with the knowledge and killed him. Necro'Khans are immortal. Our *friend* Tarkan will outlive us all."

Tzarik watched Vicdan's long fingers in Sybal's hair. He noted the inflection. "Friend?"

He already had an inkling what Vicdan would say. Tarkan wasn't Sharar. Not by a long shot. But Porshains had an ambition for unnatural things. And with their power and the unknown that surrounded them, Tzarik thought once again about exactly what he'd be unleashing on the world for Sybal's sake.

With forced calm, he said, "I've hunted Tarkan before. Should he do anything that may bring something harmful into this world, I will stop him." He began to re-string his runes onto the newer and stronger cord. He motioned for Vicdan to fetch Sybal's as well, so he could replace hers. "Sounds like you know about the rite for the Scriven. How long will it take?"

"Days, perhaps," Vicdan replied, checking his work. He smiled, pleased. "She doesn't need to heal for the scriptures to accept her, but she will need to summon, perform the five spells of necromancy. To make sure it worked."

It sounded like a runing. "And if they don't accept her?"

Vicdan made a dramatic face, moving to sit beside Tzarik. He collapsed next to the Runer with a sigh and looked around as if to make sure no one listened in. Then he pulled a small wooden jug out of his cloak. "Potheen, from Zealmor. The red woman has a cellar full." He took a long drink, winced hard, and handed it to Tzarik with a wild smile.

He'd had plenty of hard liquor before, but was not prepared for the power of the northern drink. His throat burned. When he choked and coughed, the cold air emphasized the searing sensation, only making him cough more. It was not pleasant like the araq he was used to. Unwilling to let it get the better of him, he took another long swallow before handing it back.

"Have you ever seen the runes reject someone?" Vicdan asked, continuing the conversation.

Tzarik nodded.

"I assume it's like that," Vicdan said. "With Runers, it's—what? —hours or days before you know for sure if they accept you?"

"They have to use the sword and carve their runes before they can hunt. After that first hunt, you know." Tzarik nodded, but eyed Vicdan as he took another drink.

"Necromancy is similar," Vicdan said measuredly. "But newly Scriven and newly ascended Apostles are weak. They must partake of their cannibalistic feast to gain strength back. It's perhaps one of the darkest magics."

"You know a lot about necromancy," Tzarik mused.

Vicdan smiled quickly after spilling some of the potheen down his front. He wiped his mouth and chuckled. "I must know things in order to spin a yarn or compose a ballad. Otherwise, I go hungry."

Something in the way he replied made Tzarik scan Vicdan's body, looking for a sign of a lie. The man's smooth, honey skin wasn't marked at all that he could see.

"Tarkan is sacrificing much tomorrow," Vicdan said after a moment. "And so is Zeva. But they both want it. I just wanted to make sure I wasn't the only one who saw that. And when our mutual friend finds out, I'm sure he'll pursue Tarkan all over again."

"You mean Sharar," Tzarik confirmed. "Why? He's on his own path to sorcerer."

Vicdan took another drink and made a small grunt, smiling at the burn. "A sorcerer consumes a djinn, yes? They are the highest level of demon, below only the god that created them. They can do most anything. Except *one* thing." He nudged Tzarik, looking over at him.

The Runer understood. "Raise the dead." He took the bottle from Vicdan, imagining for one moment the power a Necro'Khan and a sorcerer combined could possess. That was why Sharar wanted Tarkan so badly. He halfheartedly raised the bottle before taking a final draft. "Here's to hoping we never see that day."

THE MORNING CAME gray and still for once. At last, no wind ripped through the dry air. A soft dusting of snow clung to the rocky earth, and the air felt stagnant. Tzarik took a long moment, looking down at Sybal before Vicdan finally convinced him to leave.

Outside the stockade, Sjörna-Reks waited with Tarkan, Zeva, with her man Lokhtar in tow. A few citizens from Altevine watched, curious and confused by what their Reks was up to. As Tzarik approached, two dozen or more warriors joined, armed with axes of white or blue steel. He understood, but didn't see it as a threat. He had no intention of trying to escape with Sybal still lying prone in the cell, but he understood Sjörna-Reks's caution.

They said no words to each as they headed out after a brief meal and filling their waterskins at the well. Tzarik walked behind as Sjörna-Reks leapt to the front, transforming into the towering red wolf to lead the way. The journey over the uneven ground stretched on for hours. Tzarik twisted his ankle twice on rocks hidden in the straw-like grass. He slipped on more round ones, rolling off to the side of them and him almost falling. The ground became even more uneven and softer the closer they got to the bogs. Mist fell, green and thick around them.

"Do not follow the wisps," Sjörna-Reks mumbled a few hours later. She'd turned back into her human form.

No sooner had she said this than a soft, small white orb appeared before Tzarik's feet. He stumbled back, unsure what the thing was.

"They will lead you to the kuri," she went on. "You won't know the kuri is feeding off you until it's too late. Nightmares. Visions. Terror. Until you beg it to let you go. The only release is death, creating a new place the kuri can manifest."

The soft orb bobbed around Tzarik's feet, enticing him to follow it. In the mist, with the unsure footing, he thought it might not be the worst decision. It seemed to gesture for him to continue. His eyes drifted over the orb to the very center, the brightest part. Just as he looked, a comfort like none before instantly washed over him. Having hunted and tracked many monsters, he realized immediately what the creature had done and jerked his eyes away. His mind became clear immediately. Looking out, tiny lights dotted the bog here and there, whisking about.

"Not long now," Sjörna-Reks informed them. The marching warriors spread out a little, tramping down a wisp here and there, making the ground more even.

Vicdan jogged up beside Tzarik. "How can she tell we're almost there when we can't see—" He gasped and tripped.

Tzarik watched in mild amusement as the jongleur fell to the watery ground, but his smile stopped when Vicdan screamed. He whirled back around, hand on his scimitar. Vicdan splashed in the mud, trying to push away from something his wide eyes had locked on. Seeing the genuine terror, Tzarik ran back and hauled him up. As he did, round, white things bobbed to the surface. Skulls. Some human, some Masahk.

Vicdan moaned and swatted at a skeleton hand that had stuck to the fibers of the fur cloak. It plunked into the water with a splash and sank to float just beneath the surface. Vicdan clutched Tzarik and looked around.

"So that's what I've been stepping on," he mused.

The Runer focused harder on the earth now, too. What he'd taken for rocks and mounds of earth were dead bodies. Just below the green mist, every lump and fissure, every branch he'd snapped in the long march, was a corpse. Allowing Vicdan to shrink close, Tzarik followed the Reks deeper into the mist.

"I cannot abide corpses," Vicdan moaned. "I'd make a terrible necromancer."

At long last, they came upon more steady ground. A half circle of megaliths rose towards the sky surrounding a place of sacrifice. A raised stone platform sat in the center. Years of blood sacrifice had painted it black. Sjörna-Reks stood aside and motioned for Tarkan and Zeva to proceed.

"Tzarik, I need your hands," Tarkan said flatly.

The Runer joined them on the stone. Tarkan held a black chest, not unlike that which Tzarik carried with him at all times. Tarkan set it down and took out a vial of ash. He motioned for Tzarik to stand back and then poured it in a circle, mumbling some verse from his scriptures. Zeva stood in the center. Tzarik watched her as Tarkan cast the circle. She didn't shake. Her stoic face showed no fear. He reminded himself they weren't doing this just for him and Sybal; *they* wanted this.

"Lie down, Zeva," Tarkan instructed.

The girl did as she was told, laying down her fur cloak first so it was between her and the cold stone. When she was on her back, she unlaced her dress. Without hesitation, she slipped her slender, bronze arms out and then threw open her skirts to bare her body to the sky above. Tzarik looked away, but Tarkan took his arm, guiding it to Zeva.

"If she moves, hold her down," he instructed. He knelt, opening the black chest. Inside were bottles of black ink and a ruby blade. Tarkan cut open his wrist with the blade, making Tzarik wince. Twisting his own arm around, Tarkan closed his mouth over the wound and drank.

A little repulsed, Tzarik concentrated on making his face as placid as he could. He'd supposed necromancers used blood for their magic, but he'd never witnessed it. As he drank, Tarkan's eyes filled with red until his blue eyes vanished altogether behind the red glow. He dropped his arm, his bloody teeth gnashing as he growled the next verse. Tzarik recognized it as an ancient dialect of Porshain, but only knew every other word or so.

Empowered by his own blood, Tarkan moved over Zeva now. "The first script," he said softly, "will lock the oath to you."

"I understand," Zeva whispered back.

The air around them grew darker, like an early night fell. Tzarik glanced up just as Tarkan's ruby knife flashed. Quick as a cat, the necromancer stabbed Zeva's chest. The girl jerked under his palms and Tzarik pressed down onto her shoulders, holding her in place as Tarkan opened her body.

A horrible memory shot to the forefront of his mind. A time on

Bahratt in one of their black temples. He couldn't remember if he'd been fourteen or fifteen. He'd been on the altar then, a knife in his chest. Nefiri, the magi, had stood over him. He'd begged for Azar to come and save him.

Shoving the painful memory aside, he focused on Zeva's screams. She writhed under his palms, eyes shut tight. Finally, she gasped and closed her mouth. Something hot and wet spilled onto his fingers where he held her. Looking down, he saw her bright red blood splattering her body. So much of her blood leaked out that it brightened the swooping, swirling designs of the stone all around them. The fur cloak was drenched in it. That was when he noticed what Tarkan was doing.

The necromancer's hands plunged into her open chest. Not for the first time in his life, but for sure the most staggering, Tzarik beheld a beating heart. Deftly, Tarkan—eyes wide and flesh pale—delicately carved the necrotic scripture onto Zeva's beating heart with black ink on the ruby blade. He was so engrossed in the grotesque rite that he didn't notice when Zeva stopped screaming, going still.

Above them, a streak of green lightning cracked the sky.

"The barrier is thinning," Sjörna-Reks's voice shouted from somewhere outside the ashen circle. "Can you see it?"

Tzarik realized he couldn't see beyond the circle now. Black fog and a soundless wind cut them off from the others.

"Tzarik," Tarkan ordered. "Heal her."

Grabbing artiah, Tzarik drew it over Zeva's heart as slowly as he could. The ink set in, sealed behind a thin layer of membrane. A black tattoo formed in the shape of the script.

Tarkan closed her up deftly, growling the incantation through his strained throat. Tzarik heard the emotion choking Tarkan. He couldn't imagine the hope, agony, and desperation the necromancer felt at inflicting such wounds on the young woman he'd raised and loved. The white light from artiah ignited the dark space. Zeva's flesh mended. Not flawlessly, but quickly.

"Is that it?" Tzarik asked, hating the mysterious black shroud that hid them.

Tarkan glared up at him, unshed red tears brightening his eyes. "No."

Starting with her face, he began the long string of verses that would soon cover her entire body in black ink. Zeva moaned and tears freely flowed down into her hair as Tarkan carved the spidery scriptures into her tender skin. Every minute or so, he dumped some of the black ink—which carried a rotting scent—into his hand and wiped it over the scars, filling them. He made two or three passes, repeating the section he'd inked in. Tzarik moved to draw artiah behind him, but Tarkan stayed his hand.

"I cannot risk it," he mumbled. "Let them take to her flesh as they will." His hand shook so badly the red knife slipped out of his bloody fingers.

Tzarik retrieved it, handing it back. He forced his own hand to remain steady as he offered the knife to Tarkan. "Finish it," he said when the necromancer hesitated. He shoved the blade at Tarkan. "She won't die." He wished harder than ever that Sybal was with them. They needed her tender, feminine nature. Zeva wouldn't feel as alone. They'd had many of the same experiences. Yes, he and Tarkan had experienced the same thing. The same pain. Agony. Fear. And they'd done it alone. Sybal was still kind and caring; she'd be able to ease Zeva's torment in a way none of them had experienced. But instead, she would go alone as they had.

The necromancer went back to his task, hissing between the pauses in the verses, begging his gods to see him. To accept his gift to them.

As Tarkan kept going, elegantly slicing at Zeva's sides, inscribing the necrotic scriptures onto every inch of her body, something made the top of Tzarik's head tingle. The sulfates pulled his eyes up. He wasn't sure, but they told him eyes above, from another place, watched them. Great black and blue eyes as wide as the sky. The entity seemed pleased.

Soon, he lost track of time. His hands crusted over with Zeva's blood and he became deaf to her sporadic cries of pain and moans of agony. By the time Tarkan shouted and stood up, her blood covered the entire slate of stone they stood upon. Tzarik didn't notice the black shroud dissipate. The eyes of the Reks, Vicdan, and the warriors all fell on the three who had performed the rite. Tzarik quickly wrapped Zeva in the fur cloak to cover her naked, bloody body. He folded the end over her toes, which also bore the scriptures, black and bleeding. That was when he spotted Tarkan.

The necromancer lay in a heap on his back, lips parted, cheeks sunken; he wasn't breathing. Tzarik scrambled over the ritual stone to check his vitals. Of course, his heart did not beat, so Tzarik checked his breathing. The slightest rasping gasp issued up from Tarkan's dry throat.

"Blood," Sjörna-Reks called, whirling around to Lokhtar. "He's consumed his own for the ritual. Fool." She pointed to Vicdan.

"Wait," Vicdan started, but three towering warriors gripped him and cut his forearm, filling a goblet.

Tzarik understood as Lokhtar handed him the vessel, but couldn't help the repulsion he felt. Lifting Tarkan with one arm, he tipped the steaming blood between his lips. Having seen a lot of blood and violence in his time, Tzarik decided necrotic magic disgusted him.

THEY MADE a camp outside the bog a few hours later, since it was too dangerous to travel back in the dark. Tzarik didn't speak, but allowed Vicdan to hover close by. He had been silent and in a foul mood since the bloodletting. Tarkan came back to consciousness and sat in silence apart from Zeva. Sjörna-Reks leapt away from the camp with Lokhtar to hunt. Even upon her return, she maintained camp silence.

The embers of the campfires smoldered in the late evening when a soft coo woke Tzarik. Above him, the moon caught his eye. It was a crescent, but another crescent glowed beneath it, like a reflection in a lake. Back-to-back, the two moons made him uneasy. But the soft breath to his left roused him to what had originally woken him. Zeva stirred. He took up a waterskin and went to her. She lay on her side near one of the campfires.

Making sure she saw him approach to not startle her, he knelt next to her and helped her sit up. She winced, and he even heard her scabbing scriptures crackle under the cloak. Her hands shook too much, and her wounds were too tight for her to grip the skin, so Tzarik helped her drink.

"Thank you," she mumbled hoarsely, swallowing loudly.

"How are you feeling?" he asked, not sure what a newly Scriven necromancer might feel.

She sighed and pressed her hand to her chest. "Everything hurts. Even my insides." She blinked. Her eyes had already turned from a deep, warm brown to a glowing, pale blue.

"Looks like your scriptures have accepted you," he mused. "That might be the swiftest a black oath has taken a soul. Vicdan said it might take days."

Zeva sighed and looked up at him. Her pale eyes shone through the scabs, blood, and black ink hardening on her skin. Her hand gently moved over her face. Beneath her new scriptures, the marring from years of torture were hardly noticeable. "I was marked long ago. This will replace those scars. And you needed it," she whispered, eyes flicking to Tarkan and back. "He's waiting to see if his heart will beat. If it does, he has not been chosen as Necro'Khan." She spread her Scriven fingers, inspecting the markings. "Then he will have to make an Apostle. But that's what I want. The long life. With him."

Curious at their bond, Tzarik asked, "How do you revere him so?"

A shy smile pulled at the black cracks on her cheeks. "You know the necromancer. The user of black magic, the raiser of the dead. The wounded man whose father forced him into this darkness. I know the man beneath that shroud." She adjusted to scoot closer to Tzarik to speak more softly. "I was terrified of him when he first took me away. I thought I was going home. I saw my brother. My mother. Then he gathered me up in his black robes and whisked me away with an army of undead. He took me to obey the covenant, but loved me. He took care of me, sang to me in the night."

Tzarik snapped his head up at this, almost not believing her.

She giggled lightly at his sudden shock. "He's made sure I have never not felt loved. Valued. Safe."

"Except for Sharar?"

"A mistake," she quipped, frowning slightly now. "We suffered together at his hand, bringing us even closer. Trust me, Runer. I wanted this for so long. And it's for him as well. He craves the mantle of Necro'Khan fiercely. I can help him achieve that."

"I worry what that power might do to him," Tzarik offered guardedly.

"You don't understand him." She took another drink of water.

"I understand *you*, Zeva," he said. "Before Sybal, I would have done anything to take back my life before the runes. But it brought us together. The runes gave her to me. I'd not trade it for anything."

She smiled and reached out to touch his arm. "As a Scriven, I can summon a spirit. Help me to stand. I want to try."

As gently as he could, Tzarik lifted her onto her sore feet. She leaned heavily into him. Her blood loss had been significant; she felt weak, frail, and tiny in his arms.

"Don't you need blood to cast your spells?" he asked. He remembered Vicdan saying a newly Sriven would be weak. But he couldn't see Zeva eating sentient flesh or drinking red blood.

"Your blood won't do," she said playfully. "I want to test my new black blood. The spell will take it from my body. I'll be fine," she added forcefully. "Just keep me standing upright."

Zeva slowly pressed her palms close, but not together. She focused her eyes on the space between them and whispered a verse. The quotes from the necrotic scriptures sounded like breathy hissing to Tzarik until they vanished into silence. Beneath his fingers, he felt her muscles tighten.

"Let me see," she whispered as she finished the quote. "Just one spirit."

"I don't see anything," Tzarik whispered.

"You won't," she hissed. "Only I will see—" She gasped, cutting off her last words. "I see you!"

She quaked in his grip, so he held her tighter, pulling her against himself to steady her. He'd expected her magic to be weak, but the world of the dead came to her.

"Who are you?" she called, her eyes wide.

Tzarik readied himself for anything. He could draw atan and force the spirit into view, but he held himself back.

"I know of you," Zeva said to the ghost he could not see. "I've heard your na..." Her voice trailed off again, a tear leaked from blue eyes, and she gasped. Her focus flicked from whichever spirit she'd called up to something beyond it.

Frustrated, Tzarik grabbed his runes in his right hand and readied halat. "What is it, Zeva?"

"I see her!" Zeva shouted, lunging out of his grip, her hand shooting out to grasp something. "Sybal!" she screamed.

CHAPTER 18

APÖSTLE

Tarkan lay listening to Zeva speak. He didn't hear her words as every ounce of his effort focused inwards, listening for his heart. Waiting for the beat it drummed every so often filled him with impatience. He wanted to watch her, make sure she was all right, but he had to wait. She spoke with Tzarik, which brought him some solace.

Perhaps it had worked? He'd thought he'd be able to feel the weight of the red diamond in his chest. *You wanted her,* he growled to his god. *She's yours now. Give me what is owed!* A thrill of displeasure shot through him.

His heart beat. Never had it drummed so loud in his head as that single beat. With a cry of rage, Tarkan sat up and gripped his face as he shouted. He'd not been chosen as Necro'Khan. He shrieked a curse to the sky. The power slipped through his fingers.

"Sybal!" Zeva shouted.

He shot up to standing. Zeva teetered on her feet, reaching out, then bent backwards in a graceful arch and collapsed. Tzarik dipped, catching her, and eased her to the ground. Tarkan ran to her, the rest of the camp stirring around them.

"What was she doing?" he growled at the Runer.

"Conjuring a ghost," he replied.

A light layer of sweat shone on the Runer's brow in the strange light from the moons above.

"Did she?" Tarkan asked. Zeva was not eight hours Scriven. She should be in too much pain to summon. "She couldn't have," he tried again. "What did she see?"

Tzarik half shrugged with one shoulder, shaking. "I'm not sure. Someone she knew, and then she called Sybal's name."

Sjörna-Reks appeared, leaping out of her wolf form. She also had turned pale and pressed a hand to her heart. "I felt it," she wheezed. "She reached out, called up a spirit." She winced. "Was it him? Did she see Kjarton?"

Tarkan didn't know. He pressed his hand to Zeva's ribs and felt her heart fluttering dangerously in panic. "She's so weak, like something is taking her strength." He took her hand. The scabs on her fingers crackled under his. He'd never seen a Scriven summon so quickly. Almost like the scriptures had been waiting for her, hungry to give her their power.

"Despite the struggle, it appears that the scriptures have taken to her," Tzarik said, trying to bring comfort. "She was able to cast. She won't die in agony. She needs time to heal, to gain her strength."

Sjörna-Reks whipped her head around. All around them, bugling calls went up from wild creatures. "Vasaras is preparing to wane. We don't have time before the gods come back. Necromancer," she snarled to Tarkan. "Is it done?"

Tarkan's unbeating heart fell. A sense of fear at the confession almost stopped him. "No. I am not Necro'Khan. My heart is still flesh."

The Reks's emerald eyes flared in rage. Tarkan thought she might shift into her red wolf form and snap his neck in her fangs. Without that power, his fragile body was still at her mercy.

Zeva weakly raised her hand, shocking all three of them. They'd thought she had passed out. "Do it, Tarkan," she whispered. "You knew it from the start. Make me an Apostle. Break the script. Make the covenant scar upon my heart."

"I can't." He clenched his hands tightly. "I need blood. I cannot cast if I do not consume."

Sjörna-Reks looked around at her warriors. "I have blood, necromancer. Do it now."

As if to prove he could, Zeva sat up with a strained grunt, glaring at the Reks. She struggled. She was in pain, yes, but something else sapped her strength. Her blue eyes bore into Tarkan from her bloody face.

"Do it," she hissed. "We've come this far. Look at my eyes. The scriptures have accepted me already. You will not lose me." She reached up to Tzarik, who helped her to her feet. "I saw her, Tarkan. I saw Sybal. She's here." Her eyes flicked to Sjörna-Reks, full of conviction. "I saw Kjarton. I called him up to see if I could find him." To Tarkan she said, "It's as simple as a stab." She pulled her white—now bloody and blackened—dress down to expose the top of her chest. "I will live through it. I know it. I feel the necromancy in me. It won't take me."

The way she glared at him hurt somehow, as if the scriving rite had not just killed her innocence, but had killed the daughter he'd known. Had it changed her that much already?

"Well?" Sjörna-Reks shouted into the cold night. "Hunters are moving in. The sun will rise in an hour or so. Will you do this now?"

Tarkan hesitated.

"I am exhausted with your hesitation, little necromancer," Sjörna-Reks murmured dangerously. Her unblinking eyes never left his. She raised her left hand. With a metallic groan, her massive sword flew into her hand. "Enough with you, girl. He will give the souls I have prepared. You have failed him."

"Wait!" Zeva called, eyes wide. She ran back to Tarkan's pack and pulled out the black chest again, lifting the ruby blade from within.

"Tarkan, do it!" she screamed.

ONCE AGAIN, kneeling over her on the sacrificial stone, Tarkan mumbled prayers to his god. He begged like he never had before. *If you accept her, let her live,* he prayed in his mind. *I'm giving you all I have. The only thing I've ever loved. My one reason for living.* He hoped it pleased the gods that watched on.

Three chalices of blood let from the Reks's soldiers waited beside him. He hissed the first verse and then drank a chalice for strength. Zeva lay beneath him, face full of faith. She had no doubt.

"Never will the gods accept one flesh sacrifice," he hissed between chanting.

"They will," Zeva promised him, her face stony. "Have faith."

Holding the ruby knife over her, he whispered, and the scriptures on his hand wiggled and moved as he quoted each one. The stale wind that accompanied every necrotic spell picked up and pushed the onlookers back. He downed the second chalice of blood and a rush of hot magic surged through him. He had to stop himself from begging, "Do not take her from me," when he was, in fact, giving her to the black oath. She closed her eyes, mumbling her own prayer as he finished the third verse. He threw back the last chalice as the rite sapped his power, taking the blood from his body and sending it to his dark gods.

"Are you ready?" he asked. His hand shook.

Zeva finished her prayer and opened her eyes. "I am ready. Break my Scriven heart and unlock the powers of our pact."

Screaming for the gods to have mercy on him and Zeva, he stood up on his knees, raised the knife, and brought it down into her heart. Zeva only gasped hoarsely, arching her back in agony as the ruby blade sank into her sore muscle. He knew beyond a doubt that he'd hit the black mark on her heart, breaking it. Piercing the rune that locked the powers of every other mark on her body would open them up, giving her all the power they held. The wound from the ruby blade would form the covenant scar: the only thing that could kill a necromancer was breaking that scar, a perfect stab to the heart. Tarkan had seen many necromancers in his time die with an orichalcum blade in their heart. He'd once feared for his own scar, when Sybal had plunged her dagger into his chest over and over again.

As he held the blade in his daughter's chest, he remembered Ishmael performing this rite beneath their family home in the crypt. Tarkan had lain on an altar made of bone and blood: Ishmael's sacrifices to the necrotic gods. He'd hoped then that his gods would not want him, and that the blade in his heart would take his life. Ishmael had promised to spare his brother if Tarkan submitted to the rite. As he lay upon the gruesome altar, he'd spotted his brother's face among those beneath him. His chest had been bloodied. Ishmael had lied and tried to make an Apostle of his brother. The scriptures had denied him.

With a cry of rage and anguish, he pulled the blade from Zeva's chest, pressed his hands over the wound, and screamed a prayer into the black void. His unbeating heart ached so much he thought his own chest would rupture, splitting open from the pain. He saw Zeva as a girl, just five years old when he'd taken her from Moshav. He comforted himself with the memory of the first time she'd come to him for comfort. She'd had a nightmare that night. He'd heard stories of children needing compassion after a nightmare, but had never dreamed he'd experience it. He hadn't known what to do, but had been struck mute when she'd curled into his arms for safety. In that moment, he'd known he never wanted to let her go. She was too precious for his way of life, but he couldn't give her up.

Tarkan collapsed onto Zeva's bloody, scarred body. He embraced her tightly, remembering the small girl who'd come to him. She'd been so tiny, so beautiful. She still was. He pressed his forehead to hers, their matching marks of the star Mirzam touching. He wanted to be powerful enough to protect her forever.

Lying over her prone and still figure, Tarkan barely notice Tzarik lift him aside to draw the healing rune over Zeva.

"Wait," the necromancer said weakly, staying the Runer's hand. "We cannot cheat the healing." He fell to the side, weak from performing rite after rite. Tzarik caught him as he tipped backwards.

"When will we know if it worked?" Tzarik asked. His voice came muffled to Tarkan's ears.

"Runer," Tarkan moaned. He gripped the tops of his robes and started to pull them open. The cold air on his exposed flesh made him shake and shiver. "My heart will turn to red diamond if the rite was successful." He pressed the ruby blade into Tzarik's hand.

"I'm not—" Tzarik began, but Tarkan cut him off.

"We have no time!" His head, heavy though it was, turned to the west. "The sun will weaken the magic. I need to know now! I am not fragile. I will not bear this frailty any longer." He shoved Tzarik away and lay on his back. "If I am Necro'Khan, you have nothing to fear. You cannot kill me or break my covenant scar. My heart will be solid. It will only turn to flesh outside the cage of scriptures."

Vicdan appeared beside Tzarik. "Outside his body," he cleared up more for himself than the others. "That's why we found Ishmael the way we did."

Tarkan was half glad to see the jongleur appear. "You've stitched up my scriptures once before. Can you do it again?"

Vicdan nodded.

"Runer," Tarkan ordered Tzarik now. "Stop delaying."

Finally, Tzarik took the ruby blade and knelt over Tarkan. He motioned for Vicdan to hold him down. "This is too much blood in one night for my liking," Tzarik mumbled, slowly pressing the blade into Tarkan's chest.

"Damn it, Runer, I'm not made of glass." The slow puncturing hurt more than if Tzarik had just savagely ripped his chest open. He pressed his head into the stone as Tzarik finished cutting an opening over his heart. To his delight, his heart did not beat in panic.

Tzarik stammered something about not being able to see well.

"Put your hand beneath my ribs," Tarkan ordered. His eyes watered and streamed down his temples. He actually felt the cold wind on his lungs. "I can bear it." He would not let the pain stop him.

At last, not hesitating, Tzarik bit his glove between his teeth and pulled his long-fingered hand out. The pure torture that was the Runer's hand diving beneath his ribs was enough to rip a scream of agony from his throat. Vicdan's hands pushed hard on him, steadying him. Bloody bile rose in Tarkan's throat from the pain.

Forcing his eyes open, streaming though they were, Tarkan watched Tzarik's face above him. The Runer glared in concentration, his blue eyes dancing back and forth, hunting for what he sought. When Sybal had sprung at him two years ago in the tunnels, savagely stabbing him, he'd feared she'd sever his covenant scar. That, and the fear of forcing him to become an oath breaker, more than the fear of death, had scared him then.

A sniffle from his side made him pull away from Tzarik's face for just a moment. Zeva cried, watching him. Both of them lay on their backs, eyes meeting as the sky started to burn purple. She was alive. She looked stronger than he'd expected.

"Z-Zeva," he gasped.

She smiled, but her breath came shallowly.

"I feel it," Tzarik said at long last. "It's not beating."

"Take it in your hand," Tarkan choked.

Tarkan nearly fainted when the Runer wrapped his fingers around his heart and squeezed gently. The pain came from his open chest wound. Not his heart. He felt...nothing.

Tzarik's blue eyes widened, meeting Tarkan's.

Despite the pain, Tarkan suddenly knew no matter how much blood he lost, no matter how many blades pierced him—nothing could kill him. The realization dawned and shot a thrill through his limbs. Despite the agonizing pain, he'd live forever. The sky was doused in red as the sun finally rose, spilling crimson over the mountaintops.

Tarkan shoved Tzarik's hand out of his chest and motioned for Vicdan to stitch him up. He took in Tzarik's confused and slightly frightened visage as Vicdan went to work quickly. The younger man's lithe fingers expertly laid his flesh together and made the black markings meet.

"Take comfort, Tzarik," Tarkan whispered, all fear leaving him like breath on glass. "It is done."

He turned his head to face Zeva where she lay. Nothing could hurt them anymore. No one would dare. As far as he knew—until Sharar became a sorcerer—he was the strongest being on the map. Stronger, since even the power of a djinn could not raise the dead, or open the Deep and reach out to the gods' magic with his own bare hands. He was immortal now, like the Masahk. He'd overtaken his father.

Sjörna-Reks ran up to them, mouth agape. "Gods," she cursed softly.

For one moment, Tarkan thought about running away when she appeared. He had finally gained his power and need not bend a knee to anyone, let alone a foreign Reks. But he'd promised her. And the scriptures on his flesh warned about breaking even simple pacts with mortal beings. But it mattered little. He wanted to rip open a doorway to the Deep, prove his power to himself. If he had to submit to Sjörna-Reks for a few more days, he'd do it.

Tzarik drew the healing rune twice over Tarkan's chest. Grateful, Tarkan sat up and wrapped himself in the fur cloaks. His mind reeled with possibilities. He was still a weak body that could be physically overcome and shackled down. Necromancers often worked at a distance, raising their dead and guarding themselves that way. He'd not had that opportunity yet. So, he resigned himself to remain with

Sjörna-Reks and do as she wished. He'd fulfill his promise to her. She still needed him. She wouldn't try to harm him now, surely. But he wanted to be ready. He needed an escape. He had Tzarik, and the Runer was a strong brute, but he didn't know if the Runer would risk his own safety to run away. Not until they had Sybal, anyway.

"I never thought of you as frail, Tarkan," Tzarik murmured. "You brought Ala'Nar to its knees in a single day."

The reminder had a hint of admonition to it. He'd had an undead army then. And had not been physically shackled to Sharar.

"And I paid dearly for that," he replied darkly. "Never again." He was sure of his power now.

CHAPTER 19

THE BLÖÖD PATH

Tarkan's body shook with weakness when the thronehall at the base of the mountain range came back into view. Zeva slept on the flat of an open wagon, her skin scabbing over. The desire to rend himself from the walking mass and flee to test his new powers burned his insides. He even felt the weight of his new, hardened heart in his chest. But he saw his sorry state when he reached down to stroke Zeva's sleeping head. His bones shone through his pale, tight skin. The black veins crawled over his lean muscles and sinews like spider webs. He'd used up too much of his own blood. His legs shook, threatening to collapse if he did not rest. Zeva no doubt felt the same. Her lips parted in sleep, gasping for air. Underneath the necrotic scriptures and the fresh scars forming, the marks Sharar had left on her body had almost vanished.

As if understanding, Sjörna-Reks had her man Lokhtar usher Tarkan into a side room of the thronehall. Lokhtar carried Zeva in, laying her on the crude bed inside. A single, tiny brazier and a square window covered in wooden slats were the only other things in the room. Tarkan didn't fight and lay next to Zeva, exhaustion crushing his weak bones. He noted Tzarik and Vicdan were taken back to the stockade without too much fight. Closing his eyes, he drifted into a waking dream for just a moment before the woolen curtain over the doorway pushed open. Sjörna-Reks entered with a wooden pitcher in one hand, a goblet in the other. Her tall frame almost touched the ceiling in the small side room; she had removed her crown of antlers.

"Blood," she whispered, holding the containers out towards him. "To regain your strength. Unless you'd prefer flesh?"

Tarkan sat up and took the items, pouring himself a full goblet. He eyed the red, hot liquid. "Living?"

She nodded, watching him with wild green eyes. "Drink while she sleeps." She flicked her head towards Zeva.

He drank it down. It hit his stomach like sweet, hot, mulled wine. He chose all too often to drain his own blood for his spell work. The bit of blood Sjörna-Reks had forced Vicdan to give had long since been burned away by the rite. The more powerful magic would demand more flesh, more blood, than he'd ever consumed. Others of his tribe usually took blood from living sacrifices before performing a spell, to save their strength and spare their own blood. If the blood came from the dead, taking it in—behind the protective flesh wall of the scriptures—could open a necromancer to possession by the dead spirit.

"Consuming flesh is much more powerful," he noted when Sjörna-Reks didn't leave. He moved to pour the last of the blood into the goblet when her eyes didn't waver from him.

"You need your strength," she reasoned in her soft, gentle tone. "I have prisoners. Anything you need."

Tarkan's eyes flitted to Zeva. "I'll need three sentients for the Blood Path," he said at length. "Animals won't do this time. I'll take no chances."

Sjörna-Reks nodded, making a mental note. "Living?"

It would be stronger, but Zeva would die of anguish if he sacrificed three lives to walk the Blood Path. "Dead will do. Still stronger than animals. They need to be severed inside the ashen circle for the ritual."

She knelt before him. Even kneeling, she came to eye level with him where he sat on the bed upon the floor. She reached out and touched his shoulder, using her thumb to caress the bare part of his neck.

Confused, and a little shaken, Tarkan froze as she touched him. Flexing his left hand, he felt for any dead he might raise should she mean him harm. Even this small gesture brought a fresh wave of fatigue.

"Altevine is weak," she whispered. "I am weak. No Reks at my side. No legitimate heir." Her forest-green eyes latched onto his face when she said this. "Northica took Kjarton from me when Signar was born. He's a wildling. He cannot rule as Reks. Altevine is vulnerable."

She leaned forward, coming a few inches closer to Tarkan. He fought to not lean away from her.

"If you cannot bring back my Kjarton..." She dropped her eyes, inclining her head towards him. Her hand slowly traveled up to his face, where she sensually rubbed her thumb over his thin, pale lips.

The black blood rushed in his veins. His hand fumbled behind him until he found Zeva's hand and gripped it.

"I cannot give you what you want," he said hoarsely.

Sjörna-Reks stopped her advances and frowned, curious. "But you're Necro'Khan. You can find a way."

Tarkan shook his head, wishing she'd leave. She knew he was weak. That was why she came to him like this now. "That is why, when entering a blood pact, necromancers often invoke the law of sacrifice. To gain apprentices."

"Stealing children for your own," she said as if correcting him. The Reks's green eyes finally left his face and bored into Zeva behind him. She inhaled deeply, the tip of her nose almost touching his sunken cheek. She sighed. "I've seen one," she whispered, like a warning. "The spawn of a black oath. Runer or necromancer, it's the same. They call it a drekavac—fiendling."

"They're not sentient," Tarkan tried again. Her breath smelled like mead and her heavy lids confirmed she'd been drinking. "It cannot be your heir. They're monsters."

She sighed again, gripping the back of his neck like she might force him into a kiss, but she didn't. Shaking her head, disappointed, she stood up. Now she looked down on him with a kind of disdain. "Rest. You send that Runer into the Deep as soon as possible. Once he has his woman, you *will* go in again, as promised." She glared at Zeva. "You will. And you will bring me Kjarton."

He had no intention of reneging on his deal with her. But her threats fell on listening ears. Her fervor told him now would not be the time to remind her that bringing back a dead soul would not unfold as she imagined. What was given to the gods must always go back to the gods. They'd come for what would be stolen from their very doorstep.

"I need a living body," he replied softly. "His soul will be loose, free. A specter on this side."

Sjörna-Reks smirked, stopping in the doorway. "Fear not, my Necro'Khan. I will provide all you need to return my love to me."

$$\partial$$

Two days later, Sjörna-Reks brought three dead thralls out to the open space between her thronehall and the stockade, out of sight of most of her clan. Mostly rested and warm with living blood, Tarkan cast a circle of ash while Sjörna's men prepared the Blood Path. He drew it wide while the cries of a few onlooking thralls and warriors filled the gray skies around them. Cutting a man in two took muscle, sweat, and time. Each time the blade stuck in the bone, it made a terrible screeching sound. Tarkan steeled his heart against their agony.

As the blood of the thralls bathed the earth, a crowd gathered. "Stay back!" Sjörna-Reks commanded the growing audience. "Kjarton-Reks shall soon be among you again. I beg you not to impede me."

A herd of her warriors with their axes and long braids surrounded the ashen circle, staving off the commoners. Tarkan noted a few Runers among them. He glanced towards the stockade. Afraid Tzarik might interfere while the Blood Path victims were being prepared, he'd asked Sjörna-Reks to keep him and Sybal inside. Zeva still slept and he dared not disturb her. He hated when she watched him work.

At long last, the three victims were hewn in half, tied to stakes the size of tree trunks on either side of the circle. Each half of a sacrifice stood across from its other half. The blood leaked down, meeting in the middle. Every few seconds, a bloody organ or long intestine wetly plunked to the ground from the divided sacrifices. This made a grotesque corridor for Tarkan and Tzarik to walk as he opened the Deep.

Sjörna-Reks looked to Tarkan as he positioned himself in the center of the Path. He nodded to her, and she signaled Lokhtar to retrieve the Runer. Two others followed him to haul out the black box in which Sybal lay.

Tzarik stepped out first. His steps faltered, and his face paled when he beheld the gratuitous sight.

"This is how it's done," Tarkan said to him. He held his hand out, beckoning Tzarik to join him. Now was not the time for the Runer to succumb to his ever-growing conscience and be repulsed. After the encounter the other night, Tarkan wasn't sure what Sjörna-Reks might do if he failed this test. The smell of her breath still lingered in his nostrils. And for himself, he wanted to know if he could do it. Could he bear the powers of a Necro'Khan, or would they destroy him?

Lokhtar shoved Tzarik into the middle of the Blood Path. Tarkan faced him.

"Amidst this blood, you must swear to find and pull out the soul of only Sybal." He motioned to the two halves of the hewn men on the stakes. "Lest this be your punishment."

Tzarik's eyes darted to the halves of the dead men, taking in their tumbling bowels and loose bones. "Consider it an oath," he mumbled.

Tarkan saw clearly the Runer's hesitation, but appreciated his quick reply. This was not something he'd ever forget. "Tzarik," Tarkan said, holding his own palms close together, preparing to invoke the scriptures, "do not harbor any guilt for this rite. She was taken from you and will return. You are blameless." He watched the Runer's face for a reply. Tzarik's blue eyes still winced with uncertainty.

Taking his silence as submission, Tarkan hissed the first few words of the incantation before his words slipped into quietness. Long ago, like all Apostles, he'd memorized every verse but had never spoken all of them. Especially this rite. The words came easily. As he chanted, the black markings on his flesh crawled and moved as each one was spoken. A white haze converged over his vision, turning his eyes white as well. Behind him, Tzarik took a stumbling step back. The wind picked up around Tarkan, pushing his long black robes with whips and snaps.

Something shifted in the air around him. Far more easily than on Al'Myrah, the barrier appeared between his hands. What they'd said about Caerwren was true: the world of the gods was closer here, the barrier thinner. He reached it before he'd even finished the verses, literally feeling it on the tips of his fingers.

It appeared before him, a glowing, black doorway waiting to be pried open. He moaned as, suddenly, almost every ounce of his strength got sucked into the Deep when his fingers touched the opening. The blood from the hewn sacrifices rose off the ground and flowed into him. Panting, he felt for the fracture and gripped it. Shouting the last of the verses into the silence, he screamed, pulling open the void.

The expanse of the God Deep sprawled out before him. The structure of Altevine vanished, opening into an abyss filled with wavering spirits. Ghosts of the dead merely hovered, long rotted away even in the Deep. Despite it being a metaphysical barrier, his arms shook and his body screamed in the effort to keep the fracture open. The magic pulled the blood from his body, streaming in elegant ribbons into the Deep. His very life fed the magic. If he'd been mortal, surely this would have killed him. He needed that undead, hard heart of the Necro'Khan to open the Deep. The power overwhelmed him. The weakness brought agony he'd never experienced before. If only he'd consumed living flesh...

"Tzarik, go!" he shouted, unaware of what the scene must look like to those watching.

Reaching back behind him, he touched the Runer's chest. Tzarik's soul rushed through him, pulled by the blood magic and into the fracture. Just as the Runer's spirit entered the Deep, a terrifying feeling consumed Tarkan, like a tendril reached out to him. The lithe limb wrapped around his middle and tugged, trying to pull him into the Deep. Panic threw him backwards away from the grasping limb, his hands slipping out of the fracture. He fell to the ground, splashing into the mud and blood.

The physical world around him came back into focus as he landed hard, completely spent. He panted, unable to get a good breath into his lungs. Before him, Tzarik's body teetered and fell as well. Vicdan appeared, catching the unconscious Runer as his soulless body collapsed.

Tarkan glared into the air before them. Everything had vanished.

"Incredible," Sjörna-Reks mused breathlessly.

Tarkan whipped his head around to look at Tzarik where he lay in Vicdan's arms. It had worked. The Deep had pulled the Runer's soul into its dark world.

"How will they come back?" Vicdan cried, looking around.

Tarkan wasn't sure. "The Deep may push Tzarik out. He's a living soul, not given." He hardly had the strength to speak. His head lulled back into the mud. He couldn't worry about the Runers right now. The ritual had drained him, sapped his strength. Why? He'd expected immense strength to course through him, to be able to throw off every shackle. Fear seeped into his body along with the cold from the muddy earth. He wasn't physically strong. Why had he expected it to change him like that? Was he not Necro'Khan? What did that mantle mean if not imminent power?

Had he made a grave mistake?

Lying in the cold mud made of blood, Tarkan's troubled mind scorched his nerves.

CHAPTER 20

HÖNÖRING THE TRIAL

SYBAL'S EYES SCANNED THE EMPTY BOG BEFORE HER. THE glow of thousands of sacrificed souls made the water ripple with a soft radiance. Faint moans, sighs, and cries from the dead wafted up on the stale wind. She had to shove aside her disgust for the bog and crouch close to the surface. Something had been tracking her again while she hunted. She wanted to find it before it found her. Being devoured once by the snake god had been enough for her. Bolemesh hadn't spoken to her like other god creatures, but she had no desire to run into the spider goddess again, either.

The moonlight lit up only parts of the tree line and her eyes widened, watching for any movement. Kjarton had told her not to track it down, but she had nothing else to occupy her time. She enjoyed hunting in the Deep, cutting down spectral creatures. And she hated being hunted. She'd slain a pack of wolves the day before, avoiding the snapping and sudden ground lightning along the way. She'd gotten faster, stronger, and smarter. With nothing to emotionally compromise her, she'd become numb to the blood and gore. Gutting a monster in the Deep brought some of that feeling back. Kjarton didn't relish the hunt.

Above her, the moon touched that invisible barrier, making a mirror image of it on another side she could not see. Two crescent moons, back-to-back, looked down at her. The light was so bright, shadows played under the trees. Every trunk deflected the white light back to the moon, making it impossible for her to see the long limbs of the monster.

"The zenith of Vasaras is near," Kjarton had told her before she'd left him a few yards back. "Watch out for lightning."

One such fork of snapping green light tore up to the sky next to her where she crouched. Gasping, she jumped aside as the glowing green tear shot open like thunder and then wove shut again. The air rumbled more around her, thick with thunder. Sometimes the wind shook the branches and blew through her clothes but made no sound.

She ran towards the trees, then froze. A long, white branch or limb stuck out from behind a tall tree. It didn't look to be attached to anything and ran all the way to the ground. Could this be her monster? One of the silent winds picked up and the malignant earth shifted slightly under her feet. Her sulfates ran, screaming for her to dodge to the right. Throwing herself to the ground, a green bolt tore the air where she'd just been standing. She swore a roar and whipping tentacles reached out in a flash from the lightning.

Turning back to the woods, the branch she'd been suspicious of had vanished. "I knew it," she said resolutely into the darkness. Standing up, she marched into the woods, scimitar in hand. It had gotten so cold in the past few days that now her breath came out in puffing, white clouds. She'd never seen that happen before and had almost passed out from hours of blowing into the cold sky for her own amusement. Now she held her breath to hide from the monster.

A branch cracked to her left. Gasping for air, she slammed her back up against a tree trunk. Something high up moaned, soft and melancholy. Using just her eyes, she looked up to see a white wraith floating through the air. Tattered, long robes covered green, gossamer flesh. Its jaw hung open in an internally sad wail, eye sockets black and empty. It meant her no harm, floating among the branches. It was just lost. Confused. Since waking in the God Deep, she'd come across many wandering souls, aching spirits. She wondered if they were the ones who had been here too long.

A terrible, high screech split the air just as the wind shifted soundlessly. The gangly monster she'd been tracking materialized from the green and blue mist behind her. It had a body like a man, except where its shoulder sockets were, the torsos of other men stuck out. One long arm came from these amalgamated bodies, stretching all the way to the ground. The heads on the joint torso lulled from side to side, tongues hanging out where jaws had been fractured open. Their faces contorted in agony, screaming as the thing ran. The dominant head atop the patchwork body was like none she had ever seen before. Its jaw opened like a snake, swallowing up the lost wraith. The wraith cringed away but couldn't dodge the quick, lithe monster.

"What the hell are you?" she shouted in disgust. Sybal had been so enraptured by finally seeing the thing that she'd missed the snapping lightning behind her. The monstrosity looked down at her and roared, spitting ectoplasm all over her. Its roar sounded with every voice from the bodies it was made from.

We are one, it moaned almost like it was about to burst into wails of sorrow. *We are made by god. We are the servant of Mjordir. Our essence is in you, taken by force.* It keened piteously.

When it lunged, she leapt back to swipe and tipped into the rift.

"Shit!" she screamed.

Her body flipped, and she fell faster than if she had simply tumbled over a cliff. The rift closed above her and her body tore asunder. The agony was brief, but one she'd never forget. For a moment, everything went black, then, once again, she was drowning under the earth of the Deep. The squirming blight around her made her skin crawl. She couldn't breathe as she clawed her way to the top. She'd died again.

Bursting through, a hand seized her wrist and pulled her out. Kjarton wrapped his arms around her chest and pulled with all his might. This time, the snakelike entities in the ground wrapped around Sybal's legs, pulling her back under.

"Help me!" she screamed, clinging to Kjarton. The limbs wrenched her back down up to her thighs. They whipped out from the bog like snakes and pulled so hard her hips popped. "Don't let them pull me back under," she begged. She wasn't sure how many times she could die before she just didn't come back, forever buried like the others.

Kjarton reached to her side. "Hold on to me!" he commanded, and she did. He held his hand out to the side and his great sword whooshed into his hand. He hacked at the tentacles. A hissing, squealing sound garbled up from the blighted ground the more he severed.

A soundless wind rushed up Sybal's right side, and a dimple in the earth sucked down. "Duck left!" she called.

With a final, savage hack, Kjarton severed the thickest limb, and they both tumbled to the side as a black and green strike of lightning ripped up from the ground. This time, a heat wave shoved the ashen strands of Sybal's hair out of her face as the two sat entangled in each other's long limbs. Kjarton panted and covered his face from the hot blast.

"Thank you," Sybal breathed, disentangling herself and standing up. She reached down to pull him up.

"I told you not to hunt the mahar'nolreith," he grumbled, pushing his raven braids out of his face. "They're dangerous. One of the amalgamated creations of Mjordir, made in his image. If you want any chance to be found, you cannot keep dying. This is why I do not seek out the monsters. I gain no pleasure in killing. The Deep will be broken this next moon as the gods move between this world and ours."

"Then why have we come to this place of sacrifice?" she asked, trying to keep the accusation out of her voice. She rubbed mud out of her eyes. "You said the barrier was thinnest at places like..." Her voice trailed off and she pointed over his shoulder.

Amidst the bog, hovering just inches above the ground, a white shape appeared. No rift, no wind, just the figure manifesting out of nothing. It was a woman. Sybal took Kjarton's hand and walked towards it. She was not tall, and the closer Sybal got, the more she recognized the traits of an Al'Myrahn on her. Sybal's breath caught and her mouth popped open in awe.

The woman, more of a girl, stood with her palms almost touching, eyes wide and white. Her white garments, made of Al'Myrahn cotton, were covered under a fur cloak. She mumbled something Sybal could not hear. When she got close enough to see her long strands of dark hair, she also saw her skin. Sybal recognized the necrotic scriptures. She knew the ones on Tarkan's skin were black. They shone in glowing white opposition in the Deep.

"A necromancer?" she breathed. She took two rushed steps towards the girl. Familiarity trickled down her spine. She'd seen this girl before.

"Are you sure?" Kjarton asked, coming up alongside her. "I've never... Never seen anything like this in the deep."

Finally, the girl's words cracked through the barrier, first backwards, then coming through normally. "Kjarton?" she called. "I summon you."

Sybal froze, watching with wide eyes. "She knows you. How?"

"Kjarton?" the girl called again. "I am here with Sjörna-Reks and she desires to see you." Then she hissed a few more lines that ran forwards then backwards before they vanished into silence even as she spoke them.

Pulling away from Sybal, Kjarton stepped in front of the girl. Her brows went up and she smiled.

"I see you!" she called, though her white eyes didn't look directly at him. Her voice came muffled, like she spoke through a thick, fur cloak. "Who are you?"

"I am Kjarton-Reks," he replied. Sybal heard his voice crack as he asked the next question. "Where is Sjörna?"

The girl smiled. "I know you! I've heard your name," she said gleefully, like a child who had just turned a trick.

That was when it hit Sybal. "Zeva?" she called, rushing to Kjarton's side. "Zeva, is that you?"

The girl's white eyes flicked to Sybal. "I see her!" she shouted, inclining her head as if to speak to someone behind her. "Sybal!"

Sybal nodded. "Gods!" she swore. "What are you doing on Caerwren? Who is with you?"

But the girl winced and gasped. "I can't...hold...on!"

"Zeva, wait!" Sybal cried, reaching out to the white spirit. The girl gasped and vanished. "No, no!" Sybal screamed into the darkness, her hand still out. "Wait, come back!"

A sudden wail of rage and anguish tore her throat. Her knees gave out and she fell into the bog, screaming a lament to the dark. Kjarton knelt next to her, also shaking, but held her.

"He's here," she screamed. "I know he's here. He's looking for me." She wrapped her arms around Kjarton's neck, howling into his shoulder. Every hardened shell she'd armored herself with melted away the instant she knew Tzarik had come for her. If what Kjarton said was true, he was close on the other side. Maybe even mere inches from where she knelt in the blighted, cold earth.

She'd known that somehow Tzarik would look for her. Somehow, he'd hunt her down. And he had. From outside the Deep, such a thing must have looked impossible. He'd traveled far to the west. He'd sought out Tarkan and Zeva. He'd come looking for her. If only she'd been able to give him a sign that she was here.

Kjarton stroked her ashen hair. "*That* is why I stay close by," he whispered to her. "Perhaps I am foolish for not moving on, giving in to eternal death. But I know she's here. And so I stay, hoping one day something will slip through."

Sybal nodded, sniffling. "Then we stay. He'll find a way in. I know he will."

Kjarton pulled away, looking her in the eye. His face showed his doubt. "It would take someone very powerful to reach into the God Deep *and* get out. Should I leave, I'd be a soul, floating in nothing. A haunt. I would be satisfied in that shape, if only to see Sjörna again. Would you?"

She stood up, scanning the horizon, though she wasn't sure for what. "He'll find a way," she answered.

HE'D HONORED THE TRIAL. When Sybal had first asked for runing to be her punishment for the murder, she'd asked for the Trial of Two. She'd been clever with her request, and had shown the extent of her education. Not many knew about the Trial of Two, but it had bound him to her. Once requested, a Runer had to honor the trial and stay with the newly runed victim until released. Death brought the trial to an end, but Tzarik didn't care. Sybal had demanded the Trial of Two so that he'd stay with her. He would make good on that promise now, no matter where it took him or what he encountered on the way. Death would not stop his promise.

The world tipped around Tzarik until he fell backwards. Just when he expected to hit the ground, everything stood still. The air turned stale. Tarkan's cries faded away and hot lightning shot up from behind him. The world suddenly came into focus. Above him, a blue sun glowed listlessly behind a green fog. Nothing stood around him. The thronehall vanished, leaving only the open prairie, mountains, trees, and the cold air. Soft flakes fell from the gray sky above. The very air around him, the ground, pulsed with a deep, thrumming heartbeat. The horizon swirled and smeared, surreal and blurred. Turning back the way he'd been facing, he shouted into the silence.

When nothing answered back, he reimagined Sjörna's domain. They had traveled for hours to get to the sacrificial land. That was where Zeva had looked into the Deep, searching for Kjarton. Remembering the lay of the land, he found the way he needed to go.

Turning to the west, he took his first step into the God Deep. His boots hit the ground, firm and strong. Then they sunk into a kind of writhing ectoplasmic blight. Something akin to worms and snakes moved in the mud, making it squirm around his soles. Not daring to stand too long should the tendrils choose to pull him under, he picked up his step, marching faster over the open planes.

The runes still hung around his neck and the magic blade still hung at his side. Perhaps the black magic had helped him to cross over into the God Deep? Not caring, just grateful, Tzarik walked on for some time. Voices whispered around him, twigs snapped, and now and then, something akin to a heavy sigh rose up. But he never saw anything. He marched on, growing wary of the mysterious sounds, walking for hours before spotting anything moving that wasn't a tree or dying bush. The mist made it difficult to see more than a few yards in front of him, but the ghosts glowed.

He stopped and laid his hand on his scimitar. His eyes tracked the slowly drifting creatures. They seemed lost, floating back and forth over the moors. Then his sulfates rushed. He stopped and crouched into the tall grass.

A massive monster stood in his path mere yards away. It hadn't been there before. He drew his scimitar quickly and faced the thing. It stood tall, the body of a colossal horse and torso of a man proportionate to its larger frame. Tzarik knew one of those man-shaped hands could strangle the life out of him easily. Hanging loosely from one hand was a great axe. The long haft had two blades: one smooth and almost white, the other speckled in sigils. The veins under its black skin pulsed red and hot like embers. Small flakes of black ash hovered just over its skin. It moved amongst the ghosts, gently touching them with the tip of the sigiled end of the axe. When it did, the souls sighed heavily in relief and swirled into the axe head, where it glowed green before fluttering out.

It stopped and angled its torso to face where Tzarik hid.

Another living soul, a deep, guttural voice said in Tzarik's head. *Who dares open the Deep from the outside? What blasphemous heretic breaks into my realm?*

He tensed. He'd experienced something like this before on Xia when a creature, supposedly celestial, had spoken to him.

"Another?" he shot at the thing, still posed with his scimitar, rising out of the grass. "Can you hear me?" He realized he was speaking in Al'Myrahn. Before he corrected himself to use the tongue of Caerwren, the monster replied.

I can, it said. *Put your sword away, Runer. You do not need it while I am here. They will not harm you. I am sending them on as is my duty.*

This otherworldly monster was far less benevolent than the one he'd faced on Xia. Something about it made his sulfates tingle.

"I am looking for someone," he said to the creature. "A woman. An Al'Myrahn Runer."

The creature nodded its headless neck. *She is a living soul. She does not belong here. I will send her back to be a specter in her own world soon enough.*

"You've seen her?" Tzarik asked.

Again, the monster nodded. Without another word, it turned and pointed north, away from where Tzarik first appeared. *She comes. You must hurry. Her spawn can smell a living soul. Don't let them sink their teeth into your flesh, living one, lest you wish to be enslaved to a god for eternity.*

"Sybal?" Tzarik asked.

The creature moved its neck, shaking its invisible head. *The goddess Bolemesh. She is angry, slighted by her loss. She knows the scent of your blood. Run, Runer, run. You can find that which you seek. I will allow it. Go.*

The constant heartbeat picked up, thudding into Tzarik's ears. "Why hurry?" he asked, casting about for any danger. Shadows moved in the long grass and the trees swayed. Not realizing there was a tree line nearby, Tzarik trained his eyes on it. The line of trees swooped up a white cliff face.

Go there.

He turned back to the creature, but it had moved into the mist, leading the souls away by the glow of its inner embers. Sheathing his scimitar, he gritted his teeth and marched to the cliff. His breath came in gasps by the time he reached the top. What he saw there made him hold his breath. The earth was torn up, great gashes split the blight, and the writhing ectoplasmic tendrils wiggled out of it. Huge swaths of spider web splattered the ground and hung from the trees to his right. To his left, the cliff plummeted down. Before him, a huge mound of boulders glistened in the dying sun.

The sulfates sent a tingle down the back of his spine. Snapping his head back and forth, he looked for the danger. Nothing appeared. When he faced the rocks again, he noticed thick, grassy spines sticking out all over it. Narrowing his eyes, he moved towards it.

His heart slammed against his chest, sending a jolt of adrenaline and fear through him. The hiss of the scimitar flying out of its sheath triggered the invisible monster. The rocks shifted, suddenly sprouting eight long, jointed legs. A slobbering roar accompanied the movement. The thing leapt, fleshy mandibles snapping at Tzarik. He shouted and rolled to the side, taken by surprise. As he came back to his feet, he looked up at the thing.

What he'd mistaken as boulders in the distance rose to its full height. Towering nearly twenty feet above him, the grotesque face and body of what must have been the goddess Bolemesh came into Tzarik's view. The spider goddess roared with the sound of a million voices and arched her stinger under her belly. When she did this, Tzarik saw a white, pearlescent scar on her underbelly. He'd seen many kinds of wounds in his lifetime and knew the cut of an orichalcum scimitar when he saw it.

"She cut you, did she?" he growled to Bolemesh, smiling savagely. "She was here. It's her you're hunting." He spun his scimitar in his hand, glaring up at the goddess. "Bless yourself, monster. You'll need all the help you can get against me."

Almost like she understood, Bolemesh cried out in rage-filled agony, rearing up like a horse. Her four front legs clawed at the sky before slamming back into the earth. Tzarik removed his runes, wrapping them around his left hand. Bolemesh saw them and dived headfirst at him. Her fleshy mandibles snapped at him, flecking black ectoplasm onto him. He sliced her face, making her reel back, but then ran under her. Landing a few cuts on her legs, she curled in, stabbing at him with her stinger.

The huge, black appendage just missed him as he drew halat and got in a wound right next to where Sybal had cut the goddess. Bolemesh moved quickly. One of her eight legs crossed under, hitting him hard in his chest. He tumbled back, dropping his scimitar, and rolled painfully over the rocky ground. Just as he scrambled to his feet, her front leg smashed down onto him, pinning him like a bug to the ground. The weight of the goddess crushed the air out of him. The hairy bristles cut his palms as he shoved at it.

He looked up, and her face loomed down to his. Every grotesque detail of her too-human face came into focus. Her ember-like eyes bore into him, wild and powerful. The mandibles clicked excitedly, opening up for a long, thick, forked tongue to slip out. She languidly ran her tongue up his body to his face, making a sort of crackling, chuckling sound. Above her head, she arched her entire body to get her now-dripping stinger raised up like a scorpion. He realized what she intended to do.

Feeling with his thumb, he found buhkar in his left hand and readied the rune. With a cry of a million voices, Bolemesh moved to jab her stinger into his abdomen. Drawing the mist rune quickly,

Tzarik slipped out and leapt up. He landed on her monstrous head just long enough for her to redirect her attack. He misted again as he lost his footing and her stinger came down. The goddess struck her own skull with such ferocity, the stinger sunk to its hilt into her head.

Bolemesh reeled back, trapped in a contorted circle. She lost her balance and collapsed to the side, writhing. As she yowled, Tzarik saw her stinger poking out through the top of her mouth. A flood of tiny spiders emerged from it into her gullet. She choked, thrashing. Finally, she pulled her stinger out of her skull and collapsed again, crawling piteously back towards the forest.

Tzarik almost let her go, but imagined why the goddess had hunted Sybal, what it might have done to her. Reaching down, he scooped up his scimitar and walked easily up to the thrashing goddess. She swiped at him with her savage limbs, but he easily drew halat and buhkar to avoid them. He crushed over a dozen of her spawn as they flailed upside down in the grass. With every one, Bolemesh let out a wail of pain.

With a huge sigh, she fell one last time. Taking the chance, Tzarik spun his scimitar, arched it overhead, and brought the curve down on the goddess's neck. It sunk into her exoskeleton with a sickening, squelching crunch, but did not sever her head. He jerked it out and brought it down again and again until she stopped flailing. Black ectoplasm covered him and his sword. He panted and looked down at the still goddess.

Bolemesh roared with her million voices and snapped one last time at Tzarik. He stumbled back, but the spider collapsed once more. She didn't move and her dozens of spawn stopped skittering, lying still.

Gasping, Tzarik fell forward, his hands on his knees. His breath rattled in his throat as he realized how close he'd come to letting the monster taste his flesh. The first creature had warned him to not let them bite him. He wondered if that was what had happened to Sybal, bestowing the god-touch. He bent and picked up his scimitar.

He refastened his fur cloak and pulled the cowl over his head. The sun had set and the moon, along with its reflection at its back, rose over the mountains.

He walked out from under the trees, leaving the dead monster behind.

The night wore on as he ambled over the now frost-covered moors. More things moved in the night than before in the daytime. He'd spent too long wandering and battling the spider goddess. How long did he have before he became trapped? Or what if the powers of the Deep expelled him since he did not belong?

He was examining the moon coming over the peaks when a huge raven's shadow passed over him. His hand flew to the hilt of his scimitar and he ducked, gauging the distance to the forest. He doubted his legs could carry him fast enough to hide should the monster dive at him. The raven swooped low to the ground several yards ahead. He watched it as it came close to a figure walking along the ground.

His heart stopped. Even wrapped in patchwork furs, even far off amidst the falling snow and in the dark, he knew her. Her thick braid hung over her left shoulder. She stood tall and imposing amidst the rocky ground. Her long, lean legs marched with certainty. Breaking into a run that immediately burned his legs, he charged.

Something tugged at the back of his mind like a hook. Someone he could not see beckoned him. Pulled him. Just as he'd feared, something reached for him, shoving him out.

"Sybal!" he shouted, tearing his lungs with the effort.

Sybal stopped and turned to face him, hearing her name. Her mouth fell open as her eyes widened. She dashed towards him, her arms pumping madly at her side. "Tzarik?!" she screamed.

Other unintelligible words spilled from her mouth in a torrent of weeping babble. He didn't care. The mud of the fields swallowed up his short legs, making it impossible for him to run anymore. Grunting, he pulled his legs out with great effort and reached his hand towards her.

Sybal continued to run towards him, reciprocating his reaching hand. "No, wait!" she called.

A white-green light blasted before Tzarik's eyes, blinding him. The ground fell out from underneath him. He made out the blue of Sybal's eyes and the tears freezing on her face just as he tumbled. Her fingers almost brushed his before he fell beneath the horizon.

CHAPTER 21

THE WHITE TOUCH

TZARIK HEARD VOICES AROUND HIM, BUT HE COULD NOT force his eyes open. His heart beat rapidly in his ears in a panic he could not identify. Mentally checking in with his body, his legs ached and his palms sweated. Something trickled down his temple into his hair.

"Can you hear me?" the familiar voice of Vicdan called from far away.

Someone asked a question.

"Yes," Vicdan replied. "His heart's beating. Very rapidly."

"Why is this happening?" the voice of Sjörna-Reks asked. Her clomping strides reached Tzarik's ears. He must be inside.

Again, he tried to open his eyes. A bright, orange flare blinded him.

"We're weak!" Zeva cried from out of sight. "I haven't healed. Tarkan needs rest."

"If you'd consume," Sjörna-Reks cut in, "your strength would come back."

At last, Tzarik opened his eyes. His head fell to one side, and he beheld a crumpled form wrapped in black on the ground. Tarkan lay on the stone, eyes half closed. Zeva had her arms wrapped around him. Silent tears fell down her scarred face.

"Are you or are you not Necro'Khan?" Sjörna-Reks growled.

Tarkan didn't reply, hardly conscious. He swallowed, but his dry throat made him cough.

"Let us rest," Zeva begged. "His body is dying, sustained only by the black oath. That's the price the Necro'Khan pays. Even his father took time to ascend to the power you know the Necro'Khan for. We've had no respite. Tarkan told me how Ishmael slept for days in pools of blood to regain his strength." She held her adoptive father even tighter. "Please, let us rest. He will be strong again. I promise, I promise!"

Tzarik tried to sit up and found Vicdan's arm under him, helping him up. Once he was vertical, he noticed shackles around Zeva's and Tarkan's ankles. He followed the chains to one of the wooden pillars that held up the thronehall. His head spun when he sat up.

"Careful now," Vicdan whispered to him. "You died for a minute there. Zeva reached out to hold your spirit, afraid you might not come back."

Furious, Tzarik grunted and rubbed his blurry eyes. "I had her," he moaned. "She was there."

"Wonderful!" Vicdan bracingly clapped him on the shoulders and gave a sympathetic grimace. "Then she'll wait for you. They had to bring you back. You understand that."

Would it have been so bad if he had died in the Deep? Stayed with her? Bringing her back would mean putting her into a god-touched body. He winced, his head splitting as he thought about it. He needed a drink.

Sjönra-Reks paced like a caged wolf, glaring at the two necromancers on her stone floor. "You are weak!" she roared, her voice ringing the rafters. "A disappointment. Perhaps not worthy of my time."

Tarkan winced at her raised tone but couldn't move.

Gripping Vicdan, Tzarik strode to put himself between Sjörna-

Reks and the necromancers. He took a deep breath to steady his voice. "Give them time. We cannot imagine the toll this rite has taken." Sybal's blue eyes flashed before his mind's eyes. He gritted his teeth. "I was so close. I know your..." He choked. "I know your pain. Trust me, Reks." He couldn't hide the emotion on his face.

It had an effect on Sjörna-Reks. She drew herself up and took a long breath in, holding it to stop the roar of rage boiling up in her. Behind her, the raven carvings shone black in the firelight.

"There was a raven," he offered her. "With her."

The Reks's green eyes widened, sparkling with sudden tears. "A Vaeson raven?"

He nodded. "They were together. I think they've found each other. He was there, Sjörna-Reks. They are here."

He glanced at Zeva and Tarkan. Zeva's now blue eyes begged him to keep going, to calm the savage Reks. Her knuckles gripped Tarkan so hard, she split open her scabbing scriptures.

"They won't consume," Sjörna-Reks snapped back. "If they ate sentient flesh, their strength would return quickly."

"We won't!" Zeva cried. "Dead flesh brings the risk of possession. And I will not consume living flesh."

Tzarik's stomach turned. The more he learned about the necrotic arts, the more his distaste for it grew.

The red queen shouted, scratching at the air. Lokhtar appeared from behind the stone dais, panting lightly. A fine sheen of sweat glittered in his beard. Sjörna-Reks snapped her head towards him, glaring. He nodded.

Confused, Tzarik asked, "What is it?"

"Skarde-Reks," Sjörna-Reks growled, the snarl of the wolf inside her showing on her human face. "Where?"

"The Warpath," Lokhtar replied. "He could head to Zealmor to treat with Alasdair-Reks and Eibhlin-Reks. They say his son, Dain, is with him."

Sjörna-Reks snarled, snapping her jaw. "Hovandel?"

Lokhtar shook his head. "Our clanmen say Eilowyn-Reks has not moved since the start of Vasaras. They are too consumed with the Black Road and trade with Rhostrana." He scoffed. "City of progress. More like traitors to Caerwren. The gods will deal with Hovandel."

Tzarik noticed the Reks's change in demeanor. "They will," she agreed. "And thus I must deal with Skarde and his little thunder hawk." Her eyes flashed to the necromancers.

Tzarik braced himself should she move to harm them. But the Reks didn't. She held her head high, her antlered crown tilting up to the sky.

"They may rest until I return," she quipped. "Lokhtar, gather the Volra. I want to know what Skarde-Reks is doing in Zealmor. The Warpath is a pact with Altevine, Northica, *and* Zealmor. If he is treating with Zealmor, I deserve to know." She smiled crookedly. "If a battle is what he wants during Vasaras, then he shall have one with the broken barrier at his door." She smiled down at Tarkan who still hadn't moved. "He will give me an army. Lokhtar, see to it they cannot escape." Flicking her head to the back exit, she leapt over the fire, transforming into the huge red wolf, and galloped out of the thronehall.

The towering Caerwren warrior roughly dragged the semiconscious Tarkan back to the stockade, where he bound their hands like before, stopping them from using one component they needed to cast their spells. Separating them, he put Tarkan in one cell and Zeva next to the Masahk Runer, Ragnall. He instructed the warden to give them anything they needed to heal, and to keep them fed and strong.

His mind pulled between the Reks, the necromancers, and still filled with the image of Sybal straining to reach him, Tzarik submitted to waiting.

Two days after Sjörna-Reks left, Vicdan pulled Tzarik along with him to the stockade to wrap Zeva's wounds. The man on guard let them in, but stood just outside the cell.

"Thank you, Vicdan." Zeva sighed in relief as he massaged a white cream onto her arms before wrapping them in soft cotton. Tzarik cut the strips and handed them to Vicdan.

"Al'Myrahn cotton," Vicdan said proudly. "The Volra gave it to me when I asked to help you. Savages, reading animal guts to tell the future, but they know how to heal."

He wound her legs and let her start her torso before finishing the wrappings. In the cell beside them, Ragnall watched with mild interest. His white feathers looked rumpled and black circles surrounded his keen, blue eyes.

"Why are you helping the wolf?" he asked, his voice croaking.

Zeva looked down at Ragnall, blushing slightly. Tzarik waited for her reply. He glanced across the stockade to Tarkan, who sat with his back against the wall, eyes closed. He hissed a verse now and then, but not so much as a slight breeze stirred.

"For my father," Zeva offered. Her tone rose, showing she wasn't quite sure. "I want him to achieve that which he desires. And I can help by giving myself to the black scriptures."

Ragnall's eyes roamed up and down her scarred flesh. "Pity," he mumbled. "You must love him."

"More than anything," Zeva replied quickly.

"How cruel is love." The Masahk sighed, looking away. "Sjörna-Reks doesn't know what love is." He winced. "She thinks she does, forcing it from those around her when she wishes." He glanced to Tarkan. "Will you bring Kjarton's soul back?"

Zeva nodded.

Ragnall's shoulders slackened and he caved, leaning against the wall. "He will need a body."

Sympathy for the Runer made Tzarik give him a sorry glance but nothing more. No doubt the Masahk had been wondering why he'd been kept alive and why Sjörna-Reks used him like she did. Now they knew.

Tzarik handed Vicdan a last strip of cotton, examining Zeva as the jongleur wrapped the last of her exposed flesh. Already the black marks were partially healed. Were the scriptures like the runes? Did they take to some more quickly than to others? Despite her sapped strength, her flesh was rosy and her eyes bright. Her necrotic magic was shallow, but physically, she was healing quickly.

With Zeva bandaged, he took his leave of the stockade. Vicdan followed him out, leaving the extra medicinal items behind.

"Where are you off to brood now, Tzarik?" Vicdan asked, jogging to catch up.

Some days, a swift kick to the shins might do Vicdan good, but Tzarik restrained himself. "To find something to drink," he grunted. That was what usually helped him think.

"Then I shall join you," the jongleur volunteered with far too much gaiety.

THE RATHSKELLER they found amidst the other thatched structures of the nearby town had a mud floor and a wooden bar. Runers clogged the tables and what looked like street Volra told fortunes with bones and the entrails of small creatures in dark corners for a few coins. The entire room, despite the grates of roasting meat and succulent winter vegetables, smelled like horse piss. Every few minutes, someone called out a toast to the sun and praised it for shining down.

"You'd think they've never seen the sun," Vicdan mused, coming back with two massive wooden tankards of a red, fizzing ale.

"They hardly do," Tzarik confirmed, thinking of all the gray skies they'd seen since landing on the shore. He'd spotted thick, dark clouds on the horizon as they'd walked around the muddy town looking for a tavern or public house. They'd looked like storm clouds, but here, they probably meant snow.

Vicdan babbled on about the number of Runers, their pale skin, and how tall and broad everyone on Caerwren was. Tzarik let him chatter on. Sybal's wild eyes wouldn't stop flashing before his vision every time he blinked. Her savage scream still rang in his ears. It had taken all his strength to not demand Tarkan send him back immediately, to not rage at Zeva for pulling him out. She'd been right there. But did it matter? How did Tarkan think he could pull her soul out of the Deep? And once he did, she'd enter a god-touched body.

Tzarik's hand shook. In a sudden moment of weakness, he dropped the tankard. The red ale spilled in a graceful wave towards Vicdan.

"Steady now!" Vicdan cried, scrambling out of the way. "Liquid on these breaches in this weather and I'm sure to get frostbite. There's enough sugar in there to..." He trailed off.

Tzarik didn't hide the emotional turmoil eating away at him. He dropped his face into his hands and breathed steadily.

"That looks serious," Vicdan muttered, switching sides to sit beside him, forgetting the mead assault. He wisely didn't touch the Runer, clasping his hands instead on the wooden table before them. He shoved his portion of the ale towards Tzarik. "Whenever you're ready." He smiled.

Tzarik took the wooden mug and downed the whole thing. At first it didn't burn, just tasted sweet. Too sweet. Like drinking raw honey. Then, once he got to the fourth swallow, it seared his throat. He coughed but finished it off, recognizing the quality of the alcohol.

"That should do it." Vicdan sighed sadly, inspecting the mug when Tzarik set it down. "The great scholars say that we must let a poison out of the veins if we expect any healing."

Had Tzarik not spent a year in the far east, he wouldn't have understood the quote. He always hated those kinds of philosophical mumblings. A man should just speak plainly. So, he did.

"I saw her," he started, the burn from the drink soothing him, if only a little. "She was there." He looked down at his right hand, the one that had just brushed her fingertips. He frowned. "How do the damned necromancers intend to get her out?"

Vicdan smacked the table and turned to face Tzarik on the bench they shared. "Living souls," he supplied, looking smug at knowing the answer. "She's not dead. You're not dead. You have a physicality others don't. I imagine the wolf's lover might be more difficult. But Tarkan said it was you who would pull her out. The Deep is a reflection of our realm, yes? So we go to where she's no doubt waiting to see your sullen face again. Find her, come back to where Tarkan opened the rift, and slip through." He rubbed his chin, which needed a shave.

It sounded simple enough. But the toll it had taken on Tarkan haunted Tzarik. Seeing him crumpled on the floor, drained of his life-force, gave him pause.

"I can never repay Tarkan for what he's done," he said instead. "Or Zeva."

"She wanted this," Vicdan reminded him. He pulled out his wheel fiddle and started a slow rotation to listen to the out of tune strings. "And did you see her scars?"

The Runer nodded. "She's healing. Almost like the scriptures are taking pity on her."

"She'll be a strong necromancer," Vicdan said, as if he understood everything about their mysterious companions. His voice dropped and turned serious. "Or like they are protecting her."

Tzarik grunted. "I think Tarkan has been hunting the mantle of Necro'Khan since before we knew him."

Vicdan hissed in concern, tuning another string. "I see where this is going, Runer. Let it go. He's not a monster to be hunted. He's not your responsibility. If not him, some other Porshain would find a way. Others might have been far closer to ascension than him. At least we have rapport with this one."

That was little comfort. Tzarik had spent years minding his own business, staying out of the map's problems. It had been just as happy to oblige him. But not now. Not since Sybal.

"There is one more thing." He sighed, signaling a servant girl with a long, thick red braid to bring them more of the ale. "Do you know about the god-touched curse?"

The jongleur bit his lower lip, thinking. "The White Touch?" He rapidly tapped several keys, making the strings sing a quick, melancholy jig. "I can't recall which people, but they call it the White Touch. It's a sailor's tale from long ago about the Frozen Nation, back when explorers were trying to get around that glacial wall. Ships would journey up north to never be heard from again. Some thought they sailed off the edge of the map. Until the year 116, when Shala Diladi invented the lenses we enjoy in our telescopes to this day. He sailed north with an expedition and discovered the northern wall. Studying it from afar, he saw there was no way in. But..." Vicdan paused for dramatic effect. "Smoke rose from beyond, signaling to Diladi that some sort of sentient dwelt behind the wall on the frozen continent."

Vicdan paused again and dropped his smile. "That's not what you care about at all. Apologies, Tzarik. We still tell the myth of the black god in the north as no one has proved otherwise. I must say for myself, I never believed it. I thought gods lived in lofty clouds and castles among stars." He shivered. "Now I don't, now that we've seen them walking over the peaks of mountains like they are stepping-stones." The jongleur started to hum, turning the wheel and pressing the keys to make the instrument sing with him.

Tzarik listened to Vicdan's smooth, calming voice, allowing it to settle his rapidly beating heart. The man had a way of unconsciously soothing those who listened to him.

Taking a deep breath, he said, "My old mentor, Azar, was god-touched. I watched it slowly kill him over the four years we were together. We tried a ritual in Bahratt to remove the curse." Unconsciously, his hand went to his chest where, beneath his leather armor, a large scar traced over his heart, a permanent reminder of the horrors that came from trying to outwit a curse.

"Didn't work?" Vicdan guessed, taking the proffered tankards from the serving girl.

"Not even close," Tzarik murmured. "If there is a god in the north, it angered him that we had tried to cast off his touch. Azar and I almost died. Then..." He took a long drink. He wouldn't tell that story. Not now. "The curse overtook him. Even the magi of Bahratt and their twisted rites couldn't save him. I..." He choked. *I couldn't save him*, he finished in the privacy of his own thoughts.

Vicdan awkwardly tapped his fingers on the neck of the fiddle, clearly wanting to comfort Tzarik, but not sure if such a gesture would earn him a slap.

"What will happen to Sybal if I bring her back?" he asked so the younger man could be at ease. "I've seen it on her. Her cold skin, the ashen hair. If I bring her back, she'll suffer a fate worse than death. She'll die again, becoming a demonic servant of whatever god has hurt her."

The jongleur puffed out his cheeks and ran a hand through his shaggy dark hair. "I understand. But Tzarik, would you rather leave her there to suffer?"

"She'll be cursed, suffering, no matter where she is!" He clenched his hands to stop from pounding the table. "Saving her will do nothing."

"But she won't be alone outside that godsdamned place." Finally, Vicdan grabbed Tzarik's shoulder and forced him to face him. "She's alone in there. She's tough, strong, and brave to the point of idiocy.

But she's still alone. Do you want her to live eternity like that? Always hunted, dying again and again? Or would she want you to take the chance and save her? To be here with you?"

He'd thought of that. Tzarik's heart twisted in agony, and tears threatened to sting his eyes. He gnashed his teeth hard to bar against the welling emotion.

"Godsdamn it, Runer!" Vicdan burst, not seeing any change on Tzarik's face. "She'd rather spend a few months with you, alive, able to feel your touch, than stay forever in the God Deep. How can you not see that? Don't leave her."

The last sentence hit Tzarik hard in his wary stomach. How many times had he left her now? Why did she keep coming back? How did she have faith in him? Part of him had wondered—if he braved the Deep—if she would be vindictive, angry at him for not saving her that day on Xia. But no. She'd screamed his name, had run to him. And he had run to her.

He took a shuddering breath, gulping down the second tankard of the ale. "We need to find a way off this frozen rock," he said sternly. "Once she's back with us, we're leaving."

Vicdan beamed, pressing his hand to his chest. "We," he repeated, playing a quick, major scale.

Tzarik scoffed, taking Vicdan's tankard as well. "I'm not leaving you behind. I don't want a war with Caerwren over one abandoned Al'Myahn who won't shut up."

Vicdan reached over and took the ale back, raising it to Tzarik before taking a long drink. He sang, playing along on the wheel fiddle. "With death and the gods at our doorway, we seek Al'Myrah at last. We must away, we must away." He stopped and looked over the room at a servant girl whose huge, sapphire eyes pined for him. She held a bloody bundle in her hands. Vicdan signaled the serving girl over and offered her ten rupees for the fresh, bloody haunch of meat.

"What's that for?" Tzarik asked.

Vicdan sighed, looking at the wrapped wound on his arm. "If living blood is what our necrotic friends need, then they shall have it. I'll need my strength if I'm to be of any use, and after watching the Volra read animals guts, I am not keen to eat anything prepared in that thronehall." He winked down at Tzarik. "And I want Sybal to know how brave and sacrificial I was while trying to save her from the monsters. Maybe she'll reward me with a kiss."

Tzarik imagined strangling Vicdan while finishing off the ale.

CHAPTER 22

NÖRTHICA COMES

Zeva could not stop shaking. Looking up, she caught thick white flakes falling from the sky through the barred windows. They had given her a straw mattress, but it did little to protect her from the cold emanating from the muddy floor. Her fur cloak helped, but even it could not fend off the icy fingers of the searching wind. She leaned against the stone wall, watching Tarkan pace in his cell across the stockade. She wanted to go to him, speak to him, comfort him. The nightmares had come back to her. She saw Sharar's face behind the bars. Heard his cruel laughter as she screamed in pain from his torture. She knew Tarkan must be remembering it, too. He'd ascended to Necro'Khan, and nothing had changed. She could practically hear him abusing himself in his own mind.

She winced when a gust of wind snapped through the window.

"Pull your feet under the furs," Ragnall said from the cell beside her. The Masahk Runer did not shake, unperturbed by the cold. His soft, white feathers fluttered only from the breeze. He sat against the wall, one knee up, resting his forearm on it.

"You look stronger," she offered, pulling her feet under the folds of the fur cloak. Immediately her body heated and her toes burned, tingling from the frost. "Is your strength coming back?"

He nodded slowly, his blue eyes on her. He tilted his head,

inspecting her. The long, feathery ears that stuck out from his soft hair made it an attractive gesture. This made Zeva almost smile. She'd never had these feelings in her stomach before. They made her want to run and hide and stay to speak with him all at the same time. She wondered if the tiny feathers on his muscular arms were soft like down.

"You look better, too," he offered. "The markings suit you." He leaned forward and came to the bars between them. He held his pale hand out, the tiny feathers on his forearm glittering iridescently. "Give me your hand."

Her stomach flipped in another unfamiliar sensation as she eagerly, yet demurely, reached her hand out to his. He proffered his into her side of the bars. When her chilled, scabbing fingers touched his, she gasped.

"You're so warm!" she breathed. The stockade turned silent. Tarkan must have stopped mumbling and pacing.

Ragnall nodded. "They say Masahk carry the heat of the Alikan sun inside them always. Our blood is like a river from the sun." His right ear twitched, listening to something far away. "Despite the white blood, Alika still flows in me."

Zeva sighed in relief when Ragnall clasped his hand over hers, heat radiating off him. She sniffled and closed her eyes. The cold made her nose run. She hated it. Without thinking, Zeva laid her head against the bars, scooting closer to Ragnall. She reminded herself of their first meeting and how he'd been a brute, even leaving his old apprentice to die. She'd feared him then.

She opened her eyes to find him looking into her face. She smiled, unsure what his thoughts might be. Slowly, he raised his hand to her face. His warm skin soothed the aches from the healing scars. She suddenly wanted him to wrap himself around her and take away all the pain. She imagined being engulfed in his embrace, warm and safe with his muscular arms around her.

"If I had my runes," he whispered, "I'd draw artiah until every one of them—" He hissed suddenly, the hand on her face flexing in pain, and he cringed away, moaning.

"What's happening?" she cried, sitting up on her heels. "Ragnall?"

The Runer took a few steady breaths, his hand over his heart. "I need the hunt," he hissed.

Zeva turned to Tarkan only to find he'd been watching them. A deep scowl darkened the shadows under his hood. Before she could speak, the doors opened and the huge northern warrior, Lokhtar, entered.

"He needs help!" Zeva shouted, pointing to Ragnall. "He's hurt."

"I know," the brute growled, signaling a few guards to Tarkan. "He will go out with the Reks's Runers and be allowed to hunt. She still needs him."

A set of Runers, one near her age and one perhaps thirty-five, entered and went to Ragnall's cell. Zeva eyed them as they pulled Ragnall out and dragged him out of the stockade. Lokhtar looked down at her, coming to her door. She shrank away, unsure what his intensions were.

"Don't touch her," Tarkan snarled, twisting in the grips of his own captors.

Lokhtar ignore the necromancer and opened her door. He stood aside. "The night is going to get deathly cold. Vasaras has passed its zenith and the nights will be dangerous. Darkness will consume our skies. You are to spend a few days in the thronehall, for your safety and warmth."

Without arguing, Zeva leapt up and ran to Tarkan's side, shoving one guard off him. The guard made to shove her back, his green eyes bristling under furious auburn locks, but Lokhtar shouted a bark at the man.

"Leave her," he snarled. "Let her walk by his side. They're not going anywhere."

"Sir!" a deep voice shouted from outside. A chestnut-haired warrior with two great axes on his back ran through the stockade door, panting. "Lokhtar, Skarde-Reks and Dain Radjur-tor are coming," the man wheezed, his breath coming in thick white clouds.

Lokhtar bent his head like he might ram through the messenger. "Alone?" he quipped.

The messenger shook his head. "At least a pack of twelve swords. All on horseback. Our rangers spotted them at the roots of the Hovandel peaks and ran to warn us."

This made Lokhtar stop midstep. "Skarde-Reks was in Hovandel?"

The messenger, still gasping, shook his head and shrugged. "The rangers ran for two days to bring us this news. They are near death from exhaustion. Skarde-Reks will be upon us by midday tomorrow."

Lokhtar turned and eyed Zeva and Tarkan. "Bring the necromancers. Have the thralls brought as well. Gather some warriors to fill the thronehall. He will see the might of the red Reks."

Zeva ran to keep up with the now panicking warriors as they marched them, bound as they still were, out of the stockade and towards the thronehall. Lokhtar galloped up the stone steps to the shackled golden wolf. He knelt before it. Gripping its scruff so roughly it yelped, he roared at it, "Find mother!" and released it from its spiked chains. The golden wolf howled, confused at first, turning this way and that. When Lokhtar took a long, black whip from his belt and cracked it, repeating the command, the wolf thrust its nose into the snow and sniffed. Soon, it caught a scent and dashed away, out of the village boundaries.

"What does this mean?" Zeva asked, struggling to step high over the piling snow. "What are you going to do with us?"

"Don't worry, lass," Lokhtar grunted, plowing easily through the snow. "Do as I say and you'll be fine. Skarde-Reks will fear you. If he does not upon seeing you, he will soon."

ᘓ

ONCE INSIDE THE THRONEHALL, Zeva and Tarkan were shackled to the foot of the stone dais again. Zeva's hands being in front of her, she stood behind Tarkan to hold his cold fingers as best she could. The leather cords that wrapped their fingers had grown tight over the last day or so.

"What are they doing?" Zeva asked as a pack of thralls were herded into the thronehall and warriors of all kinds filled the space. The forges blazed and braziers lit up, filled with a wood that smelled fresh and clean when it burned.

"Forcing Skarde-Reks and Dain Radjur-tor to witness our strength," Lokhtar growled. "They have stepped outside the laws and mores of the Warpath alliance."

"Why?" Zeva asked. When Lokhtar didn't reply, she had her answer.

In the distance, behind the thronehall, a deep, echoing howl rose up from far away.

Lokhtar stopped and craned his neck. "She comes. Thank Raudnir. She'll be here by morning. Keep the forges hot. Find the Al'Myrahn Runer."

The thronehall blazed to life and heated to the point that every frostbitten finger and toe Zeva had came back to life. At first, she tried to sit up and watch the movement, but as the night wore on, sleep overcame her. Lokhtar ordered a band of thralls to bring in hay and pile furs on it for her to sleep on near the hearth. Tarkan stood by.

As she slept, her new necrotic powers manifested deep in her gut. Dreams of ghosts filled her mind. Terrors chased her down the golden halls. The gentle, evil chuckle of Sharar sounded wherever she fled. Unsure how she knew, she realized the nightmares were sapping her strength. The scriptures on her flesh squirmed, feeling like a protective shield around her. The surface of her skin tingled, telling her something was wrong. If only she could get rid of the nightmares, she'd be stronger. She could help Tarkan. Her stomach erupted in a pain so vile, she thought she'd wake, but the ethereal nightmares held her like a claw. Pain raked through her innermost parts, tearing something away from her. She twisted in pain and wanted to vomit from the effort of clinging to life. A voice, a deep voice from the stars or the depth of the earth—she couldn't tell—said this was the sacrifice for necromancy.

She woke when, all at once, the stabbing and tearing in her stomach stopped. The first thing she felt upon waking was a hot liquid crawling down her leg and the cold snow on her bare feet. Embarrassment scorched her face as she thought she'd relieved herself in front of everyone in the thronehall. But she was standing outside...

Finally able to open her eyes, she realized she clung to a man's neck, gripping his long hair in her unbound fingers. Her hands heated in a new pain. Looking up, she saw Tzarik watching her. A mixture of compassion and understanding swirled in his blue eyes. She glanced down to see a red and black river flowing from between her legs into the snow. In a final wave of cramping agony, everything else fell out of sight into the snow. The pain almost made her pass out, falling into the Runer's arms.

Her mouth popped open in horror, but no words came. She stuttered, making weeping and groaning sounds. What happened? Was all that beneath her what she thought it was? She gasped and her knees gave out as she wailed.

Tzarik caught her, fully supporting her shaking frame. He held her close, petting her long hair. He pressed his cheek into the top of her head while she wailed from the anguish into his chest. Grateful that she'd somehow appeared outside the thronehall, she let the tears flow. He must have carried her out.

"Where's—" She choked, taking a breath. "Where's Tarkan?"

He'd tried to warn her. A fresh wave of grief took her and she clung to Tzarik even tighter.

Grateful for the Runer's silence, she hoped he'd not let her go. She regripped his neck and tried to calm herself. She must look horrible, shameful.

"I'm sorry," she panted, rubbing her palms into her eyes to stave the flow of tears.

His arm went around her waist, lifting her feet out of the snow. He swung her around, one arm behind her back, the other under her knees.

Facing her now, he said softly, "Don't apologize, Zeva. The black oaths are worse for you and Sybal. I don't know why they are so vindictive to you, but you bear it well. She would know what you're going through."

She winced, one last twist of her insides relinquishing their grip. "How did you know what was happening?"

Tzarik blinked, his face stone. "Sybal told me. I saw it in a book. I made a guess."

"But Tarkan—" She couldn't stop the sob that rose in her throat.

"Zeva," Tzarik cut over her, squeezing her gently in his arms. "Tarkan may be like a father to you, and he may regret doing this to you, but he..." The Runer had to stop himself and clear his throat. "But he loves you. In his way. What's done is done. This was your choice."

Taking a little comfort in his words, she nodded. All the pain left her and now all she felt was cold. Of course, it had been her choice. But she hadn't known.

She wiped away her tears, her skin rubbing smoothly against her face. Shocked, she pulled her hand away. All her scars had healed. Now, smooth, bold inking scrawled over her flesh. It was done.

Shyly, she asked, "Will he still love me?"

Tzarik left the alley. She realized he must have carried her out for privacy. "He will," he promised. "Give him time."

"Runer!" Lokhtar's voice shouted from the thronehall around the corner. "Come quickly. Sjörna has returned just ahead of Skarde and Dain."

Tzarik used just his eyes to ask if she'd be all right.

She nodded. "Thank you, Tzarik. I owe you a debt of gratitude."

ZEVA LET Tzarik carry her into the thronehall. Thick gusts of white snow filled the air, melting over the huge hearth fire and working forges. Doors on the sides opened as Sjörna-Reks's subjects prepared to greet the other Reks. The doors behind the stone dais burst open and the huge red wolf came in. She shook her fur off and glanced around with her piercing green eyes, snapping at slow-moving thralls and maids. When she spotted Tzarik and Zeva, she snarled and transformed. Her chest heaved from panting.

"You will stand by my side," she commanded Zeva as Tzarik set her on her feet, still supporting her. "As will your father." She glared at Lokhtar and snapped her fingers, commanding him to bring the shackled Necro'Khan to her hall. She glared hard at Tzarik. "Speak once and you will lose your tongue."

Zeva clung to him. "Stay close?" she asked, begging him with her eyes.

He nodded wordlessly.

Walking slowly, the soreness still ebbing away, Zeva climbed the stone steps up to the dais where Sjörna-Reks sat herself. She scanned the scrambling movements below for Tarkan. Lokhtar pulled him along, still bound.

"Does he have to be chained so?" Zeva asked, her blue eyes not leaving him.

"I am taking no chances, my pet," Sjörna-Reks snarled, placing her antlered crown on her head. "I will not appear weak or foolish to

Skarde and his little thunder hawk." Her eyes flashed to the two-bladed axe over her throne, tracing the bite mark taken out of one.

Zeva caught something that lurked behind Sjörna-Reks's words. A malice she hadn't suspected. An age-old wound. She scurried to the edge of the dais and looked down to where Lokhtar had shackled Tarkan, arms still behind his back. At least Sjörna-Reks had not put the bridle on him. Tarkan didn't look up at her.

"Why is your skirt bloodied?" Sjörna-Reks asked Zeva suddenly, looking her up and down.

"Don't mind it," Zeva quipped, shocking herself. She looked down at her free hands, admiring her freshly healed scriptures. She liked how the black ink crawled over her arms. Lifting her skirt, she took in the lettering's curve over her calves. She hadn't cast the five spells and yet the scriptures had accepted her. She smiled. Perhaps she'd be a strong necromancer.

The back door banged open and a messenger hissed that Skarde-Reks had arrived.

Sjörna-Reks sat tall, glaring down her hall, waiting. "If you know what's good for you, girl," she mumbled darkly, "be ready to defend me."

Unsure what the tension was all about, Zeva stood strong. The scriptures to cast any of the five spells came to her; she'd memorized the verses her whole life. With each spell she thought of, a certain section of her flesh crawled, indicating where that spell lay on her body. The sensation at first made her squirm, but then she smiled. She spotted Tzarik and Vicdan in the gathered horde.

The doors burst open, curtains of snow filling the air. A huge white hawk shot into the thronehall, screaming and diving onto one of the great rafters above. The beams groaned under the weight. The hawk was colossal, filling the large space. It shook, showering those below with white flakes. Zeva's eyes widened as she beheld it and its piercing gray eyes that snapped with lightning.

A clopping of hooves brought her attention back down. A similarly white radjur the size of a horse with great, sharp, silver antlers marched with immense dignity into the halls. Its silver hooves clinked like steel when they hit the stone floor, sparking small tangles of lightning. It had the same flashing gray eyes. Leaping over the brazier, it transformed into a man so tall Zeva knew she'd only come up to his chest. His blond hair hung long down his back in dozens of tiny, interlocking braids, clasped with silver. His beard, almost to his belt, was adorned the same way. Bare arms and legs flexed in the cold air, knotted and corded with muscle as he strode. He held his left hand out to the side and a metallic whooshing preceded the appearance of two great axes soaring into his waiting palm. Once they thudded into his hands, he slung them over his broad shoulders.

Above him, the white hawk dove, landing in the shape of a younger version of the first, summoning a long sword in the same fashion. His eyes twinkled, less guarded than his father's and far more mischievous, as he looked up at the stone dais and the red Reks. Sjörna-Reks smirked down at the pair, then slowly crossed one leg over the other. She held her hand out, calling her own blade to her left hand. The simple gesture made Zeva jump, impressed.

"Sjörna-Reks," Skarde-Reks crowed, throwing his arms wide and taking in the packed thronehall. "Dramatic as ever."

"Skarde," she replied, forgoing the title they both shared. "Outside your borders, as ever."

"Bold accusation." Skarde-Reks smiled, running his hand down his long, silken beard. "Tell me, how is the Black Road? Since you've frequented it so often this Vasaras. Or have you forgotten?"

"Me?" she sneered. "I have forgotten nothing, murderer. Or has the lightning you worship on that mountain finally struck that thick skull of yours?"

The younger man, Dain, snarled and put his hand to his long sword. Zeva noted the length and thickness: that sword wasn't for hewing down a man. It was meant for something much larger.

"Peace, Dain," Skarde-Reks warned his son. His eyes slowly

roamed up to above the thrones. They took in the double-headed war axe. A small crease appeared between the Reks's eyes. With a snap of lightning, they flicked back to Sjörna-Reks. "Strigganoct has blessed me, it is true," he said, calling on the name of his thunderous dragon god. "Shall we?" He held up his enchanted axes, dropping them with a thud in the center of the hall. They stood on their heads without so much as tipping.

Dain mimicked the gesture, the tip of his great sword spearing into the dirt before the throne. Sjörna-Reks stood, handing her blade to Lokhtar, who stabbed it near the other two Vaeson weapons. This gesture must have just been a show of good faith, as either of them could summon the blades whenever they wanted.

Satisfied, Skarde-Reks looked up at the red wolf. "I come on behalf of *your* god."

Sjörna-Reks raised her head a little higher, the tines on her brow tilting upwards. Zeva could almost smell the lighting in the air coming off the two below them. She flexed her fingers, ready to act should Sjörna give any sign that she should. She reached, feeling for any dead that could come to her call.

Skarde's eyes flitted down to where Tarkan stood bound. His brow darkened. "A necromancer, Sjörna?" he asked, looking up. "I cannot pretend we in the Warpath have not heard of your hunt for such a sentient."

Zeva stiffened when his eyes fell on her.

"Two necromancers?" he went on. "I thought the ravens had lied when they said the Deep had been opened." He stopped and his eyes unfocused. "The Vorlamir must be enraged at your trespass."

"I haven't seen him," Sjörna-Reks said confidently. "No glint of his axe nor flame from his hoof."

Zeva thought a kind of static ran through her then, like right before lightning struck the ground nearby.

Dain glanced at his father, shifting his fur-lined boots. "We have," he said with a tone of caution.

"Sjörna," Skarde said, his deep voice guarded and calm. "I came to warn you—for the sake of the Warpath—but I see I am too late."

The red Reks laughed, her right hand going to the empty throne on that side. "Warn me?" Her voice was colder than the ice on the sharp peaks on the horizon.

Skarde nodded. "Your hunters have gone too close to the Empty and Hovandel. This is against the laws handed down to us by our fathers. The Warpath was forged to keep Caerwren pure, closer to our gods and the earth."

"Why do you care about Hovandel or the Empty?" she snipped back.

Skarde-Reks took a slow breath, eyes fixed on her. "Our alliance is fragile, Sjörna Wolf-tier. I need not remind you. It is for our clans we keep the Warpath. But you have ventured too far into Northica this Vasaras, trespassing into our mountain's hunting grounds. Now I know why."

"You mean Zealmor?" she cut in. "Those blue barbarians need to be hunted, Skarde Radjar-tor."

"They are our brothers and sisters in the Warpath!" the big man barked back.

Sjörna-Reks raised her chin. "Have you not heard? Eibhlin-Reks seeks a mate for her daughter, Sordika Dragon-tier." She eyed Dain. "Would be a fine match for those who worship Strigannoct. Besides, Vasaras is coming to an end. The spring will be here and the hunt will stop. The gods will sleep. What are you afraid of?"

"That you are delving into the Deep!" the other Reks suddenly shouted, taking a step towards the dais. "The Warpath is an alliance between those of us who keep the old ways. You jeopardize us all by breaking into the Deep. That is not your right. You will anger the gods even as they walk over our mountains."

Sjörna gripped the sides of her throne, throwing herself up. "You stole him from me!" she screamed, the snarl of a wolf mixing in her voice.

Zeva jumped. The spell to raise a corpse hissed through her mind and she suddenly felt the presence of a dozen buried warriors behind the thronehall waiting to rise.

"Kjarton did no harm," Sjörna growled, "and you spilled his blood on your mountain, leaving him to be eaten by your god. A kingly sacrifice that granted you the stone throne in Northica." She gasped for air, gnashing her teeth that had turned to wolf fangs. "That throne should have been my sister's."

Skarde's thick, yellow brows knit in warning. "What happened to Astrid Wolf-tier was a horrible accident," Skarde said steadily.

"On your mountain!" Sjörna snarled again. "Astrid was too strong for you! She led our wolf pack with ferocity. I gave Astrid a chance. I did Northica a favor, dispatching that bastardess you married in her stead."

Dain screamed, summoning his sword to his hand from where it stuck in the dirt. He arced it over head with a huge swooping motion like a falcon's wing. Skarde reached forward, dragging his hot-headed son back. Sjörna-Reks' eyes bulged, and her brows went up, taunting the young Vaeson with a kind of bridled madness.

"Sjörna," Skarde warned, eyeing Tarkan and Zeva in turn, "I am no fool. I see your intent. I come on behalf of the Warpath: Do not pull Kjarton from the Deep."

"You should have considered what I might do to return my love before giving him over to your god," Sjörna interrupted.

"Balance," Skarde shot back. "A sacrifice for a sacrifice. You broke the alliance first, taking my Yrsa, my white hawk, given to me by the goddess Isodel."

A melancholy overtook Skarde for just a moment. His grip on Dain turned to one of affection and worry rather than holding him back.

"I have only one son, Sjörna," Skarde tried again. "I've not found it in me to take another Vaeson wife."

"Thusly I sit alone," Sjörna shot back, indicating the empty throne. "And what of my son? Altevine is without an heir, Skarde. Will you use this weakness against me? Or would you offer me your son as a mate?" A dark, twisted smirk pulled at her red lips.

Dain growled a curse in an old Caerwren dialect Zeva didn't know. He spit onto the ground. "I'd rather die, wolf."

"We could try it that way." Sjörna leaned back into her throne, still grinning. "Vaeson mate for life. I will find a way to mate after death."

Skarde dropped the hand that held Dain's arm. "Careful, red wolf. What you speak of may bring a curse like no other upon your line. Do the other cantons know you intend to open the Deep into our land? Every vile thing, every monstrous spirit within, would spill out into our halls. A malignation."

The younger man snarled at her, pushing past his father to step closer to her. "Northica will not stand by and let you open the Deep into Caerwren," he said. "You have broken the alliance."

"How will you stop me, little hawk?" Sjörna asked, throwing her arms wide.

Dain eyed Zeva, then Tarkan.

"Touch them and my hall descends upon you," Sjörna said quickly, seeing the young man calculating.

"You've gone too far, wolf," Skarde warned for a final time. He drew in a deep breath, holding it for a moment before saying, "Our alliance is over."

"You are in no position to threaten me, radjur," Sjörna replied, but Zeva heard a change in her tone. "Do not anger me further."

Skarde-Reks raised his head and nodded, understanding that negotiations and what he'd come for were of no use. "I do not want to fight you, Sjörna. Long have our cantons been at peace, protecting the Warpath from the monsters and nightmares that walk our lands, staving off the philosophies of Hovandel and the west."

Sjörna tilted her head and shrugged. A twisted smirk distorted her face. "Give me your young son as a thrall. Let me do what I please to him. And peace may continue."

"Bitch," Dain snapped. "I'd rather die than lie with you."

"I could have it both ways." The red Reks smiled, showing her fangs. "It seems negotiations are finished, Skarde. Take your little thunder hawk and begone."

Without a look back, Skarde-Reks turned and marched with a heavy gait back up the hall and out into the white blizzard, pulling Dain in tow. They left the hall before the weapons left behind gave a metallic groan and soared out the open doors after their masters.

Once the doors shut, Sjörna-Reks collapsed against her throne. Zeva watched her, mixed emotions swirling inside her. Quite suddenly, she didn't want to stay in Altevine or near the wolf queen. She glanced at Tzarik and saw the same thoughts mirrored on his face, but with far more confliction. Sybal still hadn't been returned, and it was because of them.

Zeva turned to face Sjörna-Reks. "We must hurry," she said. "Let the Runer back into the Deep to find Sybal. The sooner we retrieve her, the sooner we find Kjarton."

But they wouldn't. Once Sybal was free and returned to her body, Zeva wanted to run.

CHAPTER 23

BACK TÖ THE DEEP

TZARIK SAT NEAR THE BLACK BOX WHERE SYBAL LAY, feeding her still body another bottle of fresh sulfates. He cut her left wrist to empty the old, but they moved slowly. Her golden hair gave way more and more to the white, ashen color of a god-touched. Her fingernails had started to turn black. Vicdan sat near, slowly turning the wheel of his instrument and humming something melancholy. He stopped every five beats to re-hum a section and change a note. The clicking of the notes and buzzing of the strings ground Tzarik's nerves with every turn.

While he watched Sybal, still and lifeless, Tzarik wanted to take her hand. Surreptitiously, he glanced at Vicdan, who didn't seem to be paying him any mind, so he reached down and held her hand. The cold in her flesh almost gave him pause, but he reminded himself that she was still alive. Their matching jade bracelets lightly clinked together in the quiet of the stockade.

"Vicdan?" he asked, cutting off a particularly long-held note from the jongleur's golden throat. "What do you know about things like this?" He took off his bracelet and tossed it to the younger man.

Vicdan caught it deftly, noting the matching one on Sybal's wrist. "Looks very Xian," he mused. "Jade, I think." He held it up to his ear and flicked the back of his nail against it hard, making a tinkling sound. "They have a story about the White Dragon and how where it once walked on the mountains with a wise man, the stone turned to jade under its claws."

He knew the story Vicdan alluded to. "So this jade could hold the essence of a god? Of magic?"

Vicdan half shrugged and nodded, handing it back. "The Masahk make such trinkets. Saying that if you give it to your love, you will always be able to find them. Especially if they're cut from the same stone. They have a similar blue stone in Alika. You'll find Masahk traders selling them in markets and festivals. Most are probably imitation, though."

Tzarik turned the bracelet in his hand over and over. He didn't know where Sybal's soul was on Caerwren. But perhaps the bracelet could lead him to her. Dare he believe in such a fantastic story? Could it help him find her?

Outside, a great bellow sang down from the mountaintops and the earth shook as some god stepped over the peaks. Perhaps it wasn't such a wild idea after all.

ƛ

Two days later, they stood outside in the blustering wind and snow while the Blood Path was set by willing Volra. Sjörna-Reks stood by, bare arms and legs stiff in the cold air, but unbothered by the snow. She glared at Tarkan as he stood at the head of the Path. Zeva waited off to the side, her eyes on Sjörna-Reks.

Tzarik walked out of the stockade with Vicdan. "Watch them," he implored Vicdan. "Don't let the Reks twist them around to doing her bidding."

Vicdan blew his cheeks out, squinting into the bright day. With the sun out and the snow on the ground, their eyes burned. "What can I do?" he asked. When Tzarik flashed his sharp eyes to him, Vicdan added, "What are you afraid will happen?"

He wasn't sure. He just knew Tarkan's ambition had showed.

And with Zeva being an Apostle, Tarkan had very little left to lose and everything to gain.

Tzarik faced Vicdan. "Just be careful. Watch her." He nodded towards the stockade where Sybal's body lay.

When they stood before the gruesome Blood Path and the onlookers, Tarkan said, "I cannot hold the rift open, Runer. Come back here by sunrise and I will open it again." His icy eyes became shrouded. "If you are there, you may come back. If not…"

"I'll be there," Tzarik promised. He tucked his runes under his armor and tightened his belt.

"Good luck, Tzarik," Vicdan called, backing away.

"May the Valravn and Raudnir bless you and watch over you," Sjörna-Reks said. "Find your Sybal and bring her back so I, too, may hold my love in my arms."

Tzarik faced Tarkan down the Blood Path. The necromancer's stone visage showed no emotion as he pressed his palms close. The scrawling on his face stirred as he chanted. His voice came out like hissing, then vanished into that unknown space. His mouth moved and his chest heaved as he breathed heavily to shout the spell, but no words could be heard. The wind burst to life, whipping Tzarik's long hair and fur cloak around him. The blood from the sacrifices lifted from the white snow, creating red rivulets around the Path, the Runer, and the necromancer.

As the black, lightning-shaped rift appeared between Tarkan's palms, Tzarik focused on the bracelet around his wrist. *Take me to her,* he prayed to the White Dragon. *If she's not here, take me to where she is.* He took one step forward and felt his body fall backwards. The green hue overtook his vision. Looking back, he watched his own body fall. Like before, Vicdan stood behind him to catch him. Stealing himself, he stepped into the Deep.

BRIGHTNESS from the day carried over into the Deep, though here, the sunlight shone with a deathly, green hue. The scream of a raven in pain and a flurry of black feathers filled Tzarik's senses as his eyes adjusted to the strange light. Ash and white cinders made the air reek, forcing him to cough. The earth shook as two titans, a black raven the size of a horse and a white snake as large as a dragon, fought. The snake had the raven in its jaws, piercing it with sharp fangs.

The raven tore at the snake with its silver talons and ripped at its eyes with its sharp beak. It cawed, "You shall not leave my shores unscathed!"

The violent entrance made Tzarik stumble back. His gut flipped as his heels dipped over a cliff edge. Lurching forward, he leapt away from the fall. The snake whipped its head, its purple eye catching sight of him.

Another foul blood! a hissing, angry voice screamed in his head. The snake stopped thrashing, the raven's wings flapping desperately.

But another living soul? the voice hissed.

Tzarik turned and ran along the edge. The snake dropped the raven and struck at Tzarik. Knowing full well he could not outrun the colossal snake, he got away from the edge and turned to face it, wrapping his runes around his left hand and drawing his scimitar in his right.

Behind the coils of the white snake, the raven fell, wounded and shrieking in pain. This one moment of taking his eyes off the snake god proved the wrong thing to do. The snake struck, but missed as Tzarik feinted just in time, forced to dodge into the snake's coils. Slashing to keep them from wrapping tightly around him, he drew buhkar to slip out. The god's angry hissing filled his head as he ran back towards the fallen raven.

These foul bloods are a canker on these sacred grounds, it hissed. Annoyed, it added, *Must go home. Xia calls me back! I am done with chase. I relinquish my claim to her soul. Another god may have her.*

But where the raven had been now lay a man with black hair,

bloodied and struggling. Tzarik could see he was a Caerwren man, most likely not a warrior. His limbs were lither and thinner. He didn't wield the massive weapons Caerwren's warriors did.

Vaeson, he thought, realizing what he'd witnessed. *Kjarton?* That meant Sybal was close.

But at the moment hot, red blood leaked from several puncture wounds all over his body. The man cried out in agony, holding his side and crawling away. Tzarik dipped down and helped haul him to his feet. The raven man's green eyes rounded in shock, taking in the runes and pearlescent blade.

"North!" the man panted. "She'll be there." Together, they ran in the opposite direction.

The few wounds Tzarik had managed to inflict on the snake god were on its soft underbelly. The orichalcum wounds had significantly slowed the snake's pursuit of them. A low, hissing laugh echoed in Tzarik's mind.

Willingly here or not, foul blood, I can have you. Come a long way, I have, chasing my sacrifice. I need to feed!

"Don't let it bite you," the raven man gasped through pained breaths.

He was far taller than Tzarik. His long, thin frame made running awkward as the Runer tried to support him. He couldn't move fast enough to outrun the wounded god. Glancing back, Tzarik knew they'd have to turn and face the monster.

"Can you fight?" he asked the man.

In reply, the man pulled his shaking hand away from his side. Tzarik could see his ribs and dark red matter through the open wound. Pulling out artiah, he drew the rune slowly over the man's side. In a soft glow of white light, the wound healed over enough to hide the inner organs and bone. Another draw, and the flesh scarred over just enough to hold.

"Just as she does," the man breathed in wonder.

"Kjarton?" he asked, confirming that he had recognized the raven Reks.

The man's brow dropped and his mouth opened in confusion, but they didn't have time to question one another. The snake struck at them hard, pushing them apart. Tzarik heard its groaning as it fought on top of its wounds. Kjarton landed a strong blow with his long, straight blade made of bone, allowing Tzarik to mist away to catch its eyes. The purple slits homed in on the short Runer.

Tzarik readied his stance, but the snake god never struck. It stopped, its tail twitching madly.

She comes... it hissed in his mind. *I am done!*

With a final spit, the god turned and burrowed into the earth, causing the ground to rock, and vanished from sight. Gasping, Tzarik caught himself on the shaky earth and went to Kjarton. Still holding his scimitar and runes, he was about to ask him where Sybal was when a voice behind, calling his name, turned him to stone.

"Tzarik?"

Whipping around, he glared into the blue, midday sun. Sybal's tall, thin form silhouetted against the green sky met his eager gaze. Her long braid, down past her backside, gave her away. He couldn't make his legs move. His brain roared for him to run to her, but his heart doubted. After all this time, as far as he'd come, could it really be her?

"Tzarik!" she screamed. She dropped into a run, her long legs bursting into motion. A string of gods' names, curses, and incoherent babble echoed from the hilltop she ran down.

The closer she got, the more he heard her weeping gasps. Her face collapsed into the throes of agony. She dropped her scimitar and threw her arms out to him.

"Please," she shouted to the sky. "Please, let this be real."

She didn't slow down. Tzarik braced himself, still not sure if this god-filled, dark world would let him have this moment. Like the last time, he expected to vanish, to be pulled back into his body.

Instead, the huge, muscled body of his apprentice slammed into him at top speed. She plowed him down and together they fell into the layer of snow over the frozen ground. She crushed him under her weight, her arms throttling him around his neck. She buried her face in his shoulder and wailed loudly. Her arms pulled him closer until he couldn't breathe, as if she wanted to pull him into her.

Finally, realizing she was very real, he reciprocated the embrace. Her ashen hair fluttered into his face. She buried her head deeper into his neck and wrapped her legs around his middle, latching onto him more tightly.

"You came for me?" she finally managed to say around sobs. She pulled back.

Looking up at her from his back, a heat like he'd never felt before rushed through his every frozen limb. His blood seared his veins with the warmth radiating from her glowing face. He couldn't stop himself from reaching up and taking her face in his hands. She smiled down, tears streaming from her eyes.

"I've found you," he breathed, brushing away the tears with his thumbs.

She nodded, sniffling, and collapsed into hugging him again. He regripped her harder, soaking up her weight on top of him.

When she pulled away again, her eyes flitted from his, to his blue lips, then back. This small gesture made his sulfates run, as if a danger had suddenly presented itself. He couldn't stop from quickly glancing at her full, pale lips in return. She swallowed, calmed her nerves, and stood up, pulling him up with her.

"Kjarton," she said, smiling now. "This is him. My mentor."

The dead Reks nodded to Tzarik, still holding his side. "She talks of nothing else."

"And Sjörna of you," Tzarik said, the mood shifting darkly.

"Sjörna?" The raven king's gray eyes widened. "My red Reks."

Tzarik nodded. "I have much to tell you." He couldn't take his hand from Sybal's. He'd not let go since she helped him to his feet. She didn't pull it away. "Is there a safe place we can stay a moment?"

Sybal nodded. "But we have to watch out for the dangers of the Deep. Follow me closely and do as I say."

ᚦ

As Sybal and Kjarton led him through the Deep, Sybal noted tracks, spider webs, and other signs of danger. He followed her footsteps and did as she told him when she and Kjarton suddenly froze and waited. He couldn't see the danger, but trusted her new experience. A slow sloshing told him some sort of two-legged entity walked up behind them. He spun, scimitar out, to see a stumbling woman making her way towards them. She had blood around her mouth and her eyes were wild with hunger.

"It can't move quickly," Sybal said easily, taking out her own scimitar. "It's a skygge, a soul that has spent too long in the Deep. They have no mind left."

Kjarton nodded to it, eyes fixed on its bloody mouth. "Follower of Crenolix. God of flesh."

Tzarik watched Sybal march up to the creature. Without so much as blinking, she severed its head. A sickening plunk sent ripples through the marsh when it hit the ground. Its eyeballs swirled to look up, moaning as its last breath dispersed on the wind.

Soon, they arrived at a small alcove of rocks where they'd made camp. Sybal did not relinquish his hand until they were safe inside the wall of stone and the fire was lit. Kjarton wrapped his wounds with cloth from a pack of mismatched supplies that looked pilfered from other poor souls in the Deep. Sybal boiled water and handed him a strange, gray flat bread.

"It's disgusting," she said heartily. "Made from mushrooms that grow in the bog, but fills you up should you feel hunger."

He took it without argument. "How far are we from Sjörna's clanland?" he asked.

Kjarton answered. "About a day's walk. We tried to stay close after..." He gave a wan smile sympathetically at Sybal. "After we saw that ghost girl."

"Zeva," Tzarik corrected. "She called you up. She and her mentor Tarkan helped me cross over."

"Tarkan?" Sybal asked, surprised. Then she stopped, a waterskin halfway to her lips. Her face paled. "How long?"

Tzarik thought for a moment. "Months." The weight of their time apart finally weighed down on him, crushing him. "Winter is halfway over on Caerwren."

Sybal shook her head, ridding it of whatever dark thought had invaded it. "But why are you here? Why have you trapped yourself here?"

"We're not trapped." He sighed, regretting the bite of the gray bread he'd just taken. It stuck to his throat and tasted like dirt. "Tarkan will open a rift at sunrise at the place I went through."

Kjarton looked out over the crags to the sun that now crawled down close the horizon. "That gives us little time. We must go now."

The Reks was right, but Tzarik couldn't tell him the truth: Kjarton would not be crossing over with them yet.

Tzarik stood up. "If what the Reks says is true, we need to move." He pulled Sybal to her feet. "I don't want to wait longer than we need to cross back over."

Sybal nodded gravely. "Wait here." She left to gather her few things and extra water for the journey.

Kjarton eyed the Runer. "Tzarik," he started, slowly. "We are spirits. Crossing over into the living realm is—"

"I know," Tzarik cut in. He shifted his feet. "I have Sybal's body. She's alive."

The Reks's eyes shone with melancholy understanding. "My body is...very much gone." He looked away.

"Sjörna has a way," Tzarik replied. "At least, she speaks as if she has a solution."

Kjarton smiled longingly. "She always did."

d

"Move!" Sybal shouted, shoving Tzarik out of the way as a black web of lightning shot up from the squirming earth. "When you feel the wind like that, see the roiling earth, listen for the crackling," she instructed. "You can smell it, too."

Tzarik leapt to his feet from where she'd shoved him to the ground. The earth in the Deep constantly twitched and writhed with unseen blight, even beneath the snow. He followed her every step after that, placing his feet where she did. Creatures moved just at the edge of his vision, but when he turned to look, nothing was there. The sulfates would rush, sending shocks of panic through him, but he couldn't see what they warned him about. Soon, his whole body grew stiff from the constant alarm.

A few moments passed when Kjarton suddenly stopped. He bent his knees and crouched. Exactly in rhythm with him, Sybal did the same, so Tzarik followed suit. He opened his mouth to ask what was going on, but caught Kjarton and Sybal communicating wordlessly. Sybal tilted her head, brows knitting quickly.

Kjarton replied with a well-rehearsed, knowing look and flicked his head to the north, where they were headed.

Sybal's shoulder fell and she looked annoyed. Then she craned her neck, looking for something.

Impressed by her new senses, Tzarik reached out with his own, feeling for anything. It didn't take but a moment for him to smell it. Again, the hot, flaming scent of ash and cinders met his nose. He'd come to associate it with the gods at this point, and he was right. The earth shook with the slow, titanic footfalls of some god passing by. Only this time, the smell was worse.

Just as he caught the wafting, hot tang of sulfur and something else he couldn't place, Sybal grabbed his shoulder. Her eyes told him to follow her, trust her. A deep, bugling screech rose from the green mist. It was far away, but Tzarik realized this was what they feared.

"It will draw the skygges to us," Kjarton whispered to Tzarik. "We must go the long way."

He glanced back at the sun. Did they have the time? He opened his mouth again to argue, but Sybal pressed her palm against his face, silencing him.

"Trust me," she whispered, leaning close.

He noticed two of her black, long lashes had also turned ashen. His heart twisted for the pain she must have been through. He nodded wordlessly.

In perfect silence, they ran low in the tall grass.

HOURS INTO THE NIGHT, Kjarton finally stopped and pointed ahead. "Her thronehall is here, somewhere."

Tzarik looked out over the marshy prairie, lit up in the light of the now full moon and the waning crescent of the second moon with its back to the first. The towering caldera cut a jagged edge against the night sky. He recognized the unique piece of land. The village and grand thronehall were not there, but the sloping earth and sharp mesa told him where they lay on the other side of the barrier.

Kjarton went about making a small fire.

Tzarik glanced up at the moon again. "I can see that second moon outside this place."

Sybal and Kjarton looked up at it. Neither had an answer.

"Be on your toes," Sybal warned, gathering dried peat for the fire. "We need the fire for warmth, but it attracts the skygge." She drew her scimitar and sat near the fire with it on her knees. Tzarik did the same, cautious of the darkness around him.

A million questions for her ate him up inside. It almost hurt to keep silent. But he didn't want to ask in front of Kjarton. He was afraid if they began to speak, his true suspicions about Sjörna-Reks and the things she'd said would come out. And Kjarton sounded still in love with the wolf. He might try to stop them if he sensed Tzarik meant to interfere with any means necessary. But if Kjarton knew what she planned to do, would he want to come back?

He glanced up at the raven Reks across the fire. He had a kindness in his eyes that Sjörna did not. And he'd taken care of Sybal this entire time without knowing who she was or that someone was coming for her. He glanced back at Sybal to find her watching him. Her blue eyes reflected the firelight attractively, the fire casting a warm hue over her paling skin and turning her white strands of hair orange.

Putting her back into her damaged body would give her only a little time. He'd be killing her again. A god-touched never lived long. Perhaps he could get her alone, speak with her.

"There," Sybal said, standing and hefting up her scimitar. "It's brought them to us."

"Who?" Tzarik asked, standing up as well.

"The amalgamation of Mjordir." She sighed. "I tracked his creation once for sport. I'm finding gods hold grudges. It's been sending these broken souls after me for some time now." She stepped out of the firelight and swung her curved blade. Something sliced and then thudded to the ground. "Stand up, boys," she said into the darkness. "We'll get no rest tonight."

CHAPTER 24

THE VÖRLAMIR

THE NIGHT PASSED JUST AS SYBAL HAD SAID IT WOULD. Mindless, sentient-shaped monsters wandered in and out of the camp all night. Drawing atan to throw light in their eyes blinded them, allowing the three of them to slice off their heads. Halat entrapped them. Tzarik lopped off one of the skygge's heads and watched it die. Then, it sank into the writhing earth of the Deep. Just as he thought they'd cleared them out, Sybal shouted and hacked at the ground.

A hand of a human man shot out of the earth, clawing as it birthed itself from the sodden ground followed by a stifled growl.

"What is this?" he cried, leaping away as one flailed to grab his ankle.

"Rebirth," Sybal called, misting out of the way of two walkers. "We don't die here in the Deep." She kicked one and sliced another, spinning an arch of black blood into the rising sun. "Kill them again," she instructed. "They'll eventually wash away underneath and crawl out somewhere else."

Gasping, his shoulders burning after the night of fending off the soul-locked, Tzarik did as she ordered. But the sun rose. They didn't have much time.

It happened like she said. Soon, fewer and fewer of the soul-locked creatures appeared. Some that did crawl out of the earth did so just to walk away.

"It's left," she panted, wiping black ectoplasm from her face.

In the distance, Tzarik wasn't sure, but he thought he saw the long, spidering legs of some sort of monster lumber into the distance.

"Runers!" Kjarton called from several yards off.

They both spun to look where he pointed. A black rift, not unlike the lightning that sprung up from the ground, appeared. Only this one didn't crackle. Tzarik recognized the opening from Tarkan.

"That's it," he called, grabbing Sybal's hand. "We have to run to it. He can't hold it for long."

The three of them dashed to the slowly opening rift. Tired, sore from being on edge all night, and ready to leave the Deep, Tzarik was able to keep up with Sybal's long-legged strides. The rift opened about a foot, and Tzarik caught sight of Tarkan on the other side. He looked strained, his cheeks sunken, and his body shaking as he pried open the world of the gods.

The air turned hot, the unmistakable scent of ash and cinder clogging Tzarik's nostrils. He'd learned in the one night spent here that that meant a god drew near. The hammering of hoofbeats rang in their ears and shook the earth. Something behind them chased them down.

Glancing over his shoulder, Tzarik spotted the headless reaper from before. It gripped its moon-shaped axe in its massive hands and charged towards the rift. It had no face, but he could tell from the urgency and wrath in its thunderous gallop that it intended harm.

"Tarkan!" he cried out. "Careful!"

He sensed the thing had come for the Necro'Khan. Tarkan's white eyes shot up from where he'd been focusing between his palms.

His chest heaved in panic, but he held fast. Zeva appeared behind him, bracing him with her own magic.

The headless beast rapidly overtook them. Sybal screamed as it leapt over their heads with ease and bore down on Tarkan. They all shouted as the Vorlamir raised its axe, rearing up on its hind hooves.

"No!" Tzarik cried, unsheathing his scimitar.

But he was too far away, despite their running. The Vorlamir swung the white side of its axe at the necromancers, forcing them to drop their hands and leap away. As they did, the rift thundered closed with a scream from Zeva.

Sybal shouted, tears tracking down her face. Her scimitar hissed as she whipped it from its leather sheath.

The Vorlamir turned to face them. The faintest bit of black blood trickled in rivulets down its crescent-shaped blade. It had hit Tarkan. "Do not draw your sword against me, little souls," it said from its headless shoulders.

Kjarton stayed the Runers, throwing his hand out to stop them. "You will lose this fight," he warned them. Glaring at Tzarik, he added, "I don't know what that will mean for you."

"He does not belong," the Vorlamir said. "If he dies here, I will take him."

"We were trying to leave," Tzarik shot back at the monster.

"And you will," it growled. Its voice rumbled like thunder from the roots of a mountain. "But not by means of the black heretics. They should not be opening the Deep like a vault to be plundered. They are not gods, though they reach for us."

"Enough!" Tzarik misted to the side and slashed at the Vorlamir with his orichalcum blade. To his surprise, he landed the blow to the horse's flank.

Enraged, the Vorlamir bucked, hitting him square in the chest. The air blasted from Tzarik as he slammed into the ground.

"Don't!" Kjarton begged again as Sybal dove into combat with it.

A harsh, rumbling laugh came from the headless torso of the

Vorlamir. It crossed blades with Sybal, sparking colorful stars where the metal met. That was when Tzarik saw it: the Vorlamir's axe blade was made of orichalcum, and familiar Xian sigils danced down the sharp side. More runes in other languages he did not know were engraved along the rest of the blade.

"Sybal!" he cried, standing up and taking up his scimitar from where it had been dropped. "Don't let him touch you with that blade."

No sooner had he said this than the Vorlamir spun the dangerous weapon in an arch over its head and brought it down. It just missed Sybal as she misted away. Tzarik got to his feet and came at the monster from behind. He drew halat towards the Vorlamir, trapping it just a moment inside a white barrier. With a nickering roar, the monster hacked at the barrier, cracking it.

Keeping his distance, Kjarton again begged them not to fight it. "You can't win," he pleaded. "Vorlamir, please. I beseech you to leave us be!"

Again the monster rumbled a laugh, finally breaking halat. Sybal came up from behind only to get a hoof kick to her face. She grunted and almost flipped head over heels, hitting the ground hard. Tzarik bent his knees, making himself as small as he could when the Vorlamir charged him again. He evaded once, but then was snatched up by the thing's great hands. The one muscled hand wrapped all the way around his neck, lifting him off the ground. With all his weight on his neck, he gagged and gasped, gripping the mighty fingers that held him. Clawing at the hand, he tried to kick the thing, but it held him out at arm's length.

"You may return," the Vorlamir said to him. "You were not given to the Deep. You should not be here."

His neck stretched painfully as he kicked into the air. The pressure built up behind his eyes.

Sybal gave a barbaric shout, but he didn't see the combat behind his watering eyes. Eventually, the Vorlamir had her pinned to the ground with his hooves, his dangerous axe pressed into her chest.

"Don't...touch her...with that," he managed around his strangled throat. He didn't know how the sigils worked, but he had a few ideas. He'd seen them in action. They seemed to take a soul away, locking them inside the sigiled blade. Maybe anywhere was better than the Deep, but he wasn't going to bet Sybal's soul on it.

"Runer," the Vorlamir said as gently as its gravelly voice would let it. "I will take you over. It is my duty to see the lost spirits to their proper place." With that, it dropped Tzarik. "This is a great mercy. Understand that. I should reap you now, taking you into my blade."

Gasping, Tzarik crumped to the ground and scrambled away from the hooves of the monster. The ground beneath them burned. He slid next to Sybal where she panted, looking up. Kjarton stood behind them, fearful, yet waiting to see what they'd do next.

"The Raven Reks," the Vorlamir said, its torso tilting up to look at Kjarton. "Given by Northica to Strigganoct, god of the northern mountain and the storms. You may not leave the Deep."

Kjarton's gray eyes pleaded with the monster, but he did not speak.

"Can you stop us?" Tzarik asked, standing up. He gripped his scimitar hard in his hand.

The Vorlamir laughed again. "I could, Runer. But I respect the white blood. And *you* were not given. I will return you to the other side."

"I'm not leaving without them," Tzarik growled back, bending his knees, ready to fight again.

The Vorlamir didn't move. Its shoulders dropped, and Tzarik thought maybe it considered him in its faceless way. Then it hummed. Reaching behind its left shoulder, it grasped something invisible to them. As it pulled, a long, straight-bladed sword with a lengthy handle and a wide hilt appeared. It wasn't steel. It glowed with a ghostly green, and a high, spectral hum emanated from it. An effulgence like mist hovered around it. With a grunt, the Vorlamir thrust the ghostly blade into the ground. A haunting cry came from the sharp edges as it buried into the malignant earth. With the long handle, the sword stood as tall as the monster.

"Runer," the Vorlamir said to Tzarik. "You came willingly to the Deep, unaware of the place you sought."

"Yes," Tzarik shot back, unsure where the monster might go with this new, far calmer conversation.

"There are tales of such men," it went on. "Ancient stories of men and woman who seek the afterlife to bring back a single soul."

Tzarik turned to pull Sybal up. He didn't release her hand when she stood; she didn't pull it away.

"Such as your kind," the Vorlamir went on, "are guilty. It is why the sulfates run through your blood." He pointed a huge finger at Sybal. "Such as her, are guilty. But I see no black mark on your soul."

Sybal quickly glanced down at him. He'd never told her about his runing. She'd asked before, but he'd only given her parts of the story.

"A different kind of Runer," the Vorlamir said. "Yet one accepted by the black oath." It tilted its headless neck up, looking back to where it had attacked Tarkan, and hummed. "Unusual. And you know the company you keep?"

"I do," Tzarik shot back.

The monster's chest rose and fell as it appeared to take a deep breath. "Very well," it said solemnly. "I will release you. But!" it said loudly when Tzarik moved to interrupt. "There will be consequences."

Tzarik clamped his fingers around Sybal's even harder. "What do you mean?"

The Vorlamir took hold of the hilt of its great, ghostly sword. "There is only one way to get to the other side of a spiritual world, Runer."

Unsure, Tzarik glanced at Kjarton and Sybal. Was it a riddle? What if he answered wrong?

The Vorlamir grunted, pulling the blade from the earth. "Death," it hissed.

At this, Sybal scoffed. "I've died many times."

"Not by my blade," the Vorlamir replied. "If I reap you, as is my task, your spirit can pass to the other side through my blade."

Sybal made a small grunt. "I've died before. You come back again and again, no matter the death you suffer."

"We do," Kjarton said softly. "But Tzarik is not dead. You are not dead entirely. Vorlamir," he called to the creature. "What will happen when a given soul, living like Sybal, returns to the realm of the living?"

"Ah, the infinity the pharaohs of Alika have delved deep for." The monster placed its axe on its back and it vanished like the ghostly blade had appeared. "To you, it will be a trial. There is only one punishment for a soul stolen from the Deep, stolen from this eternity. I fear the kind of soul you are, lady Runer." It took a deep breath into its headless neck. The veins on its bare chest smoldered like a fanned flame underneath its black flesh.

It didn't elaborate.

"And me?" Tzarik asked, overly done with the monster's cryptic talk.

"You will die here," it said. "Your first death."

His jaw dropped a little in confusion.

"Is that a risk you are willing to take, Runer?" the Vorlamir asked steadily. "Let me pierce your spirit with my blade and ferry you across within its emerald prison, among the other souls. Are you willing to die to take her soul back with you?"

Without hesitating, Tzarik spat, "Yes."

Sybal stepped forward as if to stop him, grabbing his arm. He let her, thinking he could never get enough of her touch.

"Speak plainly," she commanded the creature. "What do we have to do?"

The Vorlamir inclined its headless neck. "One day, you will answer for the heretic's actions."

"Tarkan?" Tzarik asked.

"Why?" Sybal added harshly.

The ghostly blade glowed brighter green as the Vorlamir pointed it to Sybal. "You will have enough to bear, god-touched." It slowly moved the point of its blade to Tzarik, just inches from his face. "She was given to the Deep. You called upon a dark power and a dark oath to steal her from the gods. You aided in the ascension of a mortal to that of an immortal, a gift only given by the touch or blessing of a god. Your heretic took it at the cost of living blood and flesh. One who plunders from a god cannot expect to live peacefully."

At this, Tzarik scoffed dryly. "I never have lived peacefully. Tarkan's god gifted him this power in thanks for his servitude and sacrifice. He stole nothing. Your threat's meaningless to me."

"His god is your god: fear. Every sentient has a god whether he knows it or not, Runer. Just as Layth'asad, the lion god of Al'Myrah watches over your Janna, so another watches Nah'jaha." Silently, the Vorlamir held the blade steady. When Tzarik didn't reply, it said, "Very well. As is my duty, I will reap you, killing you. Sending you to the other side."

Kjarton shifted as if to follow them. "I will not."

He didn't ask, but the Vorlamir replied, "Not by my hand. I see their intent, raven. You may yet walk on your clan's land again." It chuckled softly, a low rumble.

Tzarik reached up to where Sybal's hand lay on his arm and took hers in his. "Tell us what to do, then." He couldn't wait any longer. They were so close, and the cryptic warnings of the Deep monster wouldn't stop him.

The Vorlamir gripped the long sword with both its hands and raised it up. "These lives, created by a god, may perish but once to travel to the other side. You," he pointed the blade at Tzarik, "will taste death this one time. But you, lady Runer, have crossed once before. This is your last time."

"We've died before," Kjarton reminded the Vorlamir. "We do not fear death."

The headless monster gave another dark laugh. "Not by my hand, raven. I am no god. I am no living creature. The laws and mores of the gods do not bind me. I am everywhere; I am the only sure thing. I have come even for gods. Not one has bested me. Even the immortals have fallen to me, taken by an arrow or silence of a poison. The deaths brought on you by gods in the Deep are not final."

The Vorlamir faced the Runers again. "Are you prepared for your final death, lady Runer?"

To Tzarik's surprise, Sybal didn't panic. She didn't shake. Her face remained lax. He looked up into her blue eyes.

"You aren't afraid?" he asked. He'd been in near-death situations many times and had rarely been afraid for his own life. He feared for her, but she seemed impassive.

She shook her head slowly. "As I said, I've died many times here."

He looked away. Realizing his unspoken concern, she wrapped her arms around his neck and pulled him close. He reciprocated the embrace. Her cold reply took him by surprise. Something in her had changed. The fire that made her glow inside had dimmed. Had the woman he'd come to save suffered so much that she'd changed?

"And are you, Runer," the Vorlamir murmured, "ready for your first death?"

Tzarik nodded.

"Are you afraid?" she whispered, pressing her forehead to his.

Whether Sybal cared or not, Tzarik knew magic. They couldn't see it, he didn't understand it, but he knew something dark and magical had been agreed upon with this rite. He gathered his courage to reply. Suddenly, a sharp pain cut through his spine, cutting off all feeling to his legs. The ghostly blade shoved through his back, out through his chest, and into Sybal, pinning them together. He fell into her, his legs giving out. She held him tightly, staggering as the sword pierced them both.

"Hold on," she whispered, her breath hot on his neck.

With a mighty pull, the Vorlamir ripped the blade from them both. They fell together onto the ground, still in each other's embrace. Once again, the scent of ashes and cinders filled Tzarik's nose. He focused on Sybal's face, so close to his. A green and gray haze encroached on his vision.

"Don't leave without me," he grunted, choking on his own blood. He gripped her face.

She smiled. "You know I always find you."

CHAPTER 25

RESPITE

THIS WASN'T LIKE THE OTHER TIMES SHE'D DIED. THE world, all in black and green, spun around Sybal, pitching her soul down a spiral river. The hoofbeats of the Vorlamir filled her ears, drowning out all other sounds, chasing her down the river. Tzarik still lay in her arms and she clutched him tightly. They both glowed with a sickly green light. She opened her mouth to tell him to hold on, but a sudden rush of cold water filled her mouth and she choked. Then, without warning, something slammed into them, pulling Tzarik from her. She screamed, thrashing her arms out to feel for him in the dark.

Then, in a flash, her lungs burned and she couldn't drink in enough air. Something pressed down hard on her chest, forcing her to fight for each breath. Her stiff body wouldn't move, her eyes wouldn't open. Sensations of sounds bubbled up from all around her, muffled and unclear. Coldness radiated not from the air around her, but from her very core.

She gasped once more and finally felt her chest rise. Then, painfully, her heart thudded against her ribs. Once. Twice. The rhythm picked up, sending a wave of agony through her stiff veins with every beat. It reminded her of the Runer's death.

A hot hand touched her cheek, holding her tenderly. The warmth made her moan and lean into the hand. The longer the hot skin pressed against her cold flesh, the more she opened her eyes.

"Sybal?" voices cried all around her.

"Tzarik, what happened?" a distantly familiar, elegant voice asked to her right.

"He's hurt!" a panicked female voice called from far away. Tears and fear grated in the girl's voice.

"He won't die," a deep, womanly voice replied.

"Sybal?" Tzarik's voice called, his other hand cupping her face entirely now. At the sound of his voice, her eyes flew open.

Tzarik's warm face, blue eyes, and long, dirty black hair fell into her frame of vision. She swallowed a lump in her throat and fought to move her arms.

"I can't... I can't move my body," she wheezed. Her voice felt weak in her throat and burned.

When she spoke, his face lit up and he fell onto her, embracing her around her neck. His body radiated heat against hers. She didn't remember him feeling this warm. Trying as hard as she could, she finally moved one arm and pulled him closer. The heat melted away the chill that stiffened her. With an audible grunt of effort, she got both her arms around his neck and smothered herself in his hair. Flexing her fingers, she gripped his strands.

He sat back, pulling her up into a sitting position. Opening her eyes, she beheld a long wooden hall, fires blazing in the corners, pillars carved in the likeness of ravens and wolves. She took in the scene over Tzarik's shoulder. A woman stood before her, arms crossed, flaming red hair falling in elegant tangles down her back. She wore a foreboding crown of antlers and glared at Sybal with vibrant, emerald eyes. Beside her was a much more welcome sight: a young man with wide, brown eyes, wrinkled in worry.

"Vicdan?" she coughed, her throat and lungs weak.

"Hello, Sybal!" the younger man crowed.

Pulling away from the welcoming heat of Tzarik, she placed her hand on the side of his face and smiled at her mentor. He rarely allowed so much as a sarcastic grin to lighten his features. So when he returned her smile, pressing his forehead against hers, she burst into a delighted giggle, closing her eyes. A cold tear trickled down her cheek. Tzarik wiped it away with a warm finger.

Craning her neck, she found they both sat on a cobbled stone floor. Behind them, a young woman in white cradled an unconscious man swathed in black. The girl was covered in the necrotic scriptures. Underneath them, her face and flesh were distorted in burns and scars.

"Zeva?" Sybal whispered.

The girl looked up from the man in her arms and nodded. "Sybal," she replied.

Sybal realized the man was Tarkan. "What happened?" she asked, gripping Tzarik to signal to him she wanted to stand. He gave in to her and wrapped his arms around her middle and stood up. Her legs shook violently and her sulfates rushed to bring feeling back.

Vicdan joined Tzarik in supporting her taller frame, pulling her other arm over his shoulder. "Something attacked Tarkan and the rift closed. Then Sjörna-Reks ordered you to be brought inside, away from the Blood Path. We thought we'd lose you both. How did you come back?"

Sybal shook her head and looked down at Tzarik. They had died to cross over. "Are you all right?" she asked him.

He nodded wordlessly, eyes fixed on her. Tzarik and Vicdan lowered her onto a seat at a table near a brazier. Sybal couldn't help but groan when she sat down and finally looked around. She'd seen images of the thronehalls of Caerwren. Despite the outdated builds, the hall gave off an imposing aura. She looked around until her eyes landed on Sjörna-Reks again. The Reks eyed her with a kind of curiosity, but impatience tightened her pale skin over her bones.

The Reks dropped her arms and marched passed Zeva and Tarkan. "You may rest for three days," the Reks quipped to the necromancers. She glared down at Zeva. "Kjarton is not back yet, girl. Tell your father when he wakes that if I do not have my raven back in my arms by the third sunset, his immortality will be tested."

Zeva tightened her grip on Tarkan's body. "He will bring him back," she said stoutly. "We haven't had enough time to heal. To rest."

The Reks raised her red brows. "Consume. It is your way. If you had, all these trials would be over. He'd be strong." Her lips tightened and the bridge of her nose wrinkled into a wolven snarl. Swallowing her last words, she turned.

Before Zeva could reply, the Reks stomped out, her boots echoing against the cobbled floor.

"What's going on?" Sybal asked, flexing her fingers.

Vicdan patted her shoulder. "That's a story. Fortunately, you know someone who can spin a good yarn." He winked at her and leaned over her to look at Tzarik. "Let's get something good inside your bellies and celebrate."

Tzarik hadn't let go of her yet, but his eyes flicked to Zeva.

"I'll be fine, Runer," the girl replied despondently. She met Sybal's eyes and smiled kindly. "Welcome back, Sybal."

VICDAN LED them out of the thronehall and down into the clan's main village to a rathskeller. The walk down proved difficult with the knee-deep snow and blinding sun beating down onto the white blanket. Sybal eventually got her feet back and stopped leaning on Tzarik, but let him hold her hand. She took stock of her body, the thoughts whirling through her head, and the new emotions that coursed through her. Something had its eye on her. She knew she should have felt joy and wonder at awakening in her body, alive and well. But a black pall shadowed her return, one she couldn't place. Tzarik would expect her to behave the way she had before, so she mustered up some strength and put her mind to finding a way to show it. But she didn't have much time to contemplate before Vicdan ushered them into the rathskeller.

They'd only just found a table in a dark corner when a voice rang out to them.

"Lady Runer!" a tall, pale man with blue eyes called. Runes swung around his neck and a huge orichalcum blade shone, lashed to his back. "So, you have come back after all."

Sybal stared at the man for just a moment before she recognized him. "Korvoth?" she cried.

"I'm honored you remember me." He smiled, winking at her and clasping her arm with his big hands. He pulled her into a side embrace and clapped her shoulder with his other hand. He turned to Tzarik and greeted him similarly. "Well done, Al'Myrahns." He motioned to someone in the crowd to join. "Let's drink."

The cheer overcame Sybal and she let it carry her away rather than fight against it. Tzarik watched her, and she made sure to keep smiling. Unable to place what made her feel uneasy, she downed a shot of a clear alcohol Korvoth handed her as they all gathered around the table.

"Poitin from Zealmor," Korvoth explained when the drink forced a hard cough from Sybal. "Should get even the sulfates flowing again. Tage!" he called, beckoning again with his long arm.

Sybal looked up to see a young man in the black leather of a Runer snake his way through the crowd. He had one blue eye and one green. His long hair glowed a kind of golden-red and fell in an ocean of messy braids and silver adornments. Vicdan moved over and offered the young man a seat next to him.

"My new apprentice," Korvoth explained.

Tzarik nodded to the new Runer. "You've acquired a new apprentice since last I saw you?" he asked.

Korvoth nodded. "I've had over twelve apprentices, Tzarik. Runers come and go quickly here on Caerwren. I've had men far older than me last years and young things like Tage here last only a few weeks."

The younger Runer lowered his mismatched eyes and hid his face behind a tankard as he drank.

Sybal accepted another shot of the stuff Korvoth called poitin. This time, it hit her harder and her whole body tingled.

"She can hold her drink." Korvoth smiled, matching her shot with his own.

This gave her a small smile. She turned to Tzarik, a little more at ease thanks to the poitin. "So, we're on Caerwren? How did this come about?"

At this, Korvoth and Tage looked to Tzarik, waiting for the story.

Tzarik's eyes went to Sybal's neck. Confused, she felt her skin with her fingers. A strange scar met her searching touch.

Understanding, Sybal started the story, telling them about her fight with Wu-Zhiang. How she'd been bested. When she told the listeners how they'd beaten her, Tzarik looked away. She waited for him to ask why she'd gone back, but he held his tongue.

"You died?" Tage asked, looking at her in awe. His beardless face held adoring respect for the strange woman before him.

She tilted her head, somberly considering his question. "Something like it, anyway. But what happened after that?" She nudged Tzarik with her elbow.

Her mentor shook his head. "I'm not sure. Sharar took you."

Sybal blanched and took another drink. Had he done anything to her while she'd been in the Deep? The Al'Myrahn scholar had an unhealthy obsession with Runers.

Steadily, Tzarik told her his side of the story. How Sharar had taken him captive, his escape, and the outcome of the civil war on Xia. The Caerwren Runers watched and listened with rapt attention.

"Once I knew Sharar had sent you back to Al'Myrah, I left," he went on.

Sybal's heart broke upon hearing of Yui's death. The princess deserved better. Sybal's time on Xia had turned into one heartache after another. Running never saved them or those near them.

"And I ran into the necromancers in Singad," Vicdan chimed in. "They found you and we took you back to Ala'Nar."

Sybal half smiled at the jongleur. "Thank you. I hate to think what Sharar might have done to me otherwise."

After each of them told their tales, the table went quiet before Korvoth raised his hand to call for more drinks. He made sure to match each swallow Sybal took with one of his own.

"And this woman?" Sybal asked. "This Sjörna-Reks? What does she want?"

"She needs a Necro'Khan to pull Kjarton from the Deep," Tzarik said steadily. He rubbed his chin in thought. "The Vorlamir wouldn't bring Kjarton back like he did us. He had no body to return to. He'd be a ghost.

"Tarkan made Zeva an Apostle to gain favor with his god. It must have worked. Only a Necro'Khan is powerful enough to open the Deep and retrieve a soul. To defy death." He took a quick drink.

Korvoth turned sober at this. "Kjarton-Reks was sacrificed," he said, questioning them. "In Northica."

"What happened?" Sybal asked.

The pale Runer shrugged. "I don't meddle in the affairs of the larger clans and their Reks. Happened years ago."

Despite the dark history, something about Sjörna-Reks's persistent pursuit of Kjarton turned Sybal's belly over and made her heart flutter. She quickly became aware of Tzarik's shoulder pressed up against hers. Every desire she'd let course through her on Xia came back tenfold. She wanted to touch him, pull him against her. Would it be wrong to take just a few hours alone? Would he...?

Realizing her breathing had picked up, she looked up to see if the others had noticed. Korvoth still spoke and Tage listened intently. Vicdan, however, had his eyes on her. His lips lightly parted in a knowing smile and he winked at her. He suddenly sighed and smacked the tabletop.

"Well, young Tage, I want you to tell me your story," the jongleur cut in loudly. "You seem awfully young to have been runed, but well done on surviving it. So tell me, where were you born?"

The younger Runer stammered, looking to Korvoth for advice.

With the three engaged, Sybal stood up and pulled Tzarik with her. Glad that he followed without arguing, she tossed a few coins onto the bar and asked for a key to a room.

"What are you—?" Tzarik began, but she shot him a look that silenced him.

She grasped the key and ran up the creaky wooden steps, towing him along. Finding the room that matched the key, she shook as she unlocked it and yanked him inside. She slammed the door harder than she meant and pressed her back against it, looking at Tzarik's confused face. No breath filled her lungs as she prayed for him to understand. Tzarik was sharp and cunning when it came to the hunt. Could he not read her intentions now? She'd thought about this moment for what felt like ages. Fear took her. She'd never done this before, but thought that with him, her inexperience wouldn't matter. After all they'd been through, after all her deaths, she didn't want to wait any longer. She'd already lived longer than most Runers, had experienced more torment. No, she wouldn't wait anymore.

Suddenly, understanding dawned in his blue eyes and she saw him swallow hard. Locking eyes, they moved at the same time towards each other. They collided hard, gripping one another in a savage kiss. Sybal's head spun as she finally grasped at his muscled body. Then, the world tipped. Not like it had in the Deep, but in a wonderful, hot, rushing maelstrom.

ả

No fire blazed in the grate, but sweat soaked Sybal's skin and her heart hammered so fiercely against her chest that it thudded in her ears. Tzarik lay beside her, eyes wide and fixed on the ceiling as he gasped in rhythm with her. When he didn't speak, she said, "I've never done that before."

He swallowed and turned just his face to her, his left brow cocking upwards.

"It's true." She sighed, finally catching her breath. "It was amazing."

Tzarik smiled smugly and tucked his left arm under his head, looking satisfied.

"Don't look so please." She grinned, elbowing his exposed ribs. "Admit it, I was good, too."

"Well, it's been a while for me," he started with a small smirk. But then his face fell.

A cold trickle slithered down to her gut. He was her first, but she was not his. She almost asked about the other. Or others? But she bit her tongue, seeing the strange melancholy it brought him. She angled herself in front of him. He took the signal and put his arms around her middle, pulling her back into him. With every breath, his chest pushed into her back. His soft exhales hit the back of her neck.

After they both slowed their breathing, his hand traced the scars down her bare back. She felt the change in him immediately. His newfound hubris evaporated. She sensed it almost like his sulfates spoke directly to hers. Even though her scars brought him pain, she loved the feel of his fingers gently caressing each one and wanted him to touch her like that forever.

"This should have never happened to you," he murmured. "I should have never left you."

The fire and tingling in her belly slowly dissipated as she turned to face him; he dropped his hand. His change in emotion made her turn her attention to his body. She ran her hand over his shoulder in return. Every limb was knotted with lean muscle. His chest was broader than she'd imagined. She let her hand rest on his neck, her thumb gently stroking his angled cheek.

"I left *you*," she reminded him. "I thought if we could save the princess, my death would be worth it." She shifted towards him to displace any space until they were flesh against flesh once again. "I think I knew, even in death, you'd find me." She smiled, kissing him.

"That's a lot of faith in me," he replied.

"We always find a way back to one another."

When he didn't move to reciprocate her nearness, she lifted his arm and draped it around her middle. He then pulled her closer, leaning against the top of her head. Again, without words, she felt him want to say something but hold it back.

"What is it?" she asked softly against the sensitive flesh between his collarbone and neck. She ran her hand down his back, feeling all his scars once again. She wished her loving touches could remove every one of them, even the ones inside she could not see. Tzarik had a life haunted by hurt that she could not fathom. He bore it miserably. "Tell me," she whispered, looking up at him.

Before they'd made love, he'd hesitated, even pulled away. She hadn't noticed in the moment, her fervor overtaking her mind. He'd given in and soon joined her in the passion, but now he had that aura again.

Sitting up suddenly, she asked, "Do you regret this?"

"No," he said quickly, pulling her back down into an embrace. "I..." He struggled to find the courage and the words to tell her. She let him take his time, just happy he would open up to her. "I can't tell you. Not yet."

Tears sprang to her eyes. She was glad she lay against his chest, where he couldn't see them. "Can't or won't?" she quipped.

He held his breath. "I...don't know how." His lungs pulsed under her like he was grieving.

Guessing at what might be making him feel this way, she said, "I'm glad you were my first."

Tzarik exhaled sharply and pressed his palms to his eyes. "Damn it, Sybal," he murmured softly.

He wouldn't tell her. But she didn't care. He was here now, with her, their bodies pressed against one another. Whatever welled up inside him didn't matter. How could she make him understand?

"You told me Azar left you," she whispered. "That you didn't have the choices I did."

He didn't reply.

"You speak of him almost as if you miss him, despite what he did to you," she went on. "Do you have a good memory with him?"

At this, she heard his heart slow, but beat hard. She took that to mean that he did indeed have a good memory with his old master. "What was it?" she asked.

Tzarik took a calming breath. "Just images, really. The time I lost his scimitar." She felt his cheeks tighten as he smiled. "He'd had that damn blade since before me. Never replaced it. The curve of the orichalcum was marked with silver where it had been reforged over and over."

Sybal traced a scar gently over his stomach. "They have a word for that on Xia," she whispered, afraid he'd stop talking if she spoke too loud. "I can't recall it, but it means that the thing is better now that it has been reforged with a precious metal. It's a good thing."

Tzarik grunted, neither in agreement or disagreement. "The hilt had a mysterious gem in it." His voice softened as he relived his sparse memories. "He told me it was ice, placed there by a god. He was a fool, perhaps."

She craned around to look up at him. His eyes turned dark and distant. Wrapping her arms around him, she pulled him completely against her bare body. She tossed one long leg over his and enveloped him entirely. She didn't press him, didn't speak. The hurt she felt didn't come from him not confessing what troubled him; it was not knowing how to heal him that hurt her. So, she embraced him, vowing in her heart to never leave his side. All she could offer him was love, and wait for him to speak.

CHAPTER 26

TWÖ CURSES

TARKAN STOOD IN THE SHADOWS OF THE STOCKADE, completely invisible. He'd cast one of the five necrotic spells. They were so much simpler now and took no strength. This one turned him invisible in places where blood had been spilled. If he moved off the space, he'd be found, and would shimmer back into view. For now, he was invisible. He watched Zeva. She kept returning to comfort Ragnall, speak with him, exchange stories of travel. His stories of hunts and adventures kept her eyes locked on to him. For the time they'd been imprisoned together, Ragnall had been weak and had lacked any enthusiasm. When Sjörna-Reks allowed Zeva out, and their conversations became more frequent, he'd completely changed. Animated and wide-eyed now, the Masahk Runer's affection for his daughter was clear. He watched her slender, Scriven hand as she told some story, making her fingers undulate before her, swooping it over her head and making excited faces. He thought it must be about Rakthar, his dragon. She used to be terrified to ride the monster, but had grown to love it. Ragnall didn't watch her hand as she imitated the flight of the dragon: his eyes locked on Zeva's.

His father, Ishmael, had given him the black egg in his eighteenth year. It had seemed an age before his own Scriven ritual. He'd tended the egg in the hearth for months before it hatched. His brother had been jealous. He'd never met anyone with a dragon, and the bond the creatures could make with sentients was one of legend. Tarkan had been lucky that Rakthar had bonded so fiercely with him. When Tzarik had killed Rakthar, he couldn't let the beast go, raising it again and binding it with a script. He'd never been adept at letting things go. Perhaps it had something to do with his long life. Zeva had suffered for his inability to relinquish his hold on her. She was his weakness.

To be truly strong, Ishmael used to say, *you must love nothing, have nothing, cling to nothing. This is why I have taken Porsh from us all. We will wander the desert sands alone. That is the way of the necromancer. Only then can you fully know the power of the Necro'Khan.*

Ishmael had proven again and again that he loved nothing. Tarkan hadn't intended to love Zeva. She'd forced him to with her frightened brown eyes, the way she'd clung to him for the first time as a child, the first time she'd held his hand. His hard heart ached at the memory. And now, she gave her affection to another.

"Necromancer," Sjörna-Reks whispered from down the hall of the stockade.

Shaken that she knew he stood there, invisible as he was, he turned to face the red Reks.

"I can smell you," she offered, a small smirk turning up her lip.

He took a few steps, finding a place blood had not been spilled. He wavered into view. She swayed gently, reeking of wine. Her green eyes darted to him, squinting in the dim light when she found him. Wordlessly, she gestured him to follow her. She exited the stockade and took them back into the thronehall.

Empty now that it was night, the hall glowed with a warm, orange light from the main hearth. The sounds of lovemaking lilted down from some rooms on the upper levels. Outside, the golden wolf howled mournfully. Sjörna-Reks took her seat in her wolven throne and indicated that he should sit in the raven one. He hesitated, taking in the steely eyes of the depicted raven. Then he sat, finding no good reason to argue with the Reks.

"What were you thinking just now?" she asked, tracing the complex knots etched into the arm of her throne. "I can no longer hear a change in your ruby heart." She paused to give him a smile. "But I heard your black blood slow." She faced him, tilting her head and making her huge, antlered crown angle sharply. "Speak, necromancer," she ordered when he didn't reply quickly.

He steadied his tone, fixing his blue eyes on the ring around his finger where their blood mingled. "You unbound me, but I am not free. I am Necro'Khan, yet I feel powerless." Admitting weakness might not have been the wise thing to do. Sharar had said how much he liked Tarkan's honesty. This time, his weakness kept him from fulfilling his side of the oath.

Sjörna-Reks nodded, her face solemn. "I know. And you are weak. I thought once you ascended, you'd burst with power, shattering my clan. I want to see your strength, Tarkan. I need it. Once you are strong enough, your oath will be fulfilled."

He jolted as she reached over, taking his hand in hers. When he tried to pull back, she held him tighter. Languidly, she ran her hands over the ring that held their blood. Her lids grew heavy as she traced the markings over the back of his pale hand. Somehow, her skin shone whiter than his. Her gentle touch sent an unnerving shiver up his arm. He moved his fingers, reaching out to find something to raise. When his hand flexed, she crushed it in hers hard.

"I want you to immerse yourself in your magic," she ordered softly. "Show me the spells. I am grateful you have not raised the dead, as it would only keep you weak. But we are past waiting now. You must consume. I want you strong. Unstoppable."

He opened his thin lips to argue, but she crushed his fingers in her iron grip again. This stopped his tongue. He couldn't pull himself from her now.

"You will," she ordered. "I have given you everything you wanted, Tarkan. I am no longer bound by the oath. It is time for you to uphold your end of the pact."

He glared at her. "You made me destroy Zeva."

Sjörna-Reks smiled and gently shook her head. "No, I didn't. You chose to make her Scriven. I gave you another way, but you refused. You try to uphold the banner of righteousness with your frail courage. Weak. Tarkan, you are not righteous. Nor am I. It is time for you to give in to what you need. Why won't you?"

His blue eyes danced between her green ones. He almost argued back, but realized she was right. Zeva had asked him to not snuff out the souls Sjörna-Reks had collected in her bog. So, there they lay still. Her terrified expression in the cave outside Ala'Nar when she'd seen him consume the human heart had stopped him from doing it again. It was Zeva, not Sjörna-Reks, who held him prisoner.

"She always wanted to join me," he said at last. "I didn't want..." He choked. "I didn't want to destroy her. She deserves better."

The red Reks took in his every word, devouring him with her gaze. "When will you return to the Deep, Necro'Khan? When will you bring back my raven king?"

Her finger worked its way up his arm, pushing the sleeve of his robes aside to continue tracing the scriptures on his bare flesh. She slithered from her throne, kneeling before him. She was tall enough that she sat just below his eye level. He pressed into the back of the throne, trying to get away from her sensuous touches. Her other hand clamped to the arm of the throne, trapping him there.

"When I have rested," he whispered in reply. "Zeva must become familiar with the spells as well. Cast them. So the fresh scriptures are used."

Sjörna-Reks's hand pressed into his chest now. She held it there, her heat scorching him through his thin robes. She rose up on her knees, no longer sitting back on her heels, and leaned close to his face.

"He needs a body," she whispered.

Her breath hit his face, smelling heavily of sweet, mulled wine.

Tarkan swallowed hard. "Ragnall," he suggested. "Use Ragnall."

Sjörna-Reks stopped, biting her lower lip and lowering her head. "I suppose I've already used him. The children of Runers are..." She winced and shook her head, the bone and bead ornaments in her hair clinking as she did so.

This gave Tarkan pause. "Children?" he asked, careful to keep his tone even. Outside, the wolf had stopped howling. "Do you not have a son?"

Sjörna-Reks scoffed, smiling sadly. "Signar is a wildling. Mad. My own fault. Vaeson are not to copulate when in our animal shape. But Kjarton couldn't refuse me that night." She laughed darkly. "My son is no better than a wild dog. The offspring of Runers are hardly any better."

Sjörna-Reks slithered up closer to him. She spread his knees to sit on the throne with him. His throat went dry. He knew if Sjörna-Reks wanted to, she could snap his neck with one hand, trapped the way he was. Perhaps she was right: he should consume, get his strength back, and call up a horde of undead. If she so chose, he'd be her captive forever if he did not use his new magic to throw off her chains.

He pressed back into the wooden throne as far as he could, turning his face away from her. But her large hand gripped his chin and forced him to look into her eyes. She was so close; he saw now that tiny, star-like freckles flecked her pale cheeks and the bridge of her nose. She came closer, her knees touching the inside of his thighs.

"Are the spawn of necromancers the same?" she asked softly, grazing the tip of her nose against his sunken cheek.

"You've been drinking." He couldn't stop his breath from

hastening, knowing she heard his unease. "Yes, the same as Runers. Maybe worse," he told her.

Suddenly, he understood. She intended to use him as Kjarton's vessel. He was unsure how she'd force him to put her Reks's spirit into his own body, but he didn't want to find out. "Ragnall," he suggested again. He formed a lie quickly, desperate for it to sound sincere. "He is Masahk. A child from him would not be the same. His immortal blood would protect such a union."

Sjörna-Reks frowned, finally stopping her administrations. "I've never heard such a thing."

"Masahk keep their secrets," he went on. "On Alika, this is well known. But Runers are all but forbidden from coupling with sentients. It is part of the black oath."

The lie was terrible, but he hoped her desire for taboo couplings might help sway her wine-sodden mind. "But he couldn't stop you," he added. He swallowed hard, the heat from her warm flesh touching his cold skin.

The red Reks exhaled in a dry laugh through her nose and shook her head. "You wanted to show Zeva you were strong. But all you did was unveil your frailty to me."

She lurched forward, taking his mouth so roughly in hers that the back of his head banged against the wood. The shock froze Tarkan to the throne. She bit his lips, her sudden grip on his throat tightening until he couldn't breathe. At first, he panicked, unused to his immortal status. She inhaled deeply before breaking the kiss. She smiled, devouring with her eyes the shock he couldn't keep from his face. When his eyes flicked to the door at the end of the thronehall, she smiled, biting her lip so hard she drew a little blood.

"Fine." She sighed, standing up, giving him his space back. Something in her tone made him realize she didn't believe him. She wanted to placate him, still had control over him. Did she fear nothing? "It will be Ragnall. He's fine for a lay, anyway. I will give you two days, necromancer. Two days to spend with Zeva, make her cast, whatever you need to do to satisfy you. But you will consume to gain your strength back. Living flesh," she added when he stirred to argue. "No chance of possession. When you are strong, you will return to the Deep."

He swallowed hard, forcing his eyes to not waver from hers.

She looked down at him. "I could prostrate myself, show myself as weaker to entice you. Beg you. Weep and moan at your feet." Her eyes roamed over his frightened frame. "But that is not my way. I am strong of body. You showed yourself as complacent to gain power. And look how close you are now." She simpered. "Make me fear you. Show me the power you have gained. Don't make me force you." She smiled at a dark thought. Her fingers lightly touched his long, thin hair. "I'd enjoy it too much. I tend to destroy the things I love, along with the things that displease me. But you are an immortal body to be destroyed for eternity. If it is to be by my displeasure, then so be it."

The Reks's words hit Tarkan hard. He'd always believed he was more righteous than Ishmael and even Ashkan for not consuming living flesh. But Sjörna had shown him that if he ever wanted to throw off the chains of servitude, he needed to find the will to use the necrotic powers as they were intended. But how could he kneel to the black magic when he forced a more righteous way on Zeva? He didn't want to give in, but submitting himself to the black magic would bring him freedom from groveling to the likes of Sjörna-Reks. Once he fulfilled the blood oath, he'd be free.

Sjörna-Reks licked her lips to go on, but a strangled cry broke the cold night air. A young man shouted in alarm outside.

"Signar?" Sjörna-Reks gasped, turning to face the front of the thronehall. "Signar!" She leapt, shifting into her wolven form as she launched herself from the stone dais.

Outside, a yelping, like a wounded dog, shrieked to the skies, mixed with the cries of a boy.

"Necromancer, come!" she barked.

ȡ

Tarkan followed the red wolf at a run, bursting into the cold night air just behind her. Lokhtar met them outside, shoving past Tzarik, Sybal, and Vicdan as they trudged up the path from the village. Despite the darkness, the moon above lit up the land covered in white snow. Tarkan shivered; he'd left his fur cloak inside, but he spotted the disturbance. Set up at the foot of the path leading from the village to the thronehall were three grotesque nithing poles. Freshly butchered horse hide hung from them, the eyeless skulls staring their curse towards the hall. Tethered between the beams with his arms stretched above his head was Sjörna's wildling son, Signar, in his human form. He howled like a wolf, crying in fear under the bloody totems. Blood covered his bare chest as it rained down from the carcasses above.

"Signar." Sjörna-Reks gasped. She snapped her head to the Runers, "Find Skarde and Dain! I can smell them still."

Sybal looked down. Seeing a set of tracks, she dashed off into the darkness to follow them. Her long legs and ancestral blood carried her easily through the snow. Tzarik drew halat, shielding himself from any emanating curse from the poles, and ran to the wild boy. He swiftly cut him from the cursed totems, catching him as he fell. Rather than thank him, the wildling transformed into a golden wolf and snapped at the Runer. Tzarik fought to defend himself from the wild wolf without hurting it.

"Tarkan," Sjörna-Reks barked. "On me."

Without arguing, Tarkan ran and leapt up onto her wolven back, holding on as tight as he could with his knees and hands. Her red fur was not like regular wolf fur, course and thick. Hers was soft and thin, like her human hair. She bounded off, nearly dislodging him. He ducked low to maintain his grip, eyes streaming with tears from the cold night air cutting his face.

"When we see them," she panted. "Curse him."

One of the five spells of necromancy was putting a blight—a curse—on a sentient, object, or land. This not only brought misfortune, but would bring illness and pain to the inhabitants of the cursed place. Tarkan realized his suspicions about Sjörna-Reks were right, and she hadn't lied: she'd worked with necromancers before if she knew of the curse.

The red wolf launched herself up the rocks and frozen hills, following the scent of Sybal and the Northicans.

Behind them, Lokhtar shouted for Tzarik to leave Signar. Tarkan glanced back and witnessed five or more Northican radjur riders invade the open area before the thronehall. Lokhtar and Tzarik tried to fight them, but the Northicans overpowered them. Tarkan almost called for her to go back, but the golden wolf defended the clansmen and the Runer simply by his wild nature. Vicdan got separated from Tzarik and ran to avoid Signar's snapping jaws. Three of the radjur riders fled, not wanting to be wounded, and one went for a hostage. Since Vicdan was the only one separated, the rider galloped to the fallen jongleur and wrenched him up. With him as a captive, he rode away, whooping and crowing into the darkness.

"Necromancer," Sjörna-Reks panted, her paws thundering against the ground. "Can you see him yet?"

Tarkan turned back to their pursuit. "There!" He pointed eastward when they crested a hill, overtaking Sybal and leaving her behind. "Across the bogs. I see a white radjur and hawk."

Sjörna-Reks panted, her ribs heaving under Tarkan's thighs. "Can you curse them from here?" She slowed, howling after Skarde-Reks and Dain Radjur-tor.

Proximity mattered in the necrotic arts. "Am I Necro'Khan or not?" Tarkan growled, more to himself than to answer Sjörna-Reks. He locked eyes onto one of the figures, pressed his palms nearly together, and hissed the incantation.

The wind picked up as he commanded the black magic. Sharp ice flakes cut his eyes as he refused to blink, training them onto his victim. Hissing the verses tattooed on his body, his voice lost in the wind, he cursed the white hawk. He'd rarely cursed land or sentient. Too often it led to bounties against necromancers when the village or family discovered one loomed in their midst. He'd seen it a handful of times in his long life. His tribal brother, Ashkan, had cursed more than he should have, forcing them to flee and hide. If the one who spoke the curse was killed, the curse would be lifted. No one would come after him for this curse. He fully believed in the power and might of Sjörna-Reks.

He watched his hands turn thin and the skin grow tight over his bones as the magic took his blood. The weakness creeped up on him again. Yes, he would consume. He needed to be strong.

"Nothing happened," Sjörna-Reks growled, her hackles rising. "Curse him, necromancer!"

"I did," Tarkan replied cooly, knowing full well the son of Skarde-Reks would soon feel the effects. "Trust me, Reks. He will not see the summer."

"Will the Volra be able to stop it?" she asked, her emerald eyes following them. Sybal had almost caught up with them. She was good.

Tarkan turned to look back towards the village where Signar's howling had subsided a little. "They can try. A sachet of protection and other magics of protection will help for a time, but they will have to be refreshed for the rest of his life. Even still, Dain Radjur-tor will be weak."

A deep chuckle rumbled under Sjörna-Reks's ribs. "Good. Now I must get my Volra to remove the nithing poles before their curse takes hold."

They trotted back to the clan's village to find Lokhtar kicking Signar, trying to quiet the wolf, taking him back to where he perpetually lay shackled. Tzarik argued with the much larger man, saying they needed to go after the Northicans and Vicdan, but Tarkan didn't hear them.

Tarkan slid off Sjörna-Reks and watched her ascend the stairs, shifting back to her tall, womanly form. "Two more days, Tarkan," she reminded him, sweat glistening on her heaving chest. "Rest. Consume. Be ready to fetch me my raven king."

CHAPTER 27

KJARTON-REKS

THE NECROMANCERS HAD NOW BEEN GIVEN A ROOM IN THE thronehall, though they were still guarded. Zeva slept curled in piles of furs on a straw-stuffed mattress. The sounds of screams and guttural cries of agony outside her window penetrated her dreams. She fought to open her eyes, but a paralysis held her tight, only letting her glimpse a gleam of sunlight. Despite it being early morning, the sun only rose just enough in recent days to skirt the horizon for a few hours before sinking back down to its unknown depths. The long darkness made Zeva uneasy, and nightmares haunted her sleep more intensely than before. They still drained her energy, feeling like they sucked the very blood from her veins. She'd wake more exhausted than when she went to sleep. This dream had been the worst yet.

She dreamed they'd gone back to Al'Myrah. The hot Al'Myrahn sun had thawed her cold body out. The sand had shifted under her feet, and she could not wait to enter one of the grand cities and see the colored glass lanterns, smell the pipe smoke, and drink mint tea from golden carafes. But something was wrong. She couldn't find Tarkan. She was alone.

Zeva ran through the streets, screaming for him. Ever since leaving Moshav as a child, she'd never been parted from him for more than a few hours. They'd never spent the nights apart. The more she cried for him, the more hideous faces in the streets started to follow her. They were not kind, sentient faces. They were twisted, deformed, glaring at her and growling. Some even snapped at her, trying to bite her and pull her back into their angry horde.

"Tarkan, help me!" she wept. "Where are you?" Why had he left her? Abandoned her?

Again, she tried to open her eyes, but the dream played on, like an oily mist over the vision of her room. She couldn't sit up. Something dark moved over her. She screamed as loud as she could, knowing the shadow wanted her. Wanted to harm her. The dream took over again and familiar faces appeared in the mob coming for her. She saw the jongleur among them, coming at her with an orichalcum blade. Sybal leapt over the heads of the closest monsters, screaming for her blood. Even Tzarik was there, his face distorted and cruel.

"Why?" she cried to them, backing away. "Why are you doing this?"

Then she backed into someone. She knew the hand that grabbed her before she turned around: Tarkan. She spun, throwing her arms around him, begging him to protect her.

Sharp teeth bit into her forearm. Afraid, she looked up to see her father burying his teeth in her flesh, tearing at her. His eyes turned red with bloodlust.

With a final scream, she shot up, rolled over, and spilled out of the bed. Clutching her arm, she inspected it for bite marks. There were none. She snapped her head around, looking for Tarkan. The weak moaning from outside greeted her. Her back ached, like someone had beaten her with rods. Sighing, she took a deep breath and stood up. She felt weaker than ever before. No amount of sleep would bring her strength back. Running her hands over her arm, she reminded herself that the scriptures had taken to her. Then why had she not felt recovered? Sjörna-Reks grew impatient, but no amount of rest and blood made her feel like she could cast strongly yet. It had been too long, and they were running out of time. Something was wrong.

Just as she walked to the door, where she knew guards stood on the other side, the curtain pulled back. Tarkan stood before her, blood on his face.

"What happened?" she gasped, taking his arms in her hands. "Are you hurt?"

He shook his head, pushing her inside. He whispered, "We must be strong." He shoved a wooden plate laden with a pile of raw meat.

She winced as a dark, sticky blood covered her palms, sloshing over the side. The smell of the blood and flesh choked her. "What am I supposed to do with this?" she asked, disgusted. The dream came back strong, making her wretch.

"You know," he replied sternly. "You wanted this. You have to follow the ways of the necromancer if you are to be one. You must consume and use your spells for the oath to grow in strength. You have been too weak to cast, and yet you have, hurting yourself."

His sharp words cut to her heart. She fumbled around for the right retort.

"You must," Tarkan snapped. "Before they perish. Dead flesh opens you to possession." He reached up, touching her Scriven arm. "These protect you from the outside. But taking something inside them allows it past the barrier." His eyes flitted to the window, then back to her. "Eat. Before they die. Living flesh is strongest. Then you will perform the five spells." He turned to leave.

"But..." she started, desperate.

Tarkan whirled around, bearing down on her. "Do as I say, Zeva!" he roared. Never, in her thirteen years of being with him, had he ever looked at her with that kind of fury in his eyes.

She quelled under his striking tone, shrinking to the floor.

Tarkan immediately regretted his words, dropping his arms and closing his eyes. He knelt next to her, taking her hand and kissing her palm. "Forgive me."

She nodded but did not sink into his arms. She knew he wouldn't have snapped at her without cause. Perhaps he was afraid? She'd never seen him afraid. Even when Sharar had tortured him, Tarkan's eyes had shone with defiance. He'd changed since arriving on Caerwren. A new hunger bloomed in him, one she did not understand that made him bend a knee to the red Reks. But she still loved him.

"Our lives were the same for so long," she started, making sure her tone was kind. "I suppose the change is taking me by surprise. Yes, I wanted this. But maybe I didn't understand how quickly it would change me."

Tarkan shook his head. "It shouldn't have been like this. And I'm sorry for it. But it is now." He leaned closer to her. "Zeva, we can be strong if we follow the scriptures. Consume. And no one will imprison us again. *Use* us. We will not live in fear. Do you understand? If we do this to regain our strength, we can be free."

Reaching up, he gently caressed the burns and scars on her marred face. "No one will hurt *you* again," he added. "This happened to you because I was weak. My one task was to protect you and I failed."

For a moment, his blue eyes returned to the soft gaze she knew, and she melted into his arms. He wrapped her tightly against his chest and waited until she calmed. Then, he stood up and moved towards the door.

"Quickly," he instructed, pointing to the bloody mass in her hands. "Before they die."

He vanished. Zeva looked down at the bloody flesh and her stomach turned.

She bit her lip, gingerly picking up a sliver between her finger and thumb. "We cannot be weak again," she said, echoing Tarkan. "I will not put myself at anyone's mercy."

ᚪ

IT WAS hours before she could leave the room after. She scrubbed as best she could, but still felt the blood of the living flesh around her lips and on her hands. She cried while scrubbing herself clean until her eyes were as raw and red as the flesh she'd chewed. But the sensation of power and energy that had coursed through her after the first bite had made the others easier.

Guilt and shame made her slink out of the room and sneak out the back of the thronehall. A single guard sat outside the stockade, hammering an axe on a small forge between the thronehall and the prison. He glanced up at her as she approached but didn't stop her as she slipped into the dark, stone structure. The warden's key hung outside the stockade above the chair and table where he'd sit on watch. It clinked ominously in the biting wind as she opened the door. No other guards waited inside. The chests of items taken from prisoners sat under an unused table just inside the door. It was locked. She glanced at it and quietly stalked to the cell Ragnall lay in.

The white-feathered Masahk lay on his side, knees pulled into his chest. He moaned once and wrapped his arms around himself.

"Are you cold?" Zeva asked, wrapping her fingers around the bars of his cell.

Ragnall's long, feathered ear perked up at the sound of her voice. He rolled over carefully as if his entire body were in pain. "No," he grunted, pushing himself up into a seated position. His long, white and black wing feathers splayed out behind him like a cloak. "On Caerwren, we call it the Runer's death."

Zeva gasped. "What do you need? I don't want you to die in this cell." She pressed herself against the bars.

Ragnall shook his head. "I'd welcome death at this point. I've not been a good man, and an even worse Runer." He cringed as a fresh wave of agony washed over him. His long ears dropped as he winced. "Sjörna is not a gentle lady of the night." He tried to crack a smile, but Zeva's face fell into a horrified gawk. "And my runes... I've been parted from them for too long. But perhaps this is the best. Even for a Masahk Runer, I've lived long enough."

She glanced at the chest. Would they know if she slipped him his runes? "I can get them," she offered.

The Runer shook his head. Instead, he crawled closer to the bars and motioned for her to sit. She did, slipping her hand through to take his.

"What have you done, Zeva?" Ragnall asked, meeting her blue eyes with his. "You're different from last time. I see it. The sulfates in my veins are on fire."

The guilt roiled up inside her again, making her sick. "There are things a necromancer has to do," she began. "This is who I am now. I must partake of that life to keep me and my father safe. Just as you must."

"I see that," Ragnall whispered softly. He reached up and touched her scars like Tarkan did. "You've not led an easy life. I see it in you."

Without realizing it, she leaned into his touch, nuzzling into his palm. When she did catch herself, she didn't recoil. He didn't take his hand away. She blushed deeply.

"Do you have to?" he asked. "Are the scriptures like the runes?"

She shook her head. "Once they accept you, they keep you forever."

"Then there is no punishment like— Ugh!" Ragnall seized, curling in on himself in pain.

Zeva shot up onto her knees and gripped his shoulders through the bars as he threw his head back in a fit. "Careful!" she cried, trying to keep him from dashing his head on the stone. She strained, holding the tall Masahk up. When he came back from the spell, he collapsed against the bars. She caressed his ashen hair and ran her fingers lightly up his soft, feathered ears.

"Thank you," he panted, pressing his hand to his chest. "You are tender, Zeva. Kind." Closing his eyes for a final calming breath he whispered, "You've been good to me. Better than I deserve. It puzzles me."

She slid over the stones until her shoulder pressed through the bars against his. They sat, leaning against one another. "I will be a monster," she promised him. "Tarkan didn't want to turn me into this. I asked him to. I wanted to save him from sacrificing thousands of innocents, who don't deserve to be put into nothingness forever. I was willing to be just one sentient given."

Ragnall slipped his hand out from his cell and touched her knee gently. "But do you deserve this?" he asked.

She shrugged. "I wanted to save him."

"Zeva." Ragnall's voice turned serious now. "You are stronger than him. Look how you healed."

"I'm weak," she countered. "I feel it. But I cannot make myself consume like I should."

"But you're not weak."

She looked up at his soft, deep tone. His blue eyes sparkled in the dim light.

"The necrotic ways have taken to you. Your father sees this. He's not as strong as you."

"Yes, he is!" she argued automatically. Even to her, the words felt flat. Tarkan's confusion and rage at the lack of immediate power was obvious to her. But she couldn't admit it. If she didn't say it, maybe it'd be less true. "I don't feel strong," she said at length. "He's weak because he did not consume flesh. He did it for me."

"You *are* stronger," Ragnall argued. "Sjörna-Reks is using you. And him. I've seen how she treats those she sees value in. She is powerful, strong. I don't think your father will be able to pull out of her clutches now that he's in this deep. And he'll bind you to him."

She glared up at him, silencing his next words. "Tarkan will not let us be used again. He promised me. Once Kjarton-Reks is brought back, we'll leave. Tarkan can bring him back. He can open the Deep. We've done it once already."

The Runer shifted, coming to his knees. "I've not cared about much in my life, Zeva. But you... How can you not see what she's doing?"

Hurt at his implication of her ignorance, she pulled away from him. She had to follow Tarkan. Surely if something was going to put them in danger, Tarkan would tell her.

Ragnall went on, "With the barrier weak from Vasaras, the Deep —and everything in it—is close." He narrowed his eyes. "She may be summoning an army to take revenge on Northica, an undead horde Skarde-Reks could not help but fall to. She needs a body for Kjarton. And she's close." He suddenly gripped the bars. "Zeva, let me out. Please."

The sudden urgency in his tone touched her heart, and unchecked panic swelled in her on his behalf. "I don't understand," she whispered.

"You have to run as well," he went on, taking her hand through the bars. "She won't let you go. Whatever she's promised you is a lie. You and your father walked right into her canton and are just what she's been looking for. She'll use you to bring an army up from her bog, a whole undead swarm and the gods know what else from the Deep. I don't care about Northica, but she *will* attack Skarde-Reks. And she'll use you and your father to do it. And..." He dropped his head against the bars, his breath hitching. "She'll use my body for Kjarton."

Zeva gasped, her mind finally catching up to his. "Tarkan wouldn't have endangered me," she tried to argue.

"Zeva," Ragnall repeated. "Let me out. I'll come back for you. There's a hidden encampment under the Black Road that crosses the Empty, a whole tribe of Masahk and underground roads, called the

Court of Deliverance. Rhostrana still takes Masahk as slaves and sometimes we take the underground road to get past the Black Road and the Rhostranan slavers. There are people there in the Court who can hide you and get you off Caerwren." He covered her hands with his, pleading with his eyes. "Don't let me be his vessel. Don't let her use you and your father."

Fright shook her where she knelt. If there was danger, Tarkan would not have stayed so long. Would not have allowed Sjörna-Reks to make puppets of them. Then an idea hit her.

"I'll ask the Runers," she offered, preparing to leap up. "They perceive things I never do. And they've been so kind to me."

"Wait!" Ragnall hissed, dragging her back down. "Let me go, first."

"Ragnall—" she began.

"Zeva!" he cut over her. "I swear I'll come back for you. I won't leave you here. Ask your Runer friends for aid. But release me first. Stay near them. If you escape before I come back, look for the sign of the Court. Any place you find it means someone who lives there can help you find your way there."

Overcome with emotion and new fear, Zeva stood up. "Wait here." She pulled her fur cowl over her head, even though that would add nothing to the spell. Breathing steadily, she prepared to cast the first necrotic spell. Hissing into the air, she spoke the verses that made her walk like a vapor over land where there had been bloodshed. She wavered from sight as more than enough blood had been spilled on the prison floor.

She smiled when her body dematerialized. The sensation of standing but not seeing her legs made her teeter on her feet for just a moment. "It feels so strange," she mused. She held her hand up to eye level. Only a slight ripple showed where her hand floated before her.

Like a mist, she trotted to the door, shimmering in and out of sight as part of her foot landed on bloodless stone.

"Just the runes," Ragnall hissed when she reached for the door.

But the trunk was locked. Opening the heavy wooden door just enough to slip her hand out, Zeva stepped in a bloodstained spot to remain invisible, lifted the ring of keys, and shut the door again without the guard outside noticing. Kneeling, she unlocked the trunk and quietly threw the lid open. Inside lay Ragnall's long, orichalcum blade and his black leather string of runes, among other oddities. She scooped them up and ran back to him, tossing him the runes first.

"You are very good at that," he mused with a smile as he wrapped his belt around his middle and drew buhkar. He vanished into a haze of black mist and passed through the bars. When he materialized again, Zeva had, too.

Just that one spell drained her. She panted and wrapped her hands around one another, holding them over her chest. "I'm sorry," she wheezed. "I didn't think just one of the five spells would make me feel like this." She had just consumed living flesh as well. Why was she so weak?

Frowning slightly, Ragnall faced her. "Stand still," he ordered gently. "Something about you is not right. My blood feels your necrotic scriptures, but there's something else. I haven't been able to understand what it is about you that rushes them so."

He raised his hand and drew atan around her quickly. The soft white light pulsed out from the rune, bathing her in its magic light. He gasped and frowned, hand still raised where the runic light went out.

"What is it?" she asked, putting her hands on his chest and looking up into his face. She'd never realized how tall he stood. She'd seen him stand before, but had not been this close to him.

"Something is following you," he repeated, taking a step back, his eyes dancing over something she could not see. "I believe it's feeding on you, making you weak. Syphoning the strength you should be getting from consuming."

"Like a curse?" she asked, her gaze not wavering from his face.

The way his blue eyes narrowed, reading whatever shroud lay on her, entranced her. She slid her hand down his runeless arm, loving the softness of the tiny feathers that covered some of his pale skin.

He shook his head and pulled up his fur-lined cowl. The light from the rune faded. "Stay close to the Runers. I'll be back for you once I find a way for you to leave."

A lump so large and hard formed in Zeva's throat that she couldn't speak at all. She clung to him. These new feelings swirled in her like a maelstrom. She wanted him to run and be safe, but she wanted to hold him tight forever, too. How could she release him and cling to him at the same time? When he moved to step away, panic shot through her that she might not ever see him again and her grip tightened.

Ragnall's face softened as he smiled down at her fearful visage. It was a soft, half smile. His warm hand cupped her chin, and he quickly dove, kissing her forehead.

When he did this, heat shot through her and melted her feet to the prison floor. He pressed his forehead against hers.

"I swear I'll be back for you," he whispered. With a final kiss to the top of her head, he leapt away, drawing buhkar and vanishing into a black shroud.

Zeva's stomach flipped and she smiled, biting her lower lip hard. Her toes curled so hard in her boots that she popped the joints. Where he'd kissed her, she turned numb. Looking back into the cell, she saw he'd left behind a few long, iridescent white and black feathers. Reaching through the bars, she plucked one up and braided it into her long black hair.

Just as she opened the door to exit the stockade, Lokhtar marched towards her, grabbing her upper arm and swinging her around to march to the thronehall. She grunted at the pain of his grip.

"What are you doing?" she gasped.

"The Reks will wait no more," he growled. "She's taken your

Runers captive and will not stand to have you loose while the Necro'Khan opens the Deep."

Even as he said it, Zeva felt the wind chill and begin to swirl around the hall. Tarkan must be inside, opening the Deep again. She gasped in pain as Lokhtar jerked her harder towards the hall. He barked at two other long-haired warriors to bring Ragnall. Her stomach flipped again, but not in the pleasant way it had before.

ᚼ

A WIND TORE at Zeva's robes when they entered the thronehall. The thick smell of blood filled her nostrils as a wind of fire and ice blew through her. Tarkan stood in the midst of a new Blood Path made of sentients. She gasped at the horrific sight, entrails and limbs hanging alike down the wooden beams. She couldn't stop the scream that tore from her throat.

Sjörna-Reks walked out from behind the path. "Where is the Masahk Runer?" she barked, glaring at Zeva.

"Coming," Lokhtar replied.

Their voices could hardly be heard over the whipping roar of the wind. Zeva craned her neck as Lokhtar led her to the side of the bloody ritual. She spotted Tzarik and Sybal, arms tightly chained behind their backs. They were kneeling on the other side of the Path. She met Sybal's eyes.

"Are you all right?" Sybal called to her.

Taken aback by the woman's kindness, Zeva nodded but couldn't stop the tears that ran down her face. Ragnall was gone, and soon they'd know. Zeva turned to Sjörna-Reks where she stood behind Tarkan, her green eyes bulging in anticipation.

"Sjörna-Reks!" she called, her words almost drowned in the torrents of Tarkan's spell. "Don't bring him back." She wasn't sure what else to say. "We don't understand what opening the Deep could mean. You could bring a malignation to Caerwren that you can never expunge."

"Don't weaken now, girl," the Reks shot back.

"You said we were free to go," Sybal growled, twisting her shoulders against the bonds.

The Reks didn't reply.

In a flash of bright green light, Tarkan growled and pulled his palms apart, cracking open a rift to the Deep at the other opposite of the Blood Path.

"My Reks!" a bearded man shouted, coming in empty-handed.

Zeva gulped in fright. Sjörna-Reks whirled around, already enraged that he'd come without the prisoner.

"Where is he?" she roared.

"Gone," the man replied. "His cell is still locked."

Sjörna-Reks froze, angry tears whipping from her eyes in the necrotic wind.

Zeva's gaze moved to Tarkan where he walked down the Blood Path towards the torn opening. "What are you doing?" she screamed over the roaring wind.

Tarkan walked the path himself. Without stopping, he passed—body and soul—into the Deep.

"Tarkan!" Zeva shrieked after him, not sure what this might do to him.

Across the Path, Sybal gasped, eyes wide and fixed on something inside. "Kjarton?"

This got Sjörna-Reks's attention and she looked up, entering the head of the Path herself. Zeva could not help but feel the Reks's anticipation when she beheld her dead lover. The warrior queen melted away and something of a lovelorn woman came to her face, making her look younger, innocent. The Reks gasped, clutching her chest as more tears filled her emerald eyes. She reached her hand out towards the Deep, fingers strained with desire.

Tarkan marched a tall man with raven black hair towards the rift from inside the Deep. His face was impassive, set in determination. Zeva recognized the look: he thought they'd be done after this, just as she had. That Sjörna-Reks would let them leave. Walk away with their new power. If what Ragnall had said was true, she wouldn't. They were trapped.

"Where is the vessel?" Tarkan shouted from inside the rift.

Kjarton caught sight of Sjörna-Reks and reached out to her from inside, but Tarkan held him back. The anguish at being so close yet separated by death wracked the faces of both Rekses.

Sjörna-Reks cast about, desperate. Finally, she stopped and turned on Sybal and Tzarik.

"No, don't!" Zeva shouted before Lokhtar clamped his massive hand over her mouth.

Sybal, understanding as well, screamed and writhed in her bonds, shouting protests.

"Do it, Necro'Khan!" Sjörna-Reks shrieked. She signaled Lokhtar, who put a blade to Zeva's throat.

"You have many men at your disposal," Tarkan said. His face grew sallow, his flesh thinning rapidly the more he held the powerful spell. Softly, so Zeva thought she was the only one who could hear him, he begged, "Don't make me do this."

A thudding of hooves drew Tarkan's and Kjarton's attention. Behind them, a massive creature charged towards Tarkan. It raised a two-headed axe and roared, "Heretic!" as it bore down on him.

Panic took Tarkan over as he snapped his head between the monster and the opening.

"Do it!" Sjörna-Reks screamed. "Do this and you will be free!"

Tarkan leapt out. He flexed his long, pale fingers before crossing the threshold, reducing Kjarton's spirit to a single, green glowing orb, and held it in his palm. It hovered there, caged by the scriptures on his fingers. Once the Necro'Khan left the Deep, the tear healed, leaving the monster behind. The wind fell and a deathly quiet consumed the thronehall.

"Tarkan," Sybal begged as the Necro'Khan came to her and Tzarik, "don't do this. We saved you."

Tzarik set his face hard as he looked up into Tarkan's eyes. He didn't fight the Necro'Khan; he didn't beg.

Tarkan raised the hand that held the raven king's soul and hesitated. Zeva's heart broke for his struggle and she kicked her feet out, but couldn't loosen Lokhtar's grip.

Tarkan reached down and slipped Tzarik's runes off over his head, removing his only protection from possession.

"Please, don't!" Sybal begged.

Zeva joined in her sobs, realizing Sybal and Tzarik had had precious little time together —not more than two days at most— since she'd come back.

Tarkan dropped Kjarton's rescued spirit into the Runer's chest. Tzarik went still, eyes turning a glowing green. Using his small orichalcum blade, Tarkan cut a small script into the side of Tzarik's neck and smeared the black, sulfuric ink over it, locking Kjarton's soul inside before putting the runes back on him.

No one moved. Sybal's soft whimpers echoed gently up to the rafters as she whispered her mentor's name.

"Don't let her go," Sjörna-Reks instructed Lokhtar, pointing to Zeva. She glared a warning at Tarkan before approaching Tzarik. She unsheathed a dagger and knelt carefully in front of the possessed Runer. Lightly touching his cheek, she whispered, "Kjarton?"

Tzarik slowly stirred awake and raised his head.

"Tzarik?" Sybal begged beside him, her eyes red.

Again, Zeva's heart broke. Tzarik had come here to save Sybal. He'd only had her a few days before being torn from her again. As Zeva watched Sjörna-Reks take Tzarik's face in her hands, she realized they should not have been so desperate. Tarkan had encouraged Tzarik, had offered his god-given abilities. She glanced at her father where he stood, hunched over and gasping. He took up a large sea glass decanter and drank deeply. A trickle of blood spilled over his pale lips. She loved him. But he'd chosen the wrong path. Something detached inside her chest and a numbness took over the maelstrom of emotions fighting for dominance within her. Was this her fault?

"Sjörna?" Tzarik's voice cracked as he finally found full consciousness. His hands shook as he strained towards Sjörna-Reks. "My red queen? My wolven bride?"

With a cry of agonized delight, Sjörna-Reks fell to her knees before Tzarik and threw her arms around his neck. She cut his bonds and he returned the embrace. Then, to Zeva and Sybal's horror, Sjörna-Reks kissed him. He gripped her red locks in his black-gloved hands, entangling his fingers in them, and ravenously returned the kiss.

Beside them, Sybal soundlessly sobbed, watching the red Reks take Tzarik. Zeva didn't know how the lady Runer kept the weeping inside, but it wracked her body as she folded over, shaking, tears freshly brimming in her eyes.

Tarkan wiped his face and glared at Sjörna-Reks. "That's enough, Reks," he growled. He hovered his palms close together. His eyes turned blood red as he called up the howling, black wind.

"Don't!" Zeva warned him, finally twisting her head out from under Lokhtar's hand. But Sjörna-Reks struck first.

She flew into her wolven form, pinning Tarkan hard against the dirt floor. "Shackle him," she ordered through a spit-flecked snarl. Her voice sounded with a bark. "And bring the bridle."

"Let us go!" Zeva cried, watching her father's frail body pull against his captors. He hissed, trying to cast a single spell. "We did as you asked."

"We are not finished, necromancer," she said to Zeva. "Not yet." Satisfied that Tarkan would be restrained and that Zeva would not move, she turned to face Tzarik again.

Kjarton's eyes widened, taking in the thronehall, pulling Tzarik's face into a gaze of wonder. "I never thought I'd see these halls again." When he spotted Sybal, chained and weeping, he said, "Sjörna, release her. This Runer saved my life and..." He trailed off when Sjörna-Reks pressed her palms to his lips and kissed him to silence him.

"Trust me, my love. I will." She signaled the men to take away the prisoners. "First..."

She shoved Tzarik against one of the ornate pillars and kissed him hard, biting his lip and pinning his arms overhead.

Sybal raged as two warriors dragged her away. Zeva had half hoped Kjarton's return might save them. But his weak will bent to Sjörna-Reks.

Lokhtar followed the others out, pulling Zeva with him. They left Sjörna-Reks alone with Tzarik, possessed by Kjarton-Reks.

CHAPTER 28

ZEVA'S CURSE

A RAGE SYBAL HAD NEVER FELT IN HER TWENTY-SEVEN years seethed inside her. The enmity burned so hot, she feared the straw on the floor of her cell might be set ablaze. She distracted her mind by reliving the battles she'd won in the Deep and how it felt clambering for life out of the writhing, twisting ground. She sat, legs crossed, wrists resting on her knees, and eyes closed. Forcing herself to remember the feel of the thick, slimy ectoplasmic blight that pulled her back under the earth, she refused to imagine Sjörna-Reks's hands on Tzarik. The way she'd kissed him made Sybal's cheeks burn and split her head in agony.

Hunger didn't come to her during the days she sat in the cell. Zeva's soft weeping was the only sound outside the howling, frozen wind. She eyed the chest beside the door that held her scimitar and runes. The Runer's death did not settle in yet. Anger at Tarkan rose in her then. What kind of deal had he made with Sjörna-Reks? She didn't blame Tzarik for going along with the necromancer. He'd done it for her. She'd have to tell him that her recklessness was rubbing off on him. But Tarkan had gone willingly into the jaws of the wolf, and she couldn't see a way out now. She hated him for that, and for pulling Zeva into the darkness with him. Was he so blinded by his hunt for power that he couldn't see he was repeating what he'd tried to escape before, from Sharar? Or did he not care? Did he think the ends would justify his—and Zeva's —suffering?

On the second day, as she sat unmoving, her sulfates rushed. Something looked at her. Wanted her.

Sybal! an oddly familiar female voice shouted. *Sybal, where are you? Come to me!*

Snapping her eyes open, she caught Zeva looking at her from across the single cell that separated them. No, it hadn't been the girl. Something else had its hungry eyes on her. A tinge of disgust struck in Sybal's mind when she saw the dried blood on Zeva's fingers. She'd been consuming flesh and blood. Yes, they had been forcing her to. Sjörna-Reks had men torture Tarkan to make her eat the sentient flesh to gain her strength.

"I've always wanted to meet you," Zeva said softly. "You saved me from Sharar. Tarkan told me."

Sybal swallowed and breathed to get her white blood flowing. "Did he tell you how he destroyed my home? Rose my family up to fight me after they'd been slaughtered?"

Zeva's blue eyes rounded and tears trickled down her Scriven face. Sybal noticed how the scars on the young woman's face caught the tears, channeling them down the burns and hideous marks. She lowered her eyes, tears prickling at them.

"I'm sorry," she said softly. "Did he tell you about how I nearly killed him? Stabbed him twelve times."

At this, Zeva nodded.

"Of course he did," Sybal sighed. "Did Sharar do that to you?" She touched her own face where the disfigurement marred Zeva's.

Zeva nodded. "He hoped it would make Tarkan never disobey him again."

A sudden kinship with the girl touched Sybal. "How long did he torture you?" She tried to remember how long she'd spent in the Deep. How many times had she died?

The necromancer fiddled with a long, white feather in her hair. "Months. I thought I'd die many times. But hearing Tarkan's torture was far worse. I was trapped; I couldn't help him. I'd never heard him cry out before."

It had to have been the same for Tarkan. Sybal understood now, but it still made her angry. They were tired of being controlled, hurt. They'd been forced to endure pain by those who desired to use their power. But now that Zeva was Scriven and an Apostle, surely she would be hunted more than before. Perhaps Tarkan thought his ascension would bring him enough power to protect her. But he hadn't had a chance to escape yet.

"I'm sorry that happened to you," Sybal said. "They say suffering makes us strong. But perhaps I'd rather be weak."

"Not me," Zeva said easily. "So long as I heard Tarkan's suffering, I knew he was alive, and that kept me alive."

Sybal marveled at Zeva's tenacity. She wanted that kind of faith. She couldn't let her hate consume her. Tzarik was still alive, just trapped inside his own body.

Zeva smiled as she went on. "The djinn told me I was resilient."

Shock shot through Sybal. "You saw it?"

The necromancer nodded. "Sometimes Sharar let him walk as a human, a slave in his house."

Curious, Sybal asked, "What did it look like?"

"A man. He smelled of ash and cinder, like the gods here. I knew he was a demon, a slave to a dark god, but he didn't look like one. Like us, he was a prisoner of Sharar."

Quiet awe overtook Sybal. She'd always secretly hope that Sharar might be lying about having a djinn. Not now. She shook her head. Across the cell, Zeva sighed heavily and laid her head against the bars.

"Do you feel weak from the ritual still?" she asked the girl.

Zeva shook her head. "I've not felt strong since the Black Road.

I've consumed, even. And still my spells take everything in me. I feel like dying, but something is holding me back. Keeping me alive. Two forces inside me are battling for my strength." She pressed both her hands into her chest hard.

Sybal frowned. "There's a lot of magic here. Could you have gone near something that touched you, leaving behind a trace of a curse?"

Zeva shrugged. "It's like it's in me, blocking my spells."

"Maybe we could find some ingredients to make a tincture," Sybal suggested. "I can think of one that helps with blight within a person. But I doubt Sjörna will let us out."

The girl sighed sadly.

"We will escape, Zeva," Sybal said sternly. "I promise."

Zeva reached into the cell between them and picked up a smaller white feather. Holding her hand out, she blew gently to sail it over to Sybal. The Runer caught it and ran her fingers over the soft feather. A golden sheen wavered into the light: a Masahk feather.

The door burst open, making both women jump. Lokhtar and a handful of brutish guards appeared. They were covered in so much red blood that Lokhtar's golden beard shone redder than Sjörna-Reks's hair.

"We have hunted for three days to celebrate the return of the raven king," Lokhtar announced to them. "We have a great sacrifice for the Valravn and Raudnir."

From what she knew of the people of Caerwren and their Eldritch Hunt, Sybal guessed it was not stags they had hunted and brought in to sacrifice.

"Kjarton ordered a mass slaughter?" she asked, not believing it.

Lokhtar huffed a smirk. "The raven Reks was always softer on the people of the other clans. The wolven Reks wants fresh bodies for her horde. Sjörna-Reks will show the other cantons the power she has gained. Until the snow melts, the Eldritch Hunt will go on into these fourteen days of darkness. The gods desire blood, and they shall have it. Once we have an army for the Necro'Khan, we will take it to Northica."

Sybal glowered at the man from behind the bars. They had gone out and slaughtered perhaps hundreds of innocents from other clans to bring back for Tarkan to raise again. And for him to consume. An undead army didn't need to be large. She'd seen the devastation the Porshain could do when he was just an Apostle. Now that he was Necro'Khan, she couldn't imagine what he could do once he tried.

"Girl," Lokhtar said, pointing his bloody axe at Zeva. "Sjörna-Reks desires you come and test your skills before her. We will need you as well if we are to take the mountain."

"She's no court jester," Sybal barked, standing up. "She will not perform for your red Reks."

"Sybal, don't," Zeva begged. "They have Tarkan. And Tzarik."

Suddenly, Sybal understood why Tzarik had spent all those years alone. There was a moment when her family and her betrothed were taken that she'd felt free in the darkest sense. She had no one to lose. Nothing to protect but herself, and it had made her bold. Tzarik had been that way for dozens of years. She remembered the way he'd looked at her the first time she saw him in that courthouse where she'd stood trial. The fear on his face. The uncertainty. He knew what it meant to take her on: having something to lose.

"I go with her," Sybal snapped, drawing herself up to her full height.

Lokhtar laughed. "You are in no place to bargain."

"Or I won't raise a single body," Zeva added. "Kill us. Then what? Wait for another Porshain to wander onto your frozen rock?"

The bloodied man considered the women before half nodding and signaling his men to bind Sybal and release Zeva.

BLOOD STREAKED the white snow all around the village. Webs of it spidered in from all directions, leading to the thronehall. A severed limb fell here and there in the bloody tracks from where an unfortunate victim had been hacked to death. Beside the thronehall lay a huge, black, leathery dragon.

Zeva gasped upon noticing the creature. It blended into the dark sky.

"My own kill," Lokhtar boasted. "They retreat into their dens this time of year, but surely Raudnir will bless me for taking down a beast made in the image of Strigganoct. Northica thinks their dragon god is best, but Raudnir will feast on some of this one's flesh tonight."

Sybal had seen only two dragons in her lifetime and had no desire to battle another. But this one looked dead.

"Walk beside me, Sybal?" Zeva asked.

The necromancer was free, but Sybal was bound. Pushing past her guards, Sybal came side by side with Zeva before they entered the hall. Sybal braced herself for seeing Tzarik with Sjörna-Reks.

When the doors to the thronehall burst open, a hot wind smelling of iron pushed the women's hair back. Sybal blanched at the smell but kept her eyes open. Zeva retched and turned away. Every brazier and hearth blazed in the massive thronehall, lighting it up despite the now eternal darkness of Caerwren. Floods of clansmen moved around, roasting stags and preparing other savory food. Mead sloshed and flowed, turning the dirt on the floor to mud. In the center, a pile of perhaps thirty bodies—human and Masahk alike— were stacked up before the stone dais where Sjörna-Reks sat. In the raven throne beside her sat Tzarik. Sybal looked up at him, but knew Kjarton gazed out from behind his eyes. She lowered her eyes, unwilling to meet Kjarton's now.

"Ah, little necromancer," Sjörna-Reks called down over the clamor. She reached over and took Tzarik's hand as if he might run from her. "See what I have brought for you?"

Sybal saw the girl raise her head high, but her brows were pinched in disgust and fear.

"Just do as she says," Sybal advised. "She won't hurt Tarkan or you. She needs you." If Sjörna-Reks was going to kill anyone, it would be her. She wondered how long it would be until the Reks decided to finish her off.

Zeva cast a despairing glance at the Runer. Her lips trembled as she tried to speak.

"I know you're scared," Sybal said bracingly. "I won't let anyone hurt you. I'll find a way out." She meant it, and her voice turned to iron as she made the promise.

Below the thrones, Tarkan stood chained with his back to the stone. His arms were splayed to the sides to stop him from using his hands to cast. A bridle was clamped around his jaw like a muzzle, stopping his tongue. Sybal recalled the device and remembered the cruel, sharp edges inside that held the captor's tongue to the roof of their mouth. He looked bruised and battered. Sjörna-Reks had put him there like that to show her own strength. A wave of disgust washed over Sybal on Tarkan's behalf.

"Runer," Sjörna-Reks called down. "Join me here." It was an order.

Rolling her shoulders to lessen the tension of her bonds, Sybal let herself be led up the stone steps to stand between Sjörna and Kjarton-Reks. Kjarton looked up at her as she ascended and he offered her a grim nod.

"I don't think attacking Skarde is wise," Kjarton said with Tzarik's voice. "We should wait until the Hunt passes and the sun shines again before we declare war on our allies of the Warpath."

"Kjarton," Sjörna-Reks began, leaning across the space of their thrones. "I would burn all of Altevine—all of Caerwren—to have you by my side again."

"You might have," Zeva interrupted. "A malignation the likes of which we have never seen could come through the tears we've made in the barrier of the Deep."

Sjörna-Reks ignored her. "I have brought you back, Kjarton. I have gained powers no Reks has ever harnessed before." She gripped his chin and forced him into a hard kiss. "Skarde must know what I have done. And pay for your death."

Sybal's throat closed as she watched another woman kiss Tzarik. She forced her feet to remain nailed to the floor and not kick out at the wolven queen. Somehow, watching her touch him was worse than any death in the Deep.

Sjörna-Reks released him from the kiss and ran her hand through his hair and down to his thigh. Kjarton glanced up at Sybal for just one second, but the Runer saw it. Kjarton understood his wife's intentions, and he knew what it must be doing to Sybal. Part of her appreciated that, but it didn't matter. Kjarton's meek nature wouldn't let him stand up to the wolf on her behalf.

"Zeva," Sjörna-Reks went on. "You have been gifted a great power but have not had a moment to test it." She motioned to the pile of corpses. "Take your pick, my girl. Show my clan what you can do. Prove to me your worth."

From above, Sybal could see the entire thronehall. Zeva's eyes flicked to Tarkan, then up to her. Was she asking for permission? Zeva had a slight hunch to her shoulders. Sybal couldn't tell if it was from exhaustion or if the thought of raising her first corpse pressed down on her. But she waited for a signal from Sybal. Unsure what to do besides give in to Sjörna-Reks, Sybal nodded slightly. Zeva refocused on the dead before her, turning pale under her scriptures.

"Sjörna," Kjarton whispered, "don't make her do this."

"Don't make me tell you again, my love," the red Reks interrupted. She reached over and grasped his wrist hard in her strong hand.

Sybal trained her eyes on Zeva. As the girl chanted, her sulfates rushed. The sensation of something devouring Zeva's essence once again came to her. The more the necromancer pulled on her power, the more it ate up. She stepped forward to stop her but a keen glance from Sjörna-Reks halted her steps.

"Something isn't right," Sybal warned the Reks. Tzarik would know. She clenched her fists and watched Zeva carefully. "I sensed it before, but it's awake now, taking in her essence."

The stale, cold wind that accompanied the necrotic magic swirled around the room, snuffing a few candles and a torch. Cloaks fluttered and snapped and every strand of long hair got whipped up into the gale force wind. Sybal quickly shot Sjörna-Reks a glance. The wolven queen grinned minimally at the young necromancer.

Zeva stepped back, still chanting soundlessly, holding her palms close together. As she did, the pile of bodies shifted. A great hand stuck out, partly broken and bloodied. The corpse fought to free itself, disentangling from the others. A huge dead man rose up. His broad shoulders were thick and knotted with muscle. His long, braided hair and beard were gray from age, but no other sign of weariness rested on him. A scar ran over one eye, and both were milky white. The dead man stepped away from the pile and Zeva beckoned it to stand behind her. Once it stood at attention behind its necromancer, it dwarfed her.

Sybal exhaled softly through her nose. Zeva was strong for a new Scriven—even she could see that. In awe, she came down a few steps to be closer. Glancing sideways at Tarkan, she saw in his wild blue eyes that he thought the same. His expression told her that the scriptures had taken to her quickly. And powerfully. Despite whatever ate up her strength and being newly Scriven, Zeva was powerful. Sybal focused on Zeva's hands: every black mark had healed completely, smooth and blemish-less. That couldn't be normal. If Sybal was right and a curse did block the girl's power, then Zeva would be even stronger once they released it. Stronger than Tarkan had been when he was an Apostle.

Thinking, Sybal swallowed hard. Perhaps Zeva might be strong enough to fight against her father. Slowly, Sybal turned to look at Tarkan. He still watched his daughter, enraptured. Could she do that to them? Pit them against one another? *Can I be that cruel?* she wondered.

Sjörna-Reks flicked her wrist to one of her thralls nearby. The man took up an axe and charged Zeva. Tarkan and Sybal both cried out together. Lokhtar stopped Sybal with a stern punch to her gut. Sybal crumpled and Kjarton hurried to her, catching her. She was grateful, but pushed past her former companion to watch Zeva.

The girl shuffled away, still concentrating on her spell, and commanded her brutish, undead protector. The thrall entered combat with the undead, and Sybal knew at once that he'd lose. She'd fought undead before and knew the only way to really fell one was to stop the necromancer. They'd done it to Tarkan on several occasions, often giving chase to the fleeing necromancer.

The thrall continued to fight the undead mountain of a man, but Sybal watched Zeva. In the torch's light she slid beneath, a shadow appeared on her shoulders. Like a hand lay there. Sure this time, Sybal knew she had to stop the girl. If she could get her runes, she could draw atan and cast light on whatever haunted her. But she didn't have her runes.

At last, the thrall realized his mistake. Panting, he turned to Zeva and charged.

"Stop this now!" Sybal cried, mixing with Tarkan's strangled shouts.

"Let her find her power," Sjörna-Reks ordered.

"The necrotic magic is a consumption of life," Sybal argued. "Something is taking it from her as she tries to use it. Something is killing her."

Zeva thrust one hand away from the thrall, towards the left wall, hissing more desperately now, eyes still white. The ground shook. All sound stopped as the onlookers and the thrall stopped to feel the quake.

"What is that?" Kjarton asked.

In a flash, Sybal knew. "Get down!" she screamed, tackling Kjarton onto the stones.

Something blasted a small hole in the thatched roof, quickly followed by the snapping maw of a huge black dragon. Its long, snake-like neck slipped easily through the small opening, cascading rubble and even dislodging a single beam. The clansman inside the thronehall shouted and scattered, brandishing weapons. Some shot arrows into it, but they did nothing.

In a flash of red hair and soft fur, Sjörna-Reks shifted and howled loudly, cutting off all other sounds and calling all combatants to halt. Everyone stopped, terrified as the dragon head slipped out. With another rumble, it collapsed. Sybal glanced over Kjarton's head at Zeva. She stood now, hands down, gasping. She shook and her knees gave out.

Pushing past the Reks, Sybal ran to her. She collected Zeva in her arms and picked her up.

"Make her consume," Sjörna-Reks commanded, shifting back. She pointed to a decanter another thrall held. "Blood. Gathered for her."

Sybal glared at the thing, disgusted, but when Zeva convulsed, she reached for it. She pulled the cork out with her teeth and spit it aside, tipping the warm contents down Zeva's throat. She was pale and her cheeks had sunken. Zeva sputtered but soon drank on her own. The image disgusted Sybal.

"I can stand," Zeva offered after a moment.

Sjörna-Reks stood up, clapping and marveling. "Such power! And what quick thinking. Pity you are still so weak."

"She's not." Sybal put her arm around Zeva's waist, holding her up. "Something is haunting her. I told you. It's eating away at her and devours her even more when she uses her magic." She quickly gestured to Tarkan. "You asked too much of them too soon. Give me my runes and I will show you that something is feeding on her. We must find what it is and kill it."

The red Reks sighed and laid her hand on Tzarik's shoulders. Her fingers gently crawled up his neck and entangled themselves in his hair. Kjarton met Sybal's eyes, then cast his gaze down. He knew this hurt her.

"Fetch the runes," Sjörna-Reks ordered. A thrall ran down the hall to obey and gather the Runer's items.

A moment later, Sybal had her runes around her neck and her scimitar around her waist. She faced Zeva before the mound of bodies and held up atan. Knowing she would reveal something, she took a deep breath and drew slowly. She started with her hand above their heads, and with the first stroke, something appeared in the light of the magic rune. A soft cry of shock escaped her throat and she stumbled back. A black shape appeared, looming over Zeva. It was solid black, not a single feature visible, even in the rune light. Her eyes fixed on it. The thing stared back and slowly, a kind of grin exposed skeletal, sharp teeth.

"What is that?" she gasped, looking at the Reks as the rune light vanished. "Zeva?"

The girl sobbed gently, backing towards Tarkan. "I don't know." Unable to be held by him, she lowered herself to the ground and leaned against him. "I knew I felt something, but I didn't know what."

Sybal wracked her brain but didn't know. She hadn't hunted wide and far. She glared up at Kjarton. If only Tzarik were here. But he wasn't.

"Where have you been since coming to Caerwren?" she asked. "If we can trace your steps, maybe we can find where you picked this up." Glancing at Tarkan, she noted him begging her with his eyes. She understood his powerlessness. Tzarik was gone, so it was all up to her.

Zeva took her step by step through her journey on Caerwren, from the shore, to the moors, to the wisp she'd followed.

"A wisp?" Sjörna-Reks cut in.

That piqued something in Sybal's memory, something from a book she'd read, one that Tzarik carried with him. He'd never read it, but she had. It was all about monsters, magic users, witches and warlocks, and other creatures.

"Did you follow it?" she asked finally. Zeva nodded. "That's it," Sybal said. "It's a kuri. They mark you with their essence, feeding off you. When you die, you become a portal for them to haunt. A wisp leads you to the resting ground of the kuri, usually a graveyard or burial ground." But here on Caerwren, every mountain and plane was a burial ground.

Sjörna-Reks shifted, clenching her jaw. "I know the place." She pointed at Sybal. "Go, kill it. That's what you do, after all. I need my necromancers well in a few days' time." She jutted her arm behind her, pointing north. "We *will* ride to Skarde's mountain, and we will take the bridge. Young Dain Radjur-tor should be in the throes of his curse by now."

Sybal remembered. But she'd use this opportunity. Her heart screamed at her to make a bargain. Sjörna-Reks would never let Tarkan be unbound, and she didn't want to take Zeva with her. But she needed to know if the girl could counter Tarkan's magic if given the chance.

"Let Tzarik come with me," she said.

Kjarton looked up, slightly terrified. "Is that possible?" he began.

Sybal snapped her head to Tarkan. "You can do that."

The Necro'Khan only shifted, mute and bound.

The Reks shook her head. "I will not release him." She snapped her fingers and Lokhtar lumbered towards Zeva.

"I will try," she said quickly, turning her sad eyes to Sybal.

"No," Sjörna-Reks cried, grasping Kjarton. For once, genuine emotion wrinkled the corners of her eyes. "You cannot take him from me."

"*You* took him from me!" Sybal shrieked. Her high-pitched cry silenced every other voice in the hall.

"Sjörna," Kjarton said softly, prying her arms off him, but holding her hands. "Let this man go with her. She will come back. I'll bring them back."

The Reks's emerald eyes begged her husband to reconsider. "What if you don't come back?"

"I won't let Tzarik get hurt," Sybal swore with a growl.

Zeva stepped forward after wordlessly communicating with Tarkan with urgent glances. "Kjarton is locked inside Tzarik by the mark on his neck. Necromancers use those scripts to bind a possession or risen inside a vessel. Kjarton cannot leave the Runer's body." Zeva stopped there, glance meaningfully at Sybal, and went on. "I could release Tzarik, but only for a short time."

That was all Sybal wanted to know.

After a furtive glance at Kjarton, Sjörna-Reks bowed her head to his, kissed him, and said, "Very well. If you run, lady Runer, know that you will *not* get far." She kept her hand in Kjarton's as long as she could as he descended the stone steps to stand next to Sybal.

"Zeva," Kjarton said stoically. "When you're ready."

She touched the center of Tzarik's forehead with the sides of both hands, hovering her palms only an inch apart. With a deep breath, she whispered the verses into the wind that would put Kjarton's spirit to sleep, if only for a moment.

CHAPTER 29

THE KURT

Sybal didn't say a single word as she and Tzarik mounted their horses. She slipped her runes over her head and wrapped her belt, laden with her scimitar, around her waist. Tzarik had always been quiet, but she wished more than ever that he'd speak first, just for once. She was desperate to know what he felt. Was he angry? Did he blame her? It would be a two-day journey out to the moors where Zeva had followed the wisp, and she couldn't do it in silence. The longer she sat in the quiet, the more her sulfates rushed, telling her something watched her. Something had its eye on her. It grew to the point where she pulled the reins of her horse hard, stopping, just as they left Sjörna-Reks's clanlands. She whirled in her saddled and looked north, back the way they'd come.

"What is it?" Tzarik asked, finally breaking the silence.

Overcome by him speaking at last, she shoved the surveillance out of her mind. "Nothing. Tzarik?"

He met her eyes, but she couldn't read his face. She'd always been able to read his face, his body. She'd made him her subject over her years of training, learning his every tick and gesture. Now he was closed off, like the day she met him. It felt invasive to ask him anything now.

Being with him, silent, was worse. Her heart ached as they made camp the first night. They sat on opposite sides of the fire and wordlessly drank and ate. The quiet march continued the next day until Tzarik finally spoke.

"We need to find a midnight sun," he said as easily as if asking Sybal to fetch an egg from a henhouse.

She glanced up at him, hungry to hear his voice. "What?"

"It grows on Al'Myrah as well. Usually out of the rocks and sand. Here it's a smaller plant that grows in dry, cool areas," he went on. "Used in almost every curse-lifting talisman. Never a decoction, though. If it's boiled down to a tincture, it's very poisonous and is used for lacing arrow tips. But it will also ward off bad omens and keep most dark things at bay when paired with..." He glanced around the ground before sliding out of his saddle and kicking around a few rocks near a small mountain stream. He knelt and dug a little in the gray silt and pulled out what looked like a small black spike of quartz protruding from a natural rock. "Elder crystal," he finished. "Some dirt from the moors where the kuri lurks should help as well."

Sybal almost forgot about the painful silence with this new information. "I never took talismans seriously."

Tzarik nodded. "Potions, tinctures, plants—warlocks and witches use them most, but there's no reason we cannot." He dug out another spike of the rock he'd called elder crystal and pocketed them. "But we'll kill the thing as well and do Caerwren a favor."

Desperate to keep him talking, she tossed around for another subject, but nothing came to her frantic mind. So instead, she joined him in looking for a midnight sun. He described it as a short flower, with a rubbery stem and black petals. When he said this, she found a whole patch of nearly black grass hiding the dark flower. When she bent down, she found dozens of the blackest flowers she'd ever seen.

"I found some!" she called, almost feeling like her old self again.

Picking it without care, she stuffed a few handfuls into her own hip satchel. The flowers crunched, releasing a black secretion over her hands. The wind whipped a few strands of her ashen hair into her eyes as she knelt over it.

"Careful," he warned her again. "It's very poisonous. Can cause muteness, even blind—"

He choked as she rubbed her eye with the hand she'd used to pick the flowers, pulling strands of hair away from her face.

Realizing what he was about to say, she dove to the mountain stream and used her other hand to scoop water and rinse out her eye. She knew it was probably too late, though. With a growl, she twisted her long braid up at the back of her head and pulled the fur-lined cowl over it to hold the unruly strands in place.

"Well," she sighed, "it's just the one eye, I suppose."

Tzarik looked at her, his mouth parted in shock. "I suppose," he echoed, and almost smiled.

She blinked, wondering if the blindness would set in. Then, unable to stop herself, she sighed heavily, all the weight of their separation weighing on her. He had to feel the same way. The night in the rathskeller came back to her. His hard muscle under her hands, the way he gasped when she touched him. How he'd clung to her when she hovered above him. Her insides twisted in torment, wanting to speak. To hold him and be held by him again.

"Sybal," he said at length, over the clopping of the horses' hooves once they were on the way again. "I've missed you."

She audibly sighed in relief. Tears sprang to her eyes, almost freezing in the cold. She smelled snow on the air again. "I missed you," she choked. "So much. I thought maybe..." She swallowed the lump in her throat. "I thought maybe you didn't miss me how I did you."

He raised his dark brows and almost grinned again. "I left Xia to chase you down. Followed you to Al'Myrah and almost drowned at the hands of superstitious pirates for you. I'd not do as much for my own mother."

With that relief, she let another night-long silence fall, but this one didn't hurt as much. At least she knew he felt the same way. That night—after the fire had been lit, they'd eaten, and watched quietly as a few travelers passed them by—Sybal moved to sit by him. She took his arm and slid it around her middle before laying her head on his shoulder. When he did not reciprocate, she reached up with her other hand to tilt his head down so his cheek pressed against her head. When she did this, his face flexed against the top of her head, telling her he smiled. Drawing her knees in, she took his hand in hers and held them against her stomach, pressing them together.

"I'm bad at this," he confessed softly as the night wind howled around them. "I've had very little practice."

"You'll learn," she whispered back. "You rarely hesitate to tell me when I'm doing something wrong. That applies here. If I do something you don't like, tell me."

His hand reached up to the side of her head and gently, though hesitantly, his fingers traced through her ashen hair. She caught his chest hitch for just a moment.

"I'll be fine," she reminded him. "I don't feel any pain from the god-touch."

He sat up, taking her chin in his hand, and kissed her lips. A jolt of hot lightning cracked through her body at his initiation. She curled her toes in her boots and moved to her knees, pressing him down beneath her. Then she straddled him, unlacing his armor and kicking off her boots. When she had it off and lifted his tunic, he hissed and recoiled upward, away from the stony, ice-covered ground. Her toes touched the frosted grass as well and she cringed.

"Oh," she noted, nodding. "Sorry."

He quickly wrapped himself in his fur cloak again and actually smiled. She pulled her boots back on. Caerwren and its cold nights were ruining her desperate desires. She would be all too happy to be back on Al'Myrah, under its warm, accommodating sun.

ꭤ

"I SEE ONE!" Sybal called from the thick mist that enveloped them. She shook, not from the cold, but how it reminded her of the Deep. "Two wisps just went west." This mist only obscured her voice a little. Not like the thick, cursed brume in the Deep. "Tzarik?" she called.

"I'm here," he replied from a few yards behind her.

She knew her constantly calling his name would grate on his nerves, but she had to know where he was at all times. "Can we draw it out?" she asked.

He didn't reply.

"Tzarik!" she screamed.

"Sybal," he growled again, "I'm following a wisp."

"Wait," she whispered. "Let me. Stay where you are. When I light atan, come to me."

He grunted a reply, which she knew meant he agreed. She didn't underestimate his hunting, but she had a feeling the kuri might be drawn to her. She was fresh from the Deep and might have something still clinging to her that would draw the monster out. She slowly walked deeper into the mist over the moors. The farther she got from Tzarik, the more she felt. Then, a familiar scent hit her nostrils: ash, fire, and sulfur.

To the east, the familiar, feminine voice hissed in her mind.

Sybal swung around and looked. *What is it?* she asked the voice.

A moment of silence passed before it replied. *Mjordir, the greatest god on Caerwren. Do not tangle with him, Sybal. He will take you for himself. You are mine.*

Considered the prime god of Caerwren, Mjordir was a vicious, cruel god. She'd almost forgotten the gods walked on this side of

Caerwren. Its shape loomed dark, far away in the haze, but she made out its grotesque body. It reminded her a little of the creature she'd seen in the Deep, in that it was made up of sentient bodies. The antlers that rose off its head were arms, legs, and splayed hands of destroyed living beings. Its eyes were burning coals. It stood taller than the pines beneath its feet. The eyes almost looked like dual suns, were they not within its hideous face. How had Tzarik not seen it? Mjordir made a guttural bugling sound, then passed through an opening she could not see into the Deep.

"Shit," she hissed. They had to hurry. Turning from the east, she ran after a single wisp, willing it to take her to one of the downs where the kuri would appear. Her feet slipped over what she thought were smooth, white rocks. When she knelt to look below the mist, she found they were sentient skulls.

Here and there, the ground opened like the tiny mouths of caves, leading into tunnels underground. She froze as two white dots appeared deep inside one, looking right at her. Knowing she'd found their prey, she waited, crouched, and drew her scimitar. Holding her rune hand behind her, she drew atan and flashed a bit of light for Tzarik to follow. As his steps approached, she reminded herself that in this place, she could die. She'd become bold and reckless in the Deep, knowing she could come back if she fought hard enough.

Tzarik gave her a wide circumference, seeing the thing that watched her, and came up on top of where it might spring out. Slowly, white, round eyes never leaving her, the kuri floated up out of the burrow like it suspected she couldn't see it. Soundlessly, it then drifted towards her.

These burrows must be openings for it, she mused.

Behind the unsuspecting monster, Tzarik drew halat. She mimicked his movements, slowly backing away from the kuri. She glanced up at him and he nodded. He leapt down, and they finished drawing the shield rune, pushing them together to trap the kuri inside the magic circle. Just before Tzarik landed and the circle finished casting, the kuri hissed, its form sputtering from view, and vanished with a shriek.

"Damn it," Tzarik growled, spinning to watch his back.

Sybal moved to another burrow she'd found. "What are the chances there is more than one kuri out there and this is the one feeding on Zeva?"

"They're territorial," Tzarik replied, skittering against a rocky overcropping to check a burrow as well. "This one will hunt the moors. Another might take those shores down there. Each one of these burrows is where a victim died. It will try to lure Zeva out the longer it feeds on her, driving her to despair. That's how it expands its territory."

Understanding, Sybal scanned the misty horizon for the farthest burrow. She didn't have to look far. The black outline of the kuri appeared, hovering above the frosty grass several yards to her left. She snapped her fingers, getting Tzarik's attention before pursuing it. He broke off again to cover more ground. When she got close, the kuri drifted backwards agonizingly slowly. She followed it before she realized what it was doing.

"No, you come to me," she whispered. Concentrating, she pulled up memories of the Deep, bringing her old fear to the surface. She let her emotions roil inside her, enticing the kuri. She remembered meeting Kjarton, her first death, fighting Bolemesh. The thoughts she'd had of never seeing Tzarik again.

The kuri stopped backing away but didn't come toward her.

She thought of Tzarik's scarred chest and how she'd run her fingers over him. How he'd clenched his long fingers over her arms, pulling her into him. Remembering her attempts at seduction the night before, she smiled and almost laughed out loud.

The kuri dove at her.

With a gasp, she swung her magical steel, fending it off. With her new-found expertise, Sybal whirled and slashed at the monster, easily evading it. In combat with mortals, she'd learned how to see them signal their moves. She'd always tried it on the creatures they'd faced but had never been able to predict their movements. The spectral monsters had always been too fast or hadn't disclosed their moves. Now she saw it. She had all the time in the world and the kuri moved slowly. She drove it back to hover over a field of midnight suns. She knew fire within a ring of atan would kill most things, but she wanted to add the magical properties of the flower for added strength.

Signaling Tzarik, she got him to follow her as she drove the monster into the position she wanted it in.

"Distract it," she called.

He didn't have to try very hard. The kuri seemed uninterested in Sybal now that it had pursued her for a few moments, and it went after Tzarik instead. As it did, she whistled her horse over and took the flint and steel from its pack. She lit a small torch for fire, then ran after the monster and her mentor.

"Atan!" she called as the kuri bore down on Tzarik.

For the first time, she thought her mentor moved slowly. The kuri reached out to touch him. He quickly drew atan, knocking its formless, shadowy arm away. Fast as a cat, Sybal dashed to place herself between him and the kuri. He was too slow; he'd pick up the curse. When she stepped between them, the kuri stopped, recoiling from her in anger and hissing. She turned to offer Tzarik a playful smile, but his blue eyes looked into hers with confused horror.

Hurt a little, she spun away and shouted for him to use atan again. Together, they finally trapped the kuri over the midnight suns. Ripping a tiny vial of oil from her belt, she broke it over the flowers and threw the torch onto it. The kuri shrieked and flailed its appendages, showing a wide-open mouth for the first time. Its ghostly scream pierced Sybal's ears until she had to cover them. Then, in an explosion of black ectoplasm, the kuri perished. The black spectral ooze covered her and Tzarik.

"Burn the burrows," Tzarik quipped, calling Mamun over and

taking a small torch, dipping it into the fire Sybal had made. It burned a ghostly, magical green.

She reached down to gingerly pick her torch up, cringing from the fire. But when she grasped it, she felt no burn. Yes, the heat touched her, but her flesh merely sizzled like water in a flame. Curious, she looked up to see if Tzarik had noticed. He had. His face fell even more, and she swore his eye shone with a sudden tear. Pushing past it, she turned away from his worrying glance and set the burrows aflame. They ignited like black powder, hissing and scorching the earth, then went out.

He thinks something is wrong with you, the sweet, feminine voice in her head said sadly. *He's wrong. You're just strong now.*

The sudden voice startled Sybal. She ducked, expecting an attack. Snapping her head this way and that, she looked for the source. But it didn't come from near her, it came from inside. The voice from before. She couldn't speak to it aloud. Tzarik might worry even more, and she wasn't so sure he would be wrong.

"YOU HAVE TO SPEAK TO ME," Sybal said as they made camp the first night on their way back. "What's wrong?"

Tzarik sat on the other side of the campfire again, braiding a new leather cord for his runes. "You were fast during the hunt," he mumbled.

Nodding, she shrugged. "I've felt better each day after leaving the Deep." Annoyed with him, she stood up and came around the fire to sit next to him. He stopped braiding when she did and looked up at her.

"You're right," he sighed. "I shouldn't be separating myself from you like this. Especially since we may not have much time."

The ominous reply put her on edge. "I won't let Sjörna-Reks keep Kjarton in you," she said firmly. Unable to help herself, she leaned against him, tracing the black script on his neck. Ever since they'd been intimate, she wanted to touch him all the time, but held herself back, knowing moving too fast might push him away. "He's not like the wolf Reks. I don't think he knows who she is now. He spoke so lovingly of her, of the way she was before he was killed."

Tzarik didn't shy away from her physical intimacy. "I'm not speaking of Kjarton," he said sadly, "but of you." He reached around, pulling her long braid over her shoulder.

A tingle went through Sybal as Tzarik ran his rough fingers over her whitening strands. If only they had shelter away from the cold...

"You mean the god-touched curse," she said softly. Her eyelids grew heavy the more he touched her. His hands went to hers now. "I don't feel it."

"Perhaps not yet." He dropped his hand. "I told you about Azar. How when he found me, he was pale and ashen haired."

Sybal nodded. Of course she remembered. It had been a pure, beautiful moment of vulnerability. "So he was god-touched?"

Tzarik's eyes unfocused again, this time looking into the past. "It was our eternal hunt. To find a way to stop it. I don't know how he lasted his entire lifetime with it. He complained of the pain often, often succumbing to fits of anguish. The runes won't save you—he tried." He glared now, the fire reflecting in unshed tears. Through gnashed teeth he whispered, "Even the black rituals of Bahratt won't stop it from taking you."

She clenched the front of his black tunic and nuzzled into his chest. "I've only ever heard of Bahratt's rituals. They're described as evil. Their magi look for prophecy in rituals of torture and..." she blushed. "And in rituals of copulation."

"Sometimes both," he murmured. "But nothing came to them. So one day, Azar was gone. Taken by the god who touched him."

"What happens when it takes me?" she asked.

His breath shuddered but he tried to hide it. "I don't know."

She sat up to look at him. The corner of his mouth twitched.

With that, and the combination of his looking away, she realized he was lying.

"It called me foul," she said. "Said I belonged to another god. I don't think it will take me."

"Perhaps not that god," Tzarik countered. "It made you touched, but told me it relinquished its claim on you. Yet..." Hesitantly, he reached out and touched her white strands. "Yet the touch remains. Some monster has claim to you and is not letting go. It will—" he choked and started again. "It will take you and I cannot stop it."

"What does that mean?" she asked.

"Perhaps the god takes you, body and soul. One day, Azar was just...gone. I have seen it other times. Heard of it more. There is no timeline for how long the curse will let you live. That I am sure of."

Sybal leaned over, resting her elbows on her knees and joining him in looking into the fire. "It's a curse. There has to be a way to lift it. And you said Azar was in pain. I feel nothing. If anything, I feel faster, stronger, and more powerful than before I woke in the Deep."

Tzarik stiffened next to her. "Sybal," he said, his voice shuddering with sudden fear.

"What is—" she began, but Tzarik cut her off.

He gripped her face and pulled her into a sudden and passionate kiss so hard her lips bruised against his. Unwilling to fight his unforeseen action, she placed her hands on his neck and returned the kiss. She leaned into him, both of them panting. Then, under her palm, the necrotic script squirmed.

"Sybal," Tzarik's voice said again against her lips.

She stopped, broke the kiss, and closed her eyes, pressing her forehead to his. "Kjarton," she replied stiffly. "I'm sorry."

Pulling back, she looked into Tzarik's eyes and knew her raven companion looked back. She took the leather out of Kjarton's hands and continued Tzarik's task.

"I'm...so sorry," Kjarton said solemnly. "I couldn't stop it."

Sybal nodded, sniffling. The tears made the firelight blur her vision and she couldn't braid until she blinked. A tear released, falling onto her fingers.

Kjarton dropped his head into his hands. "I am sorry for more than that," he began. "I am sorry for Sjörna. She's not the woman I left behind. And..." He swallowed hard. "I don't know her anymore, Sybal. Perhaps...I never did. Death has changed how I see her affection. I thought she loved me. Saved me. But her eyes are wicked, a portrait of Altevine without me." He touched Tzarik's chest. "This body cannot give her an heir. So what does she want with me?" He swallowed, dropping his hand. Then he said very slowly, "She doesn't want me."

Hearing the despair in her old companion's voice, she sadly met his gaze. The sorrow on Tzarik's face churned her gut, and she reminded herself it wasn't him. She inclined her head for him to go on. She dared not trust her own voice at this moment.

"I regret coming back," he said quickly. "I knew I shouldn't have. But I loved her. I was taken from her. Stolen. And I knew she was hurting all these years."

Despite hearing Tzarik's voice, Sybal fully understood Kjarton. "I know. People do all the wrong things for love." She choked and cleared her throat. "Maybe it's all wrong. Maybe neither of us should be here."

"No," Kjarton cut in. "Not you. You belong here. With him. You were not fully gone into the Deep. He was right to come for you. And I hate that I've taken you away from him again. I feel his love for you, though he won't say it." He shut his eyes tight, a hand gripping his chest over his heart. "I know the feeling, but it's not mine. It's his. I wish it were mine!"

Kjarton was not what Sybal had expected from a Reks of Caerwren. The others were savage, forceful. Sjörna-Reks didn't show love. How could he have ever loved her? "Why?" she quipped. "Did she love you? Did she try to save you from being sacrificed?"

"I'd do it again for her," he interrupted.

"Why?" Sybal shouted this time. "She let you die, and she'll do it again. Can't you see she only wants you for her sick, twisted desires?"

He put his face in his hands. "I cannot stop myself when it comes to her. I'm not as strong as she is."

Sybal agreed with silent disgust.

"Wouldn't you do anything for Tzarik?" Kjarton asked meekly.

To stop her reply, she stood up to leave. Overhead, a flock of ravens silently cut across the moon, heading to the tree line. Sybal watched Kjarton observe them, remembering how he used to transform and fly over the Deep.

"This is not my body," he said softly. "This is not my life. No matter that it was taken early, I had one life to live. I cannot take another's." He tilted his head back to her. "No doubt she will move the moment the kuri's curse is lifted from the girl. She will be strong, and your Necro'Khan would have rested and consumed. You must hurry back before Sjörna moves."

"And you?" Sybal knew well what final words sounded like. Kjarton was preparing his own.

He stood up and moved to the bedroll Tzarik had laid out before. "I will find a way. Prepare yourself."

She watched him fade into the darkness away from her. Yes, she'd do anything for Tzarik. But those things were wild, untamed, and dark. Realizing this, she understood Kjarton, even if she loathed his weakness.

CHAPTER 30

RISEN DRAGON

Zeva followed Sjörna-Reks and her entourage out into the village of Altevine. It had been two days since the Runers left. By now, they should have reached the moors where the kuri had latched onto her. At the very least, she had two more days to wait. The barracks clinked and clanged with war forges. Sjörna's warriors wrestled one another in the snow, preparing for a fight, and tined wolves and horses were being measured for battle ware. Cauldrons of poison boiled near the forges, waiting to have arrows dipped into them. Zeva recognized the flower they had made the poison from. Midnight suns grew on Al'Myrah as well.

In her wolf form, Sjörna-Reks was followed by her wildling golden wolf, muzzled and shackled. Zeva and Tarkan marched under heavy guard behind them. The red wolf took no chances; Tarkan was still bound and his jaw bridled. Zeva walked close to him, her arm snaked through his. The strange parade drew looks from children and warriors alike throughout the main village.

She had so many things to say to the man who'd raised her: she wanted to run; they needed to leave; they were captives—just like he'd tried to avoid. She didn't blame him; she understood. But saying

these things wouldn't help. It would just enrage him, trapped help-
lessly as he was.

I don't know what to do, she thought desperately.

Sjörna-Reks led them out east towards the bogs. She didn't have
to tell the necromancers what she wanted them to do. Zeva had
thought of it the night before. She would have them raise every
spared soul from the bog and use that unkillable horde to reap her
revenge on Skarde-Reks. Part of her said to just let it happen. Once
the battle was won—and it would be, Northica didn't stand a chance
against the undead army—she and Tarkan could leave. Assuming
Sjörna-Reks let them. She prayed they'd go back to Al'Myrah and live
as they always had. But even then, Tarkan had been tracking down
his tribal brother, Ashkan, worried the other man would take the
mantle of Necro'Khan.

But there is no fear of that anymore, she thought. *Perhaps he
would give it up. Maybe we could even go to Porsh and be alone.*

But then what? Live out eternity with each other in a stale existence? Maybe the Runers would let them follow on their hunts. She
would need an alternative to offer Tarkan. He'd turned into a man
she did not recognize in the last few months. Would he so easily give
up his pursuit? For her?

They passed the last scattered homes and a longhouse for the
Volra, covered in the hewn likenesses of dragons and bears. A few
robed Volra stood outside in a circle, arms raised to the dark skies,
praying to their gods. She was about to turn away from the sacred
house when something on the well out front grabbed her eyes.
Hardly noticeable, etched under the eaves that covered the well, was a
symbol of black scales, perfectly balanced. Checking the longhouse,
she noted how none of the gods held scales in their hands like one of
the gods of Alika. On Al'Myrah, scales represented a courthouse or
justice.

The sign of the Court! She gasped but quickly averted eyes.
Checking back over her shoulder discreetly, she noted an old man

speaking quickly to a pair of half-Masahk before ushering them inside with the stealth of an assassin.

At last, a solution! Making sure to not fall behind, she began to concoct a plan to save herself and Tarkan. Sjörna-Reks left her unbound and mostly uncaged. Zeva knew it was because the Reks thought her weak. She'd shown her fragility to Sjörna-Reks, but now could use it to her advantage. They'd need to escape and run, quickly. Surely the Reks wouldn't pursue them far. And she'd never think to look in the Court of Deliverance.

"Bring me the Necro'Khan and his Apostle," Sjörna-Reks called to her warriors and shieldmaidens. They stood in the snow, facing a spine of mountains. Before the blue peeks, the bog sprawled out before them, wide, open, and frozen.

"Do not touch me," Zeva quipped when Lokhtar reached out to grab hold of her arm. "I will go willingly." She fended the others off Tarkan with a wave of her hand. In her mind, she hissed the words to raise a body. She'd have to speak it out loud to raise one fully, but she hoped having it mentally prepared might help.

"Zeva," Sjörna-Reks said, having shifted back into her human form. She threw the chain leash attached to the golden wolf to a man beside her. "You will witness the power of the man you call father so you will know the strength I have bridled."

She shoved Zeva aside and faced Tarkan. Placing her hands gently against the sides of his face, she whispered, "I will find a way, necromancer. You cannot evade me forever. I have you. Now I just have to force you."

Zeva shivered at her threat. Sjörna-Reks produced a key and clicked the lock on the back of Tarkan's head. The bridle fell off and he coughed, spitting blood onto the white snow. His thin lips were chapped and bleeding.

Sjörna-Reks held her hand out to a shieldmaiden. The woman stepped forward, offering a huge knife made of bone and her other arm. Zeva flinched as Sjörna-Reks cut at the warrior's arm, severing a chunk of her hard muscle. The woman hardly flinched, her eyes turning to steel. Sjörna-Reks's eyes didn't leave Tarkan's as she cut off a bit of her warrior for him and for Zeva.

"Make her consume," Sjörna-Reks ordered, handing the chunk to Tarkan as his chains were released.

Wordlessly, Tarkan took the bloody flesh and turned to Zeva.

Bile rose in Zeva's throat, but she took what he handed her. She bit into it, knowing she needed the strength. She needed to raise that dragon again. Maybe even scribe a locking rune on it, like Tarkan had done with his dragon to make the spell stick. Sjörna-Reks wouldn't have Tarkan scribe every corpse. In that case, the moment Tarkan stopped his concentration, they would fall. But first: safety.

The shieldmaiden swooned and collapsed on the ground. Sjörna-Reks stepped over her and faced the frozen bog below.

"Tarkan, Necro'Khan of Porsh," she said loudly. "Raise me an army worthy of Raudnir. Give me a horde of risen with which to punish Skarde-Reks and take the bridge."

The blood freezing to his pale face, Tarkan moved up to the rocky outcropping to look over into the bog. Zeva followed him. She burned to tell him her plan, to ask him to please run away with her. But something in her said he wanted to stay, to show his power.

"I will," he replied to Sjörna-Reks. "Once they rise, they will do as you bid without my voice. As promised."

Zeva whipped her head to Tarkan. Then she glanced at Sjörna-Reks. The red wolf looked all too happy to hear this.

"Do it," she ordered, taking two steps back.

Tarkan motioned Zeva to stand apart from him and she did, hovering her palms close together just as he did. Together, they chanted towards the bog. The wind blew colder now, tearing at their cloaks and kicking up the snow around them. Most of the warriors and shieldmaidens backed away, exclaiming. Sjörna-Reks stood her ground.

Zeva felt her voice torn from her throat into the wind; the scriptures on her skin writhed. No weakness consumed her. No fragility shook her knees or arms as the magic took the flesh sacrifice she'd consumed to power her spell. This almost enticed her into thinking consuming would always be the wisest decision. Without the weakness of eating up her own blood and body, the spell came easier. Even felt empowering.

The presence that had been leeching her essence had also vanished. She smiled. The Runers had done it. She was free.

Lending her power to Tarkan, she noticed the minute his lips stopped moving and he only glared down into the bog. His face twisted in a snarl and he slowly rotated his hands until his palms faced the sky. Then he languidly raised his arms up over his head and said one final line into the wind. She didn't know the variation of the spell he'd hissed, but she felt the change in the casting.

Below, a deep cracking started. It almost sounded like lightning muffled under water. White cracks spidered out over the green ice of the bog, and something writhed up from underneath the surface. Zeva stopped her spell now, knowing Tarkan was in full control. Beside them, Sjörna-Reks smiled wildly, laughing as the dozens then hundreds of bog bodies rose out of the ice and sludge. Some struggled to slither out as if the bog gave birth to them. Others crawled out easily. Once they were free of the ice and mud, they marched slowly towards the foot of the hill where they stood, waiting for commands.

"Where would you like your army, Reks?" Tarkan asked, his voice clipped by the black wind around him.

Sjörna-Reks glared north. "Have them hidden as close to Skarde's mountain as they can be. When Kjarton returns, he will remember why he loved me."

ZEVA STOOD QUIETLY near the foot of the stone dais. Sjörna-Reks had summoned her to the thronehall two days after Tarkan raised the army. The red wolf waited for Kjarton and Sybal to return for her next step. Zeva'd been separated from Tarkan, who was kept in the stockade again. Wishing she could get out and inspect the sign of the Court she'd found, she instead made her plans while she waited for the Runers to return. The first night after Tarkan raised the army, she thought about raising the dragon and fleeing. But the thought of leaving Tarkan and the Runers behind made her sick. So she waited.

Lokhtar came and retrieved her, marching her to the now all too familiar thronehall. Only a few braziers lit the huge hall, and a new kind of hopeless chill had settled over the place. Sjörna-Reks appeared from behind, a set of massive warriors marching a once again bound Tarkan in.

"This is no longer necessary," Zeva said, touching one of the chains that held him fast. "Has he not proved that he will do as you say?"

"You don't understand, little girl. Maybe one day you will." Sjörna paced across the top of the dais, hands clasped behind her back. "Unless you desire the same, do not test me. The Runers are returning." A light ignited behind her emerald eyes. "The time has come. Oh, at last."

Zeva stepped away from Tarkan to look up at Sjörna-Reks. "We will have to march on Northica with you. He may not need to speak to keep them risen any longer, but he must at least be near to command them."

Sjörna-Reks nodded, her great antlered crown making her look like a charging buck with every dip of her head.

"Reks," Zeva went on, looking up at the desperate woman. "What then? Dain is cursed. You will kill Skarde. He mentioned an alliance and the Warpath. The clans and cantons in the alliance will surely not let you walk away from attacking another in the alliance?"

"Zealmor might strike," Sjörna-Reks agreed. "But if they do,

Hovandel will side with me to protect their access to the northern islands."

Zeva frowned, shaking her head. "That's not a guarantee. You could be caught between two cantons who will want to know why you broke the alliance."

The red Reks raised her head, smiling darkly. "Fortunately for me, I have the Necro'Khan in my grasp. Once they know what they are dealing with, no clan will stand up to me. This will show my power, subjugating them all."

Zeva doubted it. Now she knew Sjörna-Reks was never going to let them go. She planned on holding on to them forever. Silently, she bowed her head and walked to Tarkan. He no longer looked weak, hungry, and tired, but he was still bound. Sighing, making up her mind, she pressed her forehead to his as they so often did.

"I'm going to get us out of here," she whispered.

Tarkan flicked his head up and she met his eyes.

"I will not let us be caught forever," she went on. "I don't care what she wants. If—" She choked on the defiance behind her words. Never had she talked to her father like she was about to now. "If you won't break us free, I will."

He shook his head against hers. She clenched her eyes shut. "You cannot break the blood oath. I've made no such oath." She forced herself to meet his eyes, wild with concern. "Trust me to free us. Don't fight me. I trust the necrotic magic you have given me. When the Runers are back—"

"Reks!" Lokhtar called, bursting through the two double doors at the front. "The Runers have returned."

Zeva's head shot up as the Reks bounded down, flying out the back door to meet Kjarton and Sybal and show her love her army. Zeva laid her hands on either side of Tarkan's face.

"I will not let you be chained like this. Not again," she swore before following the others out, Tarkan in tow.

ᚨ

THE FOREVER DARKNESS would have made it impossible to find the others were it not for the moon and its eldritch reflection in the sky lighting the white snow. Even in the night, Zeva could see far into the moors of Altevine and even make out the mountain of Northica against the star-studded sky. She spotted Sybal's ashen hair and made her way to the Runer's side.

"Sybal," Zeva said softly. She followed the Runer's gaze and saw she looked bitterly on Sjörna-Reks and Tzarik. "Thank you for hunting the kuri," she said. "I felt the moment its hold on me vanished."

Sybal nodded. "Of course, Zeva."

The pain of having Tzarik taken away again was evident in Sybal's stance, her clipped tone, and the worry in her eyes.

"Don't worry," Zeva whispered as they followed Sjörna-Reks into the village. "I have a plan."

Sybal looked down at her. "What do you mean?"

But Sjörna-Reks answered that question for her. "See, my love!" she declared, throwing her arms wide to indicate the darkness before them. With that gesture, she shifted into her red wolf and howled to the north. Her living warriors, far away with the undead, lit a perimeter of braziers. Hisses, moans, and guttural growls from the undead horde that marched out reverberated up to the starry sky. Zeva watched Kjarton's reaction.

"And look," Sjörna's wolven voice growled. Turning, she flicked her great head towards the open square before her thronehall, where a mass of more bodies was piled high.

The raven king's mouth dropped and he paled. His eyes flicked to the homes nearby, where frightened clansmen and their families cowered inside. "The people are terrified," he replied. His eyes took in the cauldrons of poison now and the rows of fresh swords from the forges. "Sjörna, no," he breathed. Kjarton turned and grasped her shoulders as she shifted back. "Why have you done this? What kind of madness has taken your soul since my death?"

"Madness?" Sjörna-Reks scoffed. "No madness, my love. I created the Necro'Khan. I harnessed his power by the oath of his own blood. For you. I brought you back to me." She smiled in confusion. "Are you not pleased?"

Zeva sensed the change in Kjarton at the same time Sybal did. Both women tensed next to each other, quickly giving each other a meaningful glance. Sjörna-Reks sensed it, too.

"No, Kjarton, my love," she cooed. "Don't fall away from me now." She lunged at him, taking his face in her hands. "I love you. I did this for you. I saved you at last. Do you blame me still for your death?"

Kjarton blanched, sighing sadly. "I never blamed you."

"I won't send you back!" Sjörna-Reks shouted, a sob growing in her throat. "I won't let you go back to the Deep. Don't make me lose you again." She kissed him hard, then savagely pulled back, glaring.

Sybal's arm instinctively went out to cover Zeva, and the necromancer let the Runer push her back. Zeva's eyes whipped to Tarkan, where two guards held him.

"Shall I show you?" Sjörna-Reks growled. She snapped her fingers and Lokhtar marched to Tarkan.

Zeva stiffened, but the big brute merely unlocked the bridle from his face. Tarkan took a deep breath and spit out a glob of blood. Sjörna-Reks marched to Tarkan, grabbed him by his arm, and forced him towards the undead mound.

"Sjörna, stop this," Kjarton called.

"If you must see my strength with your own eyes, so be it," she called back.

Unsure what Sjörna-Reks's intent was, Zeva called out to Tarkan.

"Stay, Zeva," he ordered her.

"Is she going to set the dead on her own clan?" Zeva cried in horror.

"Sjörna, don't!" Kjarton's voice cracked like thunder. The ferocity in his voice made them all stop and turn to look at the raven Reks.

"What are you doing?" Sjörna-Reks called back, suddenly afraid.

Kjarton stood apart, Tzarik's blade to his throat.

"Don't!" Sybal cried, but one of the clansmen caught her, wrestling her back. "Kjarton, don't!" she begged.

Kjarton had taken Tzarik's blade and pressed it to his own throat. "Sjörna, I should not be here. I was given to the Deep and I must return. We cannot guess what this has done to our clanlands. You don't know what you've brought to our home. I cannot stand to see you this way. What has happened to you? Why must you delve into this dark magic and seek revenge on Skarde? Is it because of me?"

Sjörna-Reks shoved Tarkan into the hands of Lokhtar and turned to face her resurrected love. "Do not make me watch you take your own life," she whispered. "Kjarton, my darling, why are you doing this to me? I love you."

Kjarton nodded, bracing himself. "Sjörna did. But you are not her. Perhaps she died with me and only the wolf remains, forever hunting. Forever raging." Kjarton swallowed hard. "I will not be the reason you throw yourself into this darkness." His eyes flicked to Sybal, apologizing with a look as tears trickled down his cheek. "I'm sorry."

"No!" Sybal screamed as Kjarton drew the blade over Tzarik's throat.

Blood splashed from the wound, melting the snow before him and soaking his clothes. He missed the black mark. Instead of releasing his spirit from Tzarik's body, he only hurt him. Zeva froze in terror. Sjörna-Reks screamed and ran back up the hill, shoving past Zeva to catch Tzarik's body as he fell to the snow. Sybal bucked wildly against her capture as well. Zeva whirled around to look at

Tarkan. A stale wind whipped up behind them all as Tarkan commanded the horde.

"Reks!" Lokhtar cried, turning to face the risen that marched slowly towards them now. He grappled Tarkan, covering his mouth with his great hand. The risen stopped, swaying on the spot. A few staggered forward, and some of the clan's warriors jumped into battle with them.

"Zeva!" Sybal shouted from where she struggled against her captor.

Understanding, she focused on the bodies she knew were piled high inside the thronehall, thinking of one in particular. With the others fighting the first horde, she was able to hiss and spit her way through the verses. A second later, the hulking mountain of a dead fighter burst out the doors and ran to its necrotic master. Zeva pointed to the man who held Sybal and it barreled towards him. Seeing the undead, wild-haired warrior, the clansman holding the Runer let go and backed away.

Sybal shot Zeva a quick glance, asking with only her eyes if she was all right. Zeva nodded and Sybal bounded up the hill to Tzarik and Sjörna-Reks. Zeva turned her brutish undead onto Lokhtar, who held Tarkan.

"Zeva, behind you!" Tarkan shouted, finally getting Lokhtar's hand off his mouth.

Zeva spun around only to see a clansman take aim at her with his bow. She didn't have time to duck before the arrow hissed towards her. Sybal gave a shout, thrusting a quickly drawn shield towards the necromancer as she galloped up the hill. The arrow splintered on the runic barrier.

A full-fledged battle broke out. Tarkan's risen returned to the fight in the second he was able to shout the last of the verses. Lokhtar, raging, gripped Tarkan by his throat and slammed him bodily into the ground. Zeva had to turn and run as a warrior came at her. She had to pull her own risen brute away from the fight to defend herself now. The warriors had seen the display: they knew they had to come at the necromancer, not their risen.

As she fought to keep herself safe, something huge and red streaked past her, snarling, "Enough of your voice!" Whipping her head back to where Kjarton had started it all, Zeva saw only Sybal holding Tzarik's body, drawing a rune over his throat. Sjörna-Reks was gone. A snarling bark behind told her where the Reks had run off to. Sjörna-Reks attacked Tarkan where he lay in the snow. Zeva couldn't hear between the distance and the din of the fight. Sjörna-Reks shifted back to her human form and gripped Tarkan's face. With the help of Lokhtar, she snatched a ladle of the boiling poison from the forge and splashed it down his throat.

A horrible, strangled cry rose from Tarkan as he clawed at Sjörna-Reks and the poison scorched his throat, taking his voice in a stream of hot, noxious rain.

Desperate, tears freezing to her face, Zeva turned to Tarkan's horde and chanted the spell quickly, taking control. She'd helped him raise them, so she already had partial control. All the risen finally moved. More warriors arrived and even a few villagers with swords appeared to fight the risen.

In a rage, Zeva reached out to more of the undead inside the thronehall and summoned them up. She choked on her mucus and tears, but pushed past it. Tarkan had stopped screaming, mute from the boiling poison. Zeva continued to defend herself with her brutish risen but got driven farther away from him. Sjörna-Reks picked up Tarkan's limp body and rushed away as her men protected her. Zeva clambered up onto her undead warrior's great shoulders as her own fresh wave of undead arrived from the thronehall. Thrusting her hands after Sjörna-Reks, she sent them towards her. This forced Sjörna-Reks to thrust Tarkan's unconscious body at Lokhtar and turn, shifting into her wolf form to fight the risen.

"I should have killed you when I had the chance," Sjörna said, snapping her wolven jaws at Zeva.

Zeva crouched, standing with one foot in the crook of her risen protector's arm and the other on his shoulder. She gripped his long, braided hair to steady herself.

"No fault of yours," Zeva shouted back. "I underestimated myself as well."

While Sjörna-Reks tore at the risen, Zeva turned back to where she remembered the dragon lay. Hissing the same verse of her necrotic scriptures, she focused on the dragon. Her risen used his hands to block a few arrows that flew her way. She was jerked around as he defended her, but she held fast, focusing on her spell. The dragon's belting roar made only a few stop and look to the skies.

Zeva directed it to Sybal, where she fought off a few clansmen. Sybal refused to leave Tzarik's side. The dragon landed hard in a puff of white snow. Sybal tried to gather up Tzarik, defend herself, and climb onto the beast, but to no avail. Zeva fought her way there and shot up the dragon's spines. After Zeva ordered her risen protector to pick up Tzarik, Sybal then clambered up behind her. With the three of them and the risen astride the great undead dragon, Zeva ordered it into the sky.

Weeping, she found Tarkan's dark form being taken away by Lokhtar. Sybal's arms embraced her hard from behind, trying to comfort her and hold Tzarik while the dragon rose. With a gasp, Zeva dropped her spell. The wind stopped, the snow settled, and the risen collapsed. A sudden exhaustion consumed her. All sound below them cut out in a single second.

"Where is Kjarton?" Sjörna's voice rang out in agony as they fled. "Where is my raven?"

CHAPTER 31

THE EMPTY

SYBAL WHIPPED HER HEAD AROUND. "WHERE ARE YOU taking us? We need to warn Northica. They're in the east. You're heading west."

Zeva ground her teeth, determined. "I need to rest in peace. You need sulfates. I know exactly who we need, and we won't find the help in Altevine. The wolf won't move until Tarkan is ready, too. We have maybe two days."

"The middle of Caerwren is called The Empty," Sybal informed her. "There's nothing there."

"That confirms it!" Zeva shouted.

Looking down, Sybal caught the dim lights of tiny farmsteads and scattered village homes. They grew further apart and fewer the more they soared west.

"I'm looking for a secret place!" Zeva shouted over the icy wind over the dragon's back. "I bet it's in The Empty. And with our dragon, we can make it to Northica before her."

Sybal tightened her grip on Tzarik, making a sound that said she wasn't sure. He woke up, grunting. Growling in frustration, she checked her belt to find no sulfates. "We left our supplies," she mumbled to Tzarik.

His hand went to his throat, fingers tracing the new scar she'd given him in exchange for his life. "Kjarton's still here," he mumbled. "I feel him."

"Zeva," Sybal said, her voice quaking a little. "Take us down. I need to wrap his wound and heal him more."

"Where I'm taking us, we will be able to," she tried again. "And he'll have sulfates."

Gnashing her teeth, Sybal clung to Tzarik harder to stop her hands from snapping at the girl. "Take us down now. I need your help. You don't know what you're looking for. You can't just fly us through this icy air until we all freeze."

The necromancer bit her bottom lip, pouting in worry before she finally nodded.

The undead dragon dove, making Sybal clamp her thighs down hard to hold on. A few lights of small farmsteads flickered about half a mile away in each direction. They were right to call the center The Empty: very little life moved.

"Is this a fire dragon?" Sybal asked, slipping an arm under Tzarik to help him down in his delirious state. She smacked his face to get him to wake up enough to inspect the dragon.

"It is," he grunted before leaning his head against her shoulder. "But it's dead. The fire in it will be out or at worst, a blighted flame."

"Very well," Sybal quipped. "Zeva, make a place to rest as best you can. Somewhere out of this wind. I'll find you," she cut in when the girl opened her mouth to protest. "I need to find dry wood and moss."

She slipped Tzarik's arm from around her to Zeva's shoulders. The temptation to kiss him made her stutter before she finally turned away into the dark prairies to search for dry wood. A few leafless trees struggled to grow tall and thick here. Their branches were dry and brittle. The few patches of moss she found were blessedly dry as well. It would do to make a fire.

Sybal! the sweet, familiar voice called to her. *You are close to me...*

"Mother?" Sybal called into the night, finally recognizing the voice that had been speaking to her. Her heart thudded to a halt. "Mother!" she tried again, louder.

Yes, she was not mistaken now. Freja's voice came to her on the wind. She stumbled over the uneven ground, snapping her head around. The voice didn't sound like it came from inside her head.

"Where are you?" she called, confused and doubting her memory. Her mother had been killed. Sybal had cut her and the rest of her family down again after Tarkan had raised them up. *You're going mad, Sybal,* she thought to herself. Had the time in the Deep twisted her mind?

You are not mad, Freja replied. *I can see you now. But I have come for a purpose: to direct your blade.*

Sybal looked up to see the sky burst into greens, yellows, and blues. A wave of mysterious light slithered across the sky to the north. She'd heard of the western skies doing such things during Osterah— the spring—but had never witnessed it. They called the lights the Herald of Beltire, since it signaled that soon warmer weather would touch the mountains. She idly wondered what summer looked like in Caerwren.

"What do you mean?" she asked, cautiously. Caerwren was too full of magic for her liking. The barrier between the mortal world and the world of the magic of the gods was too thin. This could be a trick.

I have been searching for you, Freja went on. *One who has been touched by the gods. A god-touched. And you are far superior to the others. You have been to the Deep, died there, and returned to your mortal side.*

That didn't sound like her mother at all. "What do you want

from me?" she asked, almost sure this was a god or spirit and not her loving mother.

I want your blade, Freja said. *I will direct you. Show you who to take.*

Now she knew this had to be a trick. "I cannot take a life," she said, almost smirking that even a god had not known her crime. "You know this, mother."

The voice laughed. *Nothing can harm one who has died in the Deep to return to life.* The voice faded out, barely letting her hear the last word.

"Mother!" Sybal called. No answer came. "Fool, it's not her," she reminded herself. Touching her runes around her neck, she wondered if there was any way to make the voice stop. Tossing her long, ashen braid over her shoulder, she gathered up the sticks and moss and returned to find Zeva.

THE YOUNG NECROMANCER had found a perfect place to build a camp. She'd made the undead dragon lie down and set its huge, serpentine body against the wind. One of its leathery wings spread over them, resting against a huge rock, creating a perfect and spacious tent.

"Well done," Sybal said to Zeva, remembering how touched she always felt at receiving praise. She found Tzarik lying with his back to the rock, wrapped in his fur-lined cloak.

"Kjarton is fading," Zeva said as Sybal went to work rubbing the sticks together to make fire.

"Build up a small pyre," she instructed the girl. "Fading?" she asked once Zeva obeyed. She handed Zeva some of the moss to put underneath.

"I tried to pull him up from inside Tzarik, but he's weak," the girl went on. "But unless he possesses Tzarik again, he cannot be expelled."

Sybal looked up. "You can do that?" A small ember ignited, and she rushed it to the pyre Zeva had built. She blew on it until a decent-sized flamed erupted. Then she stacked a few more sticks onto it. The heat filled the dragon-made space almost instantly, bringing relief from the cold.

"I can try," Zeva offered.

"Will it hurt him?" Sybal asked, indicating Tzarik.

Zeva pressed her lips together and almost shrugged.

Sybal sniffed and rubbed at a sudden tear in her eyes. "Kjarton was not a bad man," she mumbled, coming to Tzarik's side. He'd drifted off into some kind of sleep. She reached up and pulled the fur cowl down to pet the side of his head. She tucked his long, dirty hair behind one ear and noticed the black locking script on his neck. The scar was rough under her thumb.

"Zeva," she quipped. "I think Kjarton tried to break the mark. Would that release him?"

Zeva's large blue eyes widened. "Maybe? I'm sorry, I don't know."

Sybal shot up, shoving past Zeva, and grabbed a smoldering ember from the fire. The girl gasped a high-pitched shriek when the Runer took it up in her bare hands. Sybal gripped Tzarik's head, mumbled an apology, and pressed the ember to his neck.

Tzarik writhed at the sudden pain, eyes flying open. He landed a hard punch to Sybal before gasping and passing out from the pain. Sybal sat up, tossing the ember back into the fire. Hissing, she inspected her hands to see her flesh melted and blistering. She shook her head and moaned. Before she found something to wrap it with, the welts and dripping flesh healed over to a shiny scar.

"Oh, gods," Zeva breathed. She shuffled away from Sybal on her backside, looking on in horror. "How did you...?"

"I-I don't know," Sybal confessed, just as shaken as Zeva. She turned her hand to inspect it. The pain had disappeared. The burn hadn't vanished, but turned into a perfectly healed scar. "Zeva," Sybal said slowly, "this doesn't mean anything. There's a lot of magic here on Caerwren. I've been to the Deep. This could be nothing."

Zeva stuttered. "Of course." She relaxed a little and gestured to Tzarik. "I'll find Kjarton. His spirit might have been banished from Tzarik's body." Crawling over to Tzarik, she held her palms just an inch apart. Her eyes glassed over as she hissed into a wind that swept her voice away. "Sybal," she said, once her scriptures writhed on her face. "If I find him, do you want to speak to him?"

Inching closer to Tzarik and Zeva, Sybal nodded. "Not to condemn him. Tell him that. I want to tell him I will stop Sjörna and that I will not harm her if I can help it."

Zeva smiled sweetly despite the necrotic words dancing over her flesh and her white, glowing eyes.

Just the wind and the snapping of the flames filled their dragon-made shelter while Zeva reached out to raise the spirit of Kjarton.

"I've found him," she said breathily. "He was trying to run." Her voice came clipped from the wind. "Kjarton!" she shouted, looking up into the snow-covered land. Her voice echoed into a void Sybal could not see. "Don't. Come to me."

Sybal's stomach knotted as Zeva reached out before her like she might grab a wisp of smoke from the fire. "Is Tzarik all right?" Sybal asked, taking his hand.

Zeva nodded. "Kjarton," she said stoically. "Come back."

Sybal watched as events unfolded before Zeva that she could not see. Tzarik gasped in his unconsciousness and Zeva threw her head back. Sybal caught her before she slammed her head into the rocks. Then the girl sat up, eyes wide and terrified.

"Sybal?" Zeva gasped. "It's me, Kjarton. The necromancer invited me to speak to you."

Sybal adjusted to her knees, looking him in the eyes. "I'm so sorry," she began.

Zeva shook her head. "Don't be. This was not your doing, nor mine." Her face turned sad, and Kjarton directed her eyes to the fire. "Stop her. She doesn't know what she's doing."

Sybal sniffled. "She loved you. That's why she did this. People are mad when in love."

"I wanted to thank you," Kjarton said, lifting Sybal's chin with Zeva's hand. "For the time you spent with me in the Deep."

Sybal smiled through a fresh wave of emotion. "Thank you for saving me. For helping me get back. I wish there was more I could do for you. You don't deserve what's happened to you. You couldn't stand up to her. You needed someone to help you. To save you."

Zeva's face smiled sadly. "You can't save everyone, Sybal. Now go. Stop her. Or at least warn Northica. Skarde is like every other Reks: not innocent, but the alliance must stay strong. For the clans. We fight too much on Caerwren as it is. This is one battle we can avoid."

Sybal nodded.

"And Sybal," Kjarton said as Zeva began to sweat blood. "If a battle is avoided, you can save one life. Signar."

"Your son?" she asked, shocked.

Kjarton nodded. "Sjörna treats him like an animal. I never stood up to her in his favor. I let her hurt us too much in life. I am sure with the right hand, he could be whole in his mind again. A wolf simply needs to be tamed."

Conflicted, Sybal stammered. "We are Runers, Kjarton. That is no life for—"

"A wild wolf?" he asked, smiling. "It would be better for him...if..."

Zeva screamed, coughing. Blood flecked over Sybal's face as Kjarton's spirit vanished from the girl. Zeva collapsed forward onto Sybal. She caught the girl and held her tight. Zeva shook with fever.

"Thank you, Zeva," she mumbled, petting her hair.

"I'm so...tired...now," the girl panted. "Hungry."

Sybal glanced around. She had only a few bolts on the small

crossbow on her thigh and her scimitar. And she'd never been great at hunting. She was better than Tzarik, who had only ever hunted monsters, but not good enough to shoot something with the four bolts in the dark. They needed to sleep and then find one of those farmsteads.

"I'll feed you," Sybal promised. "Don't worry."

She laid Zeva down and wrapped her in her fur cloak before going to Tzarik. He stirred when she turned his head to inspect his neck.

"I'm glad to see your rash decisions have followed you to death and back," he mumbled with a weak grin.

Sybal scoffed in tired amusement.

"Wait," Tzarik added in a moan, his voice small and faint as he looked around. "The horses... Mamun."

"We'll go back for them," she promised, shaking her head. She drew artiah over his fresh burn. "I'm not very good at exorcisms," she confessed with a shrug. "I could have cut it, I suppose. But then you would have bled more. You're low on sulfates as it is." She ran her finger over the cut on his throat. "He did it to stop her, not to harm you."

Tzarik nodded. "I know. But he almost took me with him."

Kjarton's words came to Sybal as she drew artiah one last time. Tzarik would have two more scars to add to his collection. "He asked me to stop her."

"And we will," Tzarik agreed, trying to sit up.

Sybal grabbed his arm and pulled him up into a sitting position, then moved to sit by his side against the rock. She sat close enough that their shoulders touched under the layers of clothing.

"She thinks she does this out of love," she mused. "But she's hurting her clan."

Tzarik didn't reply, so Sybal didn't press him. Taking a chance, she leaned her head onto his shoulder and wrapped her cloak around her legs, settling in for the night. Tzarik moved his arm so she could lie down across his legs, and she did. His hand rested on her arm and sleep took her.

$$\partial$$

"I SEE A FARM," Sybal called back to Zeva. She took the lead, opting to walk on the ground so as to not frighten the people living that far out with a dragon sighting. Tzarik was weak from his wounds, hungry, and thirsty. Zeva had used the last of her strength the night before. Sybal felt the need for food and water, but had more strength than both of them.

She doubled back, helped Zeva down off her now lifeless dragon, and supported Tzarik as they walked towards the farm through a thick, blue mist.

"There," Tzarik said, pointing to a few moving shapes in the lightening darkness. The sun peeked up over the horizon just a little now that spring was on its way.

Sybal squinted and saw two forms—one clearly a man and the other a younger boy—digging far to the side of the farm's fence.

"Hello?" she called to them. "We are Runers. We've lost our way and will pay for food and water."

The man stopped digging, motioned for the boy to stay, and approached them. Sybal had Zeva cover her face as best she could, wrapping even her fingers to stop them from seeing the scriptures.

"We have a Runer," the man grunted in strange, accented Al'Myrahn. He pointed with his shovel to the hole he and the boy were digging. "Lost him to a likho just yesterday." The man was tall like the rest of his countrymen, sporting thick, black curls and an angular jaw like the people of Rom. His swarthy, weathered skin told them he had lived out here for most of his life. "I am Decimus, and that is my son, Lucius."

The boy looked up with bright green eyes through long black

curls that matched his father's. He nodded respectfully to the Runers.

"You speak Al'Myrahn?" Tzarik asked, falling into his own language for the first time in what felt like a lifetime.

Decimus nodded. "We are immigrants from Rom. Rom was settled many millennia ago by explorers from Al'Myrah. I understand your plight. Al'Myrah?" Decimus asked to be sure, looking them over. "You are far from home."

He turned and motioned for them to follow him.

"You have a likho?" Sybal asked. "I'll kill it for you if you feed us. We are hurt and in desperate need of supplies."

Decimus motioned for Lucius to get back to digging. Sybal noted the wrapped corpse near the deepening hole the boy had dug.

"Did you take his things?" she asked, eager to gather the dead Runer's effects. "He might have had a black box—"

"Lass," Decimus interrupted, "this is Caerwren. I know what a Runer's tools are. They are not so rare here as on your home continent." He turned to the fence where a mass of items hung by thick, black belts. He pulled one from the post and handed it to her. "His horse is in the pasture."

"Sira," Zeva piped up, shaking. "Was this a Masahk Runer?"

Decimus eyed her, his brows knitting as he took in her wrapped form. "Aye."

Sybal noticed Zeva visibly quake. "What was his name?"

"Morr," Decimus quipped, motioning for Lucius to help him lift the corpse. "A feline kind of Masahk or some such. Pure Alikan, too. Almost no human traits."

Zeva almost collapsed in relief. Sybal suddenly understood the girl's need to find this secret place she'd mentioned. She was looking for the Masahk Runer she'd been in prison with.

"Give us food and water," Sybal said, "and I will find this likho and dispatch it."

Decimus nodded wordlessly, dropping the dead Runer into the

hole. "We started a totem to ward it off, but it keeps coming back." He pointed towards his small hovel of a house, where a wooden statue stood out front.

"I'll take care of it," Sybal promised.

Once the Runer was buried and Sybal had found his horse, they went inside Decimus's home. The hovel resembled the thronehall a little in that the upper level was open and everything—the hearth, the beds, the kitchen—all occupied one large area. The floor was dirt. Decimus's wife was a gentle, sweet woman with red and gold hair. She served them wordlessly, offering wine, fresh bread, and a stew brimming with curious vegetables and dark meat. They didn't mind when Sybal brought in the dead Runer's black box and inserted the needle into Tzarik's arm while they sat around a fire to eat.

"What brings you to Caerwren?" Decimus asked.

"The Hunt," Tzarik said once he'd gotten his strength back. "But we've entangled ourselves with Sjörna-Reks."

Skilla, the wife, raised her brows and made quick hand gestures to Decimus, her face expressive as she went on. Decimus understood and turned back to them.

"Skilla says she has heard rumors from the ravens. She knows what you speak of."

Sybal looked in awe at the woman. "She cannot speak?"

Decimus shook his head. "The gods saw fit to take the voice of my son and my wife from his birth. But they have their ways. And she understands the animals, hearing them." He smiled up at Skilla as she prepared a tea made from a black root. "Sjörna-Reks would be mad to march on Northica with her only heir being a wildling," Decimus said offhandedly. "The clans only allow Vaeson to be Reks of the cantons. Even in more civilized cantons like Hovandel, this is the way. If she dies, some other Reks will take her clan's land."

Skilla made a quick sign, rolling her eyes. Decimus scoffed lightly.

"Perhaps," he mused, offering more wine. "We here in The

Empty hope Hovandel takes Altevine. The Warpath has remained savage too long."

With their bellies full, even Sybal could not find the mind to continue too much conversation. Decimus insisted she sleep and hunt the likho the next day. The humble farm had no other rooms besides the family's rooms, so Zeva, Sybal, and Tzarik made do with sleeping on the dirt around the hearth. Still, a roof, a fire, and hot food made it better than anything they had experienced so far on Caerwren.

Sybal removed her armor and helped Tzarik with his. He seemed more weary than usual. When they laid down, Zeva already breathing lightly, she noted his posture. He lay on his back, eyes open, jaw tense.

"What are you thinking?" she asked quietly.

To her surprise, Tzarik whispered, "Vicdan."

She frowned. "I'm sure he's talked his way out of worse situations. If Skarde-Reks hasn't sacrificed him on a cold stone by now, we'll find him." Honestly, she hadn't worried about the jongleur. She trusted his ways of survival. He no doubt was alive and well. She told Tzarik as much, his worry for the young man he usually despised taking her by surprise.

Tzarik nodded, agreeing with her, but his brows still knit slightly. Something else troubled his mind about Vicdan. She read from the way his lips moved as though he might speak that he did battle within himself, unsure of his speculation.

Knowing he wouldn't speak his thoughts unless he was sure, she said, "We'll find him."

As the night wore on and the fire dimmed, they moved closer together for warmth and safety. Sybal woke halfway through the night to find Tzarik's hand on her middle, pulling her close.

CHAPTER 32

PURSUIT

Tzarik woke to find Sybal outside, saddling up the dead Runer's horse. She took the long, straight sword off and stabbed it into the ground before pulling herself up onto the big war horse.

"Here," he grunted, handing her a set of flint and steel. "From the hearth. You'll need to heat the orichalcum to kill the likho."

"Oh?" she breathed, pushing strands of her long hair out of her face. "Thank you. I didn't know. I thought maybe fire and oil."

He shook his head. "You're half right. It's flesh and specter. You need the blade, oil, and fire."

She smiled down at him. "You've spent some time on Caerwren before?"

Reaching down, he caught one of the reins she'd dropped and handed it to her. "Crossed over it to get to Rhostrana before. Just before you, actually." He inspected the gear she'd lashed to the saddle: the dead Runer had bags of magical herbs, bottles of mixed tinctures, and a bundle of thick staves with the runes carved into them.

Behind them, a strange, warbling nickering sound came up from a nearby river. Tzarik glanced over his shoulder, then back to Sybal.

"I'm taking these," he mused, untying the long staves. "I'll put a parameter of halat around the house." He opened a smaller bag and took out a clear jar of what looked like black salt. "Taking this, too."

Sybal raised her brows, curious. "Will the runic staves keep things out?"

"I think that was his plan," Tzarik noted, heaving the staves into his arms. "Be careful. Set up a fire before you lure the likho out. Heat the metal. Don't take any chances." He ran his eyes over the bottles inside the Runer's bag again, finding a pearly black tincture. "Use this on the blade. While our metal will cut the flesh, this will weaken the spirit. Tincture of merciful creeper—a plant that grows over graves."

Sybal nodded, watching him put the tincture back. She licked her lips and turned her eyes down, biting her bottom lip. He watched her hunt for whatever words she wanted to say. Then, he decided he wouldn't let her be the one to always initiate. Quickly, he slipped her foot out of the stirrup. He stood in it himself, pulled himself up so they were at eye level, and kissed her. He took her head in his free hand to stop her from pulling away. She kissed him back and smiled under his lips.

A rock whizzed passed them, splashing in the soggy ground a few yards away. Tzarik turned to see Lucius playfully making disgusted faces at them. He exhaled lightly, almost laughing, and leapt down.

"Go on." He smacked the horse and watched Sybal vanish into the too quiet prairie, swallowed up by the mist.

Turning to Lucius, he gestured him forward. "Show me where the likho appeared."

Tzarik walked the close perimeter of the farmstead with the boy leading him to lamp posts, fallen wooden fences, and even a foreboding-looking tree near a muddy path leading away. At each place, Tzarik stabbed the sharp end of one of the rune staves into the ground, the rune facing out. As he suspected, each one had halat carved into it to shield the space behind the totem.

They worked in silence when the quiet river suddenly appeared. The water moved so smoothly over the round rocks that it made almost no sound. The water looked black. A nickering echo skipped over the rippling waves. Tzarik recognized it from before. His sulfates rushed and he held his hand out for Lucius to stop.

"Stand back," he whispered. "Do you hear hooves?"

Lucius nodded, tilting his head to listen, then held up three fingers and shrugged, confused.

"That's what I thought," Tzarik murmured. "Helhest. Go inside."

Lucious protested silently, grabbing Tzarik's cloak.

"No, you cannot stay. If you look at it, you won't see the sun rise." He shoved the boy gently, eyes scanning the river front.

The odd, three-beat hoof falls came closer. Tzarik set the bundle of staves on the ground, reached down to the bit of his tunic sticking out from under his leather armor, and tore a long strip off. Quickly, he tied it around his eyes and took deep breaths to calm his sulfates and heighten his hearing. His sight gone, the sulfates charged his other senses until he almost felt the vibration of the ground. He heard Lucius run off behind him. Helhests could be fought with orichalcum. He just had to do it blind.

Stepping over the staves, he approached the river. He gripped his scimitar in his hand and held it high, ready to strike. A deep snorting that could only come from skeletal ribs huffed behind him. He knew, even without his sight, that the thing was looking at him. Swallowing hard, he turned to face it. It nickered and hopped, pawing at the ground with its one good front leg. It's ghostly warbling calls rang out. He pulled his runes off from around his neck and gripped buhkar tightly just as the monster charged. Drawing quickly, he dodged, feeling the helhest graze his side with a set of prongs. Did everything on Caerwren come with a set of sharp horns?

As he dodged, the magic steel still gripped in his hand, he sliced at it to let it know he could harm it. The helhest whined and snorted, shocked at the hit. This enraged it more. It stamped madly, tossing its head, and charged again. This time, Tzarik went low. He slid on the muddy ground, severing one of its back legs. The helhest bugled in pain and made a kind of roaring sound. It didn't understand why its gaze was not affecting the Runer. Without warning, it charged, made a splashing sound, then all noise vanished.

Tzarik swore gently, still listening. How had the hoof beats vanished? It now lumbered and shook the earth, hobbling on its two legs, but had disappeared. Spinning on the spot, listening, Tzarik couldn't find it. Tuning in to his sulfates, they rushed up his spine. Spinning to face behind himself, he waited. Nothing.

"Where the hell are you?" he growled, listening again. He took another step and cold water filled his boots, seeping in through the soft leather. It didn't make a splash. The river was silent. Confused, not caring that he didn't know why the water cut off all sound, he realized where the helhest waited.

Raising his scimitar just in time, the weight of the huge beast bowled him over as his blade entangled with the helhest's antlers. Some reached beyond the curved scimitar and cut his shoulders where his leather pauldron and chest piece met. The helhest bellowed and bucked, taking Tzarik with it, tossing him over its shoulders. He splashed into the water soundlessly again and scrambled to his feet, drawing buhkar to make an escape. Even though he couldn't hear the thing or see it from under his blindfold, the sulfates let him feel it shake the earth as it charged. Switching to holding halat, he drew it with all his strength and shoved it out from his body like Sybal had shown him on Xia. The barrier flew at the helhest, hitting it with all its strength. A sound like dry lightning cracked, throwing him backwards.

Leaping to his feet, he dashed to where the river had splashed from the invisible creature's fall. He cut in wild arches with his scimitar. The water roiled as the thing scrambled to its feet. An angry bugle and a cloud of air snorted through wide nostrils burst out with each hit. Encouraged, he struck again and again.

Finally, when the water only splashed from his arching blade, he stopped. Panting, he kicked its corpse with his foot. It didn't move. He pulled the blindfold off and looked down. A mass of stark white bones, black, leathery skin, and gray ectoplasm sat at his feet. Sighing in relief, he gripped the antlers and pulled it out of the river. When he hauled it on shore, the slightest sound of the river came back. Very faint and dim, the sounds of the wild moors of Caerwren also came back. The sun was just peeking over the mountains now. It had to be late morning, but the ball of light had not made its way higher than that. He missed the sun.

"Gods," Zeva's voice whispered from behind him.

He turned, cold and shivering from the river water, and covered in black gore. He nodded, wiping his sword on the grass.

"What is that?" she asked, keeping her distance, hands clasped over her chest.

"Helhest," he said casually. He pointed to a brazier near the fence. "Give me some of that fire."

Without hesitating, Zeva ran to the brasier and pulled out a torch, handing it to him. Unceremoniously, Tzarik lit the beast on fire, burning its bones. He reached down and picked up the jar of black salt from before and tossed handfuls into the fire.

"Will that stop its spirit from coming back?" Zeva asked.

Tzarik nodded. "Anyone can salt and burn a corpse to stop a ghost. Most ghosts are more than just wandering spirits, though." He waded back into the river to find the leg he'd severed before. When he located it, he tossed it onto the fire and added more salt. It burned despite being soaked through. "I think this one has been around here for a long time."

"How can you tell?" Zeva asked.

Tzarik tossed in his makeshift blindfold. "If you look at a helhest, they turn you mute. It can do other things like petrify you, too. I think this one ruled this valley, muting everything with its virulent presence. Skilla may have looked upon it without knowing, through the mist or even in a reflection. If she did so while pregnant with Lucius, the spirit trait would pass to him. Specters and other such creatures are cruel like that." *Like the curse of a god-touched,* he thought bitterly.

Zeva tilted her head towards the river. "I can hear it a little now. Will the sound come back?"

"Since the river's song was silenced by the helhest, I assume it was inhabited by a naiad. She would have been affected by it."

"Oh!" Zeva cooed, clasping her hands over her heart. "I've never seen one. Do they have them on Al'Myrah?"

Tzarik nodded. "They're beautiful. But can be tricksters."

Taking up one of the atan staves, he went back to his initial task. Zeva followed him, taking the bundle from his arms to relieve him. She let him work in silence for a few totems, but he sensed she wanted to speak.

"Go on, Zeva," he said, making sure his tone was kind. "You've born much these last months. Speak."

Her blue eyes filled with sorrow. "I don't know what I should do. I've thought about everything Tarkan did for me. How he took care of me."

He slammed a totem into the ground, then turned to face the girl, sensing her hysterics growing. Putting a hand on her shoulder, he braced her.

"I told you, Tarkan loves you. If anyone else asked, I wouldn't be able to explain it. It's strange, unnatural, even. I couldn't believe it when we first met him and learned about you. I thought no necromancer could love when I couldn't."

Zeva's eyes rounded in curiosity. Then she dropped her shoulders. "But he's different now. He's been changing for so long and it frightens me. Will he do this?" She looked up again, turning pale. "Will he let Sjörna-Reks use him after he promised it wouldn't happen again? And now we're..." She choked. "We've only been separated once in my life. And I never wanted it to happen again. But he's lost himself; I can see it. I want to stop him, to bring him home. But I fear I lack the strength."

The girl's plight resonated within Tzarik. Pulling her into him, he embraced her, letting her weep in to his chest. She dropped the staves and wrapped her arms around him, crying softly. He closed his eyes, pressing his cheek against the top of her head. She was nearly a grown woman and yet she couldn't face the world as one. At her age, he'd been along for two years already, fighting monsters, struggling to survive. Not Zeva. Tarkan had kept her secluded, innocent somehow. He wished he could remove her from this, keep her that way. They stood together until she controlled her breathing and sighed.

"You do not lack the strength," he told her tenderly. "I've never seen a Runer take to the runes as quickly as these black words have to you." He cleared his throat before speaking again. "You did this—put yourself through this—for me. For Sybal. You've given me more than I can ever return to you. So I will bring him back to you. I promise."

His heart thudded excitedly in his chest. Confused, he glanced around and found Sybal leaning against the lamppost, smiling gently at the pair of them. She was also covered in black ectoplasm and carried a head with one wild eye in its face.

"Well done," he said as she approached them. He let go of Zeva and the girl embraced Sybal next.

"You look...gross," Sybal said, glancing Tzarik up and down over Zeva's head. She pet Zeva affectionately and looked around. "Run into trouble?"

Feigning nonchalance, Tzarik shook his head. He was about to reply when a huge murder of crows screamed, flying up from the prairie about a mile away. He and Sybal exchanged glances and Zeva gasped. Tzarik took his glass from his belt and looked in the direction of the fleeing crows. A tiny settlement of about ten homes and a small village belched up flames. Riders on wolves ransacked the village, bearing a green banner with a red wolf roaring on the front.

"Sjörna's men," Tzarik breathed. "Get inside!"

ꝺ

"She is coming for you," Decimus murmured, peeking out a cloth-covered window. He turned stoically to the Runers and the necromancer. "We will not die for you. They are burning the village. They will burn our home, too, until she finds you."

"She thinks you took Kjarton," Sybal said stiffly to Zeva.

"We did," Tzarik admitted, touching the scar on his throat. "But he's gone now."

Zeva looked between the two of them, her hands clasped over her chest. "Can we tell her he's gone? Maybe she'll spare them?"

Tzarik scoffed. "She won't. She's mad with revenge and drunk on her new power."

"Is Tarkan with them?" Zeva gasped, joining Decimus at the window.

"I doubt Sjörna-Reks is even there," Sybal put in. To Decimus and his family, she said, "We don't expect you to die for us. You sheltered us when we needed it most. We hunted the monsters tormenting you. We are even."

Tzarik made a note of the one horse they could take without incurring the wrath of the family. They needed to get back to the dragon and try to escape without the raiders seeing them.

Zeva spoke up quickly. "Do you know the Court of Deliverance?"

Tzarik turned to face her, confused. She looked at Decimus.

"You are not Masahk," Decimus quipped, his hands quickly fiddling with a talisman on his belt. "You will endanger the entire hidden road if you take that way."

"What is that?" Tzarik asked.

"An underground keep for Masahk avoiding the Black Road," Zeva supplied. "Ragnall told me about it."

At the mention of the name, Lucius perked up and pulled on his father's tunic, eyes wide. Decimus tried too late to silence his mute boy.

"So you know him?" Tzarik cut in. To Zeva he asked, "He was that Masahk Runer in the stockade?"

She nodded, blushing. He understood. He glanced at Sybal. Neither of them wanted to endanger the Masahk, but it would be a good place to hide and make their way to Northica. Lucius signed madly.

"What's he saying?" Tzarik asked as the smell of ash and smoke got closer. "Tell me!" he barked when Decimus hesitated.

"He says the Masahk was here. Ragnall." Decimus sighed, defeated. "He was. We gave him shelter." Back hunched, Decimus led them outside and pulled a lantern down from the post and lintel of his home. Behind the lantern, a white scrawling of a set of scales lay hidden.

"That's the sign!" Zeva chimed. "You're part of the hidden road. Please, where is he?"

Shouts from the raiders shot up from downriver, and the earth shook with the pounding of the massive wolves running towards the next farmstead.

Sybal ran to the horse and grabbed it.

"Head northwest," Decimus said. "There is a spine of mountains, near impassable, lining the shore. The entrance is there, hidden beneath an old god. But you won't make it before nightfall. The peaks are treacherous."

"We won't be walking," Tzarik said with a meaningful glance at Zeva.

She nodded, understanding. "And we won't leave you unguarded. At least for a moment." She started toward the front of the house to raise the Runer from his grave when Tzarik stopped her.

"No," he said sternly. "If you raise a body and leave it behind, they will know we were here. We cannot let them know."

"But..." Zeva started to protest, looking at the defenseless family. She stopped when the Runers didn't wait to argue. "I'm so sorry," she whispered to Decimus and his wife.

Tzarik gathered up their few remaining things and joined Sybal on the horse. The beast was huge, being a monstrous breed from Caerwren, and bore the three of them, two being smaller than Sybal, easily. Tzarik lifted Zeva up before himself.

"Thank you," Tzarik said to Decimus and his family. "I suggest you hide if you can. You cannot fight them off."

The man sighed again, taking his mute wife's hand. "We have a hiding place. We are part of the Court. If we fall, we fall, and enter the good life our god has prepared for us in Rahrgalah. But I pray we do not. Not for your sake." He glared at them. "I was always a good man."

Tzarik clicked his tongue at the horse. "May your god protect you."

"And Runer," Decimus called over the rattle of the excited horses' hooves. He spoke in Caerwren. "Speak the language of the mountains again. They will know someone from Rom aided you if you fall back into only Al'Myrahn."

"Thank you," Tzarik replied, returning to Caerwren's tongue.

They galloped away, leaving the small family to their fate. "Can you raise the dragon?" he asked as they found its hiding place not ten minutes later.

"Yes," Zeva said weakly. She began the spell.

When they dismounted the horse, Sybal took the cargo, leaving the saddle, and slapped it to make it run into the wilderness, away from the raiders.

Tzarik supported Zeva as she hissed the incantation to raise the dragon. He felt her body shrinking under his fingers until the beast woke. The idea made him sick, but he knew she'd need to consume soon if she was to make it much farther. His blood and Sybal's blood would not do.

Picking her up entirely into his arms, he followed Sybal onto the dragon. "She needs blood," he whispered to her.

Sybal directed the dragon up and into the dark sky. "Let's hope this Masahk she's fond of will find some for her and convince her to drink. We need her."

CHAPTER 33

THE COURT OF DELIVERANCE

THE BLACK WINDS HOWLED ALL AROUND THEM, BROKEN only by the waves of blue and green light weaving across the sky above. Tzarik's eyes watered even though the cutting air grew warmer than he'd ever felt it on Caerwren. The beat of the dragon's wings did not make for a smooth ride. The up and down sway was worse than any ship he'd been on in a storm. The thing's cold body between his thighs made his aching legs go numb, along with his fingers, which clutched at Zeva.

"What am I looking for?" Sybal called back to him.

Decimus had said the entrance lay under an old god. He'd seen a few of the gods, huge and smelling of fire and magic: the dragon god walking behind the mountains, its prongs scratching the sky; and the human-shaped one he and Tarkan had seen on the mountaintops. Tarkan had called it Tyrmagnar, a human man who—according to legend—ascended to godhood to save the sentients on Caerwren from Mjordir for a time.

"A skeleton," he guessed. "Something laying over the mountains, deep into the spine where it would be difficult to travel on foot."

Even with the dragon, it took them hours before they soared over the mentioned line of mountains on the northern shore. The bit of sunlight that had shone had long since set. Like a protective wall, the mountains lined the crashing shore below, trailing all the way to Northica in the east. With the clear air, Tzarik spotted a massive pyre near the top of the Northica mountain. From where they flew, it flickered like a candle in the distance.

"Holy Krishvu!" Sybal called out, reeling backwards on the neck of the dragon.

Tzarik spun to look down at where Sybal pointed. His jaw dropped a little when he saw it, too.

Just visible under feet of winter snow, what they sought came into view. Lying over a valley between two mountains, its wings spread over them like a blanket, rested the titanic skeletal remains of a god in the shape of a hawk. Its sharp beak pointed towards a small, dark opening that would have easily been missed if they'd not been looking for it from above. The many bones of its body were mostly buried in the snow, one silver talon jutting out, flashing in the green and blue borealis.

"Is our god so big?" Sybal asked, eyes glued to the glorious skeleton.

Tzarik didn't answer, not wanting to offend Sybal by reminding her he prayed to no god. The monsters of Caerwren almost made him change his mind. It made sense that if one country of people prayed to and worshiped a horde of titans like this, another would too, if not just for protection.

"Let us down here," Tzarik said, pointing his numb hand towards the sharp head of the hawk.

The black dragon stumbled on the uneven, rocky ground, slipped, and landed with a crash. Sliding to a halt, it came to rest in the side of a drift of snow. Cautiously looking up to judge whether they'd cause an avalanche, Tzarik leapt down, gathering Zeva in his arms. Her lips were blue and her skin had paled so much that the scriptures looked to be hovering above her flesh rather than etched onto it.

"Sorry," Sybal sighed, dusting some snow off her black pants. "I never learned how to fly a dragon, let alone land one."

The great beast stilled, dead once again. Zeva exhaled hard in Tzarik's arms, exhausted from all her efforts.

Tzarik had not gone five steps when a strange clinking and clattering crescendoed up from every crag and outcropping, like the knocking of bone on bone. A horrifying howl warbled up to them from the black crevasses. Sybal unsheathed her scimitar and moved before Tzarik and Zeva for protection.

"I don't feel anything," she supplied when the warning noises grew.

Tzarik didn't either. His sulfates didn't rush, his heart didn't pound. Just the natural feeling of being watched tingled his spine. Whatever made the noise didn't want to attack them, just warn them off.

No sooner had he come to this conclusion than a creature far taller than any man on Caerwren leapt out from its snowy hiding place. Its legs were strange and crooked and its head was a pure white skull. Antlers arched up from it, curving back over its shoulders. It held a massive club made of sharp bone. More like it, covered in the fur of various animals, also charged them, howling, clicking, and growling.

Panic made Tzarik fumble Zeva in his arms. He wanted to go for his sword, but he couldn't simply toss the unconscious girl into the snow. Sybal didn't move to attack either.

The creatures surrounded them, hissing now, and pressing them farther away from the head of the hawk.

"Are you Masahk?" Tzarik asked, wondering if they were just here to ward off any who accidentally wandered too close to the secret entrance.

He saw as they loomed closer that they must be. Masahk had the long, jointed legs of their animal brothers. And he now saw the skulls were worn as masks. A few of the creatures tossed their heads to one another, tilting them in curiosity. One stepped forward, pointing its bone sword at Tzarik.

"What are you doing here on our mountain, foreigner?"

"We're looking for the Court of Deliverance," Tzarik admitted easily, not seeing any danger in the truth. "A Masahk Runer named Ragnall told our companion to find him there."

The animal skull tilted down to take in Zeva. "We know her kind," it replied, drawing itself up to its full height, towering over Tzarik and even Sybal. "The red Reks has sought such as her for too long."

Tzarik nodded stoically. "We've come from Altevine. Ragnall can vouch for us."

Another Masahk came up behind the first and whispered into its ear. Tzarik thought he recognized the rabbit ears and gray fur of this Masahk. The first nodded slowly, turning back to them. It raised a fur-covered hand to its mask and lifted it. Its face had far more of the wild animal features than most Masahk born away from Alika. Soft brown fur covered its arms and face, melding seamlessly with its long, braided hair. The antlers, they saw now, grew from its own brow.

"We'll take you, but you must not see our paths," the Masahk said stiffly.

"Fine," Tzarik quipped. "Just take us to him." He motioned for Sybal to put her blade away.

Narrowing her eyes suspiciously, Sybal did as he said. Then, two more Masahk approached, blindfolding them and taking Zeva from Tzarik's arms.

∂

TZARIK COULDN'T TELL if the Masahk took them on a long, underground journey for a reason, or if they were simply trying to confuse their blinded followers. He tried to keep track of how many turns they took, what sort of ground they trod over, but after an hour, he lost count. Just minutes after the hour in the dark, a smell surged up from before them: the odor of sweat, fear, fire, and musk that comes with too many people packed into a small space. Their guides stopped them and whipped their blindfolds off. Blinking, the underground village came into Tzarik's view. Structures hewn from stone crawled along the mountain's walls and up to the stony ceiling above. Fires flickered here and there, lighting camps and forges alike. Wagons and carts rumbled past, bringing supplies, more Masahk, and livestock.

Their antlered guide pushed them forward into the throng, leading them into the village. As they went deeper, a clamoring from a road leading out of the village drew the attention of all the Masahk. A few rushed, grabbing bags of healing supplies and pots of boiling water. A caravan of brightly colored Masahk in pied clothing and golden bracelets and circlets came stumbling into the Court.

"They're hurt," Sybal noted, staying close to Tzarik. "What happened?"

"Slavers," the antlered Masahk replied, her face pinching with sadness. "Rhostrana owns part of the Black Road for their trade of black powder. They take any Masahk who dares use the main road."

Sybal's face pinched too, but in rage. "I forgot Rhostrana still dealt in the slave trade."

"It's not exactly condemned on Caerwren," the Masahk reminded her. "Nor in Alika, where they will enslave each other— especially those not fully Masahk. Perhaps it is better where you come from?"

Tzarik caught Sybal giving him a glance. They both missed Al'Myrah fiercely.

"It is," she supplied. "Slavery is against the sultana's law. Any kind of unpaid subjugation is."

"That's not to say it doesn't happen," Tzarik said, reminding her of his own bondage. He turned back to the Masahk. "Where is Ragnall?"

He held his hand out for them to return Zeva to him. They did, and he slipped a hand around her waist to support her as she was awake enough now to stand on her own. He needed to find blood for her, but didn't want to ask this Masahk for it. If he could find her something to consume without making a spectacle, that would be best.

The Masahk bowed her head, pointing behind Tzarik. "Be wary of him, Runer," she advised, turning away to help the wounded caravan. "Your Ragnall has not always been so kind."

Zeva's head popped up at the mention of Ragnall and she glanced around. "He can...help us," she said weakly.

Tzarik turned and spotted the bright white Masahk easily amongst his brethren. He stood, watching as the others rushed to help the wounded. His large blue eyes scanned the crowd, then snapped to them, their black standing out amongst the gray and brown clothing of the others. When his eyes caught Zeva, he leapt down and rushed to them.

"Ragnall!" Zeva chimed upon seeing him run to her. She disentangled herself from Tzarik and fell into the Masahk's soft, feathery arms.

Tzarik let her go, sure Ragnall cared for Zeva when he watched him catch her and pull her into an embrace. Even Sybal smiled in polite surprise.

"You're so frail," Ragnall breathed, gently touching Zeva's face. He glanced up at the Runers. "Come to my camp."

Holding Zeva, Ragnall led them away from the middle of the village towards an underground river filled with little boats. Entire roads made of water ran through the small settlements and shanty camps. Variations of boats lined the watery paths, bobbing gently. Ragnall moved to the last stone pathway that led into the settlement. A large animal-skin tent waited there. Fire in a stone circle burned before it, surrounded by furs, a square table low to the ground, and other home furnishings. A cage of wooden sticks housed three chickens and a rabbit nearby. Ragnall gestured for them all to sit. He poured a sweet mead for Tzarik and Sybal and then swiftly snapped the neck of a chicken, wringing the blood into a goblet and handing it to Zeva. The ease with which he did this did not go unnoticed. But Tzarik didn't see it as aggression. Ragnall did care for Zeva, and was not put off by her needs.

The girl took the hot blood and drank it ferociously before pausing in embarrassment. Ragnall sat very close to her, across the fire from the Runers.

"Sjörna-Reks is burning villages looking for you," he said simply. "She'll burn down all of Altevine and more until she finds you."

"Kjarton's gone," Tzarik said. "She doesn't know that. But at least while she's ravaging the land, she's not attacking Northica."

Ragnall narrowed his hawk-like eyes, curious. "Why does that matter?"

"Our friend was taken when Skarde and Dain cursed Sjörna," Tzarik said. "We can't leave him here. And as far as we know, Sjörna holds Tarkan in her clan's land still. She'll go back soon most likely, and use him to attack Northica with an undead force they cannot hope to beat. It's not that we want to defend Northica, but that Tarkan must be stopped. With her scouring the countryside, she's not headed north."

Sybal nudged him slightly, eyes fixed ahead so no one else noticed her prodding.

"We have to save him," he corrected, taking in Zeva's wide eyes.

"Your Necro'Khan?" Ragnall asked.

Tzarik nodded. "He came to help me. Zeva sacrificed herself to the necrotic scriptures for us. We owe them a debt that can never be repaid. Saving Tarkan from doing something he'll regret is the least we can do. If we save a clan in the process, so be it."

Ragnall looked down at Zeva. Tzarik saw a familiar longing in his blue eyes. The Masahk fought within himself: he was drawn to Zeva but wary of her at the same time. Tzarik also knew that if Tarkan found Ragnall's feelings out, the Masahk might have his immortal life cut short. But he'd worry about that when the time came.

"We haven't brought Sjörna to your door, have we?" Zeva asked, looking just a little more colored now.

Ragnall shook his head, his pearlescent feathers glinting in the firelight. "She's been looking for the entrance to the Court of Deliverance for two decades. She'll never find it."

"We did," Sybal put in, warning him.

He smirked. "Did you?"

Realizing that they'd only assumed the hawk head was the entrance, they didn't reply.

"Rest here," Ragnall offered. "You have no supplies. While Osterah—our spring—is here, that doesn't make your journey into our mountains any easier. I'll give you some sulfates, as I can see you are in need, and a few other supplies."

Zeva gently reached over and touched the top of his hand, begging a question with her eyes. When he met them, she blanched, eyes filling with tears, and looked away. Tzarik then followed Ragnall's understanding gaze to a few Masahk set aside from the caravan. They were dead, but still warm. They all understood, but didn't make Zeva ask. She didn't want to consume blood, let alone flesh, but she had to.

Giving them space, Tzarik stood up and nodded for Sybal to follow him to a trunk where Ragnall told them they could find sulfates. The Masahk and the necromancer slinked off into the village to gather her something more substantial to consume. Silently, Sybal found the black box and a bottle of sulfates.

"Lie down," she instructed Tzarik.

Inside the Court, the air quickly grew warm, and they were able to discard their fur cloaks. She helped him remove his armor, then eased him onto one of the many furs around the fire. When he lay down, he let out a long sigh. His back ached, his legs were tired, and his fingers finally had feeling again. He closed his eyes and let Sybal roll the sleeve of his tunic up. Her fingers prodded, looking for his white veins. He didn't speak, not wanting to ruin the one moment of silence they'd had in what felt like years.

Sybal stuck the needle into his arm and turned the bottle over, holding it so the opalescent sulfates dripped into his veins. She crossed her legs and sat next to his head, slipping the bottle into the handle of a trunk, and went to work on his knotted hair. Every time she pulled too hard on a tangle, she mumbled an apology, but he didn't care.

He drifted off, dazed at her gentle touches, but stirred when Ragnall and Zeva returned. Zeva looked almost intoxicated with relief. She sat next to Sybal, who put her arm around the girl for comfort once she was satisfied she'd pulled most of the tangles out of his grimy strands. The Masahk grabbed a black Runer's pack and went about filling it with things they'd need.

"Stay to the northern side of the spine," he instructed. "Take your dragon so you don't have to scale the peaks. But I advise you to land a mile out from the bridge so Skarde's men see you coming."

"The bridge?" Tzarik asked, a little sad at being interrupted by the other two.

"Yes," Ragnall confirmed. "Over the years, the river Tier'Morlan has cut through the mountain of Northica, dividing it in two. This happened centuries ago. Northica guards it, as it's the only passage to them and Zealmor. They're not fond of Hovandel, Gidenmore, and Rom and their more civilized ways, as you might put it. Approach the bridge and the wardens of the bridge should take you to Skarde-Reks."

"And if they don't?" Sybal asked.

"They won't kill you on sight," Ragnall offered. "They're more noble than that."

"Won't you come with us?" Zeva asked, her brows pinching.

The Masahk didn't meet her eyes, shoving things into the pack. "No," he quipped.

Tzarik couldn't help but notice Zeva's crestfallen expression. The girl looked away, her hand jumping quickly to her eye.

"Thank you for your aid," Tzarik said, taking the now full pack.

Ragnall nodded. "Stay a night or two. Rest, eat, drink. It's safe here. The wolf won't find you."

CHAPTER 34

NÖRTHICA

THE NIGHTS THEY SLEPT IN THE COURT OF DELIVERANCE, Zeva lay between the Runers, but yearned to be with Ragnall. He disappeared to help his kin on the Black Road and to hunt and came back late at night. The Court constantly buzzed with movement and caravans coming and going, but the Runers were so exhausted, they fell asleep without hesitation every night. She lay awake, waiting for him. Deep into the night, he returned with a band of other Runers. They spoke quickly and the other pair of Runers parted from him. Zeva watched Ragnall come back to his camp. He started the fire outside his large animal-skin tent, where she watched. She glanced at Tzarik and Sybal, unsure if they would allow her to sneak out to Ragnall. When she finally got the nerve up to slip away, she glanced back and caught Sybal watching her.

"I-I'm just getting some water," she mumbled quickly, stumbling over her words.

"Be careful," Sybal whispered, her glowing blue eyes never leaving Zeva.

Zeva nodded and slipped out to find Ragnall removing his cloak.

He turned when she exited the tent and his long, feathery ears perked up.

"You need to rest," he said. He pulled a bottle of blood he'd gathered for her out of his pack and glanced around quickly before giving it to her. "You need to leave in a few hours. The sun is rising."

She took the bottle when he offered it to her. He sat down on the lid of a trunk. She looked down at him. She wanted to sit next to him but couldn't make herself. Arching his back and using his long, powerful arms, he removed his loose armor and shirt. Zeva knew she should avert her eyes, but watched. She'd only seen a man shirtless once, and he'd been working outside a whorehouse in Ala'Nar. Tarkan had hissed like an angered cat when the working man had dared to touch Zeva's face.

Ragnall's body was so pale it almost matched his pearlescent feathers. Tiny, soft down covered his chest where a human man would have had coarse hair. The feathering glittered in the firelight, enticing her to feel it. His sculpted shoulders were smooth except for a few thick, corded scars. Others mapped across his chest, down his arms, and over his back. He even had what she assumed was a vampire bite on his neck. A desperation she'd never felt before rose in her belly. A fire that needed to be lit. Her mouth went dry, and she used every last bit of her strength to not reach out and touch him purely out of curiosity.

"Been struck mute?" Ragnall asked.

Zeva jumped, clutching the bottle of blood. He'd been speaking. "Yes," she said suddenly, answering a question she had not heard.

"Thank you," Ragnall replied, handing her his black box.

Confused and elated, she sat next to him, swapping the blood for the box. She held it before her chest, confused.

"Needle and thread are inside," he instructed.

Her eyes snapped to his side suddenly. She'd not noticed before, since his blood was almost the same color as his flesh and feathers. A small but deep wound bled high on his ribs under his arm. Understanding, the butterflies erupting in her stomach, she opened the box and quickly prepared the needed wares. As she did, he turned to give her easier access to the wound and raised his arm, resting it on her shoulder. Where his skin met hers, a hot sensation flared up, her partially dead blood flooding her cheeks.

"Can you come with us?" she asked, gently sticking him with the needle. He didn't flinch. She'd stitched up Tarkan before and had had to be careful to reforge the scriptures on his skin. This wound would be far easier. If only her hands would stop shaking.

Ragnall's long ears dropped a little. "I'm needed here. And I must hunt. But..." His head dropped before looking down at her. "I wish I could." His eyes roamed over her face, down her neck, then to her delicate hands at work on his wound.

His last words warmed her. They'd been affectionate when a set of bars separated them. Why was it so much harder here? "After," she began, not even sure what "after" would be or when, "I'll come find you. Maybe then...?" She swallowed hard.

"Your father would kill me," he joked, inspecting her quick work as she tied the thread off.

Zeva's heart broke just enough to take some of the color from her cheek. "I need to be with him; I need him to stop. To understand that he is strong enough to protect me, but that I can protect myself now. I fear our past has driven him mad with seeking power. He wanted that mantle, but didn't know the cost."

Ragnall turned to face her, putting one knee on either side of the trunk they sat on. Zeva's heart skipped a beat when he faced her so directly. "You sound like you're about to blame yourself. You know none of this is your fault." His hand came up to the side of her face. He rested her chin in his palm and stroked her cheek with his thumb.

She sighed and leaned her head into his hand. Unable to stop herself, she inched towards him. Taking the cue, Ragnall slipped his hand to the back of her neck and pulled her in for a kiss. Zeva gasped but let him take her in his arms. It felt just as she'd hoped. Her mind spun at finally being able to embrace him. She slithered her arms around his middle, pulling herself into him. Something stronger than the scriptures, stronger than any chiding Tarkan had given her, coursed through her. She couldn't fight it. To get closer to him, she hitched her legs up, tossing them on either side of him to lift herself onto his thighs. One of his hands roamed down her back as he continued to kiss her ravenously.

Throwing her head back, she invited his kisses down her neck while her fingers dug hard into his shoulders. He stopped then, looking up at her.

Ragnall's hesitation doused her fervor. Her cheeks burned with cold embarrassment. Turning away, she moved to flee from him.

"Wait, Zeva," he murmured. He took her hand and stayed her. She came back, allowing him to guide her onto the fur-covered ground, but kept her eyes trained on the floor.

To her surprise, he waited on her now. Shaking with fear and uncertainty, she lowered herself and rolled to be underneath him. A hot tear dripped down her temple into her hair. Ragnall wiped it gently with his thumb. Emboldened, she strained her neck up to kiss him again.

They continued to administer touches and intimate caresses until she locked eyes with him meaningfully. She loved the way he looked above her. His long, ashen hair hung around her like a curtain of tiny, decorated braids. His eyes glittered in a special way. She wondered if he noticed anything like that about her. She'd never been told by anyone other than Tarkan that she was beautiful. Pretty. She wanted to hear it.

With a sigh, he stopped and lay down next to her. Engulfing her in his arms and wrapping his legs around her from behind, he held her close, draping one of his long wings over them. A little disappointed, she allowed him to do this before giving in to the simple skin-to-skin contact. Utterly embraced by the Runer, his powerful body enveloping her, she felt wholly protected. All at once, something she'd been missing in life burned and she was satisfied.

"Why'd you stop me?" she asked, eased by the sensation.

She heard him swallow before he replied. "I've done terrible things to...sentients like you. I don't want to hurt you." His breath tickled hot against the back of her neck. His lithe, pale finger traced the scriptures on her forearm, sending a new kind of shiver jolting up her arm.

Understanding once again doused Zeva's passion. "I find that hard to believe," she whispered gently. When she'd first met him, he'd terrified her. But his trust in her, the way he encouraged her to do as she judged best, the time he asked her for aid... He'd let her feel like a woman with her own mind, able to decide her own fate. That had drawn her to him. But now, for the first time in her life, she had desires she'd only read about. And she couldn't give in to them.

Yes, that disappointed her, but if giving in meant harming him, she'd suppress those feelings. Besides, it had been a moment of heated lust. That wasn't what she wanted.

"Come with us to Al'Myrah," she offered.

He nuzzled his cheek into her long, messy hair and hummed. "Caerwren is my home. I'm only part Masahk. I don't belong in the east."

"That doesn't matter," she protested, squeezing his arms more tightly around her. "There aren't many Runers on Al'Myrah. You'd find work. And...I could be with you."

Ragnall let out a soft, pleasant laugh. "The Runer and the necromancer. What a legendary pair we'd be. They'd write songs about us. We'd be known on sight."

"And live for eternity," she added with a giggle. "Or, close enough." She was not wholly immortal. "Forever with you wouldn't be so bad."

And Tarkan? Could she give up the man who'd raised her, taken care of her, comforted her, protected her? Suddenly, tears dripped from her eyes and she couldn't help but sniffle. This was the way of life, wasn't it? Once she was older, trained, she could leave? Or would her birth father's blood oath bind her to Tarkan forever? What would happen if she left him? More powerful than the magic and oath was her love for him. That love bound her tighter than any blood oath.

"I will do what I must," she said suddenly, flatly. "I must save him from Sjörna-Reks, but then I must save myself from him." She moaned in agony. "Though it tears my heart to think of leaving him. I don't know what it will do to him."

Ragnall tightened his hold on her until she pressed hard into his chest. "That is not your concern. You've played your part for his use. What he does now is no concern of yours. It's not your burden."

Of course he was right. But leaving Tarkan would be harder than anything else she'd done in her life.

ᚨ

ONLY AN HOUR LATER, the Runers woke and quickly whirled around the camp, gathering all their wares. Ragnall led them out of the Court, this time with eyes open. He showed them to where they'd left the dragon. They mounted their packs on the dead creature.

"Remember," Ragnall said, "stay behind the spine in the north. Land far away so they don't shoot your dragon down, then walk to the bridge. They shouldn't attack you."

The Runers thanked the Masahk and left Zeva to say goodbye. Tzarik gave Sybal a knowing glance, shaking his head, but Zeva didn't mind.

"I'll come back to you," she promised. She climbed up onto the foreclaw of the dragon to reach up to the tall Masahk. Standing on the tip of her toes, she kissed him one last time. "Then we can decide what to do."

Ragnall looked at her in a pure passion before returning the kiss. "I have a few ideas," he said with a bit of a twisted grin.

She hugged him tightly, inhaling his scent of fire and snow. His hand traced down the long white feather of his that she'd braided into her hair some time ago. Smiling, heart aglow, she tore herself from him and joined the Runers on the back of the dragon. Fresh from consuming, she easily raised the beast. It came to life, shaking the snow from its leathery wings before spreading them wide. As it leapt into the air, she watched Ragnall's black-clad form grow smaller until it disappeared behind the icy peaks.

Sybal's hand gently touched Zeva's shoulder. "You're strong to leave. To go with us to Northica. To stand up to Tarkan," she affirmed.

"I know," Zeva replied, choking on the emotion. "But it hurts so much."

ा

As DIRECTED, she steered the dragon to the north, staying between the impassible mountains and the ocean. The sun peeked just over the horizon, lighting up the mountain of Northica when they found the river that cut the stone. All three of them looked in awe at the bright, turquoise water that roared through the mountain, slicing it like a hot knife through butter. The stone in Northica was not steely colored like the others. It shone white, glittering with frost. Zeva wondered if the water was so blue because it was cold. Chunks of ice rushed down the river, broken off from glaciers far away.

She guided the dragon around towards the front of the mountain, putting the howling abyss cutting through it out of sight. The river twisted and turned deeper into the mountain so that they didn't see the bridge until they arrived at the front. The sun slid across the horizon, not rising much higher before it started to dip back down hours later. They found a place not too far from a path where they lay the dragon down.

Tzarik helped the women off the dragon and they all took up their respective packs. In silence, they trudged up the mountain path. Towering, white, spear-like jags cut off every angle except directly above from sight. Sudden, perilous drops appeared around some corners, making the going slow. The sun set long before the smell of fires and life finally reached them.

Cresting a final, rocky, snow-covered ascent, the bridge came into view. The three of them stopped to take it in. Wind screamed through the broken mountain pass coupled with the crying of the river hundreds of feet below. The bridge itself reached half a mile across to where tiny fires could be seen, starting the borders of the mountain clanlands. Two huge statues stood guard at the front of the bridge. One was a man with a beard so long and intricate with braids that it drew their eyes up and down it. The man held a massive sword, the kind they'd seen only a few warriors carry, made for slaying the huge Vaeson. He pointed it into the ground with his hands clasped over the pommel. The other was a woman with wild hair. She stood as the man did, but where he held a war axe, she held a massive two-headed axe.

Tzarik narrowed his eyes at the axe. "I've seen that blade before," he mused as they marched closer. "It hangs in the thronehall of Altevine. Sjörna-Reks has it, but a large bite from some kind of monster has been taken out of one of the heads."

Zeva remembered it. It hung above the dais, behind the thrones. "She must have taken it." She glowered now, looking up at the woman guardian. "It should be returned to Northica," she suggested. "Sjörna doesn't deserve it."

As they came closer, a small group of warriors approached them on the backs of monstrous creatures. Huge creatures with hind's feet and with tusks protruding from their mouths, the mounts swayed with gentle steps as the riders came towards them. The warriors in

Northica were just as tall, broad, and thick as those in the other cantons, only these wore metal chest plates where the other clans didn't. They also protected their heads with helmets adorned with horns, antlers, and bones fashioned into the likeness of horns. Underneath the simple chest piece, leather covered little of their bare bodies. The cold did not seem to bother any native Caerwren sentient. From a distance, they looked like monsters. One of the approaching warriors drew a flail the size of Zeva herself. They stopped when the warrior produced this and waited.

"Hail, travelers," the man with the flail said cautiously. "What brings you to the Warpath and to the lip of Tier'Morlan?" He pulled up on the reins of his strange mount and examined them more, exchanging a glance with his fellow bridge warden. "And so far from your home?"

Tzarik stepped forward. "We've just escaped Altevine."

The bridge guardians exchanged another fleeting glance.

"We've come to speak to Skarde-Reks, to warn him that Sjörna-Reks is coming." He waited a beat before continuing, "With an undead army led by a Necro'Khan."

The guardians turned to each other and spoke in quick clicks and hisses—a sort of rhythmic language Zeva didn't know. By the confused glances between the Runers, they didn't either.

"And you bring such with you," the guardian holding the massive flail said to them.

"I'm here to help," Zeva said quickly. "I'm your only hope of standing up to the Necro'Khan and Sjörna-Reks. We are only just ahead of her. We have no time to delay."

The second guardian tilted her head and hissed again to the first, nodding.

"Very well," the guardian said. "As you are one who follows the necrotic gods, perhaps you can be of service to us. All is not well in Northica. We stand on a precipice, hoping for a miracle. I will show you to our Reks."

ॳ

THE CLANS of Northica lived in family groups, their homesteads spidering out from one another as their families grew. Patches of fenced-in homes and villages dotted the far-off mountain sides. Zeva and the Runers walked for hours before the guardians allowed them up onto their mounts for the more treacherous part of the journey to the thronehall atop the white mountain. The path led up into a deep basin, carved out by a moving glacier that had cut through the mountains no doubt thousands of years ago. A larger village surrounded the thronehall where life moved. Farmers, shepherds, smiths, and Runers moved in and out of the village. Somehow, Northica looked even more savage than Altevine. One Runer who had been haggling with a smith over melted orichalcum shivered and snapped around to look at Zeva. Her very presence had made his sulfates crawl. Zeva ducked her head.

Like Sjörna's thronehall, Skarde's was long, tall, and decorated with their hawk and antlered god. Sybal stopped, making Zeva almost run into her.

"What is it?" Tzarik asked when she looked around.

"Sorry," Sybal murmured, head cocked, listening for something. "My mother was Northican. I was just wondering if her family is still..."

Zeva glanced around, wondering what it must be like to go to the place of one's origin. To a place that might have been her home. "I wondered how you were so tall." She smiled up at the Runer. "Have you ever been to Northica?"

Sybal shook her head. "My mother and father had a...strained meeting and relationship before their marriage."

The bridge guardian dismounted when they reached the path leading to the hall. "Skarde-Reks stays in his hall. Dain Radjur-tor is ill and our Reks fears his son, our future Reks, will not last the spring. Speak wisely."

The guardian escorted them into the hall where, unlike Sjörna-Reks's hall that burst with sound and clatter, almost all inside stood quiet as they went about their tasks. A circle of white fur-clad Volra surrounded the main fire pit, arms raised, palm to palm, humming deeply in harmony. Seeing them, one broke off and approached quietly. The man was tall with jet black hair and skin so white it almost blended into his fur. The bone decorations clinked along his robes. Twine made from animal hide wrapped around his feet and up his bare shins.

"You bring strangers into the hall of Skarde-Reks," the Volra whispered, chastising the bridge guardian.

Without ceremony, the guardian reached behind him and grabbed Zeva hard by the arm, yanking her before him. Tzarik and Sybal both laid their hands on their scimitar hilts.

"What is she?" the guardian asked the Volra.

The man of the gods used his frozen green eyes to take in every detail of Zeva. "A follower of the old star." His cold finger prodded hard at the family symbol she and Tarkan shared on her forehead. "One who consumes the living for the dead." He traced the finger down her cheek, neck, and then arm. "Like the one who cursed Dain. A rare find, save on Al'Myrah and Alika, perhaps."

"We need an audience with Skarde-Reks," Zeva stammered, her arm throbbing in the guardian's grip.

"Yes, you do," the Volra agreed. To the warriors he said, "If you feel anything is amiss, kill them. I will take them to our Reks."

The two guardians flanked the Runers and the necromancer as the Volra led them down the thronehall, past the humming enchanters, and through the other people in the hall. Despite it being colder in Northica, the clansmen wore only animal-skin wrapped around their hips and some even bared their midsections to show off their solid muscle. Zeva had no doubt that if they desired, they could snap her neck with two fingers. No wonder they didn't fear them like others feared necromancers. Even Tzarik, with his thick arms and powerful body, looked no match for the men of Northica.

A set of wooden stairs led up behind a stone dais just like in Sjörna-Reks's hall. The top level was open and empty. War trophies, hunting kills, and other artifacts from centuries of battles and peace talks from all over the map hung or were on display in Skarde's personal room. At the back, near an open window, lay a large bed with the young prince in it. The massive form of Skarde-Reks sat next to the bed, elbows on his knees, hands clasped and pressed against his forehead. He mumbled and hissed prayers, begging his god to heal his son.

A strong wave of sympathy washed over Zeva; she signaled the Runers to stand back. Zeva approached the Reks on her own. The closer she got to the ill prince, the more her scriptures crawled, twisting her skin with an eerie sensation. When Tarkan had been hunting Ashkan, he had spoken of such a feeling when drawing near to another necromancer's curse.

Dain's long body lay flat on the bed, his skin pale and glistening with sweat. The golden circlet around his brow stood out against his white forehead. More sweat matted his long braids and the scruffy beginnings of a beard along his jaw. Zeva's heart went out to the young man as she laid her palm against his cheek, feeling for what ailed him.

"Who are you?" Skarde-Reks's deep, thunderous voice asked in a soft rumble. He'd stopped his prayers and looked up at Zeva. "Wait, I know you." He narrowed his eyes.

Zeva half expected him to go for his massive war axe that lay on the floor beside him, but he didn't. On the other side of Skarde lay a clay bowl, filled with some sort of black bile.

"You were in Sjörna's hall," Skarde went on. His red-rimmed eyes went from Zeva to the Runers behind her, then to his Volra. "You brought the friends of my enemy into my halls, Dalziel!" he roared to the Volra.

His sudden change in tone made Zeva jump. "We've come to warn you!" she cried, holding her hands up. "And to help you."

The big man, who had seemed unkillable, so powerful and full of pride when he'd entered Sjörna's halls, now crumpled again, face in his hands.

"I have only Dain," he moaned in his mountaintop accent. "My son, my warrior. When we fled Altevine, this illness followed. Dalziel promises it is not a plague. It would be like Altevine to harbor a plague."

"It is not plague," the Volra, Dalziel, assured the Reks.

"Tzarik," Zeva called back. "Have you seen a curse before?"

The Runer approached with caution and knelt by the ill prince. He touched his cheek gently with the back of his hand, feeling the temperature of his body. He turned Dain's forearm over to inspect the veins. They were black under his white skin. Tzarik noted the bowl of black bile on the other side.

"My scriptures are mad," Zeva told him. "They're crawling like ants over me."

Tzarik nodded, humming. He reached up and pulled back one of Dain's eyelids. When he did, the younger man cried out, screaming. Skarde leapt up, ready for such a fit, and held his son's shoulders down as he thrashed. Tzarik leapt back as well, out of range of Dain's mighty, swinging arms.

The Runer nodded. "His eyes are blackened. This curse has taken his mind and body." He turned to Sybal and asked, "Where are the dead Runer's things? He may have a tincture that can help."

As the Runers went through their packs, Zeva turned back to Skarde and Dain. The prince calmed, gasping and yelping piteously.

"He is not this weak man," Skarde assured them, almost weeping himself. "He is strong. He never yowled as a child. Never cried."

"Pain is not weakness," Zeva offered. "Skarde-Reks," she started again, taking a deep breath. She turned, waving her hand to stop

Tzarik and Sybal from looking for the items needed to make a protective charm. "I can heal Dain."

"Zeva?" Sybal asked, a slight warning in her voice.

Tzarik interrupted, "A necrotic curse cannot be healed. The only way to break it is to destroy the thing that sustains the curse." He stopped and dropped his eyes.

"Yes," Zeva sighed. "If Dain had been cursed by a hex bag, a totem, or some other item, we could destroy it. Necromancers curse rarely, I have heard. Because...*they* are what sustains their curses more than not." She gasped, sudden emotion swelling in her. "I have to protect him." She dropped her face into her hands and cried softly.

"What do you mean?" Skarde asked.

Sybal answered for Zeva. "Tarkan, the Necro'Khan Sjörna-Reks holds captive even now, is the one who cursed you. He is her father by a blood oath made when she was a child."

Skarde-Reks glowered, examining Zeva. She looked up to meet his eyes.

"But I can save Dain." She knelt beside the prince, taking his cold hand in hers.

"How?" Tzarik asked.

Zeva gulped. "One of the five spells of the necromancers is to take on the wounds of another."

"Zeva!" Sybal cried, running to her side and grasping her shoulders to pull her back.

Zeva threw her off. "It's Tarkan's curse. Let *me* bear it! I am near immortal; I can withstand it."

"You are *not* immortal," Tzarik reminded her, eyeing Sybal.

"Skarde-Reks," Zeva said, turning back to the Reks. "You cannot care what I do. I am your enemy. Let me take Dain's curse. I will raise you an army worthy of Northica to defend your clan from Sjörna-Reks. My father, Tarkan, has given her an army you cannot hope to defeat. Let me stand up—" A sudden sob choked her. She gasped around it, steadying herself. "Let me stand up to Tarkan. He may be more powerful than I am, but I don't think he will harm me."

"And you?" Skarde-Reks asked after looking down at Zeva for some time. "Will you harm him?"

He cannot die, she reminded herself, clenching her eyes shut tight. "Yes," she breathed aloud. "But I will not kill him. I love him. I want to save him."

Skarde-Reks took in his son, then glanced at Dalziel.

"It is true," the Volra offered. "The raven has gone; the red wolf marches. Strigganoct showed me in a vision, just as I told you three days ago."

"You also said Strigganoct would send a sign to rise against our allies," Skarde said.

"The dragon god?" Sybal asked, almost smiling. "We came here on the back of a risen dragon. Is that sign enough for you?"

"A risen dragon?" Dalziel gasped, eyes widening. He mumbled some ancient prayer, then nodded. "It must be a sign. Strigganoct himself has brought this heretic to us."

Skarde-Reks finally closed his eyes and shook his head. "Very well, little necromancer." He glowered down at Zeva. "If my son dies as you perform your heretical magic, I will not hesitate to snap your spine with my own two hands and use your cursed bones as toggles for my boots." He signaled the guardians, who drew their weapons, warding back the two Runers. "I will boil your teeth for tea and tan your hide for a banner."

Before, the threat would have rocked Zeva to her core. Now, it drove determination into her. Brow furrowed, she nodded. She opened Dain's sweat-soaked tunic and placed her hands on his chest.

"She will need to consume," Sybal warned Skarde-Reks. "Living flesh."

"And she will have none," the Reks retorted darkly.

Zeva ignored them, hissing into the black wind that picked up and howled around them, even inside. She felt it suck her words into the wind and her scriptures crawled, rebelling against taking on a fellow necromancer's curse. In her mind, she heard the scrawling over her flesh whisper to her, warning her against using her magics against a brother of the scriptures.

Then help me, she tried to bargain with the unholy text. *Give me Dain's curse and tell Tarkan I bear it.*

The magic leached the blood from her body, drying her veins as she cast the spell. Then, she felt it. Tarkan's curse filled her, crushing her heart, making her despair. The illness tried to take her, but the scriptures fended it off, protecting her. Her eyes blacked over and for a moment she saw only horrors and felt torturous pain. Then, the black magic in her cleared her eyes. Her prayers had been answered. Unsure if she'd have to repay the necrotic gods for sparing her the immediate pain, she thanked them. The curse still boiled up in her, making her shake, but it did not consume her like it had Dain.

With a scream of exhaustion, she fell backwards onto her back. Sybal broke from the guardian and lifted her up off the floor, cradling her.

"Are you all right?" she asked.

Zeva nodded. "I can bear it." She stood up, leaning on Sybal, and looked down at Dain. He didn't wake right away, but his breathing turned steady and he no longer yelped in pain and suffering.

"By the dragon's lightning," Skarde swore, falling onto his son and embracing him. He kissed Dain's forehead, then stood up. "To the mead hall, little necromancer. We must discuss your father."

CHAPTER 35

SKARDE'S TALE

SYBAL HELD ZEVA'S HAND AS THEY FOLLOWED THE NEWLY determined Reks down the stairs. He led them out to a smaller hall behind the thronehall where barrels of drink lined the walls and warriors sat, sharpening blades and sharing hunting stories. Sybal glanced at Tzarik over Zeva's head to see the same worry etched in his brows that she felt in her heart.

Skarde-Reks led them to a great table that lay empty at the front of the hall. This long, oaken slab faced the rest of the hall, giving them a view of everyone else inside. Skarde motioned for Zeva to sit across from him, and Sybal joined her. Tzarik uneasily took a seat beside the huge man. Setting his axe down, the Reks poured them mead from a wooden pitcher. He raised his stein.

Sybal looked around, spotting a few thralls in chains. They stoked the fire and bore the taunting and jeering of the Northican warriors. "Skarde-Reks?" she asked, taking the proffered stein. "You took our friend, Vicdan. Where is he?"

Skarde-Reks scoffed deep in his throat, smiling. "The bard? Couldn't stand him."

Sybal glanced up at Tzarik. Despite the worry in herself, she was glad to see him look just as concerned.

"He was our friend and companion," Tzarik said. "What have you done to him?"

"Nothing drastic," Skarde-Reks replied. "I sold him to an Alikan pirate the night before last."

"Sold?" Sybal coughed, spitting the mead back into the stein.

"Fear not." The big man smiled, handing her another stein of mead. "They were a circus of some kind. I'm sure he's doing well for himself. I couldn't stand his constant babbling. A golden throat and a silver tongue, to be sure. But by the radjur, he would not shut his lips."

Tzarik half smiled. "I understand."

Sybal rubbed her temples, moaning. Poor Vicdan. He was braver than Tzarik and others gave him credit for. He was bold. Yes, he talked a lot, but he didn't deserve to be sold to pirates.

"He defended me many times," Zeva offered. "I hope he's all right."

"He will be," Tzarik offered. "No doubt drinking on the stern of the ship, singing to a siren as we speak. Far from the dead that march on us."

Skarde-Reks nodded, taking in his thronehall, somber. "To the coming dead," he said, just loud enough for only them to hear. "May we bloody our axes on their bones."

Sybal only took a small drink but watched Zeva gulp down half the wooden stein in one go as the subject changed. The poor girl shook with anticipation and fear. Sybal took her hand to let her know she wasn't alone. Knowing Tzarik would wait all day for the Reks to speak first, she asserted herself.

"Well, Reks?" she said, tapping her long finger on the stein. "You wanted a discussion. Speak."

Skarde half-smiled weakly. "You speak like a Northican. Direct. Bull-headed."

Tzarik snorted softly, nodding into his stein to hide his face when she shot him a look.

"My mother was Northican," she replied.

"By the dragon's lightning," Skarde mused, giving her what almost looked like a proud smile. "I can see it in you now, but only just. I thought you were tall for an Al'Myrahn. Why did she leave our frozen shores?"

Sybal smiled, remembering the story her mother used to tell her as a child before bed. "My father was a sheikh. He did trade of a certain variety with Northica some years ago. He found my mother during the god wars." She stopped. When her mother, Freja, was her age, she already had two children, and had made a home and family on foreign shores. Her mother was a brave woman.

"A long war in our history," Skarde mused. "Men came from all over the map to fight on Caerwren. Many lovers met during those wars, and it took many more."

She looked up through her brows at Skarde-Reks. "All on this continent are barbarous," she said darkly. "Sjörna-Reks said you killed Kjarton." She gripped the stein hard. "I knew him for some time. He was the farthest thing from a violent man. Why? What did he do to you?" She couldn't imagine the meek, quiet raven Reks hurting even his worst enemy. Kjarton didn't have the bloodlust inside him that his people did.

Skarde-Reks took a huge breath in, the many bone trinkets and belts crossed over his chest clinking and tightening as he did. He motioned for a thrall nearby to stoke the fire and build it higher. When he finished, the hall turned much warmer.

"Kjarton was blinded by his benevolence," Skarde began. "He could never understand the cruelty that waited under the red wolf's mane. Sjörna was the eldest of ten sisters. Her father and mother were widely known warriors. Fierce. Caerwren is an old country, like Al'Myrah. But we are stubborn and have stuck to our tradition of pirating, pillaging, and fighting one another for the lands that belong to us all. The need to stray and conquer is in our blood." He lifted his hand and clenched his fist tightly to illustrate his point. "When our forefathers built the first thronehall, our spirits slept, waiting to awaken and wander again. The god war, as you call it, was a small taste of that desire to spill the blood of our brothers.

"My mother, Igrain Drake-tier, was a strong Volra prophet, and is the one who saw in a vision that we would decimate Zealmor and Altevine, and that Hovandel would not come to their aid. The weak men in Hovandel and Gidenmore call us barbarians, but we are their kin. Not wanting to destroy the clans, my father went into battle without his axe." He laid his hand on the mighty weapon and traced an elegant etching down its blade. "He killed seven warriors as he fought his way to the Reks of Zealmor. Seeing the weaponless madman, the Reks of Zealmor did not attack and instead prayed for mercy. They negotiated there upon the battlefield." Skarde smiled and drank to his long-dead father.

"He did the same with the Reks of Altevine, Sjörna's mother Sima Wolf-tier. But by the time the god wars were over, all but two of the red wolves had perished: Sjörna and her sister Astrid." Skarde's eyes drifted to the doors before them. "Imagine them, my Northican sister. Ten red wolves the size of monsters, cutting white waves into the snow of our white mountain. Wolves' blood flowing in snarling abandon. The Wolf-tier pack was magnificent. Then, they were laid to waste. That's the tribe my father created: Wolves' bane. That is who I hope for us to continue to be."

Sybal realized he was thinking of Dain. "Do the clans only follow a Vaeson?" she asked.

"The gods demand it, providing Vaeson, god-shaped," Skarde answered. "Only those made in the image of our gods may lead a clan. Our gods are the tined Radjur and Strigganoct the dragon. As Dain was born under the sign of Isodel, the white hawk, we must pay worship to her as well, since she blessed me with my son. In times of war, many are Vaeson blessed. But they lose their animal spirit if they do not take clanland. The Volra say this is how the gods ensure sacrifice and worship.

"Without a Vaeson son or daughter to lead the clan, another would take my place. I will not give up Northica to Sjörna. This land belongs to Dain once I am gone. If another Reks wishes to take it, they should do so at the end of an axe, not when it is defenseless and without its Reks." He took a quick drink. "I pity Sjörna and her wildling son. But it is the consequence she must face for her unnatural lust."

Skarde continued. "During this time, I fought in battle against Yrsa of Zealmor, the daughter of the Reks and his only child. Her brothers died in combat or to curses and plague." He smiled, stopping his story.

Sybal recognized the grin that tightened the Reks's face under his thick beard. "Love was found upon the battlefield?" She couldn't help but share his grin.

"Aye, lass," Skarde whispered, like he held a precious secret. "We call the clan people of Zealmor fire spirits. Their flesh is white as fresh snow, their hair more vibrant than Sjörna's and red as fire. Yrsa painted a black mask over her face, making the green of her eyes shine like the spring sky at night. I watched her take the heads of three men before she turned her axe on me." He sighed, still smiling. "She struck me with a spear pulled from a warrior and came to finish the job. I think she fell in love with me when I pulled it from my chest and turned it on her. We fought, landing bloody hits until our armor fell away." His smiled deepened, watering his eyes. "And on it went."

Sybal laughed lightly, shaking her head. She caught Tzarik watching her as Skarde told his tale and her sulfates rushed.

"My father," Skarde said, "started to discuss the Warpath alliance that very day. Over the next months, the Rekses of Zealmor, Altevine, and Northica did something no clan of Caerwren ever have: had civil discussion while pouring over the maps of what would soon become the Warpath and the alliance between those of us who wanted to keep Caerwren's ways alive.

"During that time, Yrsa and I behaved as dogs in spring. Meeting in secret, sharing hidden glances at feasts, hiding wherever we could to enjoy one another. But, as is the way with old, stubborn men and wild women, the Rekses could not come to agreements. So, marriage ties were offered. Astrid offered to wed me, binding Altevine and Northica—leaving Zealmor to make a proposition. I knew it would involve Yrsa. Our hidden, wild love was doomed."

Zeva made a small, sad sound. Sybal agreed.

"Sjörna is devious," Skarde murmured. "She knew Yrsa and I loved one another. But there was more; Yrsa was a bastardess. Her father had lain with a woman with no god-shape. The clans were not going to acknowledge Yrsa as a babe, but when she showed her shape not long before the wars, the clans took her in. So, when Sjörna proposed that Yrsa's father give her as a servant to Astrid in honor of our betrothal, the clans thought it the best gesture to bind the Warpath."

Sybal blanched. "How cruel. But what about Kjarton?"

Skarde nodded. "An Altevine Volra gave a prophecy just before the god wars, while the three of us were mere screaming infants. The Volra saw in a vision that a Vaeson Reks would rise from a slave and doom our alliance. It is against our sanctified laws to enslave a Vaeson lest we incur the wrath of its god."

Sybal shifted, brows pinched. "Wouldn't you know if someone is a Vaeson?" She shrugged. "Seems very obvious to me."

Skarde ran his hand over his ornate beard. "Some are born Vaeson. Other times, if a canton is without a Reks, the gods will spill their blessing out upon their people, gifting many during a full moon with their very likeness. Sometimes, they come to rule a clan. Other times they leave, going into exile; the Vilderkin, our wild brothers sharing in the image of our gods, living in the Empty or haunting the crags of our clanlands. Other times, the shape leaves them. But mated Vaeson always beget Vaeson.

"So, when the Volra saw a slave, a young thrall, rising to be Reks, the god wars erupted in full, glorious, barbaric battle. Sjörna's mother, having heard the prophecy from her own Volra, wanted to secure such a Vaeson for one of her daughters. She stole a babe from the Valravn-worshipers in her canton as war broke out and enslaved that boy in her own halls—forcing the prophecy to come to pass. In her own ways, she prepared him to be bound to one of her daughters. Sjörna showed an attraction to her mother's thrall at a young age and was the fiercest of the pack. The Reks's work was done. Kjarton believed himself to be in love with Sjörna by the time he had his freedom. Sjörna loved him with a might no hand wielding an axe has ever felt. He was her prize. Her god-given gift. Perhaps we in Zealmor and Northica did wrong to accept Kjarton-Reks. But he was a god-child. A man from a prophecy. And he was good, kind."

"That's why he won't leave her." Sybal's heart grew heavy and her stomach turned in disgust. "He loved her, true. But he was just a godtale to her. Something to be claimed and shown off. A prophecy fulfilled. But he could never see that." He was a weak man, willing to kill Tzarik in order to flee the body he'd been forced to possess.

"This is true." Skarde nodded. "The four of us grew up in the war. For twenty years, the cantons of Caerwren fought. Sometimes it was cold, other times the mountains burned with fire and the rivers turned to blood. So at last, the Warpath said, 'Enough.' Once the god wars ended and Sjörna and Kjarton were bound, Astrid and I were handfasted in Altevine, to be properly wed and consummate our marriage later in Northica. Yrsa from Zealmor was then given to Astrid as her servant, thus sealing the alliance and forging the Warpath. With the three of us united, and Rom having left the war a decade before, Hovandel and Gidenmore were satisfied. It was understood that perhaps my children would marry Zealmor Vaeson when the time came.

"But on our way back to Northica, the mountain shook. I do not know if Strigganoct was displeased or if some other god desired our demise. An avalanche the likes of which I had never seen came crashing down the mountain. Spears of ice, blankets of snow, and shards of rocks tumbled down onto our returning party. Yrsa tried to save Astrid, to find her and dig her out." Skarde hung his head, looking into his now empty stein. "We found Astrid eventually. Her spirit had long since departed.

"But Sjörna blamed me for the death of her last sister. To keep the alliance strong, I married Yrsa, uniting Northica and Zealmor and promising tribute to Altevine. By now, the Warpath knew about Kjarton and there was talk of exiling Altevine for its misdeeds. But, as was his way, when the Rekses met the raven king, they saw no evil in him and could not see how the gentle raven would bring the prophesied doom. He loved Sjörna, and she would have protected her prophecy with blood and fire. So, the alliance lived in quiet compliance for some time.

"Sjörna continued to drive the other Rekses away when her son was born a wildling."

"I've seen him," Tzarik cut in. "She keeps him chained outside like an animal."

"Did Kjarton not care for his son?" Sybal asked. She couldn't believe the man she'd known would have let his son suffer as he did.

Skarde shrugged his great shoulders sadly. "She is cruel. She forced him to copulate against their gods' laws, perhaps to have such an offspring and use it against Kjarton should he ever learn the truth and flee."

"The wildling is a prince," Tzarik corrected.

Skarde tilted his head, showing he did not agree with Tzarik. "Wildlings should not be allowed to live. It's a danger to those around it and an abomination. It cannot be tamed."

Sybal was shocked to see Tzarik glare at the Reks for his merciless comments. "Then Sjörna came for Yrsa?" she asked, returning to the story.

"Aye," Skarde sighed, pouring more mead. "Came in the shape of the red wolf during the Eldritch Hunt, took my love, and spilled her blood on our very stone steps in the name of Raudnir, the wolf god who gave her the wolven shape. You have seen the twin-headed axe in her thronehall?"

Sybal nodded, recalling the massive, gleaming blade that Sjörna kept above her thrones. The weapon was magnificent, balanced for battle and made of a white metal. She recalled the large, lupine bite in the blade. A sort of awe and respect for the mad red Reks made her push a deep breath out from her lips.

Skarde nodded sadly. "For the sake of the Warpath, I let Sjörna flee and built my wife a pyre, burying her like the warrior she was. But her blood cursed our mountain. Two of my sons died, leaving only Dain." He clenched his fist hard over his heart and bowed his head in thanks to his god. "He is everything to me, the one thing of Yrsa's that I have left. He is wise and good. A much better man than I.

"But I could not see past Yrsa's blood on my clan's land. I knew how to hurt Sjörna in return and wash away Yrsa's blood: I would take her prized possession. I stole Kjarton in the night, just as Sjörna had Yrsa." The Reks stopped here, swallowing a great lump in his throat. "He begged for mercy. Bargained his life to save Altevine. But his pleas fell on ears clogged with blood and vengeance." He looked down at his hands, spreading his fingers. "These are strong hands. Strong enough to tear the wings from a raven. And I did. I did not kill him swiftly, cutting his throat as Sjörna had Yrsa. I let him scream into the night as I tore him limb from limb."

Sybal found herself shaking, clenching her fists. "He didn't deserve that," she whispered, her voice quivering.

"True," Skarde sighed sadly. "He was the most innocent of us all. Gentle. Meek." He looked up into the rafters of his longhouse, taking another calming breath. "An ancient Reks once said, 'Redeem yourself and you shall not be spared. Live in innocence and you will be punished. The good will not survive the night.' " He sniffed defiantly. "You cannot be a righteous man and expect to live out the winter."

"That's shit," Tzarik growled.

Sybal's hand froze, lifting the stein to her lips. She would have said the same thing not a year ago. Not now... She took a drink and slammed her cup down, making Zeva jump. She'd seen that kind of proverb play out in her own life. She couldn't deny it was true: good, innocent sentients were the ones who paid the price of darkness. "How did his spirit end up in Altevine?"

"I took him there, one piece at a time, over a fortnight."

Sybal exhaled in horror, dropping her head into her hands.

"But his blood washed away Yrsa's blood, and the curse was expunged," Skarde said solemnly. "Over the years, it seems Sjörna has sought a way to bring him back. Her prized raven. And now she has. You are not the first of your kind, little necromancer, to have come through our frozen lands."

Zeva looked up, eyes brimming with tears, and sniffled. "Sjörna thinks you attacked her because you think she's weak. Because of Signar."

Skarde tilted his head quickly, not disagreeing. "The way in which the wildling was begotten is abhorrent. She would tell you that Kjarton was hers to do with as she pleased. A gift given in prophecy from the gods. But the wildling is not why we stand against her now. Trust me, lass; I know she's not weak."

"You don't deserve to be saved from her," Zeva hissed. "But she is cruel, too. All I want is Tarkan back. She's held him captive all these months. We just want to be free. We'll leave," she begged. "We'll return to Al'Myrah."

Skarde threw back the last of his mead. "I'd like nothing more than to take the Necro'Khan from Sjörna and catapult him from the highest peak in my lands. If she comes, as you say, then I have no choice. I will not let Northica be overrun with the risen dead. And you *will* help me defend the mountain."

Zeva nodded eagerly. "I am not as strong as Tarkan. Please, don't hurt him."

The big man stood up, lifting his axe onto his shoulder. "I will do my best, little necromancer. Just this once, I can spare a man."

CHAPTER 36

THE BRIDGE OF TZER'MÖRLAN

THE WARRIORS OF NORTHICA NEEDED LITTLE ROUSING. The people of Caerwren lived in constant battle, glorying in it. Over the next two days, when Skarde-Reks called for the shieldmaidens and fighters to come to arms, hordes of them marched towards the bridge. Messenger hawks rose to the higher settlements, bringing in highlanders ready for more bloodshed. Tzarik followed them out on horseback with Sybal and Zeva to scan the space where the two clans would meet. Zeva would need somewhere to hide, protected from arrows and incoming attacks, but able to see the entire bridge to direct her undead.

"Call when you find a place," Zeva said, kicking her horse and turning it sharply to head back over the bridge.

"Where are you going?" Sybal shouted after her.

"To get my dragon," the girl replied, galloping away.

Tzarik hoped he understood. She'd raise it, scribe its neck to keep it alive without her total control and concentration, like Tarkan had done.

"Sybal," he said, a thought striking him. "No doubt Tarkan will have scribed many of the risen soldiers at Sjörna-Reks's order. Going after him, taking him, won't stop them entirely. We will have to fell every undead he brings."

"They're already dead," she answered. "I can take them."

He knew she could. He'd witnessed her fight almost like a specter herself. Her new speed and strength were either a testament to her time in the Deep...or something much worse.

They climbed up the facade of the mountain, over the many statues of guardians and Rekses, who glared down at any travelers that crossed the bridge. Below, the water howled and cried, rushing past. A smooth layer of ice covered most of the bridge from the fine mist that managed to rise up before freezing. Tzarik panted with the effort of climbing the ice-covered rocks by the time they found a spot safe enough to stand on.

He looked down onto the bridge where the warriors gathered. Some roused each other with war cries and chanted responses. They banged their swords, axes, and maces against their shields, howling with the wind and water. Tzarik turned to look behind him, examining the rocky face for an escape.

"It will be dark up here," he started. "No torches. They won't know where she stands."

"We should find a few warriors to protect her anyway," Sybal added. "Perhaps Skarde will spare Dain to be her protector. He'd be safe from the slaughter."

The idea was a good one, but Tzarik knew better. "Even if Skarde-Reks agreed, a young Northican prince like Dain would not acquiesce to standing by during a battle for his mountain. Even though he's no doubt still weak, Dain will want to fight."

As they spoke, a huge gust of wind shoved their cloaks and hair back from their faces in a rhythmic beat. The scaly, black body of the dragon shot across the bridge towards them. As it did, the men and women below cheered and roared ancient prayers to their dragon god. A massive white hawk passed in the opposite direction, cutting across the bridge towards the path that led down the mountain. Dain, in his Vaeson form, flew into the dark day to scout.

Zeva guided the dragon to circle the place where Tzarik and Sybal stood. As he'd suspected, Tzarik spotted a hand-painted black script on the dragon's neck.

"I'll put her down at the end of the bridge," Zeva called. "Tzarik, she's ready for you." A small smile turned the girl's tone jovial as she announced her plan.

Tzarik raised his hand, showing he understood, and she departed to the front of the bridge. He carefully climbed back down, Sybal in tow. Skarde-Reks galloped out of the borders of his clanland astride a massive radjur buck, much like his Vaeson form. The creature stood taller than a horse, with a forest of pronged antlers arching up to the sky.

"Runers," he called, meeting them on the bridge, shouting over a bugle from his mount. "Dain has gone out to spot the enemy before they arrive. And my men are bringing our warriors. Two tribes of Vilderkin have joined us as well." He yanked the reins of the radjur and turned to look.

A line of hundreds of warriors marched up the mountain to the bridge, pulling wagons piled high with rotting corpses. In the cold, hardly any rank smell of decay rose. A small pack of Vilderkin in red war paint shouted and argued with the Northican warriors. Some of them turned to their wild shape, fangs snapping and talons flashing, but they did not come to blows. There seemed to be some dispute over the corpses.

"We burn our victorious dead," Skarde-Reks explained. "We have very few bodies to offer your little necromancer. Those who are buried with their bodies unmarked by the pyre did not die a good death and thus were not given to Strigganoct through fire. That is the way our gods allow us to enter Rahrgalah. Buried in the earth, the evil god Mjordir puts their souls into Tierheim, where they suffer for eternity. A bad death."

"Mjordir," Sybal echoed. "I saw him once. He's an amalgamated abomination of bodies and some sort of beast not unlike your radjur."

At this, Skarde-Reks frowned at Sybal. "Your eyes have beheld the evil form of Mjordir?"

Tzarik sensed immediately that this was not normal, nor something a mortal sentient should have seen. His heart gave a start as he realized his fears might be right: Sybal was changed from her time in the Deep, but he didn't know how. At least, he wasn't sure yet.

"He was foul," Sybal said, nodding.

Skarde-Reks turned from Sybal, giving Tzarik a concerned glance as he faced the procession of the dead again. "We are giving them a chance at a new death." He kicked the buck in the sides and trotted out onto the bridge to address his warriors.

"Do not fear our fallen," he said to his shieldmaidens and warriors. "The dead will be victorious! The ones buried in the earth did not earn a warrior's death and do not feast in the halls of Rahrgalah. Let us allow them to rise for one last glorious battle and earn their way out of Tierheim. Shout to Strigganoct and let every member of the wolf pack you slay be in the name of our dragon's lightning, to the glory of Isodel, the white hawk, or to be trodden under the hooves of the Radjur. Give their souls and bless our halls with their blood. May the shattering of their skulls be a sweet sound, a chorus to our mountain's strength."

As he shouted and the warriors roared in joy of the coming battle, Zeva made her way back across the bridge on her horse. The Northicans unconsciously parted, allowing her ample room to pass. Some glared up at her, wary of the Al'Myrahn stranger who would raise their dead.

Tzarik gripped the huge Northican horse's reins and it fought him only once before it allowed him to pull it towards the bridge. He missed Mamun. That horse knew his every wish, often understanding what he'd do before he did. The great black warhorse had even found him more than once when he'd abandoned it on Xia, where he'd finally given it a name after almost ten years of riding it.

Sybal followed him. They mounted and trotted to make it to the other side faster. When they crossed with Skarde-Reks, Tzarik said, "She'll need protection. Have three fighters follow her up to the alcove in the mountain, where she must be defended."

Skarde-Reks turned to glance up to where Tzarik indicated. "Of course. I will have three of my personal strongest accompany her." He motioned two men and a shieldmaiden forward and gave them the order, adding that should they need to flee, they would sound three blasts on their horns.

Skarde-Reks followed them to the end of the bridge where the dragon waited, wings outstretched and arching over its head. "You, come here," he shouted to one of his muscle-bound archers. He took the man's huge bow and a quiver of arrows. "For you, little Runer," he said, smiling. "A Northican longbow should do well from the back of a dragon. Your little crossbow won't fell a rabbit from that height."

Sensing the Reks's joke at his expense, Tzarik took the bow. The massive weapon was thick and nearly as tall as him, with a fat string covered over with a sort of wax. The arrows in the quiver were easily longer than his arm. Skarde-Reks watched him, smiling behind his beard and antlered helmet.

Making sure to keep eye contact with the Reks, Tzarik grabbed an arrow, knocked it to the string, and took a deep breath. Unwilling to be laughed at to ease the Reks's nerves before a battle, he tugged the string with all his might. The bow bent, groaning loudly like a crow in the quiet of the night.

Skarde-Reks's face fell and his eyes widened.

Feeling pride, Tzarik aimed at the front of the bridge. To his surprise, his arm did not shake with the weight of the bowstring. Spotting one of the lanterns far down the path, he calculated the decline of the hill and felt the wind that howled past him. He'd shot his own bow countless times. This one felt no different. Breathing in and holding it, he released the shaft.

The arrow made a screaming sound like a hawk as it flew, shattering the tiny lamp.

Skarde-Reks swore, using words Tzarik hadn't learned from Zeva. "Runer, that was... I can't..." Lost for words, the Reks clapped the Runer on the shoulders hard, crushing him between his massive hands. "It was well shot," he said finally.

Tzarik firmly planted the bow on the ground and leaned on it like a staff, smirking, as the Reks left him.

"Oh, yes, you're very strong." Sybal rolled her eyes, punching him hard. "Wipe that smirk off your face and let's prepare for a real fight."

They mounted the dragon, Tzarik in front and Sybal behind him. He went about wrapping the belt and quiver around his middle. The Northican warrior's belt looped his waist twice before he fastened it in front. He adjusted the quiver to be at his right side and his scimitar still on his left. Sybal wrapped artiah and halat into the palm of her hand, the others hanging down on the leather cord. Lifting her hand, she slowly moved her arm to draw halat.

"Hold on," Tzarik commanded as he kicked the dragon into flight.

No sooner had they lifted into the air than the white hawk flew towards them, crying out loudly. Just as Dain flashed past them, they saw Sjörna's army in the valley below. Riding out before the oncoming mass of risen and Altevine clansmen was a chariot. Sjörna-Reks's red mane blew wildly in the wind, as long and as bright as any banner. She cracked a whip above the beast that pulled her chariot.

An unknown sensation washed over Tzarik as he realized what poor beast she beat to pull her through the snow. Large as a warhorse, the golden wolf he'd seen chained outside her thronehall was yoked to the chariot, snapping wildly with every stroke of the whip. Pity for her wildling prince filled him. How could she be so cruel?

Scanning the horde from on high, he took in the formation. In the middle of the army rolled a massive war machine, pulled by six giant black bears. From four pillars hung a battering ram in the likeness of a screaming raven in a dive. A host of Sjörna's thralls stood chained behind it, ready to pull back the raven and let it hammer down the fortified door that stood in their way beyond the bridge.

"They plan on entering the mountain," Tzarik informed Sybal. "They won't stop if they take the bridge. They're going through Northica. Possibly on to Zealmor."

Sybal finally finished halat, giving them a long-lasting, strong shield. "Do you see him?" she asked.

He scanned the middle around the raven battering ram. "Yes." He pointed.

Tarkan stood on a wagon, securely bound with his back to a stake and surrounded by a pyre. His face was bridle-less.

"He cannot speak," Sybal said. Her grip around his middle tightened. "Sjörna-Reks forced hot poison down his throat, taking his voice after the army was risen."

Tzarik knew it didn't matter. Tarkan has made a blood pact with Sjörna. The dead would walk by her command, only held risen by his will. For the first time in some years, Tzarik fought within himself. He didn't want to harm Tarkan. The necromancer had done what he'd done to save someone he loved. No different than him. No different from Sjörna-Reks. But if he had the chance to stop Tarkan forever, should he take it? He didn't have time to wonder.

A huge arrow he hadn't seen shot towards them, launched from an archer atop the raven ram. He reeled back, but would have been too late. The arrow shattered on the halat barrier Sybal had drawn. She shoved him up from where he'd fallen onto her and smiled in chaotic relief.

"Too close," she murmured into his ear.

Tzarik wheeled the dragon back towards the bridge. "Skarde!" he called. "She's here!"

"What are they doing?" Sybal shouted over the wind that ripped at their cloaks. "Tzarik, look."

He craned around, trying to stay on the move. Nine Volra ran out before the army in sets of three. They bore a now-familiar, bloody banner and set up three nithing poles along the roots of Skarde's mountain. Tzarik wasn't sure he believed in the cursed objects, but his sulfates crawled. One of the horse hides, still fresh and wet with blood, shone golden in the dim light. Tzarik's heart froze.

Nithing poles were made of horsehide. The golden one glinted familiarly, drawing his eye to the one in the center. The cursed poles had been made from the skins of the gift horse from Xia, Sybal's white mare, and Mamun.

Rage like Tzarik had never experienced boiled his cold, white sulfates.

CHAPTER 37

AMARANTHINE

Sybal spun her head over her shoulder to look back. Zeva flexed her fingers, holding her palms just inches apart and focused on the mound of undead Northica offered her to defend their bridge. The warriors assigned to protect her stood behind, grunting and roaring in their native tongue.

"We can't let Sjörna get close," Tzarik called back to Sybal. "Once that ram is on the bridge, she'll press forward easily. Skarde's clan won't be able to get around it."

Sybal touched the scales of the undead dragon. "Is this a fire breather?"

Her mentor's head cast back and forth, inspecting the beast they rode. Finally, he nodded. "But I don't know what undead fire from the belly of a beast like this might do."

"We might have to find out," Sybal mumbled. "We can't let them get across the bridge."

A rain of howling arrows shot up at them as they swooped over the army once again. Sybal craned her neck as they turned to go back towards the bridge to look back at Zeva. Her risen now stood, shambling towards the middle of the bridge. They would be vastly outnumbered.

"Go back over Sjörna's army," Sybal called. She gripped Tzarik's shoulders and stood up.

"What are you doing?" Tzarik called, steadying himself as she wobbled.

"Giving you protection." She bent her knees deeply, getting a feeling for the up and down flying gait of the dragon. "Give them a taste of necrotic fire, away from the bridge, before they get here. Strafe the army and it will spit its fire."

For once, he didn't fight her. She had prepared a counter argument for his constant refusal to try something she suggested, but it didn't come. Gripping halat, she poised herself and drew it again as Tzarik guided the dragon back towards Sjörna's army. The red Reks roared up at them, almost sounding like a wolf even in her human form. Another barrage of arrows flew up to them at a curved angle. They shattered against the runic barrier.

The dragon reached the apex of its ascent and Sybal crouched low, gripping Tzarik's shoulders as its head snapped down. With a strange, strangled roar, the dragon spit a stream of hot fire from its undead maw. It dripped like honey rather than shooting out like she'd heard dragon fire did. When it hit the army below, it splashed, scorching them through their animal hide garments and heating their antlered helmets. They screamed and ran away, but the cursed liquid fire spilled over the rocks, flowing down the mountainside.

"Don't hit Tarkan!" Sybal shouted as the flow of fire slipped mere yards past where he was bound behind the Altevine warriors.

The flowing fire split Sjörna's army and devoured part of her undead. Behind the Runers, the Northicans cheered and roared, banging their weapons against their shields.

"Let me down," Sybal shouted. "I need to tell them to pull forward. They have to get off that bridge."

"Sybal," Tzarik began, but she reached around, covering his mouth with her hand.

"I'll be fine." She gripped his face, kissed him, then slid her legs to one side.

As the dragon came just ten feet off the ground, she slid off. Landing hard, she rolled over the stony earth, grunting as the sharp rocks pricked and sliced at her. When she scrambled to her feet and ran towards the bridge, a howl broke out from behind her. She turned to look, knowing it was Sjörna in her wolf shape, and screamed to the warriors on the bridge. Dain stood yards above, perched on the arms of one of the mighty statues.

"Don't let them on the bridge!" she shouted up. "They intend to go through Northica. They have a siege weapon!"

Dain's hawk head snapped up to look towards the horizon where, from the slope of the ground, they could not yet see the oncoming army. He cawed and lifted off, his wings shoving an icy gale towards Sybal.

Swinging her arms above her head to get Zeva's attention, she pointed towards the hill that led down, away from the bridge. The girl understood, and the risen army marched towards Sybal, off the bridge and towards Sjörna-Reks. Dain flew to the back of the bridge, signaling the masses to move forward. Satisfied, Sybal took out her scimitar and turned to face the horde.

The dragon above spewed another hot fall of necrotic fire, scorching more of the horde. Behind her, Skarde's army caught up and overtook her, spilling down the hill finally to meet their enemy.

Undead clashed with undead. Some used the weapons in their hands, rusted, old, and still covered in grave dirt. Other risen tore at each other like animals, clawing and biting. Sybal hacked a few down, now in the midst of the battle. She moved quickly, faster than she remembered she could, severing the heads of the risen. Her sulfates rushed quietly, alerting her to an attack from behind.

A rush of shining golden fur shot past her. A set of chomping, ravenous jaws just missed her arm as she spun out of the way. Sjörna-Reks had released her wolven son, setting him on Sybal. The gigantic monster spun on his paws, hackles raised, and faced her again. She fought to remember the boy's name. If she could help it, she didn't want to hurt Kjarton's son.

"Signar!" she said, remembering. "Don't do this. You don't have—"

The Vaeson prince snarled and leapt at her again, huge jaws open to catch her head. Sybal ducked with buhkar, misting underneath the wolf. He was as big as a horse. If he caught any part of her, she'd be ripped limb from limb like a gazelle in a tiger's maw.

Loving the game, the golden wolf turned, slipping only a little on the ice and taking down half a dozen risen with a swipe of his claws. He didn't seem to care who was on whose side; he just wanted to attack. With a snarl, he snapped two more risen with his teeth before turning back to her.

Realizing she'd have to ward him off, she widened her stance and prepared to make contact. The wolf shook his head, rending his last victim before pouncing at her.

"I'm sorry," she shouted as she slashed at him with all her might, misting as she leapt. The curve of her scimitar cut the wolf hard across his face. Hot blood smattered her right side, burning her eye. She blinked as the pained howl of the wolf turned to the scream of a boy.

She rubbed the blood from her eyes, cleaving two risen in the process, and saw Signar lying in the snow on his back. Bare chested in simple animal-skin leggings and no boots, the boy cried, clapping his hands to his face. His golden hair splayed out in a mess of small and tiny braids amidst gently chaotic tangles and what must have once been golden adornments. She regretted her aggressive attack, but hadn't known what else to do. She ran to him, reaching down to pull him up. Perhaps she could get him across the bridge. Would Sjörna be willing to bargain if they had her only son? Somehow she doubted it, but wanted to try.

When she reached down to take his arm, he snarled like his wolven shape and snapped at her. In his human form, this made him look like the wildling they said he was. She pulled her hand back, exclaiming in annoyance and disgust. Blood flecked from the wound on his face, spattering the snow around them. She'd slashed him from the left side of his forehead down between his eyes and to his collarbone. He bled profusely.

"Stop it!" she snapped, holding her sword up again. But the boy was too wild. He launched himself at her again, landing on her hard. With a grunt, she flipped him over. He was light, being perhaps fifteen, and she easily swung herself on top of him. Letting go of her scimitar, she gripped his throat with both hands and started to choke him. If she could get him to pass out, she could haul him over the bridge.

Signar scratched at her fingers, making odd, animal-like screams and gnashing his teeth. His bloodied face changed from rage to confusion to panic as she choked the breath out of him. A little piece of her shouted for her to stop. This wasn't his fight, his fault.

Sooner than she expected, he slowed, tears spilling down his temples. His hands dropped to his sides. Satisfied, she let go and checked he still breathed. Just as she leaned her head down to his lips to listen for breath, another howl cut through the frozen air behind her. Sybal scrambled to her feet and turned.

Sjörna-Reks marched up the hill right behind her.

"You bitch!" the red Reks growled, the wolven snarl still in her voice. "What have you done to my boy?"

Sybal scoffed, spinning her scimitar in her hand. "You don't care about him. You kept him chained outside like a dog."

Sjörna-Reks raised her head, making the antlers atop her helmet arch towards the sky behind her. "What do you know of a mother's love, Sybal?"

Shall we show her? the familiar voice of Freja said softly in her head. *Take her, Sybal. Send her to the afterlife. Give her to me. Cut her down!*

Sybal clenched her eyes closed as a fresh wave of cold shot up her spine to her head. "I can't," she groaned through the pain.

"What's that?" Sjörna-Reks asked, smirking. "Has the Deep left voices of dead ones in your head?"

Sybal looked up, shaken. "How do you know?"

Sjörna raised a pale red brow. "A guess. We here on Caerwren know about death." She lifted her axe. "Step away from my son, Sybal."

Above them, the undead dragon turned sharply. Tzarik must have seen Sjörna and her standing so close. But he didn't direct the dragon to vomit its necrotic fire. What was he waiting for? She wasn't close enough to Sjörna-Reks to be in any real danger.

Taking the chance, she snapped her head up to the dragon. Tzarik took the longbow from the saddle and aimed it down. His eyes were wide, wild with worry.

Too late, Sybal saw his target. Lokhtar aimed a similar bow behind Sjörna-Reks, and let the shaft fly just seconds before Tzarik. The red shaft from Lokhtar shot over Sjörna-Reks's shoulder. Sybal moved fast, but had stood still too long. Even with her new-found speed, the arrow found the center of her chest. The western longbow shot the arrow hard and fast. Sybal felt it drag her back, the arrow-head emerging between her shoulders and out the back of her leather armor. The feathery shaft protruded before her, like a spear in her chest. She gasped as the pain finally hit her.

Sjörna-Reks smirked as Sybal tilted and fell onto her back, snapping the bolt and sending another shock of agony through her. She lay next to Signar, who began to stir. Above, Tzarik roared her name. Her vision didn't blur, and after a few frightened thumps, her heart steadied, though it strained to continue beating. Her sulfates rushed. They tingled through her, shouting that something was wrong.

Despite the blow and the arrow protruding from her, she didn't feel the throes of death like she had before. The agony of having an arrow fly through her was real, but no gray vision came. No death rattle in her throat. Curious, she gripped the arrow. The head had broken off in her fall, so it would be safe to pull out.

More fire spilled around her, and the battle raged on. Sjörna-Reks's army came close to the lip of the bridge now. Sybal stood up, gripping the shaft. Behind Sjörna, Tzarik fought past Lokhtar having leapt from the dragon. Tzarik had one of the red arrows in his hand. He dodged Lokhtar's massive arms and shoved the bolt into his only good eye, blinding him completely. She admired Tzarik's bravery in the face of a man who could snap his spine with one hand. But her smile faded when his wide, terrified eyes landed on her with her hand still on the shaft sticking out of her chest. Sjörna-Reks looked on, just as horrified, frozen to the spot.

Looking down, Sybal saw a small trickle of her white blood spilling out. With a deep breath, she pulled the arrow out. The sensation made her grunt and double over as the wood slipped out. Quickly, she drew artiah over her wound to stop the bleeding. When she did, almost all the pain vanished. She looked up into Sjörna-Reks's horrified face. Tzarik had the same expression.

Sybal felt fine. She tossed the arrow aside and spun her scimitar in her hand, ready to fight the Reks.

But Sjörna-Reks turned, fleeing from her. She bounded down the path, transforming into her wolven form. Sybal's heart hammered as she realized the Reks ran for Tzarik. He raised his scimitar as the red wolf launched herself at him. She caught his arm in her maw and spun him around like a rag doll as she landed. Her army reached the bridge. Sybal turned to see the raven ram positioned to cross the bridge behind her. Cursing, she ran towards Tzarik.

He groaned as the Reks's teeth tore his flesh under his armor, but she noticed him concentrating on the arm in her mouth. In a flash, the wolf's head snapped back, her jaw forced open with a crack.

Tzarik fell into the snow and struggled to get up. He'd drawn halat inside her mouth, nearly breaking her jaw as the barrier appeared around his fist.

A shadow crossed over them as Dain shot down, diving at Sjörna in his hawk form. The Reks, still reeling, snapped haphazardly at the white hawk. Dain's silver talons clawed at the wolf, matching her in size. Far behind them, Skarde shouted for Dain to get back. As the Vaeson locked themselves in battle, Sybal helped Tzarik up. She caught him glancing at her chest wound.

"Tarkan's there, behind the army," she said, pointing just a few yards away. "His risen have breached the bridge. We have to get to him."

"No, look." He kicked one of the risen over and shoved its helmet off with his foot to expose the dead man's neck. There, on his white skin, a black script marked him. "She anticipated it. Or he did. They all must be marked, so he doesn't control them like he used to, as we thought."

They broke apart to fend off a few risen and wound an Altevine warrior that came at them.

"If we get to him, take him," she reasoned. "We can tell him to stop. We have Zeva. He is fighting her right now."

"Don't you think he knows that?" Tzarik grunted, fighting his way through an onslaught of risen. "We didn't raise these undead."

He was right. Tarkan knew Zeva was the only one who could raise an army like that. But he still pressed on. Had he made that choice? Had he decided to fight against Zeva? She cursed him in her mind.

"Then we take him," she tried. "Once he's away from Sjörna, he'll be safe." She didn't believe her own words as she said them.

Tzarik gave her a doubtful glance.

"The ram!" he shouted suddenly, looking up the pathway. "We have to get back."

Sybal moaned, looking back to where Tarkan stood bound.

"She's tied him to a pyre," she noted. "Sjörna wasn't planning on letting him live through this. She'll kill him, burning him alive."

A chant behind them made them stop. The ram was now crossing the bridge.

"Shit," Sybal hissed. "Where's the dragon? We're too late!"

She whirled around to see Dain and Sjörna still locked in monstrous combat. Behind her, Tzarik bent the longbow and fired at a risen about to shove a sword through the still unconscious Signar. She was about to suggest they remount when the mountain shook. She froze, and Tzarik gripped her arm to steady himself.

"What is that?" she shot as another thump rattled the mountain. The second one stilled every living warrior.

Another thump, like the steps they'd felt when they'd spotted the god walking on the earth. Far up on the mountain, Zeva's voice screamed in effort. The next thud came from the east side of the river. Every face turned as the entire horde and Skarde's army realized where the quakes came from. On the horizon—the low sun flickering through its colossal ribs—marched the skeleton of the dead giant from the side of the mountain, the man who had ascended to godhood: Tyrmagnar.

Skarde's voice rang out from the bridge. "She's raised a god!"

Tyrmagnar's fleshy, risen skeleton gripped its titanic sword and charged towards the bridge, shaking the mountain with every god-like step. The god easily stood as tall as the bridge, striding through the river. The sword in its hands was impossibly long.

"She's sending it towards the ram," Sybal gasped. "She's raised a god to protect the mountain."

CHAPTER 38

GOD-RAISER

ZEVA COULDN'T STOP THE SCREAM THAT TORE HER ENTIRE
body in two as she brought Tyrmagnar up from the mountainside
where he rested. Her hands, stretched out before her, withered away
into skeletal claws before her very eyes. Weakened, the curse flared
into life around her insides. Before her eyes went black, she swung
her arms, making Tyrmagnar strike at the battering ram. The
ascended undead raised his mighty sword and thrust it through the
pillars, severing two of the chains that held the raven ram aloft.

The thralls attached to it shouted, trying to unbind themselves.
With an upward thrust, Tyrmagnar cut the mighty ram in two,
crushing several of Sjörna's warriors underneath. With it broken, half
of it rolled back down the path, scattering her army and breaking
dozens of her undead. The raven itself got dragged on the chains
around Tyrmagnar's blade before they finally broke and were
launched into Sjörna's horde.

Then her vision went black.

Let me see him, she begged the scriptures. Her body pitched as
suddenly she saw through the eyes of Tyrmagnar, yards above the

bridge. She tipped, unbalanced on the shaky ground, but forced herself to remain standing.

"I feel his courage in me," she groaned to the shieldmaidens behind her. "It's terrifying."

"You feel Tyrmagnar?" one asked, bewildered.

Zeva nodded. "He came to me, called me. But I don't think he wanted to be raised." A sharp cut of displeasure surged through her heart, causing a stinging pain. "I'm sorry," she called to him. By instinct, she reached her hands out towards her risen. She couldn't stop the sob bubbling up in her throat. Everything hurt: her body, her skull, and her heart. She wanted Tarkan there with her. But she was alone. "I feel them all in my heart. Tarkan said they fill his mind. But mine is empty. They are all here." Her left hand hammered on her own chest. "They call me. I can hear them all."

Behind her, the shieldmaidens shuffled their feet cautiously and shared a glance.

Looking through Tyrmagnar's eyes, Zeva spotted Tarkan in the middle of a mass of the retreating horde. "I see you," she whispered, tears spilling down her cheeks. "Tarkan?" she tried to call to him.

When she remembered he wouldn't hear her, she returned to commanding the undead titan. "Take down the ram," she growled. Her arms lost all their strength with this final command. Pulling herself out of Tyrmagnar's eyes, she fell.

ᛉ

TARKAN FLAILED against his bonds as the raven ram cascaded back down the mountain, free falling. Every hit against the stone shook the mountain, sending quivering falls of snow down. The magnificent stomping of the giant sent a shudder through his entire body. It had to be Zeva.

Gasping, he tried to scream her name, but only a hoarse, breathy screech came out from his destroyed throat. He caught Sjörna's red mane flashing amongst the battle. The strange fire that spilled from the dragon's maw continued to slide down the mountain towards him. The kindling around him had been prepared by Sjörna herself before their march. He knew he couldn't be killed that way, but the torture would be immeasurable. And the scriptures would be ruined on his melted flesh. Like the runes, the necrotic holy script could be vindictive if it was ruined on the flesh of a sentient who had sworn to bear it for all eternity.

With Sjörna sufficiently distracted by the hawk prince, Tarkan tried to reach out to one of his risen. With his hands bound and no voice to command them past the initial order, none heeded his silent call. Screeching in exasperation, he tried again. How could a Necro'Khan not have total control over his own risen? Even with the blood pact, he should be able to command them. Surely the Necro'Khan did not need his voice to command his risen? His father, Ishmael, had been able to. But Ishmael had been too powerful, blighting and destroying the entire country of Porsh. That was why the other houses had risen up against him. Tarkan could not hope now to learn all Ishmael's secrets. The deepest, darkest knowledge lay waiting in Alika, in the Mahit'Onomicon, the book of the dead and other secrets of the map. If he ever truly wanted to be safe, beyond the reach of even a sorcerer, he needed that tome. He needed to be as powerful as his father. He had much to learn still.

Just as his rage mounted at not being able to call his horde, something touched his hands from behind. He grunted, writhing away from the touch, wondering if one of his risen had come to attack him. Trapped, he'd be ripped apart before he could stop it.

"Be still," a smooth voice hissed behind him. "I'm here to save you."

Tarkan snapped his head around over his shoulder. A tall, hawk-like Masahk clothed in the black of the Runers with white plumage knelt behind him. He recognized Ragnall. His long, lithe fingers made quick work of Sjörna's shackles with a pick. When the weight of the chains dropped from his arms, Tarkan raised his hands, quick as lightning. A small swarm from his horde turned and came back to him.

Behind him, Ragnall untied the yards of ropes that had trussed him to the stake. Groaning, he knew he couldn't drink his blood. Or could he? He halted, thinking as the Masahk finished untying his legs. He was Necro'Khan. The Runer blood would not kill him like it might an Apostle. But taking the black magic inside the scriptures could mean something worse. They protected him from the outside, but once blood was inside them, any magic they held could penetrate the necromancer.

Unsure, he decided it was worth the risk in this moment. He wouldn't be able to get blood from any of the warriors. They were fighting, on alert. He'd never get close enough.

His small swarm approached, waiting for his command.

"There," Ragnall breathed, tossing the last of the rope away. Before he stood up, Tarkan took a knife from one of his swarm.

Turning, he slashed the Masahk's throat. Shock paled the Masahk's already white skin. His blood glittered opalescent in the low-hanging sun. His hand went to the wound as he gurgled.

"I came...to help you," he choke, falling near the edge of the pyre.

Unable to speak, Tarkan grabbed the Masahk's fine, ashen hair and pulled his head back to catch the blood coming from his neck. The Runer was strong and shoved him off once, trying to scramble to his feet. Commanding his undead with a flick of his wrist, Tarkan grappled him and held him still.

"Why?" the Masahk wheezed, confused and terrified. "I...came... for her!"

Glaring down at the Masahk, he spit on his prone figure after the last swallow. If he found out that this filthy creature had touched Zeva, he'd be back for his body.

The Runer's white blood tasted foul. Tarkan didn't have a taste for blood and flesh like some monsters, but it was part of his magic.

Runer blood was far worse than the metal tang of red blood. It cut on the way down, then burned in his belly like a roiling poison. Disgusted, he realized it would do him more harm than good, but would give him the temporary strength he needed.

The front of the Masahk's black Runer armor was covered in white from his neck. Ragnall's eyes rolled in his head as the sleepiness of blood loss overcame him. Tarkan wiped the white from his lips and looked up to take in the battle.

The falling ram split Sjörna's horde, crushing at least a third of it. Dain had disentangled himself from Sjörna and the Runers ran madly towards their incoming dragon. The black beast flapped its wings, kicking up a maelstrom of snow. He didn't care about them. He wanted to find Zeva and Sjörna. The snow all around him turned into bright red mud, smoldering with the fire from the dragon.

The Runers mounted their beast, Tzarik shouting something, trying to turn back. Sybal wouldn't allow him. Finally, she reached down and grappled him, forcing him onto the dragon. Once they ascended, they turned to head towards the bridge. Scanning the mountainside, he spotted the huge red wolf galloping towards the bridge as well. She and her living warriors had separated themselves from his risen army and charged towards the bridge. Now was his chance.

He reached out to order his risen to attack her. Just then, something akin to a heavy sigh rose up from the masses and horde.

In one fluid motion, the risen on Skarde's side of the battle collapsed. Their bones fell from one another, flesh piling into disfigured bodies amongst the blood, snow, and rocks. The head of Tyrmagnar tipped backwards and the god dropped his blade. The giant crumbled, blessedly falling away from the bridge. With a mighty clatter that shook the snow from the mountain, the god fell into the river below.

Above, the fire dragon reeled suddenly to the left, its wings going limp and fluttering as it fell. Sybal screamed from its back as they crashed into the mountainside. The black mass that was the dragon's body landed hard and still, dead once again, pitching the Runers into the snow.

Two seconds of confused silence followed from both sides of living warriors as Northica's army was cut in half. Skarde's men started the shout but did not retreat, hammering their weapons upon shields and axe hafts. They ran madly into Sjörna's much closer living army. Dain swooped in and a white radjur with a crown of sharp antlers also charged down the bridge: Skarde in his Vaeson form. A small group of Altevine warriors made a mad dash to Tier'Morlan, diving over the edge beneath the bridge.

A necromancer's risen only fell when the necromancer released them or was stopped. Zeva would not have willingly dropped the risen dead.

Screeching in rage, fear consumed Tarkan's hard heart. He couldn't raise Zeva's dead since he had no voice. All he had were his remaining risen. Casting about, he found one of the antlered wolves Sjörna's warriors rode. He grabbed the bridle, hoarsely cursing the animal, and leapt astride it to get closer. Ahead of her risen horde, Sjörna-Reks did not stop her charge.

A clattering of hooves crossed the bridge. The huge white radjur that was Skarde charged the red wolf, its head down. The antlers came into contact hard with the muscle-bound body of the wolf. Sjörna yelped as Skarde tossed her with a powerful pitch from his thick neck. The wolf landed, rolling in the snow past Tarkan. Turning the reigns of the antlered wolf, he faced her. Gesturing with his left hand, he commanded his risen to surround her.

Sjörna-Reks stood up and shook, transforming back to her towering human form. "Signar!" she shouted, casting her crowned head to and fro. She held her hand out and her massive sword flew to it, cleaving through several living men and more risen. She caught it easily, then spotted Tarkan. Her chest rose and fell in deep gasps as she gathered herself.

"She's fallen, Tarkan," she barked over the ruckus of the battle that had moved onto the lip of the bridge. "You have nothing left. I did not do this." She tried to look sympathetic, but he saw through her tricks. "I can heal you. We can rule together. Altevine is just the start. Think of the strength you'd have. You have eternity; I do not. This will be your kingdom once I am gone. You can have any boy, girl, or Masahk as an apprentice."

He glowered at her. How dared she think Zeva was replaceable? If he had been able to speak, he'd have interrupted before that, not giving her a chance to sway him. She would have seen he wanted none but Zeva and would have made another offer. Sjörna-Reks was a fool.

"Tarkan," she began again. "Help me find my son and we can—"

With a thrust of his hand, four of the risen attacked her. She roared, tossing her massive axe out and transforming. The axe launched towards Tarkan. He ducked against the neck of the antlered wolf and the axe missed him by a foot. He glanced around quickly for Lokhtar. The man was never far from the Reks...except now. He expected an arrow to fly into his ribs or a hulking body to seize him from behind. But Lokhtar was nowhere to be found.

"I am not afraid of you, necromancer!" Sjörna-Reks roared. She'd returned to her human form, having destroyed the small mass of risen he'd set on her. "I never feared you. But her..." She raised her head up towards Skarde's mountain. "Your little woman was power beyond measure. You held her back. I saw it the moment she healed. When she raised the dragon. How could you shackle her as you did, necromancer?"

Tarkan snarled back at her for using a lesser title than he deserved.

Sjörna-Reks laughed, looking into his angry face. "You are weak. That's why I was able to control you so easily. You can only be a threat at a great distance—from the shadows. But you left an even greater vulnerability: her. Now that she's gone, *you* are stronger than ever!"

Zeva wasn't gone, he told himself. Weakened, perhaps. The Runers would protect her. He could trust them to do that. If she were gone, he'd make Sjörna pay. Make the Runers pay for abandoning her. Make Sharar pay for instilling fear in them for all these years. If Zeva were gone, he'd blight the entire map, bringing death, curses, and plagues the likes of which no people had ever seen.

In a way, Sjörna-Reks was right. He would be stronger.

If he struck her down now, it would start his reign of heresy and destruction.

Gripping the leather bridle, he steeled himself and forced the wolf to turn and walk away from Sjörna.

"You cannot walk away from me, necromancer!" she shrieked.

He half glanced over his shoulder one last time at the red Reks, her pale, white hand stretched out before like she might pull him back.

Her massive blade flew towards him. She'd called it from behind him. Panicking, he forced the antlered wolf to rear up, taking the huge blade in its gut for him. The impact knocked it backwards. Realizing it would crush him under it, he let go and tumbled, rolling several feet down the snowy hill. He wheezed and gasped, scrambling to get up. Commanding the last few risen that shambled nearby, he got to his feet and ran towards the bridge.

He was not three steps up when the scriptures on the surface of his skin began to quiver and squirm. A green, hazy blast shot up before him, opening something like the very rift he'd made before. He recognized it for what it was: an opening to the Deep. The god-thing from before stood just yards away, inside the Deep: the Vorlamir. It clutched its curved blade, facing him.

Heretic. At last, I have found you and we meet again! it boomed.

Not a single other man or woman seemed to see the rift and the reaper within. Tarkan stutter-stepped back, glancing around for an escape. The risen would be nothing to the god of death within. Behind him, Sjörna-Reks gave chase.

The scream of a thousand souls being snuffed out drew me here, the Vorlamir said. It took slow steps towards him and the open rift. Every hoof fall made fire, sparks, and ash rise from the blighted ground in the Deep. *The cry of the dead has summoned me. To take the bodies of those who died a bad death is a fell task. I have come to return them.*

Tarkan swallowed hard, his voice rasping as he tried to speak. No intelligible words came out.

I care not, the Vorlamir said, understanding his thoughts. *I have come for you. You cannot defy death upon my lands. Go elsewhere if you seek to desecrate sentient life!*

The Necro'Khan panted, craning to look around the rift for Zeva. Behind him, a wolf howled. He spun around. Sjörna galloped up to him in her wolven form and stopped, kicking snow up onto him.

"What holds you, necromancer?" she growled through her fangs.

She couldn't see it.

She lowered her head, hackles raised. "Final chance. I'll rip your body apart with my mouth." She licked her lupine lips slowly, a glint there he'd seen only once before. "You won't die, but you'll be a corpse. Like a rag doll to be stitched back together."

She glared at him. Her emerald eyes glittered in her red furred face. "Well?"

Making the strangled sounds again, he coughed. At last, he felt he could get one word out of his destroyed throat.

He glared at Sjörna. "Never," his voice rasped.

This reply did not please her. The muscles on top of her lupine skull twitched as she clenched her jaw and shook her head. "Fool," she sighed.

Her eyes flashed and she charged. Tarkan gave a strangled cry and ran towards the open rift where the Vorlamir continued his gait forward. The reaper stopped when it caught Tarkan charging towards it. Tarkan waited until he felt Sjörna's hot breath on the back of his neck before he ducked and rolled backwards. The wolf shot her neck back, snapping at him.

The pain registered before he realized she'd caught his forearm in her strong jaws. He was immortal, but could still feel every flake of snow and every tooth that pierced him. The power of her leap carried them both through the rift. Together, they crashed—body and soul —into the Deep.

CHAPTER 34

FRACTURED

The Northican men rushed past Sybal, hitting her hard. She gasped, exhausted from the battle and running up the mountain in snow up to her knees.

"Tzarik?" she called. She'd lost his small form when they'd crash-landed. "Zeva?" she called.

"Runer!" Dain shouted, flitting past her in his hawk form. "Come!"

He touched down just long enough for her to swing her leg over his huge, feathery body. She gripped the feathers of his neck and crouched down. The beat of his wings was far more graceful than the undead dragon's. He soared over the battle that was now only Altevine blood against Northican blood, both armies of risen having collapsed. She couldn't see Skarde or Sjörna. She didn't ask Dain if he knew where his father was. It wasn't the time. She scanned the ground below quickly for Tzarik. His black outline should have stuck out against the white snow. She couldn't find him.

"Here," Dain ordered, flapping quickly as he stuck his silver talons out to grip the crags. "My men say she is unwell."

Sybal leapt off the Vaeson's back. She glanced over one last time.

Something stirred on the underside of the bridge. "Dain, there are Altevine men under the bridge!" It almost looked like they were going into the river.

With a mighty caw, the hawk leapt from the crags and darted back down to his men. Sybal turned to find one female warrior left, standing over Zeva. The girl lay prone on the ground, thin, pale, and still.

"What happened?" Sybal asked, kneeling next to Zeva.

The shieldmaiden blinked, eyes shining. "She called up Tyrmagnar."

"It might have killed her," Sybal snapped, ignoring the religious reasoning.

"I felt his displeasure," the shieldmaiden insisted. "He gripped her soul in his hand and demanded to be released. She wouldn't let him go. She said she felt his courage, and it terrified her. Filled her. Said the dead were in her heart."

Half of Sybal wanted to believe the woman. She gathered up Zeva in her arms. The girl felt tiny and frail. She picked up one of Zeva's hands to examine it. It was cold and stiff.

"Zeva?" she hissed, worried. She dropped the girl's hand and gripped her face, shaking it hard. "Zeva!" she called. Zeva's black veins stood out thick and stiff under her soft skin. "We have to get down from here," Sybal ordered the shieldmaiden.

The woman nodded quickly, took up her sword, and led the way back down. Zeva was so light, Sybal only panted when she reached the bottom of the path. She glanced over at the bridge several yards away and saw the Northican warriors dashing across it, back towards the mountain. Some dropped their weapons and round shields to run faster. Even some clansmen from Altevine ran in a panic in both directions.

"What's happening?" she called. One phrase was repeated over and over as the men ran. She couldn't understand; it was jumbled in many afraid voices. "What are they screaming?" she asked.

The shieldmaiden's eyes went wide. "Black powder?" Her gray eyes flicked to the center of the bridge where everyone ran from. "Black powder!" she repeated, this time screaming.

In an instant, Sybal understood. "They're going to destroy the bridge." She spun to face it, her heart hammering against her ribs. "Tzarik!" she screamed. To the warrior, she said, "Take her," and shoved Zeva into her arms. The woman protested, but Sybal ignored her.

She slid on the blood that had turned to ice and tripped over stones on the bridge. Many called for the crazy Al'Myrahn Runer to stop and come back. She ignored them.

He risked his life for me, she wept in her head as she dashed as fast as her long legs would carry her. *Came to Caerwren for me. I won't leave him behind!*

Once the bridge was gone, the only way to the rest of Caerwren and home would be a long, grueling trek through the borders of Zealmor and the mountains there. She refused to make that journey alone. What if Tzarik was hurt? Wounded when the dragon went down? What if he was buried under the snow, suffocating?

Tears burned her eyes as she spotted a single Altevine warrior standing up on the towering walls that lined the bridge. It was nearly fifty feet across, so the tiny flame on the tip of his arrow barely registered. She slid to a stop, looking up at him.

"Sybal!" Tzarik's gruff voice called out.

Her heart hammered once—hard—against her ribs as she spotted Tzarik charging towards her from the other side. She cried out in joy and agony. He ran with a limp, one hand pressing into his thigh.

"Run!" she shouted to him. "We have to—"

The archer on the wall gave a wild yell.

"Shoot him!" Dain screamed from far away, near the mountain. "Don't let him jump!"

Sybal saw only a few archers on the other side take aim. She reached for her small crossbow, but too late. The man screamed to his god and fell backwards over the bridge, aiming up to the under-side with his fiery arrow. Panicking, she froze, torn between running to Tzarik and running back to safety.

Weeping piteously, she ran to him.

The bridge rocked with a million cracks of thunder. It didn't fall to shambles. The explosion shot up in the center of the bridge, blasting her just as she could see the blue of Tzarik's eyes. She couldn't help the instinctual yowl that broke from her. Ice and stone cut through her, and something slammed against her head, knocking her unconscious.

⚔

RUMBLINGS like a distant thunderstorm woke Sybal. A yelping of a dog in pain pierced her ringing head. Shifting, the fine white dust of ground stone fell off her in clouds. Smoke engulfed her from every direction. Her own blood smeared down her armor from a dozen places where blasted stone had torn her flesh. She felt it, but innately knew she wouldn't die.

As she pushed herself up, she remembered the Altevine warriors from before who had crawled over the side of the bridge. They must have planted the black powder, and the man with the fiery arrow had leapt to his death, igniting it. It had destroyed half the Bridge of Tier'Morlan. Cries of pain softly emitted from the white dust of the mountain.

"Tzarik?" she called, looking around. With a grunt, she pushed herself up. It hurt to breathe, and even more to shout. She must have had at least two broken ribs. Wrapping her arm around her middle, she limped towards the center of the bridge, calling for her mentor. Unable to see even five feet in front of her, she walked carefully. Every misstep, every stone under her boot, made her stumble and the sore-ness worse.

She gasped, choking on a sob as tears burned her eyes in addition to the smoke. She hadn't come this far, been resurrected, just to lose him now.

Just as the edge—jagged and still crumbling—came into view, she spotted him.

"Oh, gods, thank you!" she cried, running to him. She slid down next to him, tearing fresh wounds into her knees. She threw herself onto him, kissing his face. Her tears plopped down onto his closed eyes; he didn't stir.

"No," she murmured. She smacked his cheek gently but meaningfully. "Tzarik?" she snapped. Sitting up, she took in his body.

White blood freely trickled from the wound on his thigh he'd been pressing against before the explosion. One side of him also bled from the shards of blasted stone. Fumbling for her runes, she drew artiah over him once, quickly. Then she leaned over him again to listen for his breath. The rumbling was so loud and constant, she heard nothing. Or he did not breathe.

"Please," she begged, a fresh wave of tears splashing down her ash-covered face. "Get up. I can't go on without you. I can't. I can't!" She gritted her teeth and shook him roughly. He didn't stir. She kissed him again and again on his dry lips, pleading with any god who would listen.

Behind her, voices called out. Someone was coming.

Taking a shaky breath, she laid her head on his chest. She reached around to take his hand in hers. *From the first moment I saw you,* she thought, *before you took my blood and my life, my heart no longer belonged to me. You bound me to you that day. When you saved me.* She wrapped her other arm around his middle, hugging him tightly. "Don't think I won't find a way to save you, too. I will. You went into hell for me. You taught me well. I'll do the same a million times over, searching the underworld for you if I have to."

The scratching of boots on stone and ice filled the air as the Northican warriors rounded up the Altevine stragglers on this side of the bridge.

A hand touched her hair, gently running fingers through it. She opened her eyes.

"You are stubborn enough. I don't doubt it," Tzarik mumbled, his voice hoarse.

"Gods!" Sybal exclaimed, leaping to her knees. She grabbed the hand that had been in her hair and kissed his bloody palm. "Answer me when I call your name," she chided, smacking his face.

He smiled weakly up at her. "Can't breathe."

"Oh." She cursed and reached her arms around him, helping him up.

Dain scampered into view with a host of Northican men at his side. When he saw them, his face cracked in relief. "You're alive," he greeted them. "Father has taken the wilding prince hostage. Sjörna-Reks is missing and we can't find the Necro'Khan."

Sybal craned her neck to look back over the bridge. "I saw her just as we went down. She was headed towards Tarkan."

She looked down at Tzarik. He offered no response, but she noticed how the skin under his left eye tightened just enough. He'd seen something but wasn't going to say it here.

Dain looked over their heads to the far side of the bridge. "It will be some time before we can get across. Taking the way down behind the mountain, over the river, and back up would be longer." His eyes calculated. "I may have an idea, though. Come, Runers."

Tzarik coughed in pain, hand pressing into his chest. "What will you do with the prince?"

Sybal almost moaned out loud. Tzarik fixated on the wilding too much, she thought.

Dain held his head high. "That is for the Reks to decide. My father will deal with this once we are sure the wolven Reks and her Necro'Khan are taken care of."

"Zeva," Sybal gasped. "We need to get her to a healer," she insisted.

Dain's brows knitted ever so slightly. "Yes. Let's get you back and into safety. For now, the battle is over. Whether we have triumphed remains to be seen."

ًا

CONFUSION AND RUSHING bodies clogged the paths back into the main village. Warriors lay in the melting snow, holding wounds or tending to others. A few lithe children ran errands, bringing water, bandages, and other necessities to the front line towards the bridge. Sybal half carried Tzarik into the main circle of the village, where dozens of white-clad Volra ministered to the wounded.

Sybal couldn't find the shieldmaiden from before, so instead she brought Tzarik to a Volra healer. The Volra had thrown open the doors to his house and had moved his own table outside to use for those in need. The blood on it glittered in the sun that had not yet set. The Volra cleaned a huge blade, having just amputated an arm before she came to him.

"Do you have Runer's blood?" she asked him.

The old man nodded, the bones and beads on his long hair clinking. He pointed soundlessly with his blade behind her. She turned to look and saw a pack of black-clad Runers watching the carnage and pain. She bit her tongue. They couldn't fight. Unlike her, they had not learned to battle without killing. Or if they had, maybe they'd pretended not to in order to avoid the fight. She couldn't blame them. Not everyone in a canton must approve of the clan wars. They had an excuse, and at least they gave their supplies.

She lifted Tzarik onto the table and stabbed the needle into his arm while the Volra went to work on his leg.

"Did you see a shieldmaiden carrying a girl in white?" Sybal asked the Volra.

He nodded and pointed up towards the thronehall. "Your leg is very badly injured, Al'Myrah," he said to Tzarik. "The muscles are cut."

Sybal took out artiah. "Will this help?"

The old man winced, but nodded. "Your runic magic is not for healing. Just a quick cure in the field. The muscles will scar." He cut Tzarik's black pants all the way down to the knee and pulled the fabric open for Sybal to see the true damage.

She gasped, hand over her mouth. The wound was so deep in his thigh, she could see his bone. The muscles inside were mangled.

His leg shook, exposed to the cold air. He hissed in pain. "Feeling is starting to come back," he grunted, closing his eyes tight.

Sybal drew artiah slowly over the wound. The Volra waited while the muscles inside knit back together just enough. The old man pointed to a few white scars on the muscle.

"He will feel this for some time. Perhaps the rest of his life. But it will do." The Volra grabbed a needle and thread and stitched him up. Then he wrapped a dark violet poultice against the wound with the bandages. "Keep it clean," he warned Tzarik.

While the Volra finished with Tzarik, Sybal drew artiah over her own abrasions and felt almost immediately better. She offered Tzarik her arm as support and they headed towards the thronehall.

The hill climb made them both pant by the time they reached the great, ornate doors. The shieldmaiden stood outside, holding her arm tightly to her side while others scrambled around her.

"Lady Runer," she sighed upon seeing Sybal. Blood leaked between her fingers. "I didn't want to leave her until you arrived."

"Get tended to," Sybal said quickly. "And thank you."

She shoved her shoulder into the thick wood and pushed the doors open. The fire in the main hearth smoldered darkly. Some light came in through the windows; the sun had not set. Tzarik frowned at the hearth.

"How long did we do battle?" Confused, he squinted up at the windows and the glaring sun.

"Spring," Sybal remembered. "The sun won't set for some time.

I'd forgotten. That means the Deep is farther away. The barrier is thicker. That's good, at least."

Tzarik didn't reply, making the face he did when he wanted to say something, but wouldn't.

Sybal glanced around and spotted a body clad in white lying near the fire. The shieldmaiden had piled up furs and blankets for Zeva. Sybal rushed to her side and knelt. She took up the girl's hand in hers, stroking her pallid brow. Zeva's hand was ice cold and stiff as clay. Sybal's heart stopped.

"Oh, gods, no," she breathed. She dropped her hand and leaned down to her mouth. No breath came. Pressing her hand into Zeva's chest, she waited a long time, feeling for the infrequent beat of a necromancer's heart. Nothing but icy flesh pressed into her. "Tzarik?" she asked, looking up at him. "Did—did his curse kill her? Did he do this?"

For what she thought was perhaps the first time, Tzarik's face showed sadness. His eyes almost shone and his brows furrowed in melancholy.

"She shouldn't have raised the god," he murmured, joining her beside Zeva. He gently reached out and caressed her long, tangled hair. "I doubt she thought it would weaken her so much."

Sybal gasped a sob and ran her hand over Zeva's scarred face. "She didn't deserve any of this. Sharar's torture, being Scriven. Tarkan should have never taken her from her family."

Tzarik reached his hand over quickly and gently took hers, holding it tight. "He's gone now."

Sybal questioned him with her red-rimmed eyes.

"I saw him vanish. Sjörna with him." He rubbed at his eyes. "I can't be sure, but I smelled the Deep. I think that death god hunted Tarkan down. Came for him."

"Good," Sybal snapped.

Tzarik's voice turned soft. "In his way, he cared for her. Don't doubt that. And she loved him in a way I will never understand. She was unyielding in her loyalty to him. What they had was not for us to understand or judge."

She sniffed violently. Taking a strand of Zeva's hair, she tucked it behind her ear, which was badly deformed from burns. "I thought, maybe, that..." The lump in her throat throttled her words. "If we stopped Tarkan, we could..." She couldn't bring herself to say it. By the way Tzarik squeezed her hand, she knew he understood. "I wanted to save her."

Her heart crumbled in her chest, the shards cutting through her. She pulled her hand away and dropped her face into her palms, letting the sorrow fill her like it had over two years ago when she'd lost everything. Shuffling from across the piles of furs told her Tzarik moved. The next thing she knew, his warm body knelt beside her and enveloped her in his arms. Never had he comforted her like this before. Giving in, she leaned on him, embracing him.

Looking back at Zeva, she asked, "What should we do with her body? Are there practices we should honor her with?" Did necromancers honor their dead? She doubted it.

Tzarik leaned his cheek against the top of her head. "We could burn her on a pyre, like the clan warriors do."

At first, Sybal thought it respectful. But then she grew sick at the idea. "No," she snapped. "I will not leave even her ashes here on Caerwren. Her spirit could be trapped here, all alone, for eternity! On a foreign land, with vile gods who could steal her away. No, I will not even give her soul the chance to be tortured for eternity. She's had enough of that."

She sat up, frowning as she thought.

"Should we take her back to Porsh?" Tzarik suggested after a moment of silence filled with the crackling of the embers. "We could bury her in the family crypt. With his family."

This enraged Sybal even more. She growled through clenched teeth, grabbing at her hair. Tears mixed with mucus dripped down her face. "No. He doesn't deserve her, either! What if he comes back and finds her? Raises her? Or finds a way to resurrect her spirit? She deserves rest. She deserves to be at peace!"

Then a thought struck her.

"Ala'nar. My family home." The more she thought about it, the more she liked the idea. "Yes. I will bury her with Abdul, my brother."

Tzarik reached over, laying Zeva's hands over her middle, giving her a look of peace. "So, we go home?"

Sybal nodded, blinking out one last rivulet of tears. "Yes. We go home."

CHAPTER 40

SIGNAR WÖLF-TÖR

Days passed as Tzarik healed and Northica recovered, though none of the clan felt like the battle had been won. Sjörna-Reks's head had not been split upon a Northican axe and the Necro'Khan had vanished. Skarde told his clansmen it wasn't a victory and shouldn't be treated as one. He commanded his Volra to wrap Zeva in the dressings of honor, preserving her corpse. Bound with flowers, crystals, and other elements that kept her flesh from rotting and her hair from decay, they sealed her in a light wooden box and kept her in the thronehall where other warriors paid respects through prayers, offerings, and the burning of a candle beside her body. Sybal went to stand beside her before coming to sleep every night. She'd come back and tell Tzarik how surprised she was that so many honored Zeva. A few shieldmaidens had already composed a verse or two of a song about the lady necromancer. Tzarik knew the girl's death would be hard on Sybal. Something in her yearned for someone like that, someone she could never have. Someone to care for, mentor, teach, and love. And he could never give that to her.

On one of the dozen mornings he woke with the sun having never set, he stood on his leg to find it no longer hurt. He heard no sound from the room next to his in the upper level of the longhouse, which meant Sybal was out already. He'd not had the courage to try to enter her room and repeat their night in the rathskeller, though the desire burned like fire in him. It felt wrong with all that had gone on and with her emotions still raw.

He dressed, wrapped in a lighter wool cloak now that the icy winds of winter had passed. He walked the sloping path down from the longhouse to the bridge. Dain stood perched on one of the massive stone guardians, overseeing the work. Masons and smiths had set up workstations all along the bridge. Pulley systems hauled up huge pieces of rock from the river below. Getting closer, he took in the new bridge. Using the bones from the god below, they'd constructed the majority of the new structure.

"Do you not find it formidable?" Dain cawed from above. He leapt down, transforming before he landed.

"Won't that bring some kind of curse?" Tzarik asked. He couldn't help but smile at the prince's boldness. He had no doubt this had been his idea.

"Never." Dain smiled, crossing his arms over his huge chest. The silver circlet on his head sparkled in the sun, matching the proud glint in his gray eyes. "Tyrmagnar was a man of the clans. He protected Caerwren from Mjordir thousands of years ago, sending him to Tierheim where Mjordir awaits our souls, carried over by the Vorlamir. At least, those of us who die a bad death. Tyrmagnar will protect us."

"I'm glad to hear it."

Dain cocked a brow at the Runer. "You don't sound like it, lad."

Tzarik smiled at the address. The boy may have been tall, but he was no more than twenty years old. "Where is your father?" Tzarik asked, letting the jibe go.

"Are you ready to leave?" Dain turned and guided him back up the path towards the thronehall.

"Nearly," Tzarik mused. "Sybal has not been home in some time and is eager to leave."

"Yes, the lady Runer," Dain agreed, matching Tzarik's cautious tone now. "The unkillable."

Tzarik froze and faced the hawk prince.

"I saw her during the battle," Dain said, but no malice or ulterior motive coated his voice. "We heard about the Runer who came back from the God Deep. Risen by a Necro'Khan. We will not be able to keep this secret, Runer. Others will hear about it. The good thing about it coming from Caerwren is that most off our shores will be slow to hear it and perhaps think it is some godtale we tell to keep foreigners at bay. But the map will know. The gift of undeath is blasphemous among your people."

"Have you ever heard of such a thing?" he asked.

Dain thought for a moment. "There are those who study the gods and the afterlife who may know. But we have no such histories here."

"That's just as well. We are used to lying low," Tzarik offered. "But before we part, I must speak with Skarde-Reks concerning your Vaeson prisoner."

"TAKE SIGNAR WOLF-TOR?" Skarde boomed, leaping up from his stone throne. He'd been granting an audience with his people all day, a steady stream of his clan trickling in and out, desperate to know his next steps and taking the tasks he bestowed on them. The Runers had waited for the people to dwindle. "I have a council to hold in three days' time, Runer. I must have the wildling in my halls for my people and the people of Altevine to see. Zealmor will demand he be in the Warpath's possession."

Skarde jabbed a finger at a huge cage made from the swords and axe hafts of the fallen Altevine clansmen. Inside, the wildling crawled awkwardly on all fours in his human form, whimpering. Bruises, bloody wounds, and other signs of abuse covered his pale skin. He whined like a dog, howling and yelping. His body shook from the cold and the tips of his fingers and toes were blue.

"I *will* take the boy," Tzarik said gruffly.

Sybal snapped her head to him in disbelief. "What are you saying?"

"I will not leave him here," Tzarik continued, his brows knitting in determination. "They will kill him. Or continue to shackle him like a wild animal, using him as a show of power."

"Exactly, Runer." Skarde beamed.

"I won't leave him to be tortured here." Tzarik glared at the Reks.

"He *is* a wild animal," Skarde replied. "I understand your concern, Runer, but a child is nothing for one such as you. I can promise you," he went on when Tzarik opened his mouth to argue, "we will not torture the creature. As a wildling, his life is meaningless to Caerwren."

"He's a boy," Tzarik cut in, growling. "A part of sentient kind, a god-shaped as you say. Not a creature to be tethered and caged."

"Also the sole Reks of Altevine," Skarde added with a deepening glower.

Tzarik barked, "Even without being a Reks, his life is worth just as much as yours."

Sybal stepped up to Tzarik's side when Skarde raised his hand, preparing to summon his axe. "What are you doing? We don't need to take him."

Skarde nodded. "Leave him with us, Al'Myrah. Go home. You have more to worry about than this child."

But Tzarik couldn't. Something in him screamed to take the young Vaeson with them. He knew what it was like to be chained like an animal, to be called a creature. To be told he was worthless. The boy needed care. On the cusp of manhood, he saw in Signar something that could be tamed, that he was not simply a mindless monster. Yes, the clans of Caerwren believed he was too wild, untamable. Perhaps they knew better than him. But if he left Signar, the young Reks would be tormented for the rest of his life, never given a chance to live. He'd be murdered or sacrificed to some god of an enemy canton at best.

"I know what it's like to not be wanted," Tzarik said gruffly. "To be abandoned, shackled like an undesirable creature and told you are only worth what someone would pay for you. When my father sold me to a quadi on Bahratt, the gold the quadi offered him for me was more than generous. My father laughed. Said I was not worth half the offer. Looking me in the eye, he took a third of the offered gold and handed the chains around my neck to the quadi.

"But such thoughts are not selective of class. I watched a prince of Xia nearly succumb to years of being told he's unnecessary. But he saved his country in the end and watches over it even now, knowing he will never rule or have the honor he protects. But he took the opportunity."

He glanced sideways at Sybal.

"Someone once chased me over continents because she was alone, was desperate for guidance. I was a terrible choice."

Sybal tried to hide a weak smile but couldn't.

He looked back to Skarde. "I'd never felt anything like that pursuit; of someone wanting me so fiercely. She brought life back to me. She forced me to see her value and showed me my own. I've seen enough of Caerwren to know if I leave Signar here, he will not be safe, never given a chance to find his value. I'm sorry to strike against your customs, but you cannot tell me otherwise."

A huge sigh lifted the Reks's massive chest before he deflated. "What you say may be true, though I cannot see the worth of a wildling's life. He was conceived by force, against his father's will. Does that not count for anything?"

Tzarik silently firmed his glower at the Reks. "We cannot choose the way of our birth. He's alive now. He has worth."

Skarde averted his eyes. "I could keep him as my own. Raise him as a son. Would that placate you?"

Tzarik caught Dain tense before the prince squirmed uncomfortably beside his father.

"No," Tzarik replied. "Don't do that to Dain."

"Runer," Skarde growled, growing tired of the conversation. "The Vaeson cannot leave Caerwren. Our god-shaped are *our* blessing. Like the white hairs of Xia."

"Why could he not leave?"

"We are our secret." Skarde motioned to himself and Dain. "The rest of the map doesn't know about the Reks of the clans of Caerwren. Or if they do, they don't believe their eyes. We are a godtale to be told in rathskellers or around campfires. Even the slavers of Rhostrana do not know of us Vaeson. Can you imagine if they did? Have you seen the enslaved Masahk? The Rekses of Hovandel, Gidenmore, and Rom do not revere their Vaeson shape like we in the Warpath do. They believe they are too civilized. The Warpath keeps the gods' gift alive. Let Signar carry that banner here on our shores."

This was the only argument Tzarik took a moment to consider. It was true. He'd heard of the shape shifting monsters of Caerwren, but hadn't known they were the clan leaders. Or that they were, in fact, real. And with Rhostrana so close, there was something to fear. Signar could not control his transformations. He could turn to a horse-sized wolf at any moment while they traveled. He couldn't be kept quiet.

He glanced at Sybal. She continued to have mixed feelings twisting her face. She didn't understand what he was doing. Then, he looked at Signar, who had gone quiet. The boy gripped a sword that made up one of the bars of his cage. Red blood trickled down the blood channel of the sword. His wide, green eyes looked directly at Tzarik from behind waves of gently chaotic golden hair. For once, he was still and silent. Like he knew they discussed his fate. The cage clanked as the boy shivered.

Tzarik lost himself in the hope that glowed from the boy's eyes. Even now, he saw Signar understood. "We'll have to take that chance," he said at last.

"You will endanger every Reks of Caerwren for your feelings, Runer?" Skarde boomed, the mountain halls echoing with his thunder.

"Father," Dain finally said, cutting in. "You brought a necromancer into our midst. Took a chance to remove my curse with necrotic magic from a god no one knows."

"I'd move this mountain for you," Skarde agreed, clasping his son hardily on his shoulder. "Seeing you so weak nearly killed me."

Dain met Tzarik's eyes, but he spoke to his father. "If I were a wildling, would you risk your canton for me?"

Tzarik did not expect the emotion that immediately shone in Skarde's eyes. The big man took a deep breath and sniffled into his ornate beard. The Runer knew the answer before the Reks replied.

"Of course I would," he said, his voice thick. "You are Yrsa's son. My son. A god-shaped of thunder and lightning. You know that."

The Northican prince inclined his head. "Then let him go. You've defeated Sjörna-Reks. There is no honor to be gained in parading Signar Wolf-tor around the Warpath like a prize. He is a wildling. It would make us look weak, cruel."

Dain's words cut Skarde deep. The Reks rubbed at his eyes, then turned them to the sky, praying for guidance.

"You are right and wise, Dain," he said at length. "Runer, what will you do with him?"

"What *will* we do with him?" Sybal asked, looking shaken and confused. "Will you rune him?"

"No," Tzarik said quickly. "But there's no reason we cannot teach him to be still. To master his mind."

At this, Skarde laughed softly behind his beard. "You cannot tame a wildling, Runer. It is not in their nature. Born a wolf, he will live his life out as a wild wolf. You are a slayer of monsters, not a master of them."

Tzarik glanced to where Signar still watched them in silence. In his human form, the sight of his marred face and wild, fear-filled eyes would have turned any sentient's heart. Even now, he looked in control. If Signar could be given a chance, Tzarik knew he'd be no different from any other two-legged sentients. If they'd treated him like a wild creature since the day he was born, they had made him this way. Perhaps he was of a wild nature, but he wasn't foolish. He could be shown the way. He just needed the chance.

"I'll give him a chance to conquer himself," Tzarik answered. "He deserves to show you his worth."

Dain smiled, proud of himself, and rested his hands on his hips.

Skarde said slowly, "He *is* Reks of Altevine. Sjörna has not been found these days of scouring the mountainside. I fear she may have been taken by the mountain. Her body will not resurface until Mjordir breaks the gates of Tierheim and rides with his fell army to melt the snow once and for all. I fear the same fate for your Necro'Khan."

Tzarik winced. He knew better. When Tarkan had run from Sjörna-Reks, something had appeared that only he could see, stopping him scared in his flight. Whatever it was had made Tzarik's sulfates rush cold with warning. Then, Sjörna had launched herself at Tarkan and they'd both vanished into nothingness. He'd have bet his runes that a rift had opened and the Vorlamir had come for Tarkan. He said none of this to Skarde. Tarkan was not the Northican Reks's burden or worry.

"Yes," he said at length. "I realize Altevine is without a Reks. But Signar will do them no good as he is. That's what Sjörna believed. And you will take the clans as your own either way."

Skarde didn't argue. Instead, he raised his huge mead mug to Tzarik and took a long drink. "I have bested their wolven Reks. Our family line is long and strong. I will find a woman for Dain to marry.

She will be blessed with a god-shape, and our lands will be secured. Until then, I do not wish to anger any other Reks. I cannot risk it. I will give Altevine to the others to watch over until I have sufficient grandchildren."

Tzarik felt an ulterior motive in the large man's voice. He waited.

"When you have tamed the wildling," Skarde said, leaning onto his knees, eyeing Tzarik hard, "bring him back to his home." He smiled darkly. Tzarik guessed Skarde-Reks thought it couldn't be done. That Signar would never return. "Let him come back and take his rightful place as Reks of Altevine. He will need to be seen by his people and they will baptize him in their way. A Reks who has left our shores must prove his strength if he is to rule his canton and if his god is to smile upon him."

"And if we don't?" Tzarik asked.

Skarde's brow arched, almost daring the Runer to violate their laws. "Our gods will not let a Reks go without punishment. You have seen our gods. Do not underestimate them. Signar must come back to our shores in his seventeenth year." He gave Tzarik a knowing glance. "Signar Wolf-tor's name day is the last day of Beltire, summer. Soon he will be sixteen. You have until the first autumn moon of his seventeenth year to bring him back, tamed and ready to know his place. That is not long, Runer. Know the precious life you have taken from us, and what it could mean to Altevine to bring him back. If you don't," he warned dangerously, "Raudnir will hunt what is his. Even off his frozen shores."

Sybal shuddered beside him.

"PLEASE TELL me you didn't do this for me," Sybal growled as they saddled up their new horses just hours later.

Tzarik looked his new mount in the eye, not liking the willful glare the horse gave him. As if it knew he preferred some other beast.

Sybal was partly right, but he wasn't sure how to admit it without condescension.

"I cannot bear your sorrow," he confessed. "You are wounded in ways I do not understand yet. We can tame Signar together."

"Oh, gods," she moaned, leaning into her horse's in the side to make it let out the air it held in its lungs. She wrenched up on the saddle belt hard. "Don't you see? Abdul. Jin. Zeva. Every child I have wanted to protect is gone. I don't want another."

"Then do it for him," he shot back, matching her anger. "Don't let him stay here to be tortured, or killed as a prize in some barbaric spectacle."

He saw his words take effect on her. She bit her bottom lip, avoiding his eyes. This had to do with his childhood and she knew it. She could press him to explain. Even if he didn't understand that's where this need to save the boy came from, she would. But still he wouldn't open up to her.

"You are being cruel to me," she said, only half meaning it. "I meant what I said about Zeva. But we cannot save everyone, Tzarik."

Hearing her parrot his words from a year ago back to him cut him deep. "I'm not," he sighed. "Just him."

He took up the reins in his hand. "Let's get started. We have a long and dangerous journey ahead of us."

She followed him, eyes set on the ground. There was much more he needed to tell her, but he wanted the hot Al'Myrahn sun beating down on him and the shifting sands glittering under his boots first.

CHAPTER 41

THE FATHER OF MONSTERS

SKARDE-REKS GAVE THEM A STONE CARVED IN THE likeness of a mighty radjur and hanging from a leather cord. The talisman showed him as a messenger for Northica and commanded the captain of the small western vessel to transport the Runers and their large cargo to Moshav. Zeva's body lay in the coffin. The Northican blacksmiths had created a large cage for Signar on the back of a wagon, which they kept covered in a tightly laced tarp of hide. Not seeing the world outside the cage kept him mostly quiet, and the swaying of the cart even put him to sleep for most of the journey. That, with a combination of some herbs lacing his meals, kept him mostly docile and unconscious. Sybal insisted they keep him in the cage even when they camped at night, before they made it to the shores of Caerwren.

With the stone, Tzarik was able to find them passage without many questions asked. The crew even helped them disembark when they hit the red shores of Moshav. Tzarik didn't notice Sybal waiting on the prow of the ship while he and the crew unloaded the coffin and the cage. Signar made a snarling sound when the captain came close.

"A creature from the west," Tzarik said, brushing off the man's startled and inquiring eyes. He got the horses lashed to the large wagon before he looked up at Sybal.

Her eyes squinted towards the ghost-like city on the horizon. She almost looked sad.

"What is it?" Tzarik asked.

"It's been two years since I've seen Al'Myrah," she breathed, returning to their Al'Myrahn tongue. "After all that's happened, I'd forgotten what she looked like."

He marched into the water until he stood beside where she looked out from the rail of the small ship. Reaching up, he signaled her to take his hand. When she did, he helped her down, splashing into the golden water and red sand that was unique to Moshav. She smiled as the water lapped at her thighs.

"It's warm," she mused, smiling. "I've missed warm things."

Holding her hand, Tzarik led her onto shore, where Signar had begun to yelp and moan in his hiding place. "We have a long way to go," Tzarik said, his tongue twisting around the long-missed Al'Myrahn language. "We need to keep moving."

Sybal nodded, looking towards the city. "I thought Moshav was a wealthy province. The main city looks so...destroyed."

Remembering his last stint in Moshav, Tzarik agreed. "It's seen better days. The sheikh who runs the main city has not done much to try to keep the wealth here."

He stopped and snapped around to face the city.

"What is it?" Sybal asked, laying her hand on her scimitar.

Tzarik glared at the one golden dome of the magnificent city that was not falling into disrepair. The aureate dome glittered in the midday sun, surrounded by sandy, white walls. Did that sheikh deserve to know?

"Sybal," Tzarik began. "Zeva's brother, Sahir, is the sheikh of Moshav."

Her mouth popped open in shock. "She has family still living?" A new rage at Tarkan flared up in Sybal's icy eyes. "We have to tell him. She should be here!" She thrust a finger towards the city. "Had I known she had living family, I never would have suggested she be buried on my land."

"She shouldn't be here." His hand went to the black coffin where the young necromancer lay. He laid his palm against it as if he could comfort the dead girl inside. "Seeing her like this might enrage him. He did not speak vengefully about Tarkan when I was last here. But I cannot guess if his sentiments may have changed. Or would change if he found her Scriven...and dead."

Sybal marched to the front of the wagon and took hold of the bridle, guiding the horses towards the city. "We have to take that chance. He deserves to know the fate of his sister and the man who killed her."

Tzarik stopped, confused.

"Tarkan killed her," Sybal doubled down. "He wasted her strength. She was strong, and even Tarkan didn't know why." She glared forward. "Maybe her power scared him. Maybe it was just the power he wanted. He wasn't as strong as he thought he'd be, was he? He thought once he was Necro'Khan that all the black magic would bow to him. But it wasn't that simple, was it? Even after he pulled me from the Deep, he submitted to that wolven monster. She was blind by her love for him, seeing his smothering control as affection."

She glanced sidelong at her mentor, the rage boiling up. His stoic face didn't reply. How could he not see Tarkan had done this to Zeva?

"Why did the black magic accept her so quickly? Even healing her?"

"You weren't there before he sacrificed her," Tzarik said calmly. "Tarkan refused to give her to the scriptures. She begged him. Pleaded. I saw how it tore his once-beating heart to give her up."

This didn't sooth the raging blame she placed on the Necr'Khan. "He was to protect her. He could have said no. But he wanted this."

"She was stronger than Tarkan." Tzarik glanced towards Signar, deep in thought. "He did see that. But he didn't understand why she was. You asked why the necrotic magic took to her so swiftly? Her empathy."

Sybal frowned, confused. "I don't understand."

Tzarik's shoulders fell a little. "I know. She craved to be with him, to join him in the black magic. Perhaps the scriptures understood even when Tarkan didn't. They were drawn to her purity. It might have corrupted her eventually, but that's why she was strong. It wanted her as much as she wanted to join Tarkan within the bonds of necromancy."

An unfamiliar somberness in Tzarik's voice put Sybal on edge. Like he worried she'd do something to disappoint him. Or already had.

Going back to her original idea, she plowed ahead and said, "Sahir deserves to know what Tarkan did to Zeva."

ﺍ

THE GUARD at the door remembered Tzarik and let them into the walls of the estate. Moshav moved a little more than he remembered, filled with a few people in the market and even some Masahk travelers. The guard paid a small boy to run ahead of them and give word to the sheikh that the Runer had come back. They moved slowly through the city streets. A few citizens looked at them curiously with their grim cargo, but none spoke or even whispered.

The sheikh's home was cleaner than Tzarik remembered. Perhaps Sahir had tried to rebuild the city in recent years. To Tzarik's surprise, Sahir came out to greet them in the courtyard. Inside the cage, Signar slept, lulled to sleep by the warmth of Al'Myrah. Tzarik climbed up on their wagon and shoved the coffin to the edge. Sybal watched him, expressionless.

"The great Runer," Sahir crowed, arms crossed over the golden silks he wore. He came out from deeper inside the gold-encrusted manor. "The butcher of Ala'Nar, friend of the black magic. I have not heard of you in some time. Have you been in hiding?"

The sheikh's arrogance and greeting grated on Tzarik, but he couldn't let it anger him. He had a far worse greeting for him.

"Sahir," he said flatly. "I come in peace. I don't want to take any of your time."

"Do you miss my dungeon, Runer?" Sahir smirked.

Sybal started, glowering at the sheikh. "Dungeon?"

Tzarik gave her a glance, saying he'd tell her later. "I bring you grave news, sheikh."

To his relief, Sahir's face fell a little and his eyes shot to the coffin. "I can't imagine what you've brought." His tone came cautiously.

Tzarik signaled two men from the sheikh's household standing nearby to haul down the coffin. With a heavy heart, regretting putting the girl on display, Tzarik cracked open the coffin with his scimitar and reached in to unwrap Zeva's face. She looked peaceful. Almost asleep. Standing up, he nodded to the coffin for Sahir to look into.

With a skeptical brow raised, Sahir leaned over cautiously. His body froze. He took two more steps closer. "Is...? No. It can't be. That's not..."

Seeing genuine emotion take hold of Sahir, Tzarik knelt by Zeva and pulled the wrappings all the way off her head so her long, dark hair flowed out. He gently placed it over her shoulders.

"He's marked her," Sahir said, his voice a hiss of venom. His hand shook, hovering over her, like he didn't want to touch her. "Given her the sign of *his* family," he said in reference to the star on her forehead underneath the other tattoos. He spat through clenched teeth. "He said she was safe!"

Before Sybal could interject, Tzarik said, "He loved her. His love was twisted and incomprehensible, but he gave up everything for her."

Sahir turned from the coffin, face in his hands. He screamed into the silence, balling his fists. Tzarik let him consume his emotions before speaking.

"We brought her here to be buried with your family."

Sahir gripped his face again, crying out in rage. He seemed confused underneath his sorrow. With a final strangled cry of anguish, he marched quickly into his home.

Sybal watched him go. "At least he cares."

But something else stirred Tzarik's sulfates. "No. He's hiding something. This news should have shocked him more. He should have questions. It's almost like he expected us."

Commanding the servants to take the coffin to the family's cemetery, Tzarik followed the sheikh inside, signaling Sybal to trail him. Just inside the sandy arch was an entryway open to the gardens. A fountain bubbled sadly in the center, and off to the side, a circular seating area filled with colorful cushions waited. Sahir stood there, one hand on his hip, the other pouring a glass of arak—the white alcohol of Al'Myrah—down his throat.

"I don't know why I stayed," Sahir admitted to the room at large. "After father vanished and mother took her life, I should have left Moshav to the temple. House Hafiz has ruined Moshav. Runer," Sahir sighed without facing them. "Tell me about your adventures." His voice came thickly as he tried to distract himself from his dead sister. Tzarik didn't demand he face them, knowing he wept for her.

Holding his ground so he could see out the windows to the wagon where Signar lay, Tzarik recanted his journey since he'd last seen Sahir. Sybal exclaimed in rage when he backtracked and told her about how Sahir had held him and Vicdan as prisoners, torturing him by taking his runes and the pearlescent blade. Gradually, Sahir regained his arrogant composure and turned to face the Runers.

"Xia is quite a foreign land," he mused when Tzarik finished telling him about the long journey they'd taken. "But..." He eyed the stone pendent that hung on the outside of Tzarik's black leather. "That is Caerwren. You did not come here from Xia."

"We went to hunt," Tzarik said. Sahir did not need to know that they'd gone with Tarkan to use the Eldritch Hunt to bring Sybal back, especially when he wasn't sure if his suspicions about her new abilities and resilience were true. But the sheikh's eyes flitted to Sybal and back almost imperceptibly.

Sahir smiled deviously. "No, you didn't. I am no fool, Runer." He paced the small area, smirking. "You bring me my sister, dead, Scriven, and you bearing an oath stone from Northica, and think I will not understand?" He clicked his tongue. "Really, Runer. I may not know the details, but I have seen more than you know."

Tzarik took in the way Sahir's gait had changed. He did know something. He moved too confidently to be lying.

"We have leads to catch up on," Tzarik said at last. Sahir wouldn't give in to a game of guessing. "We just wanted to bring Zeva home."

"Hm, leads," Sahir said off-handedly, pouring himself more arak. "Then I suggest you journey to Alika."

Sybal made a small, disappointed sound and her shoulders collapsed. She didn't want to leave Al'Myrah again.

"Why?" Tzarik asked. "What's on Alika?"

Sahir drank the entire golden glass in one swallow. The hand that had been so arrogantly placed on his hip dropped. His thumb ran over the rim of his glass as he looked down. "Many things, Runer. Some that I wish were here on Al'Myrah." His head shot back up and he faced them. "The *Mahit'Onomicon* was written by an Al'Myrahn, on Alika, amidst its scholars of the dead many thousands of years ago."

Tzarik and Sybal shared a quick, uneasy glance. "You know of the Mahit'Onomicon?" Tzarik asked.

Sahir raised his brows a fraction of an inch, like he dared Tzarik to ask more.

Sybal tilted her head. "On Xia, they say the book, which they call the *Xai'de Jing*, was written by their god. It was given to a man to learn from and keep the people safe from monsters."

Sahir half shrugged. "On Xia, it was written on Xia. On Al'Myrah, it was written on Alika. Who is to say it is not the same book? Or perhaps, when the Great Continent broke apart, each land was given its own? Xian gods do not claim Al'Myrah. The titans of Caerwren do not claim Rhostrana. The point is, Lady Runer, no matter what you believe, the Dynast Pharaoh has claimed to have found the man who will read the Mahit'Onomicon, the one who can master the book and control all thirteen thousand beasts of the map. According to Alika, this man is called The Father of Monsters." He paused, then said, "Word has even reached our sultana. The eastern triangle has not yet erupted into panic, as there are no signs that such a man has been found. He'd have to be very wise, very powerful to read the Mahit'Onomicon. Someone cunning enough to enslave a djinn, perhaps?"

At this, both Runers shared a glance.

"Is that significant?" Tzarik asked. The sulfates in his veins rushed, crying out a warning. He suddenly had a feeling of familiarity. He had a guess at just the man who might crave an accolade like that, who would relish being called The Father of Monsters.

"I see by your face, you know." Sahir smiled. "Don't fear yet. First, the book must be found."

"I thought the book was at Tarkan's father's house?" Sybal interjected.

Tzarik shook his head. "We assumed so. I don't think Ishmael ever had the book."

"House Mirzam," Sahir put in. "The family who brought necromancy back to the map. House Nashira are necromancers who rallied Porshains outside Porsh against the Mirzam tribe. Nashira are necromancers just as much as the others, but the wandering tribes consider them traitors. They do not mark the outside of their bodies, but the inside. Their very bones. Thus, they are invisible to average sentients who do not know what to look for." He smiled like he'd explained the rules of a simple game for children. "My tutors used to tell me about necromancers like godtales. Things that did not exist. Mere horror stories of men who ate sentients alive to take their life's power and raise the dead."

"You sound as though you admire him," Sybal spat, disgusted.

"Did you not save his life?" Sahir asked, referencing the long tale Tzarik had relayed to him.

"I did." She held her head high. "But I did not know the monster he was capable of becoming."

Sahir smiled and laughed. "You are special, Sybal. No one but a lady like you would look at a creature like a necromancer and think they were not demons in their own way."

She scoffed venomously. "I've seen the error of my ways." She crossed her arms and stood with her legs apart, glaring down at Sahir. "So, the Dynast Pharaoh on Alika thinks he's found the one who can read and understand the Mahit'Onomicon?"

Sahir clicked his tongue, agreeing to leave her brazen attitude alone. "A sorcerer, yes. That doesn't mean the book has been found. Or that the man even really is able to read the script it's written in. Assuming it's written at all. But that's not what interested me about the news. I travel in circles much like you Runers. Ever since my father left and Tarkan stole my sister away, I've delved into the eldritch studies. Much of that comes from Alika, where they are obsessed with their dead and reincarnation and worship their god of death. And that's how I met a scholar. We had a mutual acquaintance in my old friend Tarkan. He's a scholar by the name of Abigor Sharar."

Tzarik clenched his teeth. He'd felt it, knowing it could be no one else. Sybal saw his mood shift and took a few steps closer to him.

"Don't worry; he's not here," Sahir said lazily, relishing the Runers' sudden agitation.

"Where is he?" Tzarik barked. He glanced out the window to see if their wagon still sat outside the family cemetery. It did. Feeling stupid for thinking Sharar would spring out of a dune and steal Signar, he rubbed his temples. To Sahir, he repeated his question.

The sheikh shook his head. "I'm not sure anymore. You might want to start your search in Ala'nar, however. He housed much of his experiments and research there."

Again, Tzarik felt he knew exactly where the damned scholar might set up somewhere to hide his studies. He dared not mention his suspicions to Sybal. She'd become more volatile than ever since coming back from the Deep, and her compassion had not resurfaced yet. Her kindness was missing. He'd noticed before but hoped she'd melt back into her old nature once on Al'Myrah. But the familiar shores only fueled her new bitterness. He'd take her back to her family's land, but not divulge that Sharar had most likely taken it as a hiding place.

"We cannot let him get his hands on it," Tzarik said at last.

Sahir smiled deviously. "That's not the best part. You speak of Tarkan as if he's gone."

Something in Tzarik snapped. He'd never liked Sahir, having spent days in his prison being tortured. But the way he played with their fear grated on him even more. His hand flew to his scimitar handle. He glowered at the sheikh.

"Don't, Runer," Sahir said flatly. "But I see I've upset you. Thank you for delivering my sister to me. I will tell you one last bit of information because I wish you to leave."

"Gladly," Tzarik growled.

Sahir drew himself up and clasped his hands behind his back. "Tarkan was here, not a fortnight ago. He was...not the man I remember at all."

"How?" Tzarik spat. "I saw him, body and soul, dive into the God Deep."

The sheikh smiled and even laughed. "Yes, so he told me. He's the Necro'Khan now. The ways of the Deep submit to him. You underestimate his black magic, Runer. He is a master of death and blood—life—the two things that are certain for every sentient on the map. He spoke of his life since taking Zeva. When he mentioned the scholar, I realized I had to share what I knew with him. Once I mentioned the dastardly scholar, Tarkan prepared to flee. I told him not to fear. I never mentioned my dalliance with necromancy to the pompous oaf."

Sybal glared, crossing her arms. "Did he not mention Zeva? Did he abandon her on Caerwren?"

Sahir's face finally lost a little of its luster. He expertly hid his true emotions behind an impassive mask. "No. He didn't abandon her. I saw, when he was here, that something was wrong. By my soul, I didn't ask. He must have known that she..." His voice grew too thick to speak. He smiled quickly, almost maniacally, to shove away the emotion.

"Tarkan desires the Mahit'Onomicon for himself," he went on. "He raved about being weak. Never again, he said. He promised I'd see Zeva again, so I gave him gold and sent him to Alika with all I have told you."

"See Zeva again?" The truth hit Sybal hard. "If he finds the book, he will be the most powerful being on earth."

"Second most," Tzarik corrected. "A sorcerer would be far more frightful. Inside that book lies the truth to binding and taking a djinn's powers. Tarkan knows Sharar has been hiding a djinn for some time. He wants to reap his vengeance on Sharar before he ascends to sorcerer."

"Then we should let him," Sybal spat. "He's done us nothing but harm. Let Tarkan kill him."

"And Zeva?" Tzarik asked. "What if he tries to pull her from the dead? What he if finds the Mahit'Onomicon and grows his power? We did not experience the last Necro'Khan in our lifetime. We don't know the destruction he could be capable of. And now, he has nothing to lose. No innocence tying him back."

Sybal felt Zeva's weight in her arms. She remembered the girl going to the Masahk Runer in the Court. She'd watched how shy she was. Zeva's life had been cut short the day Tarkan stole her from Moshav. Tarkan would stop at nothing until... *Until what?* she wondered. Until he covered the map in malignation? Until his grief was expunged and he paid the world back for all his suffering?

"How can we stop them both?" she asked. "Why? Sharar killed my family, but I cannot let revenge drive me. As you say, this is not our fight."

She repeated everything Tzarik used to say back to him.

Tzarik looked at Signar where he slept in the sun. "But it is. We have the chance to finish what we started in Ala'Nar. We cannot only think our lifetimes are what matters. We must make a better world for him." He nodded toward Signar. "He cannot grow up shrouded in our fear. And..." He frowned meaningfully at Sybal. "The hunt is our job. We track, learn, and kill."

"Tzarik," Sybal gasped in defeat. "Sharar has a djinn. That's a monster we could never defeat. We've witnessed Tarkan's powers. We cannot stand up to them."

The Runer steeled himself. "Your brazen courage annoyed me, Sybal," he began again. "You put yourself in danger. I feared for your life because of you. You showed that me giving up, wishing it all to end, was true weakness, not strength. I didn't have the courage to face this life. Now, I have other lives to protect."

The weight of his words hit her hard in the chest. She glanced towards where the young Reks waited. She thought back to the battle, where Signar had attacked Tzarik. When she'd taken an arrow to the chest. Slowly, she touched the spot with her fingers. What did that mean? Had Tzarik seen? *I didn't die,* she thought. *I cannot die?* Was this what the Vorlamir meant: consequences to her actions? And what about being consumed by the god-touch? There had to be answers somewhere.

"The book contains the secrets of life and death," she reiterated. "It has answers to questions we haven't even asked yet."

Confused, Tzarik nodded.

"Then we go to Alika. But not for him." She thrust a finger towards Signar. "For us."

Sahir looked between the two of them. "Let me fetch you some provisions, then."

ᘓ

The Runers will return in *Season of the Runer Book IV: The Father of Monsters*

The Runes

Artiah: The rune of healing. Drawing artiah will mend minor abrasions and heal larger wounds enough to allow escape. Artiah will also take away a small amount of pain.

Atan: The rune of light. Drawing atan will create an orb of light for all eyes to see by. Atan also reveals hidden spirits and can show disguised monsters in their true form.

Buhkar: The rune of mist. When buhkar is drawn, the Runer dissolves into a black, smokey mist able to slip between tight spaces, evade a grip, and blend into shadows easily to be undetected.

Halat: The rune of protection. When halat is drawn, the caster is safe inside a circle of protection. Anything that wishes the caster harm cannot pass the boundaries of the protective circle.

Jiun: The fury rune. Jiun—the most dangerous of the runes—turns the Runer into a berserker. Cutting off all feeling to wounds and ailments, the rune pushes the caster beyond their inhibitions. Jiun also lends temporary strength and heightened senses.

For more information about the world of the Runers, please visit www.abigaillinhardt.com/seasonoftheruner

Abi works part-time as a freelance ghostwriter, editor, audiobook narrator, and is one half of the partnership that owns Altered Reality Magazine.  She hopes to one day make these passions her full-time job while she hunts for the next bohemian adventure. She has published works of fiction, poetry, academia, and even won awards for her short stories in science fiction and horror. Her novel *The Trial of Two* was recently named an Honorable Mention in the Writer's Digest 2021 self-publishing awards and won first place in dark fantasy in The BookFest Awards. Abi is also a proud mom of two ferrets! She currently resides in Kansas.

She is one of nine children--all who share the creative spark.

Find Abi online at: www.abigaillinhardt.com

Also by Abigail Linhardt
Season of the Runer Book I: The Trial of Two
Season of the Runer Book II: Sojourn
Season of the Runer Book III: The Eldritch Hunt
Prince of MidWest
Why They Killed: A Waksha Virus Novelette
These Darker Streets
Revary (2023)